A NOVEL

AMY SOHN

SIMON & SCHUSTER

SIMON & SCHUSTER
Rockefeller Center
1230 Avenue of the Americas
New York, NY 10020

10 9 8 7 6 5 4 3 2 1

Library of Congress Cataloging-in-Publication Data
Sohn, Amy, [date]
    Run catch kiss : a novel / Amy Sohn.
       p.   cm.
    I. Title.
PS3569.O435R8   1999
813'.54—DC21   99-22057   CIP Rev.
ISBN 0-684-85302-7

Portions of this book originally appeared in
New York Press in a slightly different form.

The author wishes to thank the following individuals: John Strausbaugh, Russ Smith, Daniel Greenberg, David Rosenthal, Marysue Rucci, Will Blythe, Florence Falk, Will McGreal, Umberto Crenca, and Joe Maruzzo.

For my mother and father

With the first few words Miss Lonelyhearts had known that he would be ridiculous. By avoiding God, he had failed to tap the force in his heart and had merely written a column for his paper.

NATHANAEL WEST,
Miss Lonelyhearts

1

I WAS ONLY TWENTY-TWO and already I was infamous. I read the gossip pages with terror in my heart, certain I would find some humiliating detail about my recent downfall. I walked the streets with my eyes peeled, ever on the lookout for hidden paparazzi. I entered my local café with my sphincter tight, counting the seconds until a stranger recognized me, shouted my name, and mocked me for my crime, a crime no one understood, because of my adamant and prolonged silence on the matter.

I was the Hester Prynne of downtown. A public laughing-stock at an age when my biggest worry should have been my lack of health insurance. Shamed before my time, defamed without good cause, a huge red letter branded on my (sizable) chest.

Yet somehow it all made sense. I had always wanted to be-come someone who could walk into a room and have her reputa-tion precede her. That's what I got. In the worst way.

•

I didn't move back to New York to be a sex columnist. I wanted to be an actress. The day after graduation, I moved into my parents' apartment in Brooklyn Heights and called my agent, Faye Glass. She had represented me since I was fourteen, and helped me book a few off-off-Broadway plays and an anticrack commercial during high school, but by senior year my career wasn't exactly promising enough to make it worth postponing

11

college. So I let my contract expire, went off to Brown, and told Faye I'd be in touch in four years.

I don't think she realized I meant it literally, because when I got her on the phone that day in May and told her my name, she said, "Who?"

"Ariel Steiner," I repeated insistently. "You represented me when I was a kid. I finished college, I'm back in the city, and I want to start auditioning again."

"Oh," she said like she still wasn't sure who I was. "Come into my office sometime tomorrow and we can get reacquainted."

●

She seemed to recognize me when I walked in the door, which at first was a huge relief. Maybe her early-onset dementia wasn't as advanced as I had thought. She sat me down opposite her desk and I said, "How's the business changed since I've been away?"

"I'll tell you how *you've* changed," she said. "You're heavier. A *lot* heavier. I hate to say it, but looks are seventy-five percent of this business, and it's always going to be that way. I can't send you out for any ingenue parts until you lose fifteen pounds. Come back and see me when you've slimmed down. In the meantime, I'll submit you for fat character roles."

I nodded mutely, but as soon as I got out on the street, I started bawling. It came as something of a shock to have to put my life dream on hold all because I never got rid of my freshman fifteen. And it didn't help that I was being asked to diet when I had just graduated a college where you spend four years learning not to buy into the warped value system of the patriarchal hegemony.

The reason Faye's words were so surprising was that I'd never considered myself fat before. I was five five, 142 pounds— no slim chicken, but by no means a total porker. Guys had always considered my body more of an asset than a liability. I'm what they call zaftig: all butt, boobs, and hips. I was a late bloomer, but once I bloomed, I bloomed big. I didn't understand how the same figure that had served me so well horizontally could serve me so poorly professionally. But it didn't matter how I felt about my body. If Faye said I was fat, then I was. I had to lose the weight or choose another career, and I wasn't going to choose another career.

I'd known acting was my calling since November 1976, when I was two. My parents had taken me to my grandparents' house in Philadelphia for Thanksgiving, and after dinner the whole family gathered in the living room for the entertainment segment, where all the kids showed off their latest accomplishments. As my three-year-old cousin Eddie belted "Tie a Yellow Ribbon Round the Ole Oak Tree" into a microphone, I sat in the corner, watching them all watch him, and was seized by a jealous rage. I couldn't stand the sight of so many people paying so much attention to someone who wasn't me.

Then I got a brilliant idea. As Eddie continued to sing, I slowly and quietly began to strip off all my clothes. Everyone was so focused on him they didn't notice what I was doing. As soon as I was in the buff, I jumped in front of him with a loud "Ta-da!" and the entire room burst into fits of hysterical laughter. Eddie had been totally forgotten. They were all watching me. I didn't feel the slightest bit guilty for stealing his limelight. I just felt like justice had been served.

But now justice would have to be delayed until I lost my extra poundage. I wiped the tears off my face, bought a Slim-Fast at a Korean deli, and got on the subway home.

●

Brooklyn Heights is a quaint, old-fashioned neighborhood known for its tree-lined streets and elegant turn-of-the-century brownstones. I didn't grow up in one of those brownstones. I grew up in a three-bedroom apartment on the thirty-fifth floor of a middle-income apartment building, Silver Tower, that was built in August 1973. I once looked up Silver Tower in a Brooklyn history book and it was described as "a blot on the otherwise attractive landscape of the neighborhood."

Sad to say, that's pretty accurate. The railings on the terraces look like prison bars, the concrete is gray-brown and ribbed like a condom, and the entire phallic palace is the biggest eyesore in a twenty-block radius. The only thing that makes the apartment halfway worthwhile is the view. The terrace faces Queens, but if you lean all the way out and look toward the left, you can see the Brooklyn and Manhattan Bridges, and from my bedroom you can spot the Statue of Liberty.

When I got home, my mom was in the kitchen, chopping vegetables and listening to *All Things Considered*. "How was Faye's?" she said.

"She can't send me out on any ingenue parts till I lose fifteen pounds."

"She really said you have to lose fifteen pounds?" said my mom, horrified.

"Yeah."

"Because I think *ten* would be more than enough."

"Thanks," I said, went into my room, and shut the door. I lay down on the bed, closed my eyes, and fantasized about the day my skinny, perfect ass would be on the cover of *Rolling Stone*. It wouldn't take long. Once I lost the weight, Faye would send me on an audition for a murderous, conniving bitch part on the New York cop show *Book 'Em*. The casting director would be so blown away by my venomous appeal that she'd hire me on the spot. As soon as we shot the episode, every casting office in town would start buzzing about me, and before the show even aired, George C. Wolfe of the Public Theater would cast me in his next star-studded production—as Lady Macbeth to Will Smith's Macbeth. Once we opened, Ben Brantley would cream all over me in the *New York Times,* and Hollywood would start calling.

I'd get a walk-on in the new George Clooney vehicle shooting in New York, and then Woody would cast me as his mute fourteen-year-old mail-order bride in his Untitled Winter Project. Although I wouldn't have any actual lines, my face and body would be so expressive that I'd get nominated for a best supporting actress Oscar. I'd bring my father as my date, and when Jack Palance opened the envelope and announced me as the winner, I'd run up to the stage in strapless Chanel and they'd cut to a shot of my dad drowning in a sea of his own mucus.

I'd follow my Oscar-winning role with the girl roles in *Speed*s *4* and *5* and *Insanely Indecent Proposals.* Julia would become a has-been, Julianne a nobody, Juliette yesterday's news. Winona and Gwyneth would become my best buddies. I'd help Gwyn with her eating disorder and convince Winona to change her last name back to Horowitz, and the three of us would become the reigning Jewish Girl Power Mafia of Hollywood. Under our influence, Reform Judaism would become the most popular celebrity religion and Scientology would die out forever.

I'd start my own production company, Zaftig Pictures, and produce chick-friendly scripts with completely one-dimensional roles for men. I'd be the first woman to start asking twenty-five mil a pic. *Time* would put me on the cover, saying I was changing the rules of Hollywood. Brown would award me an honorary doctorate and I'd go back to campus to give a speech about female empowerment in a male-dominated world. All the young theaterfucks would clap wildly for me as I choked up and did a beauty pageant wave, remembering the day when Faye had told me I was Just Too Fat.

I must have dozed off, because I was awakened by my brother, Zach, standing over me, saying, "Hello, blubber." He was in his junior year at Stuyvesant High School and going through his smart-assed-prick stage.

"Mom told you?" I said.

"Yeah."

"Do *you* think I need to lose weight? Be honest."

"Well, I've never wanted to say anything to you, but you *have* put on a few pounds over the last couple years. I think the diet's a good thing. It's an excuse to make yourself more attractive." Zach could be sharp sometimes. He cracked, but he cracked wise.

We went to the dinner table and started in on our fruit cocktail, and then my dad walked in. He kissed my mother, but not me. Since I hit puberty, I haven't let him kiss me. When I was a kid we embraced all the time, but as soon as I started developing, I stopped feeling comfortable around him. Then, when I got over my puberty weirdness, I didn't know how to go back to kissing him again, because that would have been admitting I'd been wrong not to kiss him, and you can never admit to your parents that you were wrong.

"What did Faye have to say?" he asked, sitting down at the table. I told him. "I see," he said, then began contorting his eyebrows violently. He has a bushy black beard and I've never seen his lips, but I can always tell what he's feeling by his forehead.

"Don't worry," I said. "It'll be OK. It's only fifteen pounds. I don't think it'll take me that long to lose it."

"I don't either," he said. But for the rest of the meal he didn't say another word about Faye. He just asked Zach a bunch of questions about his physics class, as I shoveled down the kasha varnishkes my mom had made for me, and pretended to like it.

●

The next morning I made an appointment to interview at a temp agency on Wall Street. I had gotten its name off the front page of the Sunday *New York Times* classifieds. The ad was diabolical, but it worked. WANT TO BE A STAR? it said, in bold caps. And on the next line, in much smaller letters, "Then sign up with Dynamic Associates for flexible, temporary work."

When I walked in the office, a coiffed fortyish woman introduced herself as Frances, took me into a conference room in the back, and had me fill out some employment history forms. Then she led me into another room, where I took the typing, word processing, and grammar tests. The last was the most humiliating. It consisted of retard-level questions like "Which is correct? *(a)* Washington, d.c., *(b)* Washington, DC, *(c)* Washington, D.C., *(d)* Washington dc" and "Pick the choice that defines or is most like the word *collate. (a)* destroy, *(b)* separate, *(c)* assemble, *(d)* moisten." I wondered what they did to the people who got that one wrong. Was there a special torture room in the back where they forced you to do huge mass mailings for hours on end, until the meaning of *collate* was forever embedded in your mind?

When I finished the tests, Frances took me back into her office and tabulated my results. "You need some work on your word processing skills," she said, "but your grammar is good and you type seventy-five, which is excellent. I'm going to try to get you something for tomorrow."

By the time I got home from the agency she had already left a message on my machine about an assignment. I'd be the secretary to a financial administrator at a magazine publishing company, McGinley Ladd, at Thirty-second and Park Avenue South. The rate was $18 an hour—more than I'd gotten for any job in my life.

●

My boss greeted me in the lobby of the building. She was six feet tall with shoulder-length blond hair, and she introduced herself as Ashley Ginsburg. I could guess by that name that she was a shiksa who'd married a Jew, and despised her immediately for stealing one of our boys—my own occasional *shaygitz* suckerdom aside.

She took me upstairs to the twelfth floor and led me to my desk. It was in a small dingy room with a window overlooking Park Avenue South. "This is my office," she said, pointing to a door to the right of the desk. "Don't walk in on me unannounced or when I'm on the phone."

She showed me how to transfer a call and work the intercom, turned on my computer, gave me a user ID, and disappeared into her office. As soon as she closed the door, I called my machine to see if Faye had left a message. Nothing. For the next two and a half hours, the Corposhit didn't come out of her office once. I sat at the desk staring at my watch, looking out the window, daydreaming, and checking the machine once every fifteen minutes. At eleven-fifty, just as I was on my way out to lunch, I dialed one more time and struck gold: "Ariel, it's Faye. I got you an audition for *Book 'Em* tomorrow at six. Please call." I couldn't believe my fantasy was coming true so quickly! But when I called her back she said the role was "a chunky young woman who works as a cashier and studies part-time at City College," and I realized it might take some time before my dream became reality.

On my lunch break I took the bus to the casting office and picked up the sides. They were in a folder titled "Fat Cashier" and they weren't too inspiring. The suspected murderess had ordered produce from my grocery store and I had to explain to the cops what she looked like. I tried to rehearse the scene on the ride back to work, but it wasn't too easy to find deep motivation for lines like "All's I know is he bought radicchio."

I practiced the scene three times that night with Zach, until I felt confident about my read, and the next day after work I went into the ladies' room, changed into baggy pants and a sweatshirt, and took the bus to the audition. The waiting area was teeming with gorgeous slender girls, so I knew right away they were auditioning for the conniving murderess part. Maybe there was an advantage to going up for fat roles: the competition wasn't as stiff.

After twenty minutes the casting director finally called me into her office. There were two chairs opposite her desk—a cushy one in the center of the room and a hard-backed metal one in the corner. "Sit wherever you want," she said. I felt like Goldilocks. Would my chair choice affect my chances? Was this a secret psychology trick to see what personality type I was? I weighed my options: I knew if I chose the comfy one I'd sink down into it and give a low-energy reading, but if I sat in the metal one I'd be too far away from the casting director to connect. So I picked up the cushy one, heaved it to the corner, and moved the metal one over in its place.

"Interesting choice," she said.

"Thanks."

We ran through the scene together and when we finished she said, "You're clearly talented, and I know you could do it. Whether we cast you is simply going to depend on what the producers want. If they decide to go overweight, we'll have to go with someone else."

"Excuse me?" I said.

"If the producers want us to cast someone heavy, we're not going to go with you. You're not heavy at all." I grinned triumphantly and walked out.

The next day Faye left me a message saying I had a callback on Monday at one-fifteen at the production office in Chelsea, with the producers and director. As soon as she said the word "callback," I let out a yelp of glee. Then I hung up and rang the Corposhit on the intercom.

"Yes?" she huffed.

"I need to talk to you about something. Can I come in?"

"All right." I walked into her office. "I'm wondering if I can take a long lunch tomorrow."

"Why?"

"I'm actually an actress, and I have a callback." I couldn't resist a little self-satisfied smile.

"What's it for?"

"Book 'Em."

Her eyes bugged out. "I watch that show every week! Would you get to meet Barry Rinaldi if you got the part?"

"Yes," I said proudly. "In fact, my scene is with him. So, is that OK?"

"Sure," she said, still looking slightly incredulous. Then she suddenly seemed to realize she was being nice to her underling, reassumed her permagrimace, and said, "Close the door behind you."

●

The afternoon of the audition, I changed into the same clothes I'd worn to the first audition (they say you always should) and took the train to Chelsea. Some of the same model-type girls from the first audition were in the waiting room, stretching their legs and mouthing their lines. I sat down between two of them, trying not to be distracted by their burgeoning breasts, and read my scene over to myself. Then the casting director called me in.

Behind a long table in a huge, airy studio were four middle-aged men. I didn't let them intimidate me, though. I read the scene with even more hostile, jaded-cashier energy than I'd been able to summon the first time. At the end they smiled, impressed. That had to be good, because when they don't like you, they don't fake it.

When I got out on the street, I called Faye. "It went really well," I said. "I think I have a good chance, but the casting director said they won't cast me if they decide to go with someone heavy. She said I'm not heavy at all."

"Face it, Ariel," said Faye. "I sent you on an audition for a fat part, and *you got called back.*"

●

I didn't wind up booking it, but I wasn't discouraged. I would spend the next few months losing weight and doing the obese girl circuit, and then Faye would start sending me out on ingenue parts, and I'd take the world by storm.

But over the next month, as I stuck to my coffee, yogurt, and skinless chicken diet and narrowed to 137 pounds, Faye didn't get me one more audition. Whenever I called to check in with her, she said, "There just aren't that many character roles for young women. I'll send you out on anything you're right for. You have to just be patient and trust me."

I have never been good at being patient. Every single thing I've achieved in life has come to me because I am not a patient person. I ran for the morning-announcements position in high school with no school government experience and won because I wrote a funny campaign speech. I was always a straight-A student because I worked my ass off. My father told me when I was young that "talent is ninety-nine percent perspiration and one percent inspiration," and I took it to heart, even though he was plagiarizing Edison. So it wasn't easy to be told I had to sit tight.

Whenever I got frustrated with my acting career during high school, I would switch my focus to the only other thing I was passionate about: boys. If I didn't get called back for a play, I'd call up a cute guy in my class and flirt, and the rejection wouldn't sting so hard. I wanted to be able to utilize that technique again, but if you want to meet guys, you have to have a frame, a context, and I didn't have one. College is a frame. My boyfriend at Brown, Will, and I made eyes in Moral Problems class the first week of freshman year and went out for the next year and a half. It doesn't work like that in the city, though. If you make eyes at a hot guy on the street, he might follow you home, rape you, hack you to a million pieces, and leave you for the maggots.

So instead of trying to meet new guys, I decided to try blue-binning—recycling old ones. Whenever I had downtime at work (which was eighty percent of the time), I went through my address book and dialed my exes. I called every cock I'd caressed in summer camp, Reform Jewish youth group, and high school, but all I got were return messages from their moms, saying, "Sam's moved to Austin," or "You can reach David at his new number in Chelsea, where he's living with his girlfriend."

My temp job didn't open many romantic doors either. When you're a temp, nobody talks to you like you're a permanent resident of the planet. Besides, all the men at McGinley Ladd were rich workaholics, and I knew I couldn't have anything real with a guy who could hack the nine-to-five. I kept hoping someone from Brown would invite me to a party, but I didn't make too many friends there because I was so tied up in my relationship, so no one was calling.

Because I couldn't vent my career frustration through real-life nookie, I turned my energies to fantasizing. I stared like a hungry puppy at every male yupster who dropped a paper in the Corposhit's *in* box, trying to imagine how big their dicks were, what kind of noises they made when they came, and whether they were tit men, ass men, or pussy men. I concocted elaborate scenarios involving them sitting at important business meetings and me sucking them off under their conference tables while they tried to act normal.

At night, after dinner with my family, I would go into my room, get under the covers, and diddle the dai dai. If I couldn't sleep, I'd wank. If I was bored, I'd wank. (Once, Zach came in the room and I had to stop abruptly, but the great thing about being a chick is that no one can see your woody through the sheets.) My orgasms were pleasant enough, but my hand was a poor substitute for a bona fide bone. It was pathetic. I was making my living as a receptionist, the oldest pornographic stereotype in the book, and I didn't have anyone to role-play with. After a month in the most seminal city in the world, I was an overweight actress, an overqualified temp, and an oversexed celibate.

One muggy morning in July while I was waiting for the train at Borough Hall, I figured out a way to improve at least one aspect of my sorry life. I was leafing through magazines at the newsstand when I spotted a copy of *Backstage*. I picked it up and flipped to the Casting section. An ad caught my eye immediately: "*Lolita: Rock On.* A rock musical version of the Nabokov classic, to perform at 24th St. Stage. Seeking: Lolita, 15–25, pure but tainted, pristine but vulgar. Some singing required, but soul more important than technique." I hoped they meant it, because although I can do many things, singing is not one of them.

As soon as I got to work, I called the number in the ad. A middle-aged man answered. He had a sleazy, soft-sell voice, the kind you hear on luxury car commercials.

"I'm calling about the audition," I said. "My name's Ariel Steiner."

"I'm Gordon Gray, the director. Prepare a rock or jazz song and come in Saturday at four."

That night at dinner I told my family about the audition. My dad raised his eyebrows a little when I mentioned the word *Lolita*, then forced a smile and said, "Knock 'em dead." After dinner I locked myself in the bathroom, ran the tap water, and practiced Gershwin's "I've Got a Crush on You" into the mirror until I had more soul than JB. When I was done, I went into my room, opened the closet, and looked for an audition outfit. I picked out a polka-dot midriff for authenticity, because that's what Lolita is wearing when Humbert first catches sight of her. Then I caught a glimpse of my gut and decided against it.

●

I had to go down four flights of stairs to get to the theater. It was next to a karate center, on the bottom floor of an old church.

The waiting room was dark and smelled of cigarettes. Battered copies of *Backstage* were spread out on the floor, and a decrepit black curtain led to the theater. A blond twelve-year-old and her mother were sitting on one side of the room and a brunette in her thirties was on the other. The girl was very cute, but I could see immediately that she was no nymphet. I didn't know what to make of the brunette. I figured she was either auditioning for the role of Mrs. Haze or seriously deluded about her age range.

After a few minutes the curtain opened and a short, squat man with a white beard came out. I could tell by his voice that it was Gordon. He smiled at the girl and said, "Betsy?" The mom gave her an eager smile, Betsy went into the theater, and the curtain closed behind her. I heard her say something about "hoping to get involved in off-Broadway theater." *How clueless can she be?* I thought. This show was about as far off Broadway as you could get. You count the *offs* by the number of stairs you have to go down to get to the theater.

It was quiet for a second, and then Betsy broke into this loud, throaty version of "Hand in My Pocket" by Alanis Morissette. I looked over at Betsy's mom. She was beaming with pride. I pitied that mom. Didn't she know her kid was never going to get cast with the most brain-numbing anthem in the history of pop as her audition song?

After about fifteen seconds I heard Gordon say, "Thanks so much, Betsy. That's all we need for today." Betsy came out of the room looking vacant and dazed, and she and her mom walked out.

The brunette got called in next. She sang "On My Own" from *Les Misérables* in a shaky falsetto and she got stopped after ten seconds. The curtain opened, she left in a huff, and Gordon came out.

"You must be Ariel," he said. "I'm Gordon Gray." He extended his hand. "Nice grip."

"Thanks," I said. I never underestimate the importance of the handshake.

The theater was tiny and dark and it took a second for my eyes to adjust to the light. It looked more like a bomb shelter than a theater. There were audience seats on three sides and the stage was just an empty square area of paint-chipped concrete floor.

A wiry, fiftyish man in a beard and glasses was sitting in front row center. "This is Gene," said Gordon. "He'll be playing Humbert and helping me with the casting. Did you bring a headshot?"

I handed it to him and he sat down next to Gene. They flipped over to the résumé side and glanced at it for a second, nodding like my credits were decent, and then Gordon looked up and said, "Whenever you're ready."

I took a spot downstage center and breathed in. I tried not to think about Faye or weight or my total lack of vocal training. I was young, I was nubile, and I was gonna blow these fuckers away. I started to sing: "How glad the many millions of Toms and Dicks and Williams would be to capture me! But you had such persistence, you wore down my resistance; I fell and it was swell . . ."

They were smiling, clearly enjoying it, but I knew I had to do something bigger. On the next line I walked over to Gordon, sat on his lap, wrapped my arms around his neck, and nibbled his ear. He turned bright red and squirmed under me. That squirming was a very good sign. It meant I was affecting him, and if you want to get cast you have to make a bold impression. I would show him I could do this part if it took a lap dance. At the final line I strutted back to the stage, did a few curtsies and twirls, and finished on my knees, with my thumb in my mouth.

Gordon whispered to Gene in such an excited way that I was sure I stood a serious chance. Then they looked down at my résumé and Gordon said, "Would you mind doing an improv?" I certainly did not mind. Improv has always been one of my strongest skills. Gordon set up two chairs onstage and said, "Here's the scenario: you've just finished baby-sitting for Gene's kids, and now he's driving you home."

"I don't remember that scene from the book," I said.

"Oh, that's not in the book," Gordon said. "The show is going to be very free-form. We're envisioning it more as a riff on pedophilia than a literal interpretation of Nabokov."

That was cool. I could riff. Gene and I took our seats. He mimed a steering wheel and said, "So, were my kids good tonight?"

"Oh yes, Mr. Jones," I answered. "*Very* good. But I'm afraid *I'm* not such a good girl at all." I scooted my chair closer to him and put my hand on his thigh.

Before long I was telling him how much I hated blowing guys my own age and how frustrating it was that none of them knew how to make me come. The raunchier I got, the more flustered I made Gene. I couldn't tell how much was real and how much was pretend. Finally I said, "Well, here's my house, Mr. Jones," leaned over, and kissed him on the lips good-bye. His breath stank and there was some crust caked on his mouth corners, but I pretended to be into it. Then I pulled away, stood up, mimed slamming the car door shut, turned to Gordon, and smiled triumphantly.

"I'd like to cast you," he said.

I felt like I'd just won the Olympic gold. I couldn't even sing and I'd gotten booked as the lead in a rock musical. Clearly my charisma had paid off. But then I remembered how scant my competition had been, and my gold morphed into a bronze.

"This is going to be a very special rehearsal process," said Gordon. "Each of the performers will be given a chance to contribute material which relates to the theme of *Lolita*. It can take any form—song, story, sketch, whatever interests you. We want to examine pedophilia in our culture from all perspectives, and Lolita's is one of the most important. I'm particularly interested in having the performers use personal, autobiographical experiences in the project. So if you have anything you want to contribute, bring it to rehearsal on Monday."

When I got home from the audition the apartment was empty. My parents were at their country house in the Berkshires, and Zach was out with his friends. I went into my room, sat down in front of the computer, and tried to think of incidents from my adolescence that related to the theme of *Lolita*. Before I knew it my fingers were flying.

•

"Let's start with you, Ariel," Gordon said. It was the first rehearsal of the show, and the cast was assembled in a circle onstage: Gene; Gordon; Ted, the guy playing Quilty; Fran, the woman playing Mrs. Haze; the Push-Ups, the show's all-girl band; and me. James, the assistant director, was running late, Gordon said.

I was sweating profusely, but I tried to bite the bullet. "Um, I have two stories," I said. "The first is called 'Vanya in My Vulva.' It's about this forty-one-year-old playwright who fingered me last year at the movie *Vanya on 42nd Street*. The second is called 'Shooting Wad and Movies.' That's about this thirty-six-year-old married actor I hooked up with when I was sixteen, on the set of an NYU film. Which should I start with?"

Nobody said anything. The guys just stared at me with half-open mouths and the Push-Ups rolled their eyes. Finally Gordon cleared his throat and said, "How 'bout 'Vanya in My Vulva'?"

I took out the story.

"Roberto Pozzi and I met when I was fifteen and he was thirty-five. We were in a theater group together, and at each weekly meeting he would stare at my chest and tell me I was becoming a woman before his very eyes. One night he called me up and said he'd just written a play about a man who sodomizes and murders a crippled retarded girl he meets in Central Park. He said he wrote the little girl part with me in mind and wanted to know if I would come over to his apartment and read it with him. I said I wasn't sure, hung up, went into the living room, and asked my parents what *sodomizing* was. They wouldn't tell me.

"I never did the reading anyway, because Roberto booked a TV show in L.A. and had to move, and we didn't speak for the next four years. But junior year of college, he called me in my dorm room. He'd gotten my number from my parents. He started out asking me innocuous questions like how I liked school, but pretty soon he was asking how big my nipples were, whether my butt shook when I walked, how thick my pubic hair was, and what size bra I wore, cup and number."

Gene coughed. Gordon shifted in his seat.

"I loved these questions. Roberto was a freak, but he was a million times more exciting than all the idiot college boys I was dating. He said he'd be in New York for a few weeks around Christmas, visiting friends, and we arranged to meet at a café on MacDougal Street. I was pleased to find that his looks had only improved with age. His hair wasn't receding, he was tan and buff, he wore a long, gray wool coat and dark, clean jeans, and he kissed me on the mouth hello. We sat in the café reminiscing and then he suggested we see *Vanya on 42nd Street*.

"In the middle of the movie he started biting my ear and lip. 'Kiss me, Ariel, kiss me,' he said. 'I want you to kiss me. Turn to me and kiss me, baby. Come on, kiss me.' I did, but Roberto was a biter and biters really turn me off. I kept closing my mouth to hint that I liked to be kissed soft and sweet, instead of hard and rough, but he kept gnawing the tip of my tongue."

Right on the word *tongue* I saw someone come through the curtain into the theater, and as soon as I saw him a current shot straight from my heart to my hole. He was in his early thirties, medium height, in a hip-length leather jacket, and he had mussed yellow hair and Buddy Holly glasses. His glasses and strut made it clear he thought he was hot shit on a silver platter. It's always the cockiest guys who nerd themselves down because nerding yourself down is a way of saying, I'm so hot I can dress like a dork and women will *still* find me good looking. I was not turned off by his hotshitism, though. No indeed. I have always been a sucker for guys who think they're hot shit because I want to be the one woman to turn them into the weak fucks they really are.

He took a seat in the front row of the audience, and I struggled for a few seconds to find my place in the story.

"Then Roberto put his hand on my leg and up my skirt and

rubbed my underpants. He slid his fingers under the panties and stuck one inside. I closed my eyes, and when I opened them I saw Wallace Shawn on the screen, lisping his way through a mournful monologue. I wondered if I was the only one watching Wallace Shawn who had a finger up her crack."

I glanced at Buddy Holly. He was smiling.

"When the movie was over we walked down the street holding hands. We headed up Sixth Avenue to Balducci's and he bought me jelly beans and cheese. I liked him buying me things. It didn't matter that he was leaving, a biter, and a highly unstable choice in the long run. It was a warm pleasure to walk down the street on the arm of a man who knew the importance of a nice wool coat, who had good teeth, clear skin, and thick hair. Who smelled like old Aramis, called me 'baby,' and walked briskly with his arm linked in mine. My life was like a Charlie perfume ad. With a very sick twist."

I looked up. "That's it."

It was quiet. One of the Push-Ups glared at me and lit a cigarette. Gene and Gordon grinned uncomfortably, and Buddy Holly crossed his legs.

"Excellent, Ariel, excellent," said Gordon. "There's some real good stuff there. Real good stuff."

"I agree," said Gene. "You've got some vivid, potent material there. Your writing is so firm, and stark, and tight. I think she should read the other story, Gordon. What do you think?"

"I think so too," said Gordon. "This is James Delaney, everyone. The assistant director. Ariel's just finished reading a tantalizing tale about an experience with an older man, James."

"I'm sorry I came late," said James.

●

"Have you copyrighted your stories?" he asked, as I packed them into my bag. It was the end of rehearsal and everyone had left the theater except us.

"No, I just wrote them a few nights ago, for the show. Why?"

"You might want to consider it, in case you ever submit them somewhere. There's a lot of theft in literary magazines these days. You could submit something somewhere, have it rejected by an editorial assistant, then see it pop up under her name in another publication months later. Happens all the time."

"Jeez," I said innocently. "I had no idea that was so common. You wouldn't happen to have the number for the Copyright Office, would you?"

"As a matter of fact, I do. Not with me, but at home."

"Maybe you could . . . give me your number, then. And I could call you for the number of the office."

As he started to reach for the Pilot V5 Extra Fine pen protruding from his shirt pocket, my sexual frustration balled up into a fist and punched me in the face. I shot my hand out and grabbed the pen myself, letting my fingers rest against his chest for a second as I pulled. I glanced at him quickly to see his reaction. He looked half intrigued, half afraid. Maybe writing those stories had been a wiser move than I knew.

●

That night under the covers, I pretended my vagina was the trash compactor in *Star Wars* and James was this tiny Han Solo trapped inside me. The hotter I got, the faster my walls began to close and the harder he had to struggle to get out. After a few minutes he found this pole in there and desperately tried to pry me open with it, but it was to no avail. Each move he made only intensified my arousal and crushed him further. I was going to suffocate that little fucker with brute Chewbacca strength. As I finally began to come, I imagined myself shooting his miniature carcass out of me across the room. As soon as he landed he began to grow to human size—still dressed as Han Solo, except in Buddy Holly glasses. He climbed on top of me, fucked me slowly and expertly, collapsed with a sigh, and hummed "Everyday" softly into my ear until I fell asleep.

●

The next morning at work, I couldn't stop thinking about James. I kept getting this image of him walking into the theater, and each time I got it, I'd wetten and sweat. When a guy makes you wetten and sweat each time you think of him, it kind of makes you want to call him. So I left a message on his machine saying I was calling for the number of the Copyright Office. A little while later he called back.

"Good morning, Ashley Ginsburg's office, Ariel Steiner speaking. How may I assist you?"

"Mmmm," he said. "You have such a sexy phone voice."

I loved that compliment. My voice has always been the attribute I'm most proud of. The only part of my job I enjoyed was answering the phone, since it let me put on a little show for each caller. I always tried to cultivate a pleasant, welcoming, and perfectly well modulated tone.

"I'm glad you think so," I said. "I work hard on it. I think good phone manners are essential to establishing the credibility of a place of work. Are you calling to give me the Copyright number?"

"Yes. But I also . . . had another agenda. I wanted to know if you'd like to get a drink with me tomorrow night, since we have rehearsal off."

I wrote "YES!!!!!!" in huge letters on my blotter.

"That sounds fine," I said.

"Good. Let's go to Corner Bar, at West Fourth and West Eleventh. At ten, say. And I want you to bring those stories."

"Why?"

"Because as I watched you read last night, I could see that you possessed something . . . something highly alluring. If you got onstage and performed those stories for an audience of men, I am certain that you would *electrify*. I would just love to . . . *present* you. To be a part of you turning men on. To *assist* with that task." He was quiet. All I could hear was his heavy breath. I wondered if he had something in his hand.

"What about women, though? Would women be allowed in the theater?"

"Yes. The women would be jealous once they saw how the men were responding to you. They would come on to their men that night harder than ever and the men would make love to them thinking of you. The sex would be so good that the women would feel grateful to you. You have this incredible erotic energy, which should be put onstage for other people to watch. You have something powerful and hot and big."

There was something bizarre about James's vision, but he thought I was sexy and that flattered me. Besides, maybe he was on to something with this one-woman-show idea. We could tour the globe together and wow crowds from Houston to Hamburg. Critics would dub me the Jewish Madonna, the thinking girl's Robin Byrd, the straight Holly Hughes. After a few months on the road James would fall in love with my brilliance and propose. I'd insist that he convert to Judaism, we'd get hitched in Temple Emanu-El before a crowd of thousands and immediately have a litter of slightly off-balance children.

I'd drop the smut tales and start doing performance art about the joys of motherhood, and it would be even more provocative than before. Everyone who watched me would suddenly want to become parents, and it would set off a worldwide population explosion that would go down in history as the Steiner Effect.

"I should go," said James.

"OK," I said.

"I'm looking forward to tomorrow. I think it will be a highly entertaining evening, for both of us."

"I hope so."

●

That night at rehearsal, Gene played a composition he'd written on his French horn, entitled "Lovely Lolita," and James read a long, rambling poem about a deer hunter. It was boring and pretentious and made me lose some artistic respect for him, but it didn't diminish my lust. At the end of the night I waved good-bye to him casually so no one would know there was something budding between us.

After work the next day I stopped in the Village to browse for shoes. I was passing by Patricia Field, this transvestite store on Eighth Street, when in the center of the window I spotted a long, shiny black flip wig with the hair curled up at the ends. I went inside. "Where are the wigs?" I asked the hulking she-man behind the counter.

"Upstairs," she said in a German accent that sounded fabricated. At the top of the stairs was a counter with a row of wigs behind it. A tall, severe-looking queen was behind it, fitting a girl my age with the very wig I wanted. It didn't look too good on her. She had pale skin and small features and it was too big for her face. I felt sure it would look better on me because I have large features and a large head. The girl shook her head no, the queen took off the wig, and I stepped up to the counter.

"Excuse me," I said. "How much is that one?"

"A hundred," she said, primping it up.

There was no way in hell I could afford it. But I had to see it on me. I knew she would probably hate me for trying on something I wasn't planning to buy, but I didn't care. Her job frustration was her problem, not mine. "I'd like to put it on."

I sat down in the swivel chair behind the counter. She turned me so my back was to the mirror, fitted me with the wig, then spun me around so I could see my reflection.

Suddenly I was a raven-haired knockout. My skin looked visibly pinker. Usually it looks green because of my Russian Jewish ancestry. My mother's always called it olive, but it's really closer to chartreuse. My eyes looked bright and alive and my torso seemed slimmer.

"You look like Mary Richards," said the queen.

"Who's that?"

"Oh, honey. You never saw *The Mary Tyler Moore Show*?"

"It was kind of before my time," I said, blushing. "But thanks anyway. I'm glad I look like her."

She fluffed the wig and made the ends curl out more dramatically. I ran my fingers through the hair as if it were my own, but the gesture looked distinctly false in the mirror. I tried again, and the second time it looked more natural.

I couldn't stop looking at the new me. I loved her. I felt gorgeous and available and on top of the world. Then I remembered the price. "You can take it off now," I said. She sneered, removed the wig, and put it back on the dummy head. I trudged down the stairs without looking back.

When I got outside I noticed a bank machine across the street. Suddenly I heard Robin Williams's voice in my head saying, *"Carpe diem."* The only reason I saw *Dead Poets Society* was for the young hottie quotient, but that line has always rung truer than true. I looked at the display wig in the window, then back across the street at the cash machine, and, well, I *carp*ed that *diem*.

The queen was visibly delighted when I told her I'd take it. I knew she'd probably get a handsome commission. She trimmed the wig a bit, said, "If you tweeze your brows it'll look even better," and started to put it in a plastic bag.

"No," I said. "I'll wear it."

As soon as I got out on the street, I felt like a new woman. Men turned and stared. I didn't know if they were staring because they thought I was hot or because they knew it was a wig, but it didn't really matter. They were looking.

●

When I got home from the store I raced to my room and opened my closet. There was no doubt in my mind that I should wear the wig on the date, because it seemed like just the sort of thing James would enjoy. But I needed a dress to go with it: something saucy yet simultaneously demure. Cute hot, not slut hot. I combed through my clothes until my eyes fell upon a bright white number.

It was the nurse dress I'd bought junior year for Halloween at the Providence Salvation Army, also known as the fashion locus of the Western world. I had found it in the uniforms section, and when I got back to my dorm I hemmed it to ass length and went to a party. I didn't stop getting compliments the whole night. I felt like a porno movie come to life. And James was a highly pornographic man.

After dinner I showered, tweezed my eyebrows, bleached my

mustache, and put on some lipstick, the wig, the dress, and my brown platform heels. I slipped on a boiled-wool car coat, put the stories in a fake-alligator-leather lunch-box handbag, and went to the front door. My mom came out of the kitchen. "What did you do to your hair?"

"It's a wig," I said.

"Leo! Zach! You gotta see this!"

My dad and Zach emerged from Zach's room, where they'd been surfing the Net.

"Oh, dear God," said my dad.

"It's not real!" said my mom. "It's a wig!"

"You look like one of those Hasidic women," said Zach.

"I'm trying to look like Mary Richards."

"You don't look like Mary!" laughed my dad. "You look more like one of the daughters in *Fiddler on the Roof*. How ya doing, Chava? Why aren't your legs covered?" My mom laughed and so did Zach, and then the three of them broke into the chorus of "Sunrise, Sunset."

"Leave me alone!" I snapped, went out the door, and slammed it behind me. I felt a little guilty for being such a bitch, but it was such a mood killer to be dressed like a looker and have to deal with a naggy family.

●

When I got out of the subway I stopped at a newsstand and bought a pack of American Spirit cigarettes, the natural, nonaddictive kind. I've always thought their motto should be "They'll kill you, but slowly." I don't really like smoking but I like the way I look smoking. I buy cigarettes whenever I want to feel sexy or jaded, then smoke one or two and throw the rest of the pack out.

I lit up, walked to the bar, and cupped my hands against the window to see if I could spot James. He was sitting right by the window, sipping a glass of beer. I pushed the door open and posed in the doorway, the cigarette hand poised against the jamb, the other on my hip. I looked straight at him and said, "I'm not a smoker, but I play one on TV." He lifted his head and smiled. So did some of the other patrons. That was a little embarrassing, but I knew I had to own the moment.

I approached him in the sultriest strut I could muster, trying not to stumble in my platform heels, feeling glad I'd worn control-top panty hose.

"That's a gorgeous wig," he said.

"How'd you know it was a wig?"

"It's crooked. I can see your hairline." I pulled it down. "What would you like to drink?"

I was about to say a Bass, but I thought it might sound unfeminine, so instead I said, "How about a whiskey sour?" I'd never had one before but it seemed like just the kind of drink a swinging single woman might order.

He beckoned the bartender over. "Another Bass please, and a whiskey sour."

"I don't have any sour mix," said the bartender a bit gruffly, looking at me. "I can give you whiskey, lemon juice, and sugar." Suddenly I realized my faux pas: a whiskey sour was a bourgeois drink—and this was not a bourgeois bar. There was sawdust on the floor and a few rickety tables in the back, and all the other patrons were haggard old men.

"Just make it two Basses," I mumbled.

The bartender brought the beers and James and I went to a table in the back. "Can I help you with your coat?" he asked.

"Sure. That's sweet of you."

"It's not as altruistic as you think," he said, easing it off my shoulders. "Do you know where the tradition of men helping women with their coats comes from?"

"No."

"From men wanting to rub against women's rears. It's a classic masking of an ageless urge." I waited for him to press himself against me but he just pulled the coat off and sat down across from me.

"Did you bring the stories?" he said.

"Yes."

"Why don't you read me one?"

I reached for my handbag and took out "Shooting Wad and Movies." He came across the table and sat down next to me.

"Why did you move?" I asked.

"Because I want to watch you from the side. That way, when you look at me, you'll have to peer over your shoulder. I find it very sexy when a woman peers over her shoulder at me. Did you ever notice how women in fashion advertisements are posed that way?"

"No."

"It's because that's the mammalian come-hither look, from the days we were four-legged creatures and did it from behind." James was revealing himself to be severely deranged, but I'm never intrigued unless the guy's somewhat deranged.

I looked down at the papers.

"I first met Mitchell Sorensen on the set of an NYU graduate film we had both been cast in. It was about a young girl's budding friendship with the school janitor."

As I continued to read, James watched me closely. If I lifted my hand to brush the wig from my face, he stared at my hand. If I licked my lips because my mouth was getting dry, he stared at my tongue. He watched me like watching me was a cottage industry.

When I finished the story, he said, "Now, why don't you take out the other one?"

"But you heard it at rehearsal," I said. "Why do you want to hear it again?"

"It'll help me get performance ideas."

I was in a predicament I could not have anticipated: James was turning out to be more interested in my talent than my *talent*. Suddenly, someone turned on the jukebox. Loud Sinatra came on. "Let's go somewhere quieter," said James. I was relieved. Maybe the change of pace would make him forget about the stories.

We went to a Greek diner and sat down in a booth, side by side. When the waiter came I ordered a coffee and James ordered a grapefruit. That made me slightly uncomfortable. I'd never met a man who ordered grapefruit. He spooned out a wedge, munched it, and said, "Please read."

"I don't want to anymore," I said.

"I think you should."

"Why?"

"It's good for you."

"No, it's not. I know what's good for me and I can tell you that's not it. What would be good would be if you took me home with you."

"But you have so much tension inside you right now. That tense energy is exactly what I want to put onstage. It's what makes you so sexy—that desire, that fervor. I want you to play with what it feels like not to have any release."

"I *want* release!"

He spooned out another wedge, chewed it slowly, sighed, and said, "All right. Let me help you with your coat."

●

He had his own place on Christopher, with a loft bed. There was a brown leather couch, a TV across from it, and an armchair in the far corner, by the window. To the left of the front door was a kitchen with a butcher-block island. "What do you do for a living?" I asked.

"I'm a carpenter." Boy oh boy. He worked with his hands. I wanted to jump him, but I had to play it cool.

He went into the kitchen, poured himself some whiskey, and offered me a glass. I took a sip. It burned my throat but I tried not to wince. He sat on the couch. I put down the drink and started to climb up the ladder to the bed, hoping he would follow. But he tugged on my leg and said sternly, "You can't go up there. It's private."

I wished he'd put it more politely, but politeness is so overrated. I sat down next to him and leaned in to kiss him. He kissed back a little, but his tongue was fat and lazy and he didn't seem to take any pleasure in the contact. Then he pulled away, stood up, and crossed over to the armchair.

"What are you doing?" I asked.

"My primary interest is in watching men watch you. That's why I wanted to meet you in a bar. Did you notice how all the men looked at you when you took off your coat?"

"Sort of."

"That's because you have something very special. You exude sex. And men can smell that. You will walk down the streets and they will sniff it in you. You should stare into the eyes of men on the streets and enjoy how much they will want you."

I wanted to believe I had that much power. I wanted to believe I was the kind of girl who made men crazy, even if I was too fat to be an ingenue, even if this was my first date since I'd come to the city.

He kept talking, and I stuck my hand down my stockings. Between his dirty talk and the buildup from the diner, it only took me about ten minutes.

"I came," I said after. (I don't make any loud noises. I never do.)

"I'm glad," he said.

I thought about leaving but I didn't feel ready. I wanted to arouse him, and since he wouldn't let me touch him, I decided to try another way. I stood up by the couch and slowly unzipped the front of my nurse dress. I slid it off my shoulders and threw it on the floor, till I was standing in front of him in just my panty hose and Minimizer bra. I unsnapped my bra slowly, dropped it on the floor too, and ran my fingers up and down my breasts, like a stripper in a movie.

He opened his mouth and watched me, and then he unzipped his pants, took it out, and began to stroke it. I kept moving around, pretending "Fever" was playing in the background, and from time to time I would reach my hand up and flip the wig like it was real. His blinds were up and it was dark outside, so I could see my reflection in the window. In that black wig, with my bra off, in my stockings and platform heels, I was a glam queen. I was beautiful.

After several minutes he leaned his head back hard and fast against the chair with a thump and shot it out all over his hand and pants. I went to the bathroom and got a Kleenex. As I handed it to him he looked up at me with sad, round eyes and whispered, "You found my weakness." I put my dress back on and he walked me to a cab, but when I tried to kiss him good night, he turned his face away again.

•

On the ride home I thought about what I had done. I didn't like how he'd refused to kiss me or let me in his bed, but I really liked that line about me finding his weakness. That meant I'd made him vulnerable. That meant he was into me.

When I got back to the apartment it was one in the morning and the house was quiet. I tiptoed past my parents' bedroom toward mine. "Did you have a good time?" my mom called out.

I felt a pang of guilt that she'd been awake worrying about me and that I'd been such a bitch on my way out the door. "Yes," I said. "Really good."

I went into the bathroom and took off the wig. I looked in the mirror and my real hair looked strange framing my face.

2

WHEN I CAME INTO WORK the next morning, the Corposhit was waiting with a stack of papers for me to copy. It was rare for her to be giving me stuff to do. That's the irony of temping: they never give you enough work but they can't stand to see you doing nothing, so your main responsibility is pretending to be busy. It wouldn't be so bad if you sat down at your desk and your boss said, "Hi. I've got nothing for you to do today. Absolutely nothing. Feel free to paint your nails, masturbate, or pick your ass." But it doesn't happen that way. If your boss notices that you're not doing anything, then *her* lack of responsibility becomes so glaringly obvious that she gets pissed—and blames you for her own inability to move up the corporate ladder.

Each day I would occupy myself with the various fake-busy tasks: surfing the Internet, playing computer solitaire, calling in for messages, taking frequent bathroom trips to stare in the mirror at my steadily sagging rear, and reading magazines and newspapers under the desk. Usually I read the *Times*, but today I had been planning to read the *City Week*.

The *Week* was the *Village Voice*'s main competitor and it was distributed free on Wednesdays in green metal boxes on every corner in downtown Manhattan. My dad had introduced me to it when I was fourteen. He came home from work one night and plopped down a copy on my floor, open to a syndicated question-and-answer column called "The Skinny Puppy," by a guy named

Simon LeGros. Readers sent in questions about anything they didn't understand ("What is the function of male nipples?" or "How did the flipping-the-bird gesture originate?"), and he gave long, fascinating answers. When I finished reading the column I turned to the film reviews, and then I looked up my horoscope and glanced at a few of the comics. The entire paper was quirky but endearing, and I felt like I was discovering a well-kept city secret. From then on I started picking it up myself on the way home from school. When I went to Brown, my dad would mail me clippings from time to time, and now that I was back in the city I read the paper every week.

Like the *Voice,* it had lots of X-rated ads and a Personals section, but unlike the *Voice,* its political bent was just to the right of Mussolini. The editor in chief, Steve Jensen, in his column, "Knee-Jerk Asshole," wrote diatribes against Bill Clinton interspersed with two-sentence reviews of tony Tribeca restaurants, and tons of readers wrote in regularly to call him a fascist neocon. In addition to Jensen, there were three autobiographical columnists: Len Hyman, a neurotic suburban dad ("The Nebbish"), Dave Nadick, a depressed suicidal with a degenerative nerve disease ("Wasted"), and Stu Pfeffer, a young punk rocker ("The Mosh Pit"). Each week they would regale readers with their latest sagas—Hyman taking his daughter to her first day of kindergarten, Nadick throwing himself in front of a car, Pfeffer squeezing some girl's tits at a CBGB show. I loved tuning in to the different pathetic lives each week. It made me feel like I wasn't doing so badly.

I put down my bag, took the papers from the Corposhit, and headed to the copy room very slowly so I could keep her waiting if she had something else for me to do. When I got there I stuck the papers in the copying tray, but after only one copy the machine jammed. I opened every single door in the machine, searching for the offending paper, but I couldn't find it. Just as I was about to smash my fist into the glass I heard someone say, "Do you need some help?" I turned around. A thin, tall girl with shoulder-length black hair, burgundy lipstick, and a small tattoo on her left hand was standing behind me.

"I think I do," I said.

She strode over to the machine, opened a door on the side I hadn't noticed, violently ripped out a piece of paper, and slammed the door shut. "Sometimes you just have to be brutal with it."

"I wouldn't want to be on your shit list," I said.

"No, you wouldn't," she said.

"Are you a temp?"

"Yeah. How'd you guess?"

"The tattoo. I'm a temp too. Ariel Steiner."

"Sara Green." We shook hands. "What do you think of this place?"

"I hate it. I hate doing nothing and I hate doing work, because both drive me crazy."

"Me too. I was in the International Socialist Organization in college, and now I'm licking the asshole of corporate America."

"I was in the ISO too! Where'd you go to school?"

"Columbia. You?"

"Brown."

"What are you—actress, opera singer, or musician?"

"Actress. What about you?"

"I'm a rock star in training. I'm studying accordion and writing my own songs. You want to see my cubicle?"

"OK."

Hers was one floor down. She'd been using our copy machine because hers was broken. On her bulletin board, she had Clash, Sex Pistols, and Replacements stickers, and there were headphones plugged into her CD-ROM. "Does your boss mind when you listen to music?" I asked.

"He doesn't know. I only do it when his door's closed, and only in one ear so I can hear if he's coming."

I noticed a pink message slip on the desk with some typewritten words on it. "You *type* your boss's messages?" I asked incredulously.

"No," she said and handed me the slip. Under the words *While You Were Out* she had typed, in neat bold caps, I THOUGHT ABOUT WAYS TO KILL YOU. I asked if she wanted to come to lunch.

●

I always ate my lunch in the Met Life building because they had performances on a stage in the mezzanine each day between twelve and one—big bands, ballroom dancing, and barbershop quartets. When Sara and I got there, a gorgeous svelte couple from a midtown dance center was demonstrating the tango. We found a seat on the bleachers and then Sara took out a Yoo-Hoo and a tuna sandwich on Wonder bread, and I took out a yogurt and a rice cake.

"I wish I were that woman," I said, staring out at the dancers. "A cruel, vicious chick who won't take no for an answer."

"Me too," said Sara. "But my love life sucks a horse's penis. A couple weeks ago, my friend Liz set me up with this sculptor she knew. I met him for drinks at BarCode, and twenty minutes later we were sixty-nining on his mattress. We had the most sensuous and electrifying three-week affair, but one morning he called to say his ex-girlfriend had come back into town from Prague and he'd decided to get back together with her."

"That's awful."

"Not really. Because a couple days later, I was sitting in this café on Avenue A by my apartment, writing lyrics, when this très Keith Richardsesque rocker in a polyester button-down started making eyes at me. Twenty minutes later we were sixty-nining on his mattress. But a few nights later we were fooling around, and when I asked if I could tie him to the headboard, he jumped out of bed and started pacing up and down the room, saying that was just a little too weird to be believed, was I some kind of pervert or something? I was like, '*Some*one's a closet submissive.' "

"You said that?"

"No. Thought it. I just watched him pace around for a while, and then I was like, 'Are you gonna get back in bed so we can talk about this, or are you comfortable just being a raging asshole?' "

"You *said* that?"

"No. Thought it. I didn't say anything. I got up, put on my clothes, and went to my ex-boyfriend Jon's apartment in Hell's Kitchen. We've been having a really jagged breakup."

"When did you break up?"

"Six years ago. We were high school sweethearts in Paramus, where I'm from, but he went to NYU, so we kept seeing each other on and off throughout college. We're trying to stop fucking, but it's not easy. You know. The ties that bind."

"Yeah," I said. "My boyfriend at Brown—Will—and I kept having sex for four months after he dumped me."

"Why'd he dump you?"

"I cheated on him with Bo Rodriguez, the president of Students Against Classist Oppression."

"And your boyfriend walked in on you?"

"No. I hooked up with Bo at a party, fall of freshman year, right after Will and I started going out, but I didn't tell Will till the end of the semester. The guilt just got to be too much and I confessed, one morning in his bed. He pushed me off onto the floor and said he felt like he could never trust me again. But he didn't break up with me either. We went out for another year and had this really mutually abusive relationship where all we did was fight and fuck. He finally dumped me January of sophomore year, claiming he couldn't trust me anymore, but we slept together on and off till May."

"Guys are weird about their girlfriends sleeping with other guys."

"I didn't sleep with Bo. We only went to second."

"That's ridiculous. Your boyfriend freaked because of a make-out?"

"His father left his mother for another woman, so his views on fidelity were kind of loaded."

She nodded understandingly. I was spilling my guts, but it didn't feel strange. Sara made me feel like I could never one-up her in the dysfunction department. By the time we were on our way back to work, she had informed me that at different points in her life she'd been suicidal, bulimic, on Prozac, president of her temple youth group, knocked up, doped up, coked up, institutionalized, and a member of NA, OA, AA, and Phi Beta Kappa. In light of her past, I decided she wouldn't be too weirded out if I told her about James.

"It sounds like he's bad news," she said. "I think he's a provocateur."

"What's that?"

"Someone who walks into a bar, sees two guys in a brawl, hands one of them a gun, then leaves."

"Am I the guy he hands the gun to, or the guy about to get shot?"

"It's not an exact metaphor. I'm just saying, he likes to push buttons. If you want your buttons pushed, then go for it. But if you're looking for a boyfriend, you're probably gonna need to find a guy who doesn't have serious issues about letting you in his bed."

●

James did turn out to be bad news. That night at rehearsal he didn't say a word to me, and whenever he caught me looking at him, he looked away. I had thought my finding his weakness would make him like me more, not less. It didn't make any sense. I didn't understand how his intrigue could turn so quickly to disgust.

When he was on his way out the door, I ran up to him and said, "Can we talk for a second?"

"No," he said and rushed out. I called him when I got home, but the machine picked up, so I left a message. He never called back.

I left half a dozen more messages over the next few weeks, but he didn't return any of them. He would pretend to act normal when we were rehearsing, but he never spoke to me during any of the breaks. I tried to forget about him and pour myself into the role. Sometimes it worked. I would be running a scene with Gene and get so involved in it that I'd forget James was watching. But there were other times when I would catch James's eye in the audience, lose focus, and have to call for my line.

One night about a week before the show was set to open, the phone rang at twelve-forty-five. My parents and Zach had already gone to sleep and I was just drifting off myself. I raced into the living room and picked up the cordless.

"Hello?" I said.

"Listen," he said, "someone's been calling me around one in the morning the past couple nights, then hanging up when I answer. Was it you?"

I didn't know which pissed me off more, the fact that he was presumptuous enough to call and ask if I'd been harassing him or the fact that he had no idea how presumptuous he was. I knew hating him wasn't much better for my mental health than pining after him, but it felt like a step in the right direction.

"I'm sorry to disappoint you, James," I said as haughtily as I could, "but it wasn't me." And I hung up quickly, before he could say anything back.

●

Despite James, *Lolita: Rock On* was a huge success. We ran the first two weekends of August and were sold out almost every night. I got to dance and sing and play my clarinet, my car scene with Gene was the highlight of the evening, and most of the dialogue from "Vanya in My Vulva" made it into the final script. We served the audience free beer and wine at the door and deliberately started each performance half an hour late so they all had time to get happy.

Gene had instructed me, whenever I wasn't onstage, to go around the audience and interact with people. That was my favorite part of doing the show. I'd sit on a hot guy's lap, put my arms around his neck, and whisper, "I really like you," into his ear until his girlfriend started to give me dirty looks, and then I'd move on to the next guy.

Because of the lap sitting and the "Vanya" story, I was a little nervous about inviting my parents. The day before we opened I sat them down at the dinner table and said, "Some of the material in the show might make you uncomfortable. If you don't want to come, I won't feel offended." So they didn't. And I *was* offended, but I didn't give them a hard time because I didn't know how to explain that even though I had told them not to feel obligated, they should have felt obligated anyway.

Sara saw the show three times. She said my performance put that Kubrick chick's to shame. I opted not to invite Faye, though. She was sixty years old—and she wasn't a hip sixty, either. If she saw the show she'd think I was trashy, not talented.

One night I was on my way out of the theater when someone tapped me on the arm. I turned around and this lanky guy with curly brown hair said, "I just wanted to tell you how incredible I thought you were."

Hmm, I thought.

"Thanks a lot. I appreciate it." He had a slightly upturned nose, and a dried white piece of snot was poised delicately on the end of one of its hairs. I wasn't disgusted, though. I was charmed. He was handsome but human.

"It says in the program that you contributed some of the material in the show," he said. "Which parts?"

"The car scene, and that story I told about *Vanya on 42nd Street.*"

"I thought you wrote that. It was my favorite monologue in the play."

"Thanks," I said again. He smiled at me, but I couldn't think of anything else to say. How could I make a move on a random audience member without coming off as completely desperate? Before I could figure it out, though, someone else came up to congratulate me. I turned away for a second, and when I looked back the guy was gone.

●

As soon as the show closed, I started looking for an apartment. I had saved over $2,000 and decided it was time to get my own place. I knew I wanted to live in Brooklyn—not just because it was cheaper than Manhattan but because I had always taken pride in my bridge-and-tunnel origins. Not that Brooklyn Heights was ghetto central—it's the most stuck-up, Waspy neighborhood in the borough—but at least it wasn't the Upper East Side. I had to hold on to what little street credibility I was born with, by staying on the wrong side of the tracks. I was a middle-class girl with working-class aspirations.

One afternoon when the Corposhit was out at a meeting, I logged on to the *Village Voice* classifieds (that was how Sara found her apartment) and typed in "Brooklyn studios." The fifth listing down read, "CARROLL GARDENS—Lg studio on safe, tree-lined st, 5 bls from F. Sunny, lg closet, hwd fls, $750/mo. Call Al Casanova."

That last name had to be an omen. Maybe this guy would

bring good luck to my love life. I made an appointment to see it after work and called Sara to ask if she'd come along.

When we got out of the subway I liked the neighborhood immediately. The streets were quiet and wide and filled with trees, and in every front yard was a statue of the Virgin Mary. Old women were sitting on stoops staring at the people going by, men in undershirts were leaning their heads out of upstairs windows, kids were playing hockey, and yuppie moms were wheeling babies in strollers.

The brownstone was on Clinton Street, at the corner of Luquer, just a few blocks from the Brooklyn-Queens Expressway. We rang the bell and a bulky guy in his mid-forties came to answer.

"I'm Ariel," I said.

"I'm Al." He looked at Sara disdainfully. "You didn't say anything about a roommate. I can't have that. It's too small for two people."

"She's just my friend," I said. "The apartment's for me."

"Oh," he said, eyeing her like he still didn't believe me, and leading us inside. The hallway was musty and smelled of cat. There was a radiator to the right of the door, and leaning precariously on top of it was a statue of a young boy with golden hair and a rosary around his neck.

"Who's that?" I said.

"Saint Christopher," he said. I decided not to put a mezuzah on my doorpost.

"I live on the bottom floor, with my brother Carl," he said, heading up the stairs. "We don't want anyone noisy and we don't want any funny business. He works very long hours and he needs peace and quiet when he comes home."

"What does he do?" said Sara.

"He's a funeral director."

"What do *you* do?" I said.

"Oh, I can't work," he said gravely.

"Why not?"

"I have a bum leg. I broke it on a construction job eight years ago and it's given me horrible pain since then. But I'm suing the city and I have a feeling we're going to settle any day now."

"When did you sue?" asked Sara.

"Right after it happened. Nineteen eighty-eight."

When we got to the top of the stairs I noticed a three-foot-high cylindrical-shaped indentation in the wall. "Did there used to be a statue there?" I asked Al.

"No," he said. "Every apartment in Carroll Gardens has one of those. That's so your coffin can clear the corner when you die.

The houses in this neighborhood were meant to be lived in for a lifetime." I liked that ethos—but I wasn't sure I wanted Al to be the one who carried me out.

He opened the apartment door, and I took a deep breath and walked in. It was cozy and bright. On the right side of the room were two windows overlooking the backyard, with a view of the BQE. On the left was an eat-in kitchen, a large closet, and a tiny bathroom with a Home Depot Formica sink and a blue tub and toilet. While I was running the faucet Sara came in. "What do you think?" I whispered.

"I think it's a steal," she said.

I walked over to Al and said, "I'll take it."

•

By the time I moved, I was down to 129 pounds. No Karen Carpenter, but certainly skinny enough to show Faye I stood a chance at ingenue parts. So, one day on my lunch break I changed into high red go-go boots, a brown miniskirt, and a tight black T-shirt and took the bus to her office. When I took off my jacket she said she couldn't believe the transformation and would start sending me out on vapid-hot-girl parts immediately.

Two days later she got me an audition. It was for a new NBC sitcom to be produced by Phil Nathanson, creator of the hit eighties sitcom about disgruntled postal workers, *Return to Sender*. The new show was called *Dem's da Breaks* and it was about a working-class widow named Gina who gets into an Ivy League college at age forty-five, goes back to school, and experiences severe culture clash with the ruling class. My role was Bridget, a series regular, a rich, smart college girl in Gina's class, the cynical, snobbish contrast to her homegrown wisdom. "They want a young Dorothy Parker, a Gen X Fran Lebowitz," Faye told me on the phone. "Sarcastic, funny, and jaded."

"Sounds great," I said.

"Wear a little makeup when you go. It'll make you look pretty."

I picked up the sides after work. In the scene, Bridget arrives in an empty classroom, finds Gina sitting in the front row, and says, "Are you the cleaning woman?" Gina explains that she's a student and goes on to give Bridget a long, comic lecture about class consciousness. By the end, the two of them are on their way to becoming good friends. It was cheesy and obvious, but some of the lines were sharp, and I felt like I could nail it.

The audition was scheduled for a Saturday afternoon. I spent the morning going through the script, and then I pinned my hair back slick to my head and into a bun, put on a full face of makeup, and changed into a zip-up ribbed black top with fake fur collars, and a brown miniskirt, with the platform heels. I felt like a smart slut. A rich prima donna. A Mia Sara Jessica.

When I got to the audition, there were dozens of other, markedly less Semitic-looking Fran Lebowitzes sitting in the hallway, fixing their makeup and reading the sides. I even recognized a few of them from the *Book 'Em* audition. I signed in, and a few minutes later a pregnant blond woman in overalls came out of the office and called my name.

The audition room was long and bright, with high ceilings. Sitting all the way at the end, with a video camera behind him, was a fifteen-year-old boy.

"This is Kevin," said the casting director. "He'll be reading with you."

"You mean . . . he's Gina, the working-class widow?"

"Yes." Was it bring-your-son-to-work day or something? How was I supposed to build a believable relationship when I was acting with a *kid*—and a guy?

She stood behind the camera and peered into the lens. "First we'll do a rehearsal and then we'll do a take. Did you learn the lines?"

"No. Was I supposed to?"

"Of course you were."

I felt the floor slip out from beneath my feet. "I'm sorry, my agent didn't say anything about that, so I—"

"This is a TV audition," she said. "You should always learn the lines." I'd been on TV auditions in high school and not learned the lines and never had a casting director complain, but I didn't feel this was the time to point that out. "If you have to," she said, "then try it on book. Whenever you're ready."

My read was decent, but when I was done she said, "I'm really losing your face in the script. Why don't you try it, just once, without looking at the lines? It's such a short scene. Put the sides down, slate your name, and go for it." She gave me a perky smile.

I gingerly laid the pages on the floor. She went behind the camera. The red light of doom came on. "Slate, please."

"Ariel Steiner," I said, like it was the beginning of my eulogy. Then I looked down at my hands for a moment, desperately trying to channel my misery into snobbery, gave Eddie Haskell a patronizing glare, imagining that he was female, Italian, and forty-five, and opened my mouth.

Nothing came out. I'd completely blanked. Very daintily, I leaned down out of frame, picked up the script, looked at the first line, put the script back on the floor, and said, "Are you the cleaning woman?" with as much narrow-minded maliciousness as I could well up.

But this time I was even worse than the first. Joke after joke came out whiny and desperate—because all my energy was going toward trying to get the words right.

"You do know the lines," said the casting director when I finished. "Try it again, and this time you can keep the script on your lap."

She was trying to be encouraging, but I hated her anyway. I hated her for talking down to me, for forcing me to do the scene off book, and for making me audition with a child. But I knew it wouldn't serve me to get angry. I took a deep breath to calm myself and got a whiff of my own BO, so foul it almost knocked me out. I could feel my mascara beginning to trickle down my face.

My next time through I remembered all the lines, but I still wasn't funny, because I was so tense. I had lost all desire to please her or please myself. Halfway through the scene I began to give a deliberately monotonal read. It became a sick game: how hard could I make this woman struggle to like me?

At the end she gave me a plastic smile and walked me out. I glanced quickly at all the other hopefuls, who knew to memorize their lines and wear waterproof mascara, and I wanted to whip out an Uzi and gun them down in one clean round.

I didn't cry when I got out on the street, though. I just figured you win some, you lose some, and at least I'd learned my lesson: don't ever go on a TV audition unmemorized again. But then I started to fantasize that maybe, just maybe, despite my atrocious read, I'd book the part anyway. One of my theater professors at Brown used to tell our class these industry legends about now-famous people who gave bad auditions but were discovered because some casting director saw the charisma within that would be certain to make them stars.

I could see it now. Phil Nathanson would be sitting in his sunny Burbank office smoking a Cohiba as he watched tramp after talentless tramp attempt to be funny and smart at the same time. As the thousandth chippy of the day slated her name, his fat round head would begin to droop, and then suddenly I'd appear on the screen. Through his filthy, wax-filled ears he'd hear the words "Ariel Steiner" and something about the pure, vulnerable timbre in my voice would make him jerk his head up toward the monitor. As I blanked on my first line and leaned out of frame to look at the script, the moment would have such unrehearsed comic charm that a smile of delight would creep across Phil's jowls. As I stumbled pathetically through the rest of the take, his smile would turn to a chuckle, and the chuckle to a howl of delight. "Why, she's the young Dorothy Parker!" he'd shout, rising to his feet. "The Gen X Fran Lebowitz! Sarcastic! Funny! Jaded! She can't act to save her life, but her natural sardonic style is exactly what I'm looking for!"

Then he'd race to his red emergency phone, the one he used only for very special occasions, like the time he discovered the *Return to Sender* superstar, Fred Hanson, and he'd lean down and shout to his coproducer and brother-in-law, "Stan—get your ass in here!" Two seconds later Stan would run into the office, and as they watched my second take they'd cry simultaneously, "Hello, new It Girl!"

"This chick's the future of TV!" Stan would exclaim.

"I know!" Phil would reply. And then he'd get right on the phone to Faye and cast me on the spot, and I'd be on my way to taking the world by storm.

But then I realized how naive I was being. I was trying to convince myself that it was precisely my *lack* of preparedness, my *in*ability to follow the rules that would mark me as someone who wasn't afraid to make bold choices. But that was just plain stupid. Forgetting to learn my lines wasn't a bold choice, it was a suicidal one. Phil probably wouldn't even get to see my audition anyway, because they'd weed me out before the tapes even made it back to L.A. I walked to a pay phone, called Sara, and asked if she'd meet me for a drink.

●

We decided to go to BarNacle. We'd gone there a few times before. It was on Ludlow, south of Houston, and they had booths and a pool table in the back, pop art on the walls, and two pinball machines in the front. The only times we went there were before nine on weekends, or on weeknights. It had been listed in *Let's Go New York*, and if you went late on a weekend there were so many Germans you felt like you'd walked into a Nazi youth convention.

When I walked in I spotted Sara at the bar talking to a skinny guy with dark skin. I was glad I was dressed like a vapid hot girl. The guy smiled at me, and Sara said, "Hey, Ar. This is Josh Malansky. We went to Columbia together. We bumped into each other on the street and I asked if he wanted to join us."

Malansky. He had to be a tribesman. Which was a definite perk. Since the age of fifteen I have not been able to spend more than ten minutes with a guy I'm attracted to without wondering if he's Jewish. As soon as I find out that he is, I start fantasizing about our future together. An image floats into my head of the two of us getting married under a *huppah*, my parents shedding tears of joy and him smashing a glass beneath his feet.

It's not like I won't get naked with a goy. I totally will. It's just that deep down, I won't ever feel like we could have Future Potential. He could be my Perfect Goy, but not my Perfect Guy. We could fuck like wild boars, but no matter how good the *shtup*, I'll spend half the time trying to fight the image of my parents weeping when I tell them I've met a *shaygitz*, disowning me, and the two of us getting married in a Vegas shotgun church teeming with grimy white-trash couples.

I sat down on a stool next to Josh and ordered a Jameson on the rocks. Sara had gotten me into Jameson. She said it made you look tough as nails and not to be messed with. I hated the taste but I figured that was the price I had to pay.

As the bartender set my glass down, I noticed that Josh was drinking a nonalcoholic beer. That intrigued me. Maybe alcohol had done something brutal to him. The only quality that turns me on more than Yidhood is a troubled and tormented past.

"What do you do, Josh?" I asked.

"I drum in three bands and work at the Kinko's on Houston Street."

"Is it true what they say about drummers?"

"What?"

"That they're all off-balance, unstable, and combustible, like in *Spinal Tap*?"

"It's not a totally groundless stereotype," he said, grinning. "Most of the drummers I know are like that. You guys want to hear a joke?"

"Sure," I said.

"What do you call a guy who hangs out with musicians?"

"What?"

"A drummer." I smiled. Sara snort-laughed. "What does it mean when the drummer is drooling out of both sides of his mouth?"

"What?"

"It means the stage is level."

"Very good," Sara said.

"But what about the stereotype that drummers mooch off their girlfriends?" I asked. "Is *that* true?"

"Sometimes," he said.

"Are *you* mooching off a girlfriend?"

"I don't have a girlfriend." Sara gave me a look, then started to get up.

"I've, um . . . gotta go practice accordion," she said. "Nice to run into you, Josh. Call me later, Ar."

Josh and I grinned at each other awkwardly and he ordered another nonalcoholic. "Are you a teetotaler?" I asked.

"Yeah. I stopped drinking a couple months ago. I was traveling in South America and drinking every night and I got in this really bad brawl in Lima. That's how I got this." He pointed to a two-inch-long scar running down his left cheek. My vaginal canal immediately got fifty feet longer. Ever since I saw Charles Bukowski's acned author shot in the back of *Women*, I've had a fetish for men with bad skin. The more pockmarked, the better. Edward James Olmos, Tommy Lee Jones, James Woods, Dennis Miller, Bill Murray—they all make me crazy with lust.

"I have a scar on my chin," I said. "I fell off a bike when I was twelve." I tilted my head up to show him. I can always gauge my potential with a guy according to his reaction to my chin scar. If he's into it, I know we could spend our lives together. If not, there's no hope at all.

"Nice," he said, nodding approvingly. "I think scars are sexy. They show character."

I was putty in this cat's hands, and it only got better as the evening went on. He was from Telluride, he'd been traveling for the past seven months, and he was living in Williamsburg with some friends. He had a loud, wild laugh and a quick, easy smile, and overall he seemed like a much better potential boyfriend than James.

On my third Jameson I suggested we move to a booth in the back. When we got to the booth I sat down and he lay with his head on my lap and closed his eyes. I wanted to scream but instead I acted casual. I picked up a *Village Voice* sitting on the table, thumbed through the pages, and deliberately let them brush against his hands.

After a while he reached for my hand and put it on his, keeping his eyes closed. We stayed like that for about ten minutes, and then I decided to make a bolder move. I put my other hand against his face and stroked his rubbery skin and scar and lips. He opened his eyes and pulled my face toward his.

Wow. His lips were malleable and since his beer was nonalcoholic, he tasted good. I helped him sit up so I could lie on top of him and then we kissed and dry-humped for a while on the seat. I didn't care if anyone saw. He was exactly what I'd been looking for: scarred, teetotalling, Jewish, and under me. I asked if he wanted to come over.

It was a humid August night and our subway wasn't air-conditioned, so when we got out at Carroll Street we bought two juices at the deli across from the station and drank them on the walk to my apartment. When we got upstairs I put the leftover juices in the refrigerator, turned out the light, and switched on the patio lanterns strung along the ceiling.

I hoped Josh wouldn't think my decor was immature. My bed, a futon, had a cheap green-and-magenta plaid blanket on it. To the right of the bed was a card table with my computer on top, and a gray metal folding chair I got at Staples. Between the windows was a particleboard bookcase, and by the right window was my makeshift entertainment center—CD towers, two milk crates with my TV and CD player on top of them, and wooden speakers my parents had bought in the seventies. Facing the TV was another futon, in couch position, but for some reason the mattress never seemed to stay on the frame, so you could only sit on it for about five minutes before you slid onto the floor.

If the furniture wasn't collegiate enough, the posters were. But luckily I'd relegated the most offending to the kitchen: the Matisse of the dancing girls, *The Kiss*, and Bob Marley. Above my bed was Bob Dylan in *Don't Look Back*, and on the other wall were Johnny Depp in *Dead Man*; album covers of Joan Armatrading, *Track Record*, Jim Croce, *Time in a Bottle*, and Johnny Cash, *Ragged Old Flag*; a framed copy of the Bukowski photo; a publicity shot from *Say Anything...* of John Cusack embracing Ione Skye; and a lithograph my grandmother had given me of an old Yiddish saying: *"Beser tsu shtarbn shteyendig vi tsu lebn oyf di kni'es."*

"What does that mean?" said Josh, staring up at it.

" 'Better to die standing than to live on your knees,' " I said. "Not that I'm opposed to living on my knees every once in a while, though. For a *really good cause.*"

He turned red and headed for the CD towers. That made me nervous. I always want guys to compliment me on my collection because most guys think girls have no taste in music, and I want to be one of the few who do. Some guys get off on my Rufus and Chaka Khan, others my Sebadoh or Coltrane, but what impresses nearly all of them is my Dylan collection: I have fourteen of his albums.

My fandom began senior year of Brown, when I saw him in *Don't Look Back* on a date with this ISO guy named Jason Levin. As soon as Bob appeared on the screen, fey, thick lipped, and young, I had a fantasy that still gets me going today: I'd knock out

Jason, race into the film, and leap into my sweetheart's arms. He'd drop his "Subterranean Homesick Blues" cue cards so he could catch me, carry me back to his hotel room, pick up his guitar, and croon "One Too Many Mornings," "Visions of Johanna," and "It's Alright, Ma (I'm Only Bleeding)," in that order. At the end of the medley I'd set his guitar in his stand, remove his sunglasses and boots, unzip his tight dark jeans, and pull him on top of me. He'd rip off my clothes, shake his head from side to side, and say, "Mama, you been on my mind."

"Don't I know it," I'd coo back, and then I'd pull his sizable Semitic sex straight into me and he'd fuck his music into my hole, up to my heart and mouth. I'd feel his brilliance and pathos swirling around inside me and it would be so intense I'd explode in a fabulous o. As soon as I started throbbing, he'd start shooting, and together we'd tremble joyously, him weak for my love, me weak for his genius. As our dual eruptions finally began to fade into the wild blazing night, he'd moan nasally, "Joan Baez don't hold a candle to you, babe," before withdrawing, reaching for the harmonica holder on the nightstand, and lighting a fag. I'd cough, and he'd put his hand on my cheek and stare at me lovingly, marveling at our spiritual and carnal connection.

But suddenly, with a swift V-8–style smack to the forehead, he'd remember he had to get back to the movie. We'd race back to the street scene and kiss good-bye, as Allen Ginsberg eyed us with interest. The audience in the movie theater would suddenly wonder *(a)* where Bob had been for the last forty-five minutes and *(b)* what this chick was doing in the flick. As they rubbed their eyes to make sure they weren't imagining it, I'd leap off the screen back into my seat. Jason would regain consciousness and Bob would start the song again, periodically lifting his sunglasses to wink right at me, so I knew he'd never forget.

"I like your collection," said Josh.

"Thanks," I said. "What do you want to listen to?"

When he said, "How 'bout *Nashville Skyline*?" my heart soared up to the water-stained ceiling, because that album has always been one of my all-time favorites. Jason and I used to lie on his bed and listen over and over to the part on "Girl from the North Country" where Dylan screws up the lyrics, and laugh about it together. Ever since then, I'd been convinced my Perfect Guy would notice that part, too.

I pulled out the disk and stuck it in the player. Then I got under the covers and Josh got under them next to me. I took off some of my clothes. He took off all of his. He looked even skinnier naked, which made me a little nervous. I'd done the small guy thing before and it was kind of scary. I've got enough to think about in bed that I don't need to add accidentally suffocating my partner to the list.

But his body was soft, and so was his mouth, and after a while my asphyxiation fears flew away. When it got to the fuckup in the song, he said, "I love this part." I was ready to walk down the aisle then and there.

We rolled around under the covers and suddenly he popped the question. "Do you have any . . . ?"

I didn't, but I knew one of us could just go to the market on Court Street and get some. At the same time, I was afraid that if I gave it up that easily, he might lose interest. So I said, "No, I don't. I'm sorry. But even if I did, I'm not sure I'd want to anyway. I like you too much. I want us to wait. It's not that I'm not hot for you. I am. I definitely want to sleep with you in the future. Just . . . not yet."

"Me too," he said. We leaned toward each other and kissed more. The breeze wafted in. We fell asleep on top of the blanket because it was so warm.

●

When I woke up he was putting on his clothes. I looked at the clock. It was eight-thirty. "Where are you going?"

"I have a lot of shit to do today."

"But it's Sunday. I was hoping we could go get breakfast together."

"I have to build some shelves."

"Oh."

"But give me your phone number."

I wrote it down for him and he wrote his for me. I put on my robe and followed him downstairs to the door. He put his hand on the doorknob, then turned around abruptly, like he was having a change of heart, and said, "Ariel?"

All my worries slid away. He wasn't walking out on me after all. He would lift my chin with the crook of his finger like in a 1940s movie, tilt my face up, kiss me passionately, and say, "I changed my mind. I *do* want to stay, and not just for the day—for my life!"

"Yes?" I said, gazing at him with bedroom eyes.

"Can I get my juice from your refrigerator?"

●

As I stood in the shower scrubbing my armpits, I replayed the night in my head. Josh seemed to *like* me, not just want me, so I didn't get what I could possibly have done wrong. Maybe he was a closet asshole. Maybe underneath the nice-guy exterior all he really wanted was the nookie, and when he didn't get it, he flew.

Or maybe it had nothing to do with what I had said. Maybe I smelled. I'd recently switched to this all-natural deodorant, Tom's, because Sara had told me regular deodorant gives you breast cancer, and the new deodorant always seemed to wear off by the end of the day. What if he'd secretly been repelled by my odor? Or my underwear? I'd been wearing the high-waisted granny kind when we got into bed because I only owned three pairs of sexy underwear and they were all dirty, but the granny underwear had come off so quickly I didn't think he'd gotten a chance to see it. Then again, maybe I was overreacting. There was always a possibility that he really *did* have to go build shelves. He had given me his phone number, after all.

I got dressed, bought a newspaper at the grocery store down the block, and walked to this café on Smith Street I liked to go to called The Fall that had kitschy-antique furniture and bookshelves with free books. All these twenty-something couples with nice shoes and funky glasses were drinking coffee, reading the Sunday *Times,* and playing footsie under the tables. I walked past them toward the counter, ordered a bagel-with-scrambled and a coffee, then sat down on a couch. I opened my paper to the Weddings pages, and started to read the boxed wedding of the week. The bride and bridegroom had met at a dinner party, fallen instantly in love, and later discovered that his mother and her father had once gone on a date. It was so disgustingly romantic I had to close the paper.

I wanted someone to talk to, kiss, read the Sunday *Times* with, order coffee for. Where was my funky-glasses guy? My footsie player? My young, slender, brilliant-artist type? If I wasn't grossly deformed or retarded, if there was nothing officially wrong with me, why had it been so long since I'd had a boyfriend?

My post-Will liaisons had included a blond water-polo player with a perfect body who took me on one date, then, the following week, fell in love with an emaciated compulsive exerciser; a white freshman with dreads who had gorgeous cheekbones but a major THC problem; Jason, the socialist, who went out with me for two months, then decided he was categorically opposed to monogamy; and Tell, an occasionally cross-dressing punk rock grad student who thanked me for helping him realize that all women are evil.

I knew logically that it might take some time to meet my Perfect Guy, but I was terrified it would never happen. What if I was still living alone in my Carroll Gardens studio at age forty-five? Sara would have a house out in Greenwich, a stockbroker husband, and a litter of kids and cats, and I'd still be frequenting the same East Village bars we used to go to together. And then my chances of getting married would be smaller than my chances of getting killed in a terrorist attack.

I felt like I'd been born at the wrong time. Deep down, I was really a shtetl girl. I didn't want the pogroms, I just wanted the certainty. I wished I could hire a yenta to set me up with my own personal Motel the Tailor—a sensitive, doting, slightly more attractive version of Austin Pendleton—so we could spend our lives together and I'd never be lonely again.

On the walk home from the café I looked at the Halloween decorations in front of all the houses. It was only September, but they do holidays early in Carroll Gardens. Every front yard was decorated with gravestones, skeletons, spiderwebs, plastic pumpkins, ghosts, and goblins. Some even had microchips that played ghoulish laughter all day long. I felt like the ghosts were mocking me for not having a boyfriend, for being alone when everyone else in the world was attached.

As soon as I got upstairs, I called Josh. He was home. "I was just calling to say I had a really good time last night," I said haltingly.

"Me too."

"But you left so early this morning. Did I say something, or—"

"Ariel . . ." When a guy begins a sentence with your name, you know the next words out of his mouth are going to be pretty damn ugly. "I've been through a lot of difficult things over the past few years, which I can't really go into in detail. I had a really good time with you, but I don't know if I'm ready to get into anything serious. I don't want to lose you as a friend, though." And then he slid me the Whopper: "But no matter what winds up happening, you can bet on one thing."

"What's that?"

"We'll always be great somethings."

Everything became glaringly clear. The "great somethings" line is the oldest in the book. Just as I was thinking it couldn't possibly get any worse, he served me the Arch Deluxe: "I think it's just a case of being in the right place at the wrong time."

"I guess it is," I said. "Well, nice knowing you." As I started to hang up, I thought I heard him say, "You're the best," but when I said, "What?" he said, "Get some rest."

That night Sara took me to BarF. She said I wouldn't feel so bad about Josh once I saw how many other fish were in the sea. BarF was on Fifth, between A and B. It had a good indie-rock jukebox, a pool table, and three-dollar pints. I used to go there in high school, and the place would be filled with fifteen-year-old boys. Since Giuliani, though, they'd started carding, and now it was mostly twenty-something hipsters, Irish immigrants, and aging bikers.

We sat down at the bar, sipped our Jamesons, and moaned about the cruel, vicious nature of love. Just as the liquor was going to my head, this sideburned hipster sat down next to us and asked Sara her name. Her eyes widened and she sat up straighter in her seat, dropped her voice an octave, and said, "Sara."

"I'm Jonah," he said.

She gestured toward me. "This is Ariel."

He nodded curtly, turned back to her, and said, "Do you live around here?"

"Yeah."

"Do you want to go out for coffee sometime?"

"Sure." She scribbled down her number and he went to the back to play pool.

Almost every time Sara and I went out, it was the same story. We'd be in the midst of an intense conversation when a Camel-smoking coolio would saunter up to us and hit on her. I knew it wasn't fair to blame her for being so attractive, but I did. There are pretty girls and there are messenger girls, and I've always been a messenger girl.

In high school I had this tall, gorgeous girlfriend, Rebecca, who would take me out to ska shows, and every time we went to one some hot guy would pull me aside and ask if she had a boyfriend. I would have him wait a second, and then I'd go back to her and point him out. If she liked him, I would tell him he could approach her. If she didn't, I'd tell him she had a boyfriend.

The worst thing about being a messenger girl is that you can't ever let on that you're bitter about it. Because then you're not just ugly, but an ugly bitch. So you have to play it cool, like you're just not the girlie type, like there's nothing you love more than relaying messages for your pretty friend. So after a while I stopped dressing up when Rebecca and I went out. Instead I just played up my sidekickability by wearing baggy jeans, making lewd jokes with the guys, and pretending I was just there for the music.

It wasn't like I never hooked up on my own. I did—but the guys always made me promise not to tell anyone what we'd done.

They all gave the same explanation for their discretion (they didn't want their friends to tease them), but I knew the real reason: they were ashamed. It was one thing for them to want me, it was another thing for them to let the world know they did. It never occurred to me that they might be total dicks who weren't worth my time. I was so flattered that they were interested that I was content to let them define the terms.

With Sara, though, I couldn't even console myself with the knowledge that I was getting secret action, because I wasn't. I was nothing more than the pretty girl's friend. I knew part of the reason was my face. I have two huge, deep dimples and round, squishy cheeks, and people always think I'm younger than I am. But I didn't want to have to vamp up in order to get noticed. I wanted a guy to think I was attractive despite the fact that I looked like Shirley Temple. I wanted a guy to see that my tits were *way* bigger than Sara's—even if I always wore loose clothes. But guys in their twenties just aren't that creative. If you don't display, you go home alone. So as Sara distributed her digits to half the male population of the East Village, I bantered with the bartenders and pretended not to care.

By the end of the summer my life was nothing like the working girl's dream I'd been convinced it would be. My acting career was turning out to be a bust (since *Dem's da Breaks*, Faye had only gotten me one audition, for "Zelda, the ugly sister," in a Jewish Rep production called *The Two Gentlewomen of Vilna*), my best friend was getting all the guys, and I was spending my nights jerking off to the rumble of trucks going over the BQE.

But one morning in mid-September, Sara invited me to see a movie Nick Fenster directed, and I became convinced my life was going to turn around. Nick Fenster's hand had been imprinted on the Hollywood Boulevard of my pussy since I first saw him and Seismic Cunt in concert at Chaise Lounge, senior year of high school. The moment I caught sight of his bobbing Adam's apple, huge *schnoz*, acne scars, and six-foot frame, I was slayed. Courtney Love said rock is dick, and although I have zero respect for that sutured sell-out, I totally agree with that statement. When a guy can impress you with what he does onstage, you can't help but wonder what he'd look like coming inside you.

The next day I bought all four of the Seismic Cunt albums, and listened to them whenever I was depressed or lonely. That summer the band broke up, though, and I hadn't heard any news about Nick or the band till now. Maybe it was an omen that Sara had asked me to the movie. Maybe Nick would show up at the screening and I would get a chance to meet him face-to-face.

When I got home from work, I changed into white tights, a white, orange, and blue flowery dress with bell sleeves and a bell bottom, and knee-high red go-go boots, and then I went to meet Sara. The movie was long and insipid and focused on a bunch of sheep hunters out in the woods. It didn't have much of a plot, but it had an excellent rock sound track, composed by Nick. Despite the fact that it was pure fluff, the audience laughed extra hard at all the jokes and gave it a standing ovation at the end. It was obvious that everyone there wanted to fuck Nick or be Nick.

After the flick, Sara and I went to the bar next door to the movie theater. As I tried to signal the bartender, I spotted the man of my dreams. Standing catty-corner to my quivering kitty, talking to a bunch of nondescript hangers-on, was Nick Fenster in the flesh.

I squeezed Sara's arm. "Ten o'clock," I said.

"He's staring right at you," she said.

"Are you fucking with me?"

"Would I fuck with you about a matter as grave as this?"

I shot a glance at him. She had not been fucking with me. Out of the legions of lipsticked, bulimic groupies in the bar, Nick Fenster had chosen to look at *me*. But I couldn't play it too easy. I turned my face away and ordered two Jamesons. Sara slipped me a Camel Filter. She knew I was in serious need of mystique, and nothing gives a dame mystique like a death wish.

As she proceeded to tell me how weird she felt about having fucked her ex-boyfriend Jon again the night before, I began to grow supremely conscious of how I looked listening to her. Aware of my every eyebrow raise, nod, and ash flick. I could feel Nick's eyes a-laying on me. Just as Sara was getting unnecessarily explicit, I saw him leave the hangers-on. He seemed to be heading straight for us. Moments later I was face-to-face with his gaunt, sunken cheeks.

"Hi," he drawled. One of his trademarks was his deep-fried voice. He sounded like a slowed-down record player all the time.

"Hi, Nick," I said like I knew him. "Great movie."

"You liked it?"

"I *loved* it. But the seats in the theater were so uncomfortable! My *ass* is killing me!" He nodded, smiled halfheartedly, and began walking away.

Sara hooked him back, though. "Nick!" she called after him. He ambled back over. "There was something about the film I didn't get."

"What?"

"The sheep in the film were all dead before they got killed. The hunters never shot any real live sheep."

"I know," he said, rolling his eyes. "That's why the last line is Frank saying, 'Is that a live sheep over there?' He was spotting a live sheep. Did you catch that?"

"Oh, I caught it," said Sara. I hadn't caught it, because I'd spent most of the movie craning my neck to the balcony behind me to see if he was sitting in the VIP section, but I nodded like I *had* caught it. I waited for him to say something else, but without so much as a "Catch you later" he slipped out the door.

"That was so weird," I told Sara. "*He* came up to *us,* but then he acted like *we* were annoying *him*. It was so passive-aggressive."

"I know," she said. "He's so desperate for attention he approaches his own groupies before they approach him, but he's so embarrassed by his desperation that he has to make sure he's the one who leaves first."

She went back to dissecting her relationship with Jon, but it was hard for me to listen. All I could think about was Nick, Nick, Nick. My tall, emaciated smoker. My Renaissance man. His natty hair and bony, bony knees.

On our first date I'd so impress him with my intellect and wit that he'd realize how different I was from the fake-titted supermodels he'd dated before. He'd see that what he really wanted was a real girl, with a zaftig body and things to say, and instantly fall hook, line, and sinker. I'd teach him world history, reinstill his faith in Judaism, and give him a reason to live. The sex would be the hottest I'd ever known. I'd come every time. But I'd rest easy knowing the main reason he loved me was for my brain. My innocent background and Ivy degree would be the perfect complement to the rocky road of his childhood and his years in the school of hard knocks.

He'd put me in all his films and they'd all begin winning the biggest awards. He'd be the Cassavetes to my Rowlands, the Bergman to my Ullman, the Godard to my Seberg. After several years, though, his balding and erection difficulties would begin to get on my nerves. I'd realize that what I needed was a guy my own age, and I'd file for divorce—coldly, calmly, and without any warning.

He would fall into a deep depression and make lots of movies that were bad because I wasn't in them. But I'd keep acting in lots of movies that were good because Nick hadn't directed them. I'd write a book called *Leaving Nick* and everyone would buy it. He'd write one called *Losing Ariel* but no one would buy it. He would become known to the world as Ariel Steiner's ex-husband and have to support himself with sporadic appearances on tabloid

TV, where he'd discuss the misery of having been loved and left by such a mankiller. I'd go on to conquer the world in every conceivable way, grateful that he had helped me back when I was just a nobody, yet aware that I could have done it all without him.

When I turned seventy-five, I would receive a Lifetime Achievement Award at the Oscars. "You worship me, you really worship me," I'd tell my cloying legions, thanking God, my parents, and everyone who helped me along the way—except Nick. On my way out of the ceremony a wizened, geriatric hunchback would hobble up to me and my twenty-five-year-old personal trainer/boyfriend, Lothario, and whisper my name. The hunchback's stench would be nauseating but I would not vomit because I had spent so many years working to help smelly hunger victims in Third World countries.

As the old man came closer, I would see that it was Nick. Gaunt and pathetic, shit stains on his pants, saliva dripping down his face. "I still love you, Ariel," he'd croak. I'd dash into the car with Lothario, quickly hitting the automatic door lock. Suddenly Nick would spasm in pain, cry out my name again, stagger forward, and drop dead on the hood of my limo.

"Morty," I'd call to my chauffeur, opening the partition. "Put on the wipers."

As we watched Nick get swished off my windshield, Lothario and I would smile ruefully, and as the limo pulled away I'd look out the window at Nick's crippled, dead body on the sidewalk and cluck, "Poor, poor thing." Lothario would pat my thigh lovingly. I'd give his huge Italian member a hearty squeeze and he would lift my gown and eat me out vigorously and expertly until I erupted in the best orgasm of my life, or at least of my seventies.

When I got home from the bar, I took out the white pages. I didn't expect Nick to be listed, but he was. There was no address, but there was a number. I looked at my watch. It was well past midnight, but I knew he was a night owl and severely doubted I'd wake him.

I dialed. A machine picked up, with that unmistakable voice. He said I could press pound if I wanted to leave a fax. I imagined him lying naked next to me, whispering, "Press pound, baby. Press pound."

I kept my message brief. "Hi, Nick. I met you at the movie. I told you my ass hurt. I was wearing a white dress with bell sleeves and a bell bottom." I left my number, hung up, and got in bed. Right as I was drifting off, the phone rang.

"Hello?" I said.

"Did I wake you?"

"No," I said, trying to sound relaxed. "Not at all. I'm surprised you called. I didn't expect you to call me back."

"I try to call everyone back."

That was a little pretentious, but I tried not to let it turn me off.

"So you liked the movie, huh?"

"I sure did," I lied. "It was funny. Why'd you come up to me tonight?"

" 'Cause I thought you were cute." Those were the words I'd been creaming to hear.

"But why'd you walk away when I mentioned how badly my ass hurt?"

"To stop myself from making a dumb joke. Tell me more about your bottom."

"Well . . . once I mooned somebody. This boyfriend of mine in college. We were in his dorm room and he was watching *60 Minutes*. I wanted him to pay attention to me so I stood right in front of the TV and mooned him. I like mooning. But people think it's weird when a woman moons. Funny when a guy does and gross when a girl does."

"I always thought it was the opposite—nasty when guys do it, funny when girls do."

"Maybe you're right. Listen, how would you like to get together and talk about mooning some more?"

"All right. Come to my apartment Friday at midnight. I'll be in the studio till then, recording a movie sound track. I live at eighty-nine Lispenard Street, buzzer number five."

"What should I wear?"

"Wear that white dress again."

"What kind of *underwear* should I wear?"

"Something see-through."

"Gee, Nick, the closest thing I have to see-through underwear would be *no* underwear."

He was quiet a second, and then he murmured, "Wow."

"What?"

"Now you got me horny."

"Really?" I smiled gleefully. "So how's your *shotgun*, Nick?"

"It, uh . . . it really *is* a shot gun now."

"I'm glad," I said. "Well, it's getting late. I should go to sleep. But I don't want *you* to go to sleep right away. OK?"

"What do you mean?"

"I think you know what I mean."

He chuckled and said, "You're a good kid."

I hung up and threw myself down on my futon. I couldn't fucking believe it. Right at that very moment, Nick Fenster had his dick in his hand thinking of me. There had always been this huge gap between my fantasy life and my real life, and suddenly the gap was closing. I turned over onto my pillow and visions of Nick fucking me from behind on the back of a dead sheep jumping over a fence danced in my head.

●

Friday night I changed into the white dress and went to his apartment. I wore underwear because Sara told me to. "It's the hot-and-cold thing men go crazy for," she said. "Gratify him in one way but not in the other."

Nick's apartment was a fifth-floor walk-up, so I was winded by the time I got there. He opened the door. "I thought I was gonna die before I made it here," I panted.

"You're too melodramatic," he said. It wasn't the most auspicious beginning.

The place was immaculately decorated, with a slanted ceiling, a black leather couch, and tons of fancy recording equipment. As I looked around the room he sprawled out on the couch and whined, "Jesus, I'm exhausted." I couldn't tell if he was talking to me or himself, and then I realized he might not know the difference.

"Why are you exhausted?"

"I've been up late every night this week recording this sound track. Fred Wilson is such a prick."

"Who's he?" I said, taking off my coat and sitting next to him.

"The director of the movie. He did that indie film *Breaking the Maiden*."

"I loved that movie. Why's he a prick?"

"He looks over my shoulder the whole time we're trying to record. I can't work under those conditions. He reins in all my creativity. Wanna hear what we worked on tonight?"

"Sure."

He got a remote control off one of his shelves and jerked it toward the DAT player. Soft acoustic guitar music came out. It was pleasant. "So, what do you think?"

"I like it."

"Do you know my music?"

"Yes. I have all your albums. I first saw you play at Chaise Lounge in November ninety-one."

"That was a lousy show."

"No it wasn't! As soon as you sang the opening line of "Pop

Goes the Cherry," I knew I would meet you someday. 'Thank me, spank me, wank me, yank me. Let me kiss your cute pink hole. Lay me, slay me, pay me, weigh me—'"

"Stop it! I hate that song. I can't even listen to it anymore."

"But it's one of your best!"

"I don't even keep the CD in my apartment. Bad karma." He upped the volume on the player. "This is the music for the opening credits. The shot is a sunrise." He propped his legs on my lap but kept his head turned toward the DAT. He didn't seem to want to acknowledge that he was making a play for me. It was the same dynamic he'd exhibited in the bar when he'd come over to Sara and me, then left as though we'd been bothering him.

But who was I to complain? A rock star, albeit a minor one, had invited me to his apartment—and I was busy psychoanalyzing him.

"You hungry?" he said.

"A little."

"I'm starving. My assistant was supposed to leave food in the refrigerator but he forgot. I gotta get rid of him. He's more of a harm than a help. There's a great oyster place on Greenwich we can order from, but they don't deliver. You'd have to take a cab over, have the cabby wait outside the restaurant, and pick up the food."

If Nick had been a friend, the I-buy, you-fly thing wouldn't have bothered me in the slightest. But because he *paid* someone to do precisely the kind of thing he was asking me to do, I didn't want to do it. It made me feel like a hired whore.

"Why don't we go together?" I asked.

"I'm exhausted, honey. I gotta take a bath. If you don't want to go, that's OK. It just means we can't eat anything."

I didn't like that "honey," but I knew the food would be good, and plus, there was no way he was going to get it himself. Besides, it wasn't like he was asking me to walk there. All I had to do was hail a cab. I was being way too sensitive. I told him I'd go.

He picked up the phone and ordered oysters, lobster, and chicken, with rice and greens, mashed potatoes, and French fries. Then he stood up, yawned, and said, "I'm gonna get in the bath. You should leave in ten minutes."

I followed him into the bathroom. He ran the water and began to strip. His body was long and lean, not too muscular, not too skinny. I had masturbated to the thought of this moment on and off for the past five years, but he took his clothes off so casually and quickly that I didn't get turned on. This wasn't the way it was supposed to work. He was supposed to strip sexily, slowly, staring at me all the while, then carry me to his bed, play me like a Stradivarius, and tell me afterward that it was much more than sex; he'd fallen head over heels.

He opened his medicine chest, took out some Rogaine, and squeezed a few drops of it onto his bald spot.

"Does that stuff work?" I asked.

"It doesn't make it come back, but it definitely stops the loss."

"Do you worry about the side effects? I've heard it can be bad for your heart."

"I shot heroin into my veins for eight years, sweetheart. I'm not too worried about the dangers of Rogaine." Suddenly the thought of sleeping with him seemed a tad less appealing.

He slid himself in the tub and I knelt beside him and watched him soap up. "Your penis looks like a little boy's," I said.

"What do you mean?" he asked, turning to me and glaring.

"Well, it's so wiggly, and cute. It reminds me of a boy's. Not that it's small. Not at all. I just mean it reminds me of a boy's . . . personalitywise."

"Have you seen a lot of little boys' penises?" he growled.

"No. Um, maybe I should go get the food."

"There's a hundred bucks and a set of keys on the kitchen counter. Lock the door behind you before you go. I don't want to get ax-murdered."

"I don't think there are that many ax murderers hanging out in Tribeca."

"Neither do I, but if there's just one, I bet I'm first on his list."

●

When I got back to the apartment, Nick was still in the bath. "Put the food on some plates!" he yelled. "I'll be out in a minute!"

As I was setting the plates down on the coffee table he came in, wearing a white terry-cloth robe. He looked huge and manly in that robe and I wished the night would suddenly turn from disappointing to exciting.

I handed him his food and we dug in simultaneously. The oysters slid smoothly down my throat, the potatoes were fluffed and garlicky, the chicken juicy and rich. But I knew it would make a pretty sad statement if my only good memory of the night was the meal.

When we finished eating he propped his legs up on my lap again. I leaned over to kiss him. He jerked his head away. Did every guy in the city over thirty have a kissing issue—or just the ones *I* went out with?

"You're like Julia Roberts in *Pretty Woman*," I said.

"I didn't see it."

"She never kisses her johns, because if she kisses them she might get vulnerable and fall in love with them."

"I'm not afraid of being vulnerable. I just don't like kissing."

"Oh," I said, then darted in again.

"Now, why would you do that, right after I said I don't like it?"

"To change your mind?"

He laughed scornfully, reached his hand into the V neck of my dress, and fondled my tit. "You have nice breasts."

I closed my eyes and tried to enjoy the feeling of his hand, but it wasn't easy without the smooch. It felt mechanical and disconnected. Maybe he would change his lip policy if I got him more excited. I put my hand on his cock and worked it. It got hard, but not completely. We kept making out in this halfhearted style, my hand around his cock, his hand in my dress, our faces three feet apart, until he pulled away and said, "I'm exhausted. I gotta sleep. You should go home, honey."

That was it? A good meal and a copped feel? No candlelight, no lovemaking, no downtown celebrity gossip? No revelation of the deep-rooted self-hatred and insecurity that came with fame? No "Thanks for getting the food"? The evening had been a disappointment in every conceivable way. At least on the phone I'd felt like I'd had some sway. I had turned him on—all with the sound of my voice. I wanted it to be like that again. *I* wanted to call the wad shots.

I stood up and put on my coat and we walked to the door. "Thank you so much for having me, Nick," I said. "I had a great time."

"No problem."

"It's such a shame that you have to go to sleep, though," I said slowly.

"Why?"

"There are so many things I would have loved to have done with you."

"Like what?" he asked, his eyes narrowing.

"Well, for one, it was a big mistake to have worn this dress tonight. I wish I'd worn my nurse dress instead."

"*Nurse dress?*" His half boner was peeking out of the slightly open robe.

"Yeah. It's so short it barely covers my ass." He pulled his robe open and began to stroke, bending his head down so his ear was closer to my mouth. "I would've worn it with white stockings, a white garter belt, and no underwear." He was steadily jerking off now with no shame. "You could have bent me right over, grabbed me by the hips, and plowed it into me standing up, just like you are now. I would have been so tight for you, Nick, so wet and ready and red. It really is a travesty—"

"Can I come on your dress?"

"No! It cost thirty-five dollars!"

"Then you should go." He closed his robe, opened the door, and locked it behind me.

●

In the morning I called Sara. "I'm not surprised that's how it ended," she said.

"What do you mean?"

"When we talked to him after the movie I had a feeling he was a narcissistic prick."

"Why didn't you tell me not to go?"

"Would you have listened?"

"No."

"There's your answer."

"Thanks."

"Listen, don't work yourself up about it. Just look on the bright side. At least you didn't go down on him. Then you would have felt *really* shitty about yourself."

She had a point, but somehow I didn't feel too consoled. I just felt like a moron for being dumb enough to think Nick would fall for me. He was a rock star. They were supposed to be dicks. It was part of the job description. I had an uncanny knack for getting worked up over guys who had *asshole* and *scumbag* written all over their foreheads, but I was always surprised when they proved themselves the jerks I should have known they were from the start. It was the dating version of that old joke "The food was horrible—and the portions were so small!" I couldn't get enough of the most unsuitable men. Maybe I just hadn't met the right one yet. If I could only find the *right* addicted, commitment-phobic, misogynist, misanthropic, tortured, narcissistic artist, I was certain I could make him marry me.

●

That night I convinced Sara to come with me to a bar in Cobble Hill I'd passed a few times, called BarOoklyn. I figured I might have an easier time meeting guys on Brooklyn turf than Manhattan. She picked me up at my apartment at nine, we ate at an Italian place on Smith Street, and then headed up the street toward the bar. When we were a few blocks away these two teenage black guys came out of nowhere. "Excuse me, miss. Do you have the time?" said one of them.

I looked at my watch and said, "Eleven-forty," and as I said it, I thought, *Boy, it's late. We shouldn't be out here this time of night.*

We kept walking and they followed, and then we crossed the street and they did too. When we got to the other side, the first guy got in front of us, the other got behind us, and the front guy said, "This is a stickup. He has a gun. Take out all your money and give it to me."

My money was in his hand in five seconds flat, but Sara had to fumble for a while to get hers because she had a cigarette in one hand and her wallet was lodged deep in her pocket for safekeeping. The front guy said, "You're not moving fast enough, you're not moving fast enough," and for one brief moment I thought they were gonna pop us, but when he said, "Keep walking and don't look back," I knew we'd survive.

We walked as fast as we could down the block, making sure not to turn our heads around, and suddenly Sara started crying. It was weird. I'd never seen her cry before. Her cheeks got all blotchy and red and she looked like a little girl.

"It could have been worse," I said, hugging her. "At least we're not hurt. Let's take a cab to the bar and forget this happened."

"We *can't* get a cab. We don't have any *money.*"

She was right, and I felt like an idiot for forgetting the main event that had just taken place. We went to a cash machine on Atlantic and Court, and as my money was spewing out I thought, *Gee, I'm lucky. All they got from me was twenty dollars, and I can go get twenty more right where the first twenty came from.*

But when we got to the bar, everyone was laughing in such a carefree way that I felt like spitting in their drinks. Sara ordered two beers for us, and while we were waiting this guy came up to her and said, "I like your boots." She was wearing knee-high black leather boots and a miniskirt.

The first thing I thought was, *Why can't a guy just for once notice me and not her?* and the second thing I thought was, *I bet she's gonna tell him we were mugged, because she tells all strange guys the intimate details of her life.* I started counting to five in my head, and at four she said, "I really don't feel like talking right now. My friend and I just got mugged."

"Oh my God, that sucks!" said the guy. "Are you OK? What happened?"

She started to tell him, but then our drinks came and I said, "I'm going to the back," and she said, "I'll come with you." There was a pool table in the back room and only one name was on the chalkboard, so I scribbled mine down underneath. (Sara never played pool because she said she sucked at it.)

My opponent turned out to be a loose-cannon sleaze who introduced himself as Jimmy. After he broke, he sunk three in a row. On my first turn I made a decent shot, a bank off the side. "You're not bad," he said, giving me a smarmy smile. I rolled my eyes, feeling cocky, but on my next shot, an easy one, I missed. He sunk his next four in a row, then went for the eight ball. But it didn't go in. Maybe I had a chance. I sunk one and another, but then I accidentally sunk the eight. "Fuck!" I shouted.

"Good game," snickered Jimmy.

Sara and I went back to the front of the bar with our beers, but all the bar stools were taken, so we had to sip our drinks in a little nook by the phone. Suddenly the pool sleaze came up to us and smiled. "Would you please leave us alone?" I said. "My friend and I are trying to have a conversation here."

"I wanted to use the fucking *phone*!" he shouted drunkenly. "I wasn't even *thinking* about talking to you! Who the fuck do you bitches think you are?"

We moved away, the guy still yelling after us, and I realized there's no justice in the foul-smelling urinal of a city, because everybody will slice you one way or another.

"Let's go home," I said to Sara. We took a car service to my apartment. I lent her a T-shirt to sleep in, and we got in bed.

"Are you going to tell your parents about the mugging?" she said.

"I don't think so," I said. "They'd freak out."

"So would mine," she said.

We said good night and rolled over so we were back to back. Her body was warm and for a second I wanted to turn toward her so she could hold me and make everything OK. It wasn't a sexual longing; I just wanted to be touched. But I had a feeling an impassioned bear hug in bed might not be the wisest move for our friendship, so I stayed put. She fell asleep a few minutes later. I lay awake a long time, listening to her snore.

●

On the train home from work Monday night I was overwhelmed by this piss stench. Now, smelling piss on the trains was nothing new, except usually the odor comes from a specific person, so once you figure out who it is you can just move away. This time, though, I couldn't pinpoint its source. I looked around at the other passengers to see if any of them were smelling it too, but no one seemed to, so I told myself it was just paranoid, flighty white postmugging angst making me fabricate the stink.

I breathed through my mouth, leaned back in my seat, and thought, *None of these small travails like getting mugged or smelling piss on the train would be so bad if I only had a boyfriend.* And right as I was thinking this, a totally lovey-dovey, Park-Slope-written-all-over-their-faces couple across from me put down their paperbacks and nuzzled noses.

The only thing that gave me hope was the jug of Carlo Rossi I had waiting in my refrigerator. As soon as I got home I poured myself a glass, made spaghetti and marinara sauce (it's the only thing I can cook), sat on the couch, and turned on the TV. *Sleepless in Seattle* was on. It was that scene where Tom Hanks finds his son in the Empire State Building observatory, hugs him passionately, and says, "We're doing OK, aren't we? I haven't done anything really stupid, have I? Have I screwed it up for the both of us?" and his son shakes his head no and hugs him back. I always get busted up when I watch that part. The only thing that gets me blubbering harder is the final scene of *Lucas.*

I sat there watching the movie, tears rolling down my face, and then I took a deep breath and thought, *What can I do to cheer myself up?* I went to my bag, took out my address book, and flipped through the boys' names in it. The first prospect I came across was Tim Berman, this performance artist a year ahead of me at Brown I'd always been vaguely attracted to. After he graduated he'd moved to the Lower East Side, and I'd heard a rumor that he was dating a girl from his year named Vanessa, but then someone told me they'd had a brutal breakup. I said to myself, *I'm gonna call him and invite him to have a drink with me right now and he is going to be home and say yes, and my life is finally going to start picking up.*

The phone rang four times before a machine clicked on. A woman's voice said, "Vanessa and Tim aren't home right now, but leave us a message and we'll call you back."

This is a rat race, I thought, *and I am a crippled rat with a leg dragging behind me, smearing blood all along the little twisted maze. All those other rats have gotten their Havarti and are twitching their noses at me, laughing cruel, heartless little rat laughs.*

The next name I found was Zeke Feder, a somewhat assholic yet highly entertaining egomaniac I slept with senior year of high school. We used to have long philosophical conversations about the differences between men and women and we would spar and joke and sometimes it was sort of fun.

"Hello?" he said.

"It's Ariel Steiner," I said. "How've you been?"

"Pretty good," he said.

"I heard you dropped out of Vassar."

"Yeah."

"What have you been doing since then?"

"I just recorded a rap album. It's coming out on Universal next month under my professional name, MC Ezekiel. What about you?"

"I'm a temp and I got mugged this weekend."

"That sucks."

"Do you want to get together sometime and catch up?"

"Sure."

"We could meet in a diner and I could put my hand on your lap under the table so no one else could see. How does that sound? Would you like that?"

Suddenly the phone got staticky and I couldn't hear anything, and then he said faintly, "Could you hold on a second?"

"What?"

"I have to change the channel on my phone. It's a cordless."

It went on like that for the next ten minutes. As I tried desperately to coo innuendo, he kept interrupting me to change the channel on the phone. I didn't feel too good about myself, being put on hold in the middle of my own phone sex, so finally I gave up, hung up, and crawled into bed. I pulled the covers over my head and imagined I had a blow-up boyfriend to inflate on the nights I really needed a shoulder to cry on. He would have a very medium-sized penis I could play with if I wanted to, but nothing huge or uncircumcised. I would lie next to him and bury my head in his soft longish hair and he would kiss me softly and sweetly, without any excess saliva or beer breath. I would tell him the wretched story of the mugging and the piss and he would listen very quietly and then fuck me if I wanted him to but not if I didn't, and in the morning I would wake up next to him and eat breakfast staring into his eyes. As soon as he started turning into a Real Boyfriend, though, with complex needs, concerns, neuroses, and complaints, I would just pull out the plug like he was a beach toy and he would very quickly, without any ceremony or complaint, deflate with a whiny hiss. Then I would fold him up carefully, squeeze out all the air bubbles, and put him under the pillow till the next shit-caked, piss-soaked weekend.

I lay in bed for a long time, thinking. I thought about my

screwy love life, and how much I hated temping, and how I hadn't gotten cast in anything since *Lolita*. I looked at my pictures of Joan and Bob and Bukowski and Cash, and then I looked at my computer. The last time I'd used it was when I wrote "Vanya in My Vulva."

I slowly climbed out of bed and went toward it. I turned it on and typed the words "The Blow-Up Boyfriend." And then I wrote a story about the mugging, the piss, my fantasy man, and the overall suck quotient of my summer in the city. When I was done, I printed it out and read it over to myself.

It was good—good enough to make me wonder if maybe I was banging my head against the wrong brick wall. If after three months in the city the only thing I could call my own was my misery, why not try to put it to use? I had always wanted to make it as an actress, but more important, I had wanted to *make it*. I was tired of being a failure at every single thing I tried. If I sent my story somewhere, I had nothing to lose. At worst, it would be rejected. At best, it would be published, I'd get some exposure and maybe it would lead to more opportunities.

I had to think of a good place to submit it, though. Someplace that would appreciate a depressing urban tale of loneliness and degradation. And then it hit me. The *City Week*. I knew that rag better than any in town. Its entire bent was depressing urban tales. "The Blow-Up Boyfriend" was right up their alley.

Who knew what the story might lead to? Maybe some bigwig publisher would catch wind of it and sign me up to write a memoir. I'd fly to Paris to find myself and some subject matter, and promptly fall in love with a French Jewish fireman who would become my muse, my Nin, my Toklas. I'd chronicle our intense, torrid affair in a juicy tell-all, *Matieu and Me,* and the book would become an international best-seller. But within months he'd grow so envious of my success that the next time his wagon got called to fight a fire, he'd distractedly aim the hose at the wrong house, and as a result seven innocent children would die. To save Matieu and the town I'd break off the relationship and hop on a train bound south.

I'd publish a book a year, all about my adventures as a broad abroad, chronicling my luscious affairs with half the male population of the continent, comparing NATO men to non-NATO, Eastern bloc to Western. The books would be prurient but heartfelt, hilarious and astute, naming truths no one else was brave enough to name, bringing tears and laughter to the hearts of the lonely, changing people's minds, livening their spirits. I'd collect a Pulitzer, Nobel, and MacArthur along the way, but through it all

I'd remain totally humble. I'd die single but happy, fulfilled by my work if not my men, proud to have been able to move people with the staggering power of my prose.

I stapled the story together and typed a cover letter—"Dear Mr. Jensen, I hope you like this. There's more where it came from"—and went out to mail it.

3

On Thursday morning I got this message on my machine: "Ariel, Bill Turner. Associate editor, *City Week*. We'd like to publish your story in 'I-Level,' our section for freelance pieces. Can you bring it in on a disk tomorrow?"

I called Sara to tell her the good news and she screamed so loud I had to hold the receiver away from my ear. I hung up and started to dial my dad, but then I remembered the part about the phone sex and decided against it.

●

That night, as I loaded "The Blow-Up Boyfriend" onto a disk, I got an idea. Why not put a second story on there too and ask Turner to take a look at it? He'd never know what else I had up my sleeve if I didn't show him. When someone gives you an inch, you've got to take a mile.

I needed to come up with something good, though. Something better than the first one. Something powerful, and hot, and big . . . James. An hour and a half later I had a second story: "The Mammalian Come-Hither."

●

The *City Week* offices were on two floors of a converted factory in SoHo, on the corner of Broadway and Broome. I took the elevator up to the fourth floor and walked down a long, winding

71

hallway till I came to the entrance. To the left of the door were several huge stacks of the *Week* in metal holders. Straight ahead was a high forest green counter, and behind it was a girl in her late twenties with dyed white-blond hair.

"I'm Ariel Steiner," I said. "I'm here to see Bill Turner."

She looked me up and down and said, "Blow-up boyfriend, huh?"

"Yeah."

"You should market that idea. I'm Corinne Riley, the senior editor."

"Nice to meet you."

She stood up, led me a few feet away to a small glass office, and pointed at a tall, thin guy in his late thirties who was sitting behind a computer. He had big bushy eyebrows and a widow's peak.

"I'm Ariel Steiner," I said.

He stood up, shook my hand, and said, "Nice grip."

I had to think of a good comeback, something that would crystallize me in his mind as a fast-talking, clever, bad-assed chick—someone as hot as her stories. "It's from all those hand jobs," I said. He reddened and I thought, *If I can make this guy blush that easily it's gotta bode well for my future at this institution.*

I took my disk out and handed it to him. "The document's called 'blowup,' " I said, "but there's a second one on there I was hoping you'd look at as well."

He arched a brow and said, "What's it called?"

" 'Hither.' " He chuckled and loaded them both onto the computer.

●

The morning "The Blow-Up Boyfriend" ran, September 25, was also my twenty-second birthday. I woke up feeling revved, but the rest of the day was hell on wheels. When I arrived at my desk, the Corposhit was ringing me on the intercom. "Come into my office," she huffed. "I have some papers I need you to fax to Jeff McCoyd at Erhard, Lieb."

I walked in. "I want you to fax pages four and five only, with a cover sheet," she said, handing me the pages. "Make sure you spell *Lieb* right on the fax."

"Is it listed in the Rolodex?"

"Don't bother me with these questions." That was the response she always gave when I asked her about the higher-order functions of temping.

I went back to my desk, dialed information to get the number, then called the firm and asked the receptionist to spell it. "E-R-H-A-R-D comma, L-I-E-B comma, T-U-R-N-E-R ampersand sign, Y-A-T-E-S, and then L period L period P period," she told me.

"Jesus, how stupid does she think I am?" I wondered. Then I answered my own question.

I asked to be connected to Jeff McCoyd's secretary. She gave me the firm's fax number, I went to the fax machine down the hall, sent it, and came back to my desk. Thirty seconds later, the Corposhit emerged from her office. "Did you get the number?"

"Yes. McCoyd's secretary said to fax it to the general number for the firm, so I did."

"Oh no, no, no," she said. "You need the direct number."

"But his secretary said to use the general one."

"His secretary is a *temp*."

"So am *I*," I said, half hoping she'd fire me for my insolence.

"Call and get his direct number, and fax it again," she said and went into her office.

I went through the whole routine again. Then I took the dictionary out of my top drawer and began to read it under the desk, starting at page one: "**abacist** *n*. A person skilled in using the abacus." Fascinating. I'd always wondered what they called those people.

The Corposhit came out of her office. I dropped the dictionary on the floor with a thud. "Do you have the pages you just faxed to Erhard, Lieb?" I handed them to her. "This isn't what you were supposed to fax. I said pages two and three. You faxed four and five."

"You said four and five. I'm sure of it."

"Fax him pages two and three with an apology for faxing him the wrong pages."

"Do you want the apology on letterhead?"

"Yes."

"Should it be a memo or a letter?"

"Don't bother me with these questions." She spun on her heel and went back into her office. I typed up the apology, faxed it, then went back to my desk. The intercom rang.

"Yes?"

"Do you have a copy of the apology you just messengered? I'd like one for my files."

"You mean faxed. You told me to fax it."

"No I didn't. I wanted it messengered."

Suddenly I was no longer sure if the Corposhit was the insane one or if I was. When, over the course of a day, everyone with whom you interact treats you like you have a mental deficiency, you cannot help but begin to wonder if maybe they are right.

"I really think you said to fax it," I said. "But I can messenger it too."

By the time I was finished, I was dizzy and sweating. All I wanted to do was read my story in the paper so I could comfort myself with the fact that even though I was nothing more than a temp to the Corposhit, I had something going for me on the side that she didn't know about.

At noon on the button, I dashed out of the building, ran to the *City Week* distribution box on the corner, pulled out the paper, and opened to the table of contents. There it was, halfway down:

> I-Level:
> *The Blow-Up Boyfriend* by Ariel Steiner . . . p. 37

I quickly turned to thirty-seven. At the top of the page was the title and my name, in the trademark *City Week* font, and in the center of the text was an illustration of a pixieish girl humping an inflatable man. Underneath it was the caption "Blow me (up)." I read it from beginning to end, standing on the corner, and just as I was about to leave, this middle-aged suit came up to the box and pulled out a copy of the paper. I glanced at him for a second, imagining him going home that night and reading the story, completely unaware that he'd exchanged glances with the very girl who wrote it. I was known but anonymous at the same time, and I liked being both.

●

I met Sara at the Met Life building for lunch, and she read "The Blow-Up Boyfriend" while we listened to a doo-wop group and I ate a Hostess cupcake she'd bought in honor of my birthday. When she finished, I said, "What did you think?"

"I don't know," she said dully.

"What do you mean?"

"For one, I don't like my pseudonym."

"What's wrong with it?"

"*Farrah?* People are going to think I'm some frosted, drug-addicted bimbo. And do you really think I"—she peered down at the page—" 'tell all strange guys the intimate details of my life'?"

I had to think quickly. "Uh . . . *of course* not," I said. "That's an exaggeration. That character isn't you. She's fictitious. I just made that part up about the protagonist being jealous so the story would have a darker tone."

"How stupid do you think I am? It's so obvious you feel that way about me! I wish you'd had the guts to tell me face-to-face instead of publishing it in the newspaper!"

"I *don't* feel that way about you! I'm sorry I didn't let you know about it in advance. I should have. But I swear, she's not you."

She harumphed, took a sip of her Coke, and turned her head toward the singers on the stage.

●

When I got back to work there were three messages on my machine.

My dad: "I picked up a copy of the *City Week* on my way to lunch today, and as I sat down in the cafeteria and opened the paper, I caught sight of something very odd. My own last name. Above the words 'The Blow-Up Boyfriend.' Why didn't you tell us you were mugged? Also, should I show it to mom? I think she'd be proud to see your name in print, but I'm worried the . . . content . . . might upset her."

My mom: "Dad faxed me the article. Were you hurt in this mugging? Did you file a report? Come over for dinner tonight. Oh—and Happy Birthday!"

And Turner: "Hey Ariel. Our editor in chief, Steve Jensen, and I read your second story, and we'd like to run it too. We're wondering if you could come into the office sometime this evening and meet with us."

Suddenly I forgot all about my parents' frenzied tones. It sounded like Turner wanted to offer me a column. If he did, then I'd be more than an unemployed actress who'd gotten one measly story published. I'd be a Real Writer. But maybe I was reading too much into his message. Maybe he just wanted me to submit another piece. I had to fight my Brown-bred instinct to deconstruct, and wait to hear what he had to say.

●

When I got to the *Week*, Corinne wasn't at the front desk, so I headed straight for Turner's office. He greeted me at his door, then led me down the hall into Jensen's office. It was a huge white room with floor-to-ceiling windows and an incredible view of lower Manhattan. Jensen was in his early forties, short and fair, with thick glasses and cropped brown hair. He was sitting behind a huge, messy desk, which made him look even smaller, and his feet were propped up on it. He stood up to shake my hand and I noticed he had one crossed eye. I tried to look in the normal one but I kept staring at the crossed one instead. I felt like I was on *Columbo*.

"Have a seat," he said. Turner and I sat down side by side on the couch opposite the desk. I sunk down so deep I had to crane my neck to see Jensen.

"We liked your piece very much," said Jensen. "And we think this could be the beginning of a fruitful relationship. Do you read the paper regularly?"

"Of course."

"What do you think of it?"

I didn't know whether to kiss ass or show chutzpah. I decided to do some of both. "Well," I said, "I think its greatest strength is its first-person component, the columns, the fact that you can tune in to different lives each week. What I don't like about it is that all those lives are men's. You've got a masthead full of whiny, angst-ridden boys. Some neurotic, some slackish, but all male. It's tiresome. The way I see it, your columnists are my boyfriends."

Turner chuckled. Jensen didn't. "You're right about the lack of female voices," said Jensen. "That's one of the reasons we're interested in you. How would you feel about doing a weekly column?"

I felt like vomiting. How could I write a column about my life when I didn't even *have* a life? But Bukowski didn't turn down *Open City* when they offered him "Notes of a Dirty Old Man." Dylan didn't say no to Columbia when they gave him his first recording contract. These guys were making me a whopper of an offer. And when somebody makes you a whopper of an offer, you take it. Especially in a dog-eat-dog town.

"I'd . . . love to," I said. "But I'm not sure what you want it to be about."

Turner and Jensen exchanged glances, like they found it amusing that I didn't know my own angle. "The same stuff the first two were about," said Turner. "The weekly struggles of a single girl in the city. A *Perils of Pauline* from a slacker slut perspective. We're seeing it as 'Reality Bites My Ass.' What do you do for a living?"

"I'm a temp and an actress. A temptress."

This time, neither one smiled. "That's what we want it to be about," said Jensen. "Going on auditions. Temping. But most of all, getting laid. Or trying to. Do you know who Suzanne Long is?"

"No."

"She writes a column for the *New York Gazette*," said Turner, "about the mating rituals of elite thirty-something Manhattanites. 'WASP Nights,' it's called. We're seeing you as the rent-stabilized Suzanne Long."

"You can write about whatever you want," said Jensen, "as long as it's true. We're a newspaper. We run journalism, not fiction."

"Of course," said Turner, "any record of an actual event is going to contain some element of distortion. We're not asking you to wire yourself every time you go out. Just try to stick to basic facts of your life."

"OK."

"I already thought of a title for the column," said Jensen. " 'Run Catch Kiss.' Like the children's game, where the girls chase the boys and kiss them when they catch them. We'll subtitle it 'True Confessions of a Single Girl.' Your illustrator will be Tessa Tallner, the woman who drew the 'Blow-Up Boyfriend' illo. We have a feeling you're going to be eminently illustratable."

"We'll run 'The Mammalian Come-Hither' next Wednesday as your first official column," said Turner. "You'll get us your next one the Monday before it runs. If you have E-mail, you can send it in that way, as long as it's here by nine Monday morning. That leaves you eleven days to come up with something. Think that's enough time?"

"Absolutely," I lied.

There was only one issue they hadn't addressed. It wasn't the most important, but it mattered.

"You'll get two hundred bucks a week," said Jensen.

"Does that include prophylactics?" I asked.

"No," said Jensen, deadpan, standing up and shaking my hand.

"Steve," I said, "I don't know how to th—"

"No thanks necessary," he said. "Just go get busy."

●

Jensen's admonition stuck in my head the whole subway ride to my parents'. What exactly did he mean? Would I have to become a barfly, go to the diviest pubs in town, and come on to different men each night, just to stock up on potential material? What if none of them wanted to sleep with me?

But what made me far more nervous than the prospect of not getting any dates was the prospect of telling my parents about the column. I'd had very bad experiences in the past when I'd tried confiding in them about my sex life. Their birds-and-bees strategy with Zach and me had been a strange combination of total openness and total avoidance. Every morning until I was thirteen, my dad would take a bath, then walk down the hallway to the bed-room completely naked. I'd be sitting at the kitchen table with Zach, drinking my orange juice, when out of the corner of my eye I'd catch sight of my father's loping phallus swinging noncha-lantly as he approached. Zach would bury his head in his cereal, but I'd steal furtive glances at the measuring rod by which I would judge all the others, wondering if they were all that dark, that bald. Eventually my mom would spot him, come out of the kitchen, and say, "Leo—have you ever heard of a towel?" and he'd dash into the bedroom with a look of chagrin.

At night when he came home from work, he would go into the living room, take off his pants, and sit down at the dinner table in his Fruit of the Looms. Sometimes a neighbor would ring the doorbell and he'd have to run into the bedroom and hide be-fore we opened the door.

My mom wasn't as much of a nudist as he was, but she was nauseatingly crunchy when it came to talking about sex. When I was in eighth grade she started buying me sex books and putting them on my bed: *Period*; *Our Bodies, Ourselves*; and *Girltalk: All the Stuff Your Sister Never Told You*. She always said her mom never talked to her about sex, and she had vowed to be different with her own daughter. I would study these books diligently, and at night when she came in to kiss me good night I would ask fol-low-up questions like "Does *blow job* mean you blow on it?" and she would frown a little and then explain.

That summer I went off to summer camp for children of left-leaning parents, and one day this skater named Flip Goldin, who could catch his own spit in his mouth, asked me to be his girlfriend. The first few days of the relationship, all we did was French at good night time, but then one morning he con-vinced me to cut activity period and we went to my bunk and sat on my bed.

We'd been kissing for about ten minutes when he put his hand on one of my breasts. I hadn't even started wearing a bra yet and I was afraid he'd be disappointed when he saw how little I had to offer.

"They're small," I said, pushing his hand away.

"That's OK," he said, and then he slid it under my shirt and ran it over my nipple. My skin tingled and my breath got short, and I knew I'd found an A.M. activity I enjoyed. A week later we were sneaking off into the woods regularly so he could finger me and I could give him head.

When I got home from camp I told my mom I'd had a boyfriend, but I didn't give her any details. I didn't think she'd be too happy if she knew I'd been orally devirginated before my bat mitzvah.

The summer after ninth grade, I got a job as a mother's helper for two-year-old twins in Rehoboth Beach, Delaware, and lost my virginity to an eighteen-year-old stoner surfer. He didn't have any condoms, so we didn't use anything. I didn't get pregnant but I was so afraid of AIDS that in the winter, after the six-month window, I went for an HIV test at a clinic in Tribeca. It turned out negative, but the experience of getting tested was so harrowing that I decided to tell my parents. I felt sure they would be supportive, and I saw telling them as a way of bringing them closer.

I sat them down at the kitchen table one night after Zach had gone to sleep, and told them the whole story: losing my virginity to a near stranger, the sex being horrible, worrying that I was pregnant, not being pregnant, going for the HIV test, waiting for the results. As I talked, my dad started running his hand through his hair, which is what he always does when he gets tense. My mom stared at him running his hand through his hair, which is what she always does when she gets tense. When I finished, he said, "No one said you have to tell your parents *every*thing," went into the bedroom, and shut the door.

"He's just worried about you," said my mom, following him into the room.

I had told them the truth because I wanted them to know me, see who I was, and love me anyway, love me more, even. But instead they'd made it clear that when it came to certain areas of my life, they'd rather be left in the dark. Now I had to tell them I'd gotten a weekly column about my sex life for a paper with a quarter of a million circulation. I was not looking forward to dinner.

●

When I opened the apartment door, my mom, dad, and Zach were at the table, sipping zucchini soup. By the smirk on Zach's face I could tell he'd read my story too. I sat down.

"Happy Birthday," said my mom.

"Were you really mugged?" said my dad.

"Yes," I said. "But it wasn't that bad. They only got about twenty bucks from each of us. And I don't even think it was a real gun. Sara thinks it was the guy's finger."

"Why didn't you tell us?" asked my mom.

"I didn't want to worry you."

"You should have told us," she said.

"And you shouldn't go out late at night," said my dad.

"It wasn't that late. And I'm OK. Really."

It was bizarre, but I found myself feeling sort of glad they were so upset about the mugging. I was hoping it might make them forget about the phone sex.

"What about the rest of the story?" said Zach, grinning snidely. "Was the other stuff true too?"

But before I could come up with an evasive answer, my dad said, "Zach. The extent to which Ariel fictionalized real-life events in that story is her own business, not ours. She doesn't have to tell us how much is true. I, for one, would rather not know." I knew he was lying about his reasons for not wanting to know, but I appreciated the gesture nonetheless.

"Thanks, dad," I said.

"How'd you get it published?" said my mom.

They were very impressed when I told them. Part of me wanted to leave on an up note, not tell them about the column, and hope they never read the paper again. But I'm not very good at avoidance. So I gulped and said, "I have something to tell you guys." They turned to me expectantly. "I had a meeting at the *City Week* today. They're running another piece I wrote next Wednesday, and they've asked me to start writing a weekly column for them."

"*Mazel tov!*" said my mom. "What's it going to be about?"

"My life. I can write about whatever I want. Auditions. Wacky interactions. Temping."

"What are they calling it?" asked my dad.

" 'Run Catch Kiss.' "

"What does that have to do with temping?" asked Zach.

"Well," I said, glaring at him, "the focus is actually supposed to be on my . . . dating life."

"What dating life?" smirked Zach.

"The one that's about to begin."

"I don't get it," said my dad. "They want you to go out with guys and write about them?"

"Yeah."

My parents exchanged a worried glance across the table, and then my mom smiled perkily and said, "That's certainly an . . . *inventive* idea."

"Can't wait to see what you come up with," said my dad.

"Me neither," said Zach.

●

When I got home I tried to write, but I couldn't think of any good column ideas. So I called Sara. "I know this might not make you too happy, in light of our fight today," I said, "but the *City Week* just offered me a regular column." The line was quiet. "Hello?"

"That's incredible news," she said. "We should go out and celebrate."

"So you're not mad at me anymore?"

"No. Just don't ever write about me again without my permission. Otherwise I'll stop speaking to you."

"Deal."

We met at BarF.

"What's the emphasis supposed to be on?" she said as I sat down next to her.

"Sex."

"So you're the staff whore."

"I—"

"How much are you getting?"

"Two hundred a week."

"That's a lot less than a whore would get." She glanced at the pool table in the back. "Do you see any potential . . . subjects? What about him?" A twentyish guy was coming out of the men's room and heading past the pool table toward us. He was tall, with curly brown hair, and I knew I knew him from somewhere but I wasn't sure where. As he came closer, I remembered. It was the audience member who had come up to me after *Lolita: Rock On.*

I knew it was fate that he was here on this night. I had wanted him, and now we were crossing paths again, just when I needed subject matter. He sat down at the corner of the bar and I caught his eye.

"Lolita," he said.

"Ariel, actually. Where'd you go that night? You disappeared."

"I had a friend waiting for me outside. He was in a really bad mood because his girlfriend had just broken up with him, so he wanted to leave right away. I tried to say good-bye to you but you were talking to someone else, so I figured I'd just slip out. I didn't mean to be rude." Suddenly I saw his eyes shift from me to Sara.

"I'm sorry," I said. "This is my friend Sara. What's your name, anyway?"

"Michael." He stood up and sat down on a stool next to Sara's.

"I know this sounds like a line," she said, turning to him, "but you look really familiar."

"Yeah?" he said.

"I think I saw you on the subway about two weeks ago. I was

sitting across from you on the downtown Six? Around five-thirty? And I was staring at you because you look just like this guy I knew in college, who had four fingers. I was trying to look at your hand to see how many you had, but it was tucked under your arm and I couldn't see. We both got off at Astor, and when you stood up, I saw that you had five fingers and that's how I knew you weren't him."

I had heard a lot of bad pickup stories in my life, but Sara had sunk to new lows. I couldn't believe she would concoct a tale this far-fetched and completely unbelievable—all in the interest of hitting on someone.

"Wait a second," said Michael, nodding enthusiastically. "I think I do remember. You were wearing a long, dark skirt, right? And you have a tattoo on your hand of the number four." She showed him her hand and grinned triumphantly. "I knew a guy with four fingers once," he said. "His name was Richie Paducca. He lived down the block from me in Brookline."

"That's the guy!" she screamed. "Richie Paducca! He went to Columbia!"

"Yeah, he did go to Columbia. Blond hair, short? The missing finger was a birth defect?"

"That's him! This is too weird! I see you on the subway, think you're someone else, and then it turns out you know the someone else I'm thinking about! This is unbelievable!"

"It sure is," I said.

For the next twenty minutes the two of them kept chatting, intermittently throwing questions toward me in a feeble attempt to make me feel like I was part of the conversation. But it's obvious when two people would rather be alone. It was like watching a dick and a pussy talking. I had met Michael first and Sara had stolen him right out of my hands. I'd been cock-blocked—and on my birthday to boot. I stood up, said good-bye, and took a cab home alone.

●

The next day at lunch, Sara gave me the scrumptious details about Michael's stupendous pussy-licking skills, and I had to sit there and pretend to be interested. I wanted to tell her how pissed I was that she had cock-blocked me, but I didn't feel like we knew each other well enough for me to have a right to be mad. It wasn't like Michael was an ex-boyfriend of mine or anything. He was just a random hottie who happened to be into her more than me. But after a few minutes of acting like everything was fine, I found myself feeling so angry that I couldn't look at her. As she went on about Michael, I stared straight ahead like a sullen teenager and gave monosyllabic responses. "What's going on, Ariel?" she finally asked.

"What do you mean?" I said.

"You're acting like a freak. Are you upset about something?"

"No," I said.

But she knew something was up because she didn't call once the whole weekend. And on Monday at lunch, when I got down to the lobby, which was where we usually met, she wasn't waiting for me. I had lost my only friend, but I didn't know how to get her back. I was too ashamed to tell her how I felt, too proud to admit to my jealousy.

The worst part of our breakup was the timing. She had left me with no one to go out with—right when I was in need of fodder. I thought about going out alone, but it seemed too desperate. When two girls go out together, they look cool. But when a girl goes out by herself, she looks pathetic. So every night that week, while Sara was probably lying spread-eagled on her bed, I was watching TV, chugging Carlo Rossi, rereading *Notes of a Dirty Old Man*, and praying some guy from my past would call me out of the blue so I could have an interaction worthy of a column.

On Wednesday at noon I went to the *City Week* box and took out a copy of the paper. On the bottom of the front page, nestled between the teasers *Nadick's Latest Bender, p. 18* and *Hyman Tries Treatment for His OCD, p. 19*, was the following:

"I STOOD UP BY THE COUCH AND SLOWLY UNZIPPED THE FRONT of my nurse dress. I slid it off my shoulders and threw it on the floor, till I was standing in front of him in just my panty hose and Minimizer bra. I unsnapped my bra slowly, dropped it on the floor too, and ran my fingers up and down my breasts, like a stripper in a movie . . ." A new column by Ariel Steiner, "Run Catch Kiss," debuts, p. 21.

I could only imagine the look on my parents' faces when they read that. But what was worse than the teaser was the cartoon. In the center of page twenty-one, above the caption "Comic Strip," was a picture of the same pixieish girl from last week, pinching her nipples in front of a guy jerking off. The illustrator drew James's penis superlong, pointing straight up into the air, with little accents around it so it looked like it was shaking, and she drew me with a mole above my lip, short dark hair, and two erect little boobs sticking straight out. This Tessa Tallner chick was even more perverted than *I* was.

When I finished reading the story, I turned to "The Mail":

Ariel Steiner's derision of uncircumcision ("I-Level," 9/25) is yet another indication of the incredible bias we natural men have to face. Had Steiner railed out against Black guys, or Jewish guys, dozens of people would have written in to brand her a bigot. Why should there be a double standard when it comes to us? We foreskinned Franks, who count among us such luminaries as Elvis Presley, Tony Danza, and Charlton Heston, will no longer stand for such narrow-minded prejudice.

JEFFREY THOMASON, *Upper East Side*

Dear Ariel Steiner,
    Why settle for a blow-up boyfriend when you can have a real one? I'm well hung, women tell me I'm a good kisser, and you seem like just the kind of girl I'm looking to meet: an honest dirty talker, with a sense of humor too. My number's in the phone book. And no, I'm not a psycho.

JERRY LUPINO, *Bronx*

As soon as I got back from lunch, I checked my machine to see if Lupino had called. Nada. It was a little disappointing. But I called the phone company and made my number unpublished anyway, hoping to thwart the next perv's wicked plans.

Later that afternoon a heavy breather *did* call. My dad. "Should I show this one to mom?" he asked. "I know she's going to ask me to." The *City Week* was available only in Manhattan, and my mom's office was in Brooklyn Heights, around the corner from my parents' building. She ran her own business, selling children's videos mail-order to schools and libraries.

"Maybe you shouldn't," I said.

"I'm having a hard time here," he said. "The illustration was unsettling enough, but it was the subtitle above the column that got to me the most. I don't know if I want to think of what I read as a true confession."

"I thought you said the truth quotient was *my* business and no one else's."

"I lied. Are you making stuff up or aren't you? How can they call it true if it's not?"

"Maybe you shouldn't read the column at all. I mean, if it makes you so uncomfortable—"

"I can't stop reading it! I don't have that much self-restraint!"

"Well, then please do me one favor: don't talk to me about what you read and what you haven't. Because maybe I don't want to know . . . how much you know."

"That's an interesting point you make. There's an element of your *own* shame here that I hadn't even considered. I was just thinking about *my* shame, and mom's. I think you've made a perfectly fair request, and I'll do my best to honor it." I wasn't sure I believed him.

●

For the next few weeks, as Sara and I kept up our mutual silent treatment, I was forced to keep mining my past. I knew my columns were supposed to be true confessions, but Jensen and Turner never said anything about chronological accuracy. So my next three were about Josh ("Great Somethings"), Jason, the ISO guy ("Share the Wealth"), and Tell, the cross-dressing punk ("Glen or Glenda"). I made it out like each affair had lasted only a week, and for the last two I changed the names of streets and restaurants so it sounded like the stories had happened in New York, not Providence. The illustrations were: me standing naked, staring at a naked guy with sideburns and an erect penis; me getting eaten out in a classroom with a poster of Marx in the background; and me blowing a guy who was wearing a wig.

Every Monday night when I got home from work there would be an E-mail from Turner: "Dear Traci Lords— Keep it up. If you know what I mean," or, "You are one sick chick—and I mean that as the highest compliment." Evidently my wool pulling was working. In Turner's mind I was a hot, swinging single girl. He had no idea what a lame-ass homebody I really was.

The readers' responses were just as strong as Turner's, but unfortunately, in both directions:

I love you, Ariel Steiner. You get me off every week, with grace and style. I wish the paper printed a picture of you so I could see what you look like.

ERNIE LAYNE, *Far Rockaway*

P.S. Why aren't you listed?

If Ariel Steiner came over to my house and did a striptease, I wouldn't blow her off. I'd propose.

FREDDIE ASSISI, *Chelsea*

Thank you, Ariel Steiner. How useful it is to know that when I want to spill some seed, I no longer have to spring five bucks for a *Hustler*. I can just pick up a free copy of the *Week* and use it for the same purpose. And because it's on newsprint, it happens to make excellent toilet paper as well.

NATHAN SHERMAN, *Forest Hills*

Who did Ariel Steiner sleep with to get her column?

LINDA SALLE, *Upper West Side*

When I read that last letter, I had to close the paper and take a few deep breaths. I had known *City Week* readers wrote the most venomous letters in town; I just hadn't been prepared for them to whack me so hard and so soon. But at the same time, the invective felt oddly familiar. While I had never been ridiculed *in print* before, the experience of being humiliated before an audience of thousands was not exactly new for me.

In the fall of ninth grade, my drama teacher, Mrs. Hopper, announced to our class that there was an Arts Day coming up, where any interested students could act or sing or dance in front of the entire school. She had a book of famous movie scenes on her desk and said we could borrow it if we wanted to. I leafed through it on the subway and found a scene from *The Graduate*. It was the one where Benjamin drives Mrs. Robinson home from the party, she insists that he come into the house with her, and then seduces him.

I had seen the movie a few months before, at a girlfriend's house, and as I watched Anne Bancroft flick her long cigarettes and clink ice cubes in her bourbon, I'd been struck with monumental awe. I wanted to be just like Mrs. Robinson when I grew up: husky voiced, poised, leggy, and nicotine addicted. An alcoholic, neurotic seductress, the ultimate man manipulator, with a heart as sharp as her nails.

There was a cute, obnoxious kid in my class named Nate who I'd had a crush on for quite some time. He was known for his loud mouth and quick wit. The day after I read the scene, I approached him at recess and asked if he had ever seen *The Gradu-*

ate. "Only about four hundred times," he said. "It's my all-time favorite movie. Why?"

"Well, there's this Arts Day coming up next month, and I was wondering if you'd want to do a scene from it with me."

"Me? Play Benjamin? That's my life dream. I'd be honored."

For the next three weeks we rehearsed in the hallways every day after school. Nate was a natural and he already knew most of the lines because he'd seen the film so many times. When we began our work on the last page, though, we hit a brick wall. The movie version of the scene ends like this: Benjamin stands in Mrs. Robinson's daughter Elaine's room, looking up at a portrait on the wall. Mrs. Robinson enters naked and locks the door behind her. He sees her reflection in the glass of Elaine's picture, then just as she tells him, "I find you very attractive," he hears Mr. Robinson's car pulling into the driveway, frantically unlocks the door, and runs down the stairs.

Since there was no way I was going to walk onstage naked, Nate suggested an alternate ending. In the final, climactic moment, I could step behind a shoulder-high flat, remove my dress (under which I'd be wearing a strapless bra), and pull him down behind the flat on the last line. I loved the idea. We tried it out that day and rehearsed it over and over again until we were thrilled with the effect.

The afternoon of the performance, Nate and I paced in the hallway outside the auditorium. Through the door, we watched the house lights dim and the stage lights come up, and then we entered through the center aisle, like we were coming up the driveway of the house. Suddenly I was transformed into Anne Bancroft. It didn't matter that my Mrs. Robinson dress was torn, ill fitting, and found in a bin of rags in the back of the auditorium. I was hoarse and leggy, and the school was watching.

When we got to the part where I stepped behind the flat and took off the dress, a murmur passed through the audience. I had these puppies in the palm of my hand. "I find you very attractive," I cooed, and pulled Nate down behind the flat, waiting for thunderous applause. None came. The kids didn't know it was over. "What should we do?" whispered Nate.

"Wait. They'll figure it out eventually."

They didn't. Still utter silence. It was painful. "It's over!" he shouted, but it was a large auditorium and nobody heard him. "This is ridiculous," he said. "I'm leaving."

"No, don't," I said, but he didn't listen. He stood up abruptly, so abruptly that he knocked over the flat. Suddenly I found myself trembling, half nude and squatting, in stockings and a bargain-basement bra, in front of twelve hundred of my closest friends. I looked out in terror and watched the audience break into a villainous roar, a roar of pure ridicule, so unabashedly evil it was heartbreaking. I could see it pass like a wave from the front row all the way up to the balcony, slowly but surely, until every single kid was guffawing at me, openmouthed.

I got the joke. The tables had been turned. The seductress was naked and ashamed, and the underdog had emerged the victor. I grabbed my dress and covered my front with it desperately, then sidestepped off the stage into the wings, my knees weak, my world caving in before me.

When I cried to my mother that night about what had happened, she said, "Don't worry. They'll forget about it within a few days." But I knew that even if the ridicule only lasted a week, it was the worst possible week for it to happen. The day after Arts Day was the official starting date of the campaign for school government office. I was running for correspondence vice president, the morning-announcements person, and I'd already gotten a thousand pencils embossed with ARIEL STEINER FOR CORRESPON-DENCE VP.

I arrived at school the next morning trying to make like nothing had happened, handed the pencils out to my homeroom classmates, and said, "I hope you vote for me." The boys took them, leered at me, and said things like "Of course I'll vote for you. Out of all the candidates, you're the only one who's exposed her agenda." The jokes were stupid and obvious, but they got me in the gut. Every single person who took a pencil made a jab about my visibility.

When I stood up on the auditorium stage again, a week later, to make my campaign speech, I heard a male voice in the balcony yell, "Hey, perky!" I knew he wasn't referring to my personality. But I bit my lip, dove into my oratory, and wound up winning the election. Not by a landslide, but by enough for me to wonder if maybe the *Graduate* scene had been partially responsible for my victory.

Maybe it was the same with the letters to the newspaper. If I was riling people up, I had to be doing something right. Controversy had worked for Madonna; why not me? As Dorothy Parker said, "Better to have people say nasty shit about you than nothing at all." Or something like that.

Whenever I read a particularly scathing attack on me in "The Mail," I wondered whether Faye was reading it too. But she never called to say she knew about my double life, so I assumed she didn't. Of course, she never called *anyway,* since she was such a lousy agent. She hadn't sent me on a single audition since *The Two Gentlewomen of Vilna*. One part of me wanted to tell her about my new career, so she could plug me to casting directors as The Controversial *City Week* Columnist, but the other part knew that would require her *reading* me. Faye would be horrified if she read the stuff I was writing. So I kept my mouth shut and hoped she wouldn't glance twice at the green boxes on the corners.

After a month of writing "Run Catch Kiss," I had become the vamp the city loved to hate. There was just one problem. I hadn't actually done any running, catching, or kissing. I had earned a reputation without leaving my apartment—but I *wanted* to be leaving my apartment! All that mining had made me nostalgic. I needed some present-day play.

Maybe my fears about looking desperate were old-fashioned. It was the nineties; women could go to bars by themselves without seeming like hos. Besides, there was an advantage to the fact that Sara and I weren't speaking anymore: I might look hotter without her sitting next to me.

The night "Glen or Glenda" came out, I changed into the same mini and tee I'd worn to show Faye my new body, and took the train to BarF. It was only about eight by the time I got there, so it wasn't too crowded. A couple of hipster boys were playing pool, but they didn't look up when I walked in the door.

I sat down at the bar and ordered a Jameson, trying to look like a confident, self-important sex columnist who frequented pubs alone all the time. But as five minutes went by, then ten, then thirty, without a single guy approaching, I began to get supremely depressed. What did I have to do to get some attention? Bare my breasts? Fellate my shot glass?

Suddenly a middle-aged guy with a white beard, a Harley-Davidson T-shirt, and a bandanna on his head sat next to me and said, "Can I buy you a drink?"

"No thanks," I said. The state of my love life had turned out to be worse than I thought: the only guy I could get to come on to me was Uncle Jesse from *The Dukes of Hazzard*.

I glanced at the two pool players in the back. One was lining up a shot and had his ass to me, and the other was busy putting songs on the jukebox. I sighed, went out the door and headed down First Avenue to the F stop.

Run Catch Kiss
True Confessions of a Single Girl
Ariel Steiner
The World Series Struck Me Out

I'm walking down First Avenue the other night when I pass a bodega. A bunch of Dominican men are clustered around a TV screen inside, so I go in to see what they're watching. It's Game Four of the World Series, the Yankees vs. the Braves. I lean against the counter and look at the screen, and within minutes I'm hooked on the game.

In the eighth inning, Jim Leyritz hits a homer that ties it—and the entire bodega erupts in loud cheering. I'm in the midst of giving a high five to the man behind the counter when a skinny V-necked boy comes in, with a beer in one hand and a smoke in the other. His hair is high, as are my hopes. He stands next to me, looks at the TV, and begins cheering and jeering with such goofy enthusiasm that the Dominicans laugh at him. I laugh too, and then I look at him for a second and go, "Do you really like the Yankees that much, or are you just acting?"

"Funny you should say that," he says. "Because I'm in acting grad school. Tomorrow for class we each have to do an independent activity. I'm making an audiotape of the first part of the game, when the Yanks were losing 6–0. I'm going to play the tape onstage while I clip my toenails, and react with disappointment. But if the Yanks wind up winning, then there'll be a whole underlying ironic truth behind my sad reaction."

"Where'd you go to undergrad?" I ask.

"Williams?" he up-talks, raising his voice on the second syllable like it's a question.

I hate up-talkers. Nothing irritates me more than people who raise the pitch of their voices at the end of declarative statements. So I say, "The way you just said that was so pretentious. If Williams were an obscure school that nobody had ever heard of, it would be justifiable for you to say it like that: 'Williams? It's a farming school? In Iowa? With two hundred students?' But Williams is well known. So when you raise your voice like that—as if to say, 'Williams? Are you familiar with it?'—it plays me for a fool. Which I most certainly am not."

"Where'd you go to school?"

"BROWN!"

He raises his eyebrows like he likes how far I've flown off the handle. I'm glad my bantering style hasn't turned him off, because if I can't banter with a guy, there's no way in hell I can have a future with him. As the game goes on, the two of us eye each other surreptitiously, and I start to think less and less about the Series and more and more about him. In the ninth inning, we introduce ourselves. His name's Darren.

A shout goes up from the men in the 10th, as Bernie Williams gets walked and the bases are loaded. Then Wade Boggs walks too, so it's 7–6 Yanks, and the guys whoop and holler like it's the second coming. I think how baseball is kind of like sex, because it's not a consistently high-energy sport. There are these intermittent surges of excitement every once in a while, followed by a steady lull for a few minutes, until the next surge comes again.

During one of the lulls I look at Darren and say, half sexy, half kidding, "You're fun to watch the game with."

He says, *"Oh, Ariel!!"* in a fake lusty voice, but I can tell it's not entirely a joke.

The Yankees win the game and everyone embraces and cheers because now the Series is tied. I kiss this old guy who's sitting on a crate, and then I look at Darren expectantly. But he doesn't kiss me. He just smiles. We go outside and he lights a cigarette. I notice that he holds it awkwardly, like he's not really a smoker, and I figure he probably picked up smoking so he'd fit in better in acting school.

I ask if he'll walk me to the F, and when we get to the station I lean against the entrance and stare down the street, stalling for time. He looks at me for a while, then grabs my face with two hands and kisses me with the intensity and purpose of a line drive. Every few seconds while he's kissing me, I get distracted and start thinking about the possibility of the Yankees winning the Series. I start to wonder whether Darren and I will celebrate the victory together and how romantic it will be if we do.

Suddenly he stops kissing me and says, "Maybe we should go somewhere."

I decide to play hard to get. "I don't know," I say. "It's kind of late. Maybe I should just get on the train and go home."

"OK," he says. "Nice meeting you."

Damn, I think. *Reverse psychology never works.*

"Come to think of it," I say quickly, "I changed my mind. Maybe we *should* go somewhere."

He says he lives on Pitt Street and I say that sounds like a fine destination to me. We head toward his house, stopping every few blocks to make out. I don't know if it's the joy of watching the Yankees win or the unseasonable humidity in the air, but I'm in an incredibly romantic mood. Every time we have to stop for a light, we turn to each other and suck face. We've been walking for about ten minutes when we come to a wall with *Streit's Matzoh* painted on it.

"Wow, a matzoh factory," I say, stopping to stare at the wall. "Are you Jewish?"

"Half."

Yes. "So am I. Can I kiss you against the matzoh wall? It would really turn me on."

"Sure."

I lean him against the wall and press myself against his boner. I'm Linda Fiorentino in a Jewish *Last Seduction,* kneading the bread of his affliction. My Red Sea is parting for his rising staff and I hope this night will be different from the others.

He lives in a remarkably clean two-bedroom. When I compliment him on it, he says his roommate's a dominatrix, so every couple days, a different man pays her to let him come over and straighten up. We go into his room and dive onto his futon. I slide my hand down his pants and pull out his dick. It's large and pale and angled to the right. I pump it while he kisses my breasts. After a little while, he asks if he should get a condom. I say I don't want to have sex and he looks sort of disappointed. That makes me feel guilty, so I say, "You can come on my chest."

He smiles, goes over to a cabinet, and comes back with this white stuff in a bottle. "What's that?" I ask. "Come that you saved?"

He laughs like that's the funniest joke he'd heard in a long time and says, "No. Clinique." As soon as the word "Clinique" comes out of his mouth, I find myself questioning his sexual orientation. But then I remind myself it's the '90s, and in the '90s, *all* men are vain.

He props himself up above me, we rub the Clinique all over his dick, and I squeeze my tits as hard as I can around it, which isn't easy since my hands are slippery from the lotion. He rocks back and forth between them for a while, then comes all over my neck. We lie on our sides looking at each other. I smile a Meg Ryan smile, stroke his high hair, and say, "Wouldn't it be funny if someday we got married, then went back to the bodega, and all the men remembered the night we met there?"

He slits his eyes, rolls onto his back, and stares at the ceiling. You know something's wrong when they turn from you to the ceiling.

"In case you're wondering," I say, "I didn't mean . . . I wasn't suggesting you *actually* marry me. It was just a momentary mindless fantasy I was sharing with you. I guess a girl's not supposed to share those fantasies because it could scare a guy away, huh?"

"It sure could." He stares at the ceiling a little longer, then turns his back to me and goes to sleep.

I don't fall asleep right away, because I'm so worried I said the wrong thing. But then I tell myself I'm reading too much into it. I made him laugh. He stopped on corners to kiss me. We bantered. When you have that good a time with somebody there's no single thing they could take as the Wrong Thing.

In the morning I kiss him a little and he kisses me back. I look for signs of the wanting-the-girl-to-leave thing going but I don't see any. We trade numbers and get dressed. He puts on wide-wale corduroys. I stroke the wales and tell him how sexy wide-wale corduroys are on a good-looking man. He belts his pants and I can see the outline of his thing through them. I pat it and it gets firm. We start to make out again, but we have to go, so we go.

I link arms with him as we walk to the train station, and when we get there he kisses me good-bye. To insure that he doesn't think I'm needy, I don't ask him to call me. Instead I go, "See you around," very casually and head down the stairs.

That afternoon I leave a message on his machine, telling him I'll be at the bodega at night watching Game Five if he wants to come. The Yankees win again, but somehow the victory just doesn't taste as good as before, because he doesn't show up. I call him the next day and leave another message saying I'll be watching Game Six Saturday night. He never calls back. I go anyway, and the Yankees win the Series. The city is jumping for joy. Cars are honking and people are drinking on the street. I stand at a pay phone outside the bodega, putting the same quarter into the phone again and again, thanking God for Tollsaver.

All day Sunday I think about the hookup, trying to figure out how one single comment could have sent him flying off like a foul ball. Every time I pass a pay phone I dial his number and hang up when I get the machine. I tell myself hanging up on the machine isn't as bad as leaving a message because he has no sure way of knowing it's me, but then I realize he *has* to know it's me because who else but a woman scorned would call and hang up that many times in a row?

I finally decide to stop calling, but I still can't get him out of my mind. Sunday night I watch a fight on TV, enjoying the blood and gore, and I realize boxing is a much better metaphor for sex than baseball.

The night the column came out, I decided to call Sara. I needed to talk to her about Aaron (his real name), but it wasn't just that. I wanted to be her friend again. It seemed stupid to avoid her when I missed having her in my life.

When she picked up the phone, she sounded like she'd been crying. "It's me," I said. "Are you OK?"

"Not exactly," she moaned. "Michael just dumped me."

"Why?"

"He said he didn't feel like we had a future, because he could only have futures with women who made him feel vulnerable, and I didn't make him feel vulnerable enough!"

Suddenly I didn't feel jealous about Michael anymore. I just felt sorry for her. How could I envy her when the cock she'd blocked had turned out to be so flaccid?

"I'm sorry," I said. "And I'm sorry I was mean."

"Why were you?" she said, sniffling.

"I had a crush on Michael, and when he turned out to be into you instead of me, I hated you for it."

"Well, look what came of it!"

"I know. He sounds like an asshole."

"But he's an asshole I miss!" She blew her nose loudly. "I fucking went to his house and made him chicken soup when he was sick! I paid for all our meals because he never had any money! And now he's ending it because I wasn't evil enough? What kind of twisted world are we living in?"

"I know what you mean," I said. "I recently had a similar experience."

"Yeah, I read it. I could relate."

"Maybe we should go out tonight. Do you have plans?"

"How could I have plans? I just got dumped!"

"OK, OK. Where should we go?"

"BarBarella. It's on First between Seventh and Eighth. It's my new living room."

●

She couldn't have picked a better meeting place. In the window were bright neon signs advertising different beers, and hanging from the ceiling were Christmas lights, holly, and crepe-paper balls. There was a sink in the back (the bathrooms were too small to have their own), two bookshelves, a few clunky wooden tables, and a jukebox. The clientele was a mix of new hipster and old dive—T-shirted boys rubbing elbows with haggard sixty-year-old women. The bartender was a tough-looking chick with large breasts, peroxided hair, and black glasses.

Sara ordered the drinks and I went to check out the juke-box. I selected a medley of sob-story music—Nina Simone's cover of "I Shall Be Released," Tom Waits's "I Wish I Was in New Orleans," and Dylan's "You're Gonna Make Me Lonesome When You Go"—then sat back down next to Sara at the bar.

"What do you think the solution is with these guys?" I asked her. "Are we supposed to be cold and abusive? Is that what they want?"

"I think so. Most men are really self-loathing. They're looking for women who will hate them as much as they already hate themselves."

"I don't loathe men. I love them!"

"I know, but you can't make that clear too early on. I don't think it was the wisest idea to bring up marriage on the first date."

"I wasn't bringing it up seriously! It was a joke. A fantasy. A funny thought. If he didn't get that, then he's the fucked one!"

"Didn't you read *The Rules*?"

"That book is crap."

"It's not. It picks up on a true dynamic. Guys love the thrill of the chase, so you have to watch your step. As soon as you start pushing, he loses interest. You already violated three of the Rules with that guy: 'Don't Call Him and Rarely Return His Calls,' 'Let Him Take the Lead,' and 'Don't Open Up Too Fast.' "

"Do you really believe that stuff?"

"Yeah."

"Are *you* going to be distant the next time you meet a guy you like?"

"I'm not going to try to meet anyone new. I'm seeing Jon tomorrow night."

•

The next morning at my desk, I thought about what Sara had said. Had I ruined everything with Aaron—all because I'd pursued him so aggressively? When Ione Skye broke up with John Cusack in *Say Anything...*, he held up a huge boom box beneath her window and blasted "In Your Eyes" by Peter Gabriel. That's how he told her to take him back. And of course, she eventually did. Why was it sexy for John to pursue Ione that way, but insane for me to do so with Aaron? Why couldn't he see me as a John Cusack, instead of a Glenn Close?

But then it occurred to me that I might not have to follow *The Rules* in order to make use of them. Maybe I could utilize them another way: by making my next column a scathing, bitter satire of the entire vomitrocious philosophy. I opened my top drawer, put a notepad on my lap, and started to scribble. By lunchtime, I had finished.

RUN CATCH KISS

True Confessions of a Single Girl

ARIEL STEINER

The Drools: Time-Tested Secrets for Stalking Your Mr. Right

Drool #1: Approach strange men in cafés and bars. Walk right up to every guy you like and tell him you find him attractive. Very attractive. Explain that you have not been fucked in a very long time. Tell him you had a boyfriend once but he left you because you mailed him a lock of your pubic hair for Valentine's Day. When he blushes or looks the other way, grab his face and say, "I'm talking to you, dick." If he says he's taken, snort and say, "Ha. You haven't been taken till you've been taken by me." If he tries to plow past you, throw yourself on his shoulder, holding fast to his waist. Beat his back and wail, "I'm no quitter!" until he brings you back to his house.

Drool #2: Spill your guts to him as soon as possible. On the first date, try to bring up your hopes for the future right away. Explain that he can move in with you whenever he feels comfortable; there's no need to hesitate at all. Outline how important it is to you to have children, and suggest that the two of you get started immediately.

Drool #3: Call him at least four times a night, just to say hello. While you're at work, leave messages every hour or so on his answering machine or voice mail. For example, "Hi. Can't get you out of my mind. Being with you makes me feel like a pig in shit."

Drool #4: Try to see him three times a day. If he's not sure he wants to see you that often, tell him he has no choice. If he tries to break up with you, send him black balloons that say, *Hell hath no fury.* Find out which new girls he's dating and hire somebody to off them. Lurk in the back rows at their funerals. Don't give in to getting over. Fight and fight until he's yours. If he leaves the state, follow him. Never let him get more than half a mile away. Change your identity. Wear a wig. Get a face-lift. Move in right next door to his new house. Approach him in a bar the exact same way you did the first time, explaining how you have not been fucked in a very long time. When he says you remind him of his old girlfriend, throw your head back and laugh. Heh heh heh heh heh.

———————————

4

AFTER READING your last few columns, Ariel Steiner, my initial conclusion was that you must be suffering from a total lack of confidence. But after further consideration, I realized you're not the one at fault. Your parents are! I cannot fathom what type of abuse they must have heaped on you to make you grow into such a miserable, self-destructive hussy.

FRED SADOWSKY, *West Village*

P.S. Why aren't you listed?

The reason I never called Ariel Steiner back after we hooked up ("The World Series Struck Me Out," 10/30) was because she's completely deranged. I might have been interested in seeing her again if she hadn't called and hung up on my answering machine so many times right after we met. Who wants to date someone that obsessive? And for the record, my cock tilts to the left, not the right. Evidently, Steiner's mental problems extend beyond the realm of emotional instability into penile dyslexia.

AARON "DARREN" WALKER, *Lower East Side*

100   It was the day "The Drools" came out, and Sara and I were on the Met Life bleachers listening to an opera singer. "Say something comforting," I said, putting down the paper.

She thought for a second, then said, "It was an honest mistake. Do you label the cock tilt from *his* perspective—or your own?"

"*That* was supposed to be comforting?" I sputtered.

"What do you want me to say? You *chose* to take this job. You have to live with the consequences. Just try to remember what Dorothy Parker said. 'Better to—'"

"I know," I said. "I know."

●

When I got back from lunch, my dad called. "Who is that asshole Sadowsky?" he growled.

"Sadowsky?" I said. "What about Aaron?"

"That letter didn't bother me so much. It must have been humiliating for *you*, but he didn't mention mom and me. So, what should I do? Should I write a response, saying we raised you well?"

"No!"

"*Did* we raise you well?"

"What do you mean?"

"Are you really that unstable?"

"Does the word *satire* mean anything to you?"

"I knew it was satirical. I just wasn't sure how much."

"Remember that conversation where I asked you not to tell me what you read?"

"Yes, but you've got to throw me a bone. Larry Stanley's beginning to drive me insane."

"Who's he?"

"This guy in my office. Every Wednesday afternoon he walks up to my desk with the paper, says, 'Hey, Leo—listen to this!' and reads the raciest portions of your column to me in a very loud voice so all the other systems analysts can hear."

"What do you say when he does that?"

"I say it's not fair to quote you out of context."

I had to hand it to my dad. He was holding on to his sanity in the face of an extremely difficult situation. He was in a horrifying Jewish parent predicament: his child had been awarded the Pulitzer Prize . . . in pornography. The proud-father side of him must have wanted to gush to his coworkers about my newfound success, but the staid conservative side must have been deeply ashamed about the area of my expertise.

"I know this is hard for you," I said.

"It's not me you should be worried about. It's Mom. She wants us to get buttons that say, IT'S ALL FICTION, so we can flash them at dinner parties when people ask how much is true."

●

That night when I got home, I found a *City Week* envelope in my mailbox. Inside were three letters addressed to me care of the *Week,* which Turner had forwarded:

Dear Ariel,
   My friends call me Mary because of my milky-white status. I am thirty-two years old and have yet to penetrate a woman. But it's not because I'm gay. I'm just shy. Do you have any advice on how I might gain some confidence when talking to the fairer sex? Perhaps we could discuss this over a drink. But don't get me wrong. This is not a come-on. I'm far too shy to be capable of coming on to you. I just think you might be able to help me out.
                                                    CHRISTOPHER HINKLE

Dear Ariel,
   I await your column each week like a junkie awaits his fix, like a dog awaits his walk, like a baby awaits his mother's teat. Each Wednesday after work, I race to the *City Week* distribution box at the corner of my office building, my forehead glistening with sweat, my lips moist with expectation. I open the metal door, withdraw the paper with trembling fingers, then get on the subway, open straight to "Run Catch Kiss," and indulge myself in your latest tale. When I reach the final line, my heart grows heavy as I realize with dismay that seven long days must pass before you can be mine again.
                                                              TED BARROW
P.S. Don't print this in the paper. I have a girlfriend.

Hey Ariel—
   It seems pretty clear which side of the banquet table you sit on, generally speaking, but do you ever switch?
                                                          MYRA GALITSIS

I didn't feel so lousy about the letters in "The Mail" after that. I had fans—even if they didn't write in to the paper to say so.

And I had friends—even if I'd never meet any of them face-to-face. I read each letter a few times over, stuck them in a file folder, and slid it under the futon in case I ever needed something to cheer me up.

Then I went out to meet Sara. Her accordion teacher, Evan, was playing at BarBie, a rock club on Avenue B, and she'd invited me to come. When I got to the show I found her in the front row, smoking and dancing wildly to the music. The sound was unlike anything I'd heard before—circusy and jazzy both, with weird instruments: violin, mandolin, cello, electric bass, bassoon, and drums. Evan was tall and emaciated, with stringy dark hair and pale shiny skin. He played with incredible intensity, his fingers moving like lightning, his head bowed and intent, a cigarette dangling from his lips. In between songs he would lean down his head, speak shyly into a tiny microphone planted inside the accordion to introduce the next number, then ask someone in the audience for a light. He came off as a cross between a twelve-year-old girl and a bad-ass rocker, and that combination sucked me in.

At the end of the first set Sara and I went up to the bar to buy drinks. Suddenly I spotted Evan coming toward us. "Hey, Evan," said Sara, pulling him over. "This is Ariel."

"Sara told me she knew you," he said. "I'm a huge fan."

"Really?" I said, my upper and lower mouths both widening with glee. It's a major ego trip when you go from *being* a groupie to *having* one—all within the span of a few weeks.

One of Evan's band members signaled him from the stage and Evan nodded back at him. "I should go," he said. "But after the show a bunch of us are going to head over to BarNey Rubble to hear two hard-core bands play. You girls want to come?"

"Actually," said Sara, "I'm meeting Jon, but maybe Ariel wants to."

"OK," I said.

"Good," said Evan and went back to the stage for the next set.

●

"I really liked the gig," I said as we headed up the street together. He walked in one of those effeminate swaggers that's more often a sign of Bowie worship than any latent leanings. "It was funny when you spoke into your accordion."

He smiled. "That's funny you thought it was funny. It wasn't planned. We just didn't have enough mikes." He took a packet of Drum out of his jeans with his right hand, removed a rolled cigarette, stuck it in his mouth, and lit it, all while keeping his left hand in his pocket.

"Are you doing that with one hand to impress me with your manual dexterity?" I asked.

"No," he said, pulling his left hand out. He was holding a key chain attached to a small canister of Mace. "I keep my finger on the trigger at all times, so I'm ready if somebody fucks with me. I'm so skinny that ruffians tend to seek me out. I was mugged eight times before I got the idea to carry Mace."

"That's horrible. Have you always been skinny?"

"Yeah. Most people think it's because I snort h, but it's really because of my Scottish ancestry."

"So you don't snort h?"

"No, I do, but I was skinny before I started."

Now, I'd gone out with my share of stoners and drunks, but heroin was another thing altogether. It was enough to freak me out in a big way. He must have noticed the shock on my face because he quickly added, "I don't do it that often. Just once in a while. I'm trying to stop, actually."

At least he was trying to quit. At least he knew it wasn't good for him. Maybe I was making a mountain out of a molehill. This was modern-day New York City. I couldn't be too judgmental.

"It is such a thrill to be meeting you in the flesh," he said. "But I'm kind of embarrassed I told you I was a fan. I feel like maybe I gave you the wrong idea about me."

"What would that be?"

"That I was some sort of loony who was only interested in you because he wanted you to write about him."

"Are you?"

"I wouldn't *mind* it if my name appeared in the column," he said, blushing, "but that's not my main motivation."

"What is?"

"I just thought, I mean, from reading you, you sounded like someone I wanted to know."

"Biblically?" I asked hopefully.

He smiled. "I just mean you just seem like an honest person. I've been wondering what you looked like since I started reading you. And I guess I was a little scared when Sara said you were a friend of hers, because I thought I might meet you someday and not be attracted to you, and I didn't want that to happen. But then when she introduced you to me, I was relieved, because, I . . . was."

This guy was stroking me in more ways than one. Boosting my feminine ego and artistic ego all in one fell swoop. But I was nervous. I felt like I had some sort of vampish reputation to live up to and I didn't know if I could. What if he only wanted me because he thought I was easy? Maybe it was best not to jump the gun in the make-out department. I was hot for him, though. I didn't want to have to pull a Pollyanna on principle, then miss out on decent action. I decided to play it by ear. Forget the fact that he'd read me before he met me, and pretend it was a sweet, normal, *Our Town*ish kind of date. With a sex columnist Emily and a junkie George.

●

BarNey Rubble was very hard rock. The music was way too loud and the crowd tattooed and leathered. It wasn't my scene at all. But I bopped my head to the music so Evan would think I was as tough and downtown as he was.

When the set ended, he said, "You want to come over to my place?" His apartment was a huge, beat-down loft above a restaurant, on First between Third and Fourth. There weren't any posters on the walls, the floor was covered with dust, and the only thing to sit on was a ratty tweed sofa with the stuffing coming out. As I headed for the couch, I realized I was shivering. "Why is it so cold in here?" I asked.

"My heat and electricity got cut off. My roommates and I haven't paid our bills in a while. So we're stealing the upstairs neighbor's electricity"—he pointed to an extension cord stuck through a hole in his ceiling—"but we haven't figured out how to steal heat."

I nodded and sat down. "I think I'm going to snort some h," he said. "Do you want some?"

"No, thanks," I said. "I'm kind of a prude when it comes to drugs."

"That's cool," he said. He went over to a card table on the other side of the room. I turned my head to the side so I couldn't see because I was afraid it might be too upsetting. I'd never seen someone snort coke, much less heroin. The hard drug scene at Brown was pretty private. If you didn't partake, you didn't witness.

A few minutes later he sat down next to me. His pupils were a little dilated, but aside from that he seemed the same.

"Have you ever shot up?" I asked.

"No, never. I'm stupid, but not that stupid." I believed him because I wanted to fuck him and I had to believe him to fuck him.

"Have you been tested?"

"Yeah. You?"

"Yeah." I'd been tested three times, but the last one was fall of freshman year, when I first started going out with Will. Since then, I had sucked the unrubbered cock of four guys who claimed they were negative—but let only one of them come in my mouth; let two guys enter unprotected for about four seconds before I made them pull out and put on condoms; and got eaten by a guy who used to shoot up but had gotten tested regularly since and claimed he was OK. So I wasn't lying, but I wasn't a hundred percent sure of my current status, either. And I didn't think Evan was lying, but for all I knew, his last test had been too long ago to matter. The presex sexual-history discussion is a pretty bogus exercise. You each say you're clean, but you don't discuss when the tests were or what you've done since, and you pretend telling each other you're disease free is as good as knowing for sure.

Evan got up and put on a CD—Fred Frith, he said—sat down, covered our laps with a blanket, and took my hand in his. I rubbed his thumb. It was cold. He leaned in and kissed me. His lips felt good but his tongue was slightly bitter and suddenly I got scared I'd get high from tasting the smack.

"Could I get high from kissing you?" I asked.

"No. It's already been metabolized into my bloodstream."

We kissed more. He caressed my breast, outside my shirt. I put my hand on his crotch.

"It's the smack," he said, pulling back.

"Oh."

"But maybe tomorrow, when I'm not . . . what are you doing tomorrow night?"

"Nothing."

"Why don't I come to your place, then? I tend bar till midnight and I can come over right after."

"OK," I said. I wrote down my address for him, and then he walked me to a cab.

●

As soon as he came over the next night, we got on my bed. Things were getting pretty steamy when he leaned to the side and reached for his pants.

"Are you getting a Drum?" I asked.

"No. A condom."

He unwrapped it, rolled it on, got on top of me, pumped for about three minutes, then collapsed on my chest. It was the first New York City, postcollege, independent-single-girl sex I'd had, and sad to say, it was pretty disappointing. Sex is often that way for me. I'm much more entranced by the idea of it than the act itself. Not that I haven't had good sex. I totally have. But only with Will. That was because *(a)* I cared about him and *(b)* either I jerked myself off during it or he did, so I came.

My first time was awful, though. I met the surfer on the boardwalk in Rehoboth Beach on one of my nights off from baby-sitting the twins. He was eighteen years old, from rural Pennsylvania, and he was spending the summer smoking pot, surfing, and living in a house with some friends. We would meet at ten or eleven, play Skee-Ball or ride the Ferris wheel, and then make out on one of the benches on the boardwalk. One night he suggested we go down to the beach, and we lay on the sand in the dark. He fingered me for a few minutes and asked if he could put it in.

I was incredibly curious about sex because I had done everything else with Flip Goldin at camp and I had this idea that it would feel like fireworks—gorgeous and explosive and romantic all at once. But I was scared, too, so I said, "I'm a virgin," hoping he might retract the offer.

He didn't. He just said, "That's OK."

"Do you have a condom?"

"No, but don't worry. I'll pull out."

And even though I had learned in health ed never to do it without protection, I was afraid that if I told him no, he would never offer again and I'd lose my chance to learn what it was like. So I said, "OK," and closed my eyes. He moved my bathing suit to the side with his hand, then heaved himself onto me and put it in. This searing pain shot right through me. It wasn't a fast pain, like a Band-Aid rip-off, that came and went instantly. It was slow and grating and it didn't wane with time. I tilted my head back and gritted my teeth, praying it would get better, but it didn't. Finally I started to cry. He didn't notice.

"I think you should stop," I said. He pulled out and lay next to me with a loud sigh. "What is it?" I asked.

"It's just that I really want to come."

And I wanted him to be happy. Even though I hardly knew him, I didn't want to stand in the way of him having his way. I wanted him to like it even though it was killing me because then he would like me and I wanted to be liked.

So I said, "Maybe we can try it again," and he got back on top of me and kept going. It hurt a little less, but it definitely didn't feel like fireworks. After a few minutes he yanked it out abruptly and left a warm wet spot on the stomach of my bathing suit. I pulled my shorts up and stood to go, but when I reached in my pocket for the key to my bike lock, I couldn't find it. It had slipped out into the sand.

The bike wasn't mine; it was the twins' mother's, and I was terrified she'd fire me if I told her I'd lost the key. So the surfer and I spent twenty-five minutes running our fingers through the sand, trying to find it, and I started crying—not just about the key but about the fact that my first time had turned out to be such a whopping disappointment. He rubbed my back and said, "Don't worry. I'll find the key and walk the bike back to your house." I told him where I lived and went home.

When I got upstairs I locked myself in the bathroom, ran a shower, and took off my clothes. The crotch of my suit was stained with blood and sand. I got in the shower and held the suit up to the showerhead, trying to will the night out of my mind. I had never expected it to be that ugly. I'd expected it to be perfect and clean like in all the movies. My devirginator was supposed to be as sweet and doting as John Cusack with Ione under that blanket in the backseat of his Malibu. He wasn't supposed to be a stoner moron.

I dried off, put on my nightgown, and slid into bed, under the cool sheets. I heard this ticking out my window and looked down. It was him, wheeling the bike into the driveway. I put my nose to the window screen and he smiled and waved, and for one brief moment I didn't feel so bad about the sex, because even though it had been awful, he'd been gentleman enough to look for the key. That was how it had been with almost every guy since then, too. They could be ninety-nine percent asshole and one percent sweet, and the one percent was always enough for me to justify staying.

Evan pulled out, slid the condom off, and set it on the floor next to the bed. "I'm sorry I came so soon," he said.

"That's OK," I said. I got up to pee so I wouldn't get a urinary tract infection, and when I got back he'd fallen asleep.

•

Friday night I invited him to see a movie at the Quad about these heavy-metal teens who murdered some little boys. In the middle of the movie he reached for my hand and stroked it. Suddenly I wasn't so upset about the sex being bad. If he was stroking my hand voluntarily it meant he had to be thinking romantic thoughts.

I immediately started fantasizing about the two of us spending the rest of our lives together. With my love to guide him he'd slowly evolve from junkie accordionist to responsible boyfriend. He'd go on Nicorette, join NA, and educate himself about female sexual pleasure. We'd buy a factory in Williamsburg and convert it to a living space, and have Jewish Scottish kids who were smart but tough, wise but rocking. He'd said himself he wouldn't mind if I wrote about him, so my column would transform from a diary of a single girl into a portrait of hipster monogamy.

I'd write weekly rants on the difficulties of finding vintage clothes for kids and earplugs small enough for five-year-olds. Thurston and Kim and Jon and Cristina would all become huge fans, the *Week* would raise my salary to a thousand a pop, and Williamsburg would replace Chelsea as the hottest celebrity 'hood in the city. Evan would take care of the kids during the day while I wrote, and I'd take care of them at night while he performed. It would be an ideal, reciprocal coupling, and whenever people asked how we met, we would tell them the incredible story of how he started out as my fan, became my lover, then turned his life around and went sober all because of my pure and noble affection.

When we got out of the movie theater, I wrapped my arms around his neck and kissed him long and hard. He writhed out of my embrace and said, "I think I'm going to go back to my apartment and practice for a little while. But my friend Kath is having a birthday party in the financial district tonight. Why don't you meet me there around midnight?" He gave me the address and walked briskly down the street.

It wasn't so easy for me to imagine us having children after that. But I didn't let myself get discouraged. I was as uninvested as he was. I wasn't Just Another Desperate Single Girl Looking for a Boyfriend; I was Ariel Steiner, a highly successful young woman with her own weekly column in the hottest city in the world. I had strangers sending me fan letters. I was unlisted. Evan was nothing but a paltry, pathetic reader, lucky I'd given him the time of day. If anyone was the less besotted party, it was me. Besides, he'd approached me first. And it's always the pursuer, not the pursued, who gets dumped in the end.

When I got to Kath's apartment, I found Evan sitting on the couch and groping along the floor. "What are you doing?" I asked.

"Looking for my Valium. I'm coming down off smack. I dropped the Valium on the floor a few minutes ago and now I can't find it."

"What does it look like?"

"It's small and white and has a little v cut out of it." I looked around the room, found it a few feet away, and handed it to him.

"Thanks," he said and swallowed it without water.

After the party we took a cab back to my place. Once we got up to my room, he zonked out in my bed. I was kind of disappointed we weren't going to get another chance to have sex, but I told myself it wasn't his fault. He had drug problems. I couldn't blame him for falling asleep.

The next night he called at three-thirty in the morning. "I was wondering if I could come over. I've been thinking about you."

All my bad feelings about him flew away. This was romance right out of a John Hughes movie. He was stopping by in the middle of the night because he couldn't get me out of his mind. It didn't get much more sappy than that.

He rang my buzzer about forty-five minutes later, and I went down to get the door. Al was standing in the foyer in his undershirt, peering out through the glass at him. "He rang my doorbell," he said angrily.

Oh God. This cat was going to get me evicted. "I'm sorry, Al," I said. "It's my, um, cousin. He must have been confused. I'm really sorry. I promise this won't happen again."

"It better not," he said and went back into his apartment.

I opened the door. "You woke up my landlord!" I hissed. "Didn't you see my name on the buzzer? It's marked pretty clearly!"

"I guess I didn't."

We went upstairs and sat down at the kitchen table. "Thanks for letting me come over so late," he said. "I'm high and I couldn't sleep. Do you have any alcohol? I need something to calm me down."

"Evan," I said, "did you come because you were thinking about me, or because you couldn't fall asleep?"

"Both," he said. I heard the *Jeopardy!* wrong-answer buzzer go off in my head. But I poured him a glass of Carlo Rossi anyway, because I am a generous soul.

By his fourth glass, he was babbling hard—about how he really should stop snorting h but it was such a good high, a much better high than coke, and so cheap, too. Then he said, "I've been having the weirdest nods lately."

"Nods?"

"Waking dreams induced by smack. Jim Carroll wrote a whole book about it, *The Book of Nods*." He started to detail some of Carroll's nods. I tried to listen, but I didn't give a fuck about Jim Carroll's nods. The reason addicts make lousy boyfriends is not because they can't get it up or commit, but because the only subject that interests them is how good their drugs make them feel. All they ever want to talk about is what geniuses Hunter S. Thompson, Carlos Castaneda, and Jim Carroll were. A girl can hear only so much about Thompson, Castaneda, and Carroll before she starts to get a little bit bored.

"Let's go to bed," I said, in the hopes that it might quiet him down. We moved to the futon and started fooling around. He rolled on a jimmy and I sat on top of him. This time I played with myself in the hopes that I might come, but I felt self-conscious, and he could only get half hard, so after twenty minutes it became clear that neither of us would be throwing a lump anytime in the millennium. Finally he sighed and said, "I don't think I can come because of the smack."

"OK," I said, held onto the rim, and climbed off. He took off the condom. We lay there silently. I wanted something between us to work. I wanted to excite him—even though I wasn't so sure I *liked* him. I put my hand on it. It woke up. I crawled down and took it in my mouth. It was bitter from the spermicide, but I was diligent, and within just a few minutes he rewarded me for my efforts.

"So, did you like that?" I said, sliding up next to him.

"Yeah," he said. And then he blinked and said, "Want to hear something really weird?"

"OK."

"This afternoon I got together with this buddy of mine, Ray, and when he came up the street to meet me, I noticed he had Saran Wrap sticking out the back of his shirt." I tried to figure out how this related to the act that had just transpired. Was he going to tell me Ray had used the Saran Wrap as a prophylactic with a girl, forgotten to remove it, then shifted around in bed postact so it somehow got stuck on his shoulders?

"Go on," I said.

"So I was staring at the Saran Wrap, trying to figure out what it was doing on his back, and then I noticed he had this tattoo under it, this huge black tattoo of a crow. I knew he was planning on getting a tattoo, but I can't believe he got such a big one!"

Suddenly I realized the story had no blow job connection at all. I had wanted him to say, "Want to hear something really weird? That was the best head I've ever gotten in my life!" or "Want to hear something really weird? I was in a relationship for three years and the sucking I got from her did not come close to approximating what I just got from you." I didn't want to hear about the crow on his stupid friend's back. I had given him head and he had given me a tattoo tale. I'd witnessed postejaculatory temporary-retardation syndrome many times before, but never had I seen this dire a case.

"That's . . . a really funny story," I said.

"I know," he said, rolled over, and fell asleep.

The next morning we got dressed and went to a diner on Court Street for breakfast. He ordered coffee, eggs, and a Bud. "How can you drink a coffee and a Bud at the same time?" I said. "Don't they cancel each other out?"

"No," he said. "The coffee is to wake me up and the Bud is the hair of the dog that bit me."

"I see."

"Ariel . . ."

Warning number one.

"Yes?"

"I don't know if it's such a good idea for us to keep seeing each other."

Sayonara city.

"Why's that?"

"I've been feeling really loopy lately, about h and whether I should keep doing it. It's kind of a crazy time and I feel like I need to be on my own for a while."

"So you've been feeling loopy because of the heroin, but not because of me."

"No."

"No you haven't been feeling loopy about me, or no you have been?"

"I have been." *Oof.* "I wanted to talk to you about it last night. That's why I came over. But then I got kind of wasted and I couldn't say it. When I first met you I didn't think you wanted a relationship. I mean, you're a sex columnist. Why would you want a boyfriend? But then it became pretty clear that you did, and I just can't handle that now. I really need to focus on myself and my music. Let's go out for coffee, though. I'll call you." He stood up, kissed me on the cheek, put some money on the table, and headed for the door.

Suddenly I forgot about his boring conversation, bad habit, erection problems, and lack of head appreciation. I didn't realize that by dumping me he might be doing both of us a very big favor. All I could think was, *I can't believe I let him end it first.* I was tired of being rejected. *I* wanted to be the one to cut a date short because I had band practice or shelves to build. I wanted to cock my head and say a guy's name in a faux polite tone, then dump him flat on his flabby ass.

Because when it came right down to it, I didn't resent Evan so much as want to *be* him. I envied my assholes. All they cared about was their work and themselves. They didn't need relationships to make them happy. They were never looking for anything long-term, so they never got hurt. I wanted to learn to be that recklessly self-important, to have such incredible drive and direction that relationships were unwanted diversions. I wanted to be an isolationist commitmentphobe. A jaded jade. I wanted to be a guy.

Maybe my column could help me sprout the penis I'd been envying my whole sorry life. I could view it as my band, my shelves. My Main Thing. If I saw myself as a scientist instead of a sap, then I could turn the boys from my tormentors to my experiments. Just like Evan said, I was a sex columnist. What did I need a boyfriend for? I wasn't a reject; I was a swinger. I wasn't a loser; I just didn't believe in monogamy. It wasn't that I couldn't *get* a boyfriend; if I got one, I'd lose my job.

When I got home from the diner I wrote a column about Evan, but I altered a few of the relevant details: I didn't mention that he'd been a fan (so my readers wouldn't get any ideas), I changed his name to Kevin, said *I'd* broken up with him because of his heroin problem, and said the one time he'd been hard enough to fuck, I came. It was the last fiction that was most important. There was no way I could let my readers know my saddest true confession of all: ever since I was a teenager, my orgasms had been as elusive as the boys themselves.

I didn't have my first till freshman year of college, when I was eighteen. Not that I hadn't tried before. Throughout high school I had diddled away under the covers late at night fairly frequently, in the hopes that I'd someday be able to join that Special Girls Club. But I was always so tense and angry at myself while I did it that I couldn't get there. There were two main reasons I wanted to come: (1) I thought it would be the most exciting physical experience of my life and (2) all my girlfriends could. I've always wanted to be the best at everything, and it killed me that in the coming department I lagged behind.

I tried to get my friends to give me specifics on exactly what happened when you came, but they all gave the same infuriating answer: "I can't explain it, but you'll know when you have one." I hated hearing that. It was so vague. And the few girls who tried to be more articulate gave such differing explanations of what it felt like that they weren't much help either. Some called it a wave, others a shudder or an explosion.

The boys I fooled around with were even more clueless than I was. Most didn't seem aware that there *was* a Red Button down there, much less seem interested in finding it. Instead, they'd utilize the plunger technique, which went something like this: (1) Shove as many fingers as far up as possible. (2) Move them around aimlessly for several minutes, as though tickling a kitten's neck. (3) Stop whenever you grow bored and not a moment later.

But because I didn't even know what to do myself, I wasn't able to give much coaching to the few guys who knew what a clit was. Inevitably I would let them diddle away for a while, then sigh, pat their shoulders, and say, "That's OK. You can stop now." I kept hoping one of them would protest and say, "No, I don't want to. It's really important to me to make you feel good." But instead they'd give me these relieved looks, then ask if I'd mind blowing them. And down I'd go. I figured *some*one should get some satisfaction, and if it wasn't going to be me, it might as well be them.

Will, my boyfriend at Brown, got me closer than any guy before. He tweaked and licked, tickled and poked for hours on end, to no avail. But as frustrated as I was, there was a part of me that didn't really want a guy to be the first to get me there. I felt like it would be an injustice—because I'd always believed a woman should be master of her own ceremony.

One late night in his dorm room, a few months after we started going out, before he found out about the Bo Rodriguez makeout, Will presented me with two paperback books: *My Secret Garden* by Nancy Friday and *For Yourself: The Fulfillment of Female Sexuality* by Lonnie Barbach. There was a picture of Lonnie Barbach on the back of her book. She was Semitic looking, mustachioed, and young. I was sure this sister Jewess could help me. The first sentence of the book was, "So you've never had an orgasm, or you don't think you have." I nearly wept with joy.

For the next three weeks, with the help of Barbach and Friday, I embarked on my emission impossible. I tweaked myself as often as I could, anytime I had a spare hour—but without fruition. One afternoon Will came over to my room. We put on our favorite mix tape, the one with "The Weakness in Me," "Cowgirl in the Sand," "Rock Me Again & Again & Again & Again & Again & Again," and "Tell Me Something Good," got in bed, and got to work. Those songs riled me up. When Will finally left to go to the library, I closed the door behind him, still feeling dazed and on edge, and decided it was time to make the kitty purr.

I stopped the mix tape, stood in front of my CD collection, pulled out Sly and the Family Stone's *Fresh,* and slid it into the player. I got back under the covers and told myself I wasn't going to try to come. I was going to listen to the music, relax, and enjoy the ride. I'd been going at it for about thirty-five minutes when suddenly, right in the middle of "Que Sera, Sera," something strange happened. I began to feel like my cunt wanted to sneeze. I tried to relax into the feeling, and breathe slowly and calmly. I listened to the funk and kept wanking—not fast and mad, but slow and gentle, nice and easy. The sneeze feeling got more and more intense, until finally it happened. The clap. The wave. The shudder. It was this very slight, very brief eruption, and it didn't last more than five seconds, but it was the biggest victory of my life.

I raced to the library and breathlessly told Will the good news. He shut his book, we went back to his room, and got to work. It took almost an hour, but with my coaching and his persistence, he finally rocked my Gibraltar.

That was the beginning of a new phase of our sex life. As I got better at making myself come, he got better at making me come too. I even got to the point where I could pop during sex—but only if somebody was buffing the muff while we were going at it. That hand reliance bothered me. I wanted my sex with Will to be exactly like in the movies. You didn't see Tom Cruise reach down to diddle Kelly McGillis in *Top Gun* or Richard Gere tweak Debra Winger in *An Officer and a Gentleman*. OK. Maybe Tom and Dick aren't the choicest examples of raging male heterosexual power, but it still bugged me. I wanted to come from cock and cock alone, because I had this idea in my head that Real Women could.

Will bought *For Each Other,* the sequel to *For Yourself,* and we tried lovemaking techniques that were supposed to be conducive to female orgasm. We put a pillow under my butt so my clit would be angled against his pelvic bone, but although it felt good, I couldn't make the hurdle. I tried riding him and angling forward. We tried doggie so he could stimulate my G-spot. Over the course of the whole relationship, though, it just didn't happen. And with every guy since then, the only way I'd been able to come during sex was with the help of somebody's hand.

But I couldn't say any of that in the column. I wanted my readers to think of me as a nouveau Erica Jong, and Jong came from fucking. Or at least her protagonist did. Even after she stopped loving her husband, Bennett, Isadora Wing still whooped when they *shtup*ped. And she came with her lover Adrian, too—although he couldn't always get it up. If my readers knew about my orgasm deficiencies, good-bye nouveau Jong. Hello pathetic ho. They'd think I wasn't just a slut but a frigid slut. They'd pity me. And I didn't want to be pitied. I wanted to be envied. So I gave my readers what I knew they wanted: lies.

●

When I finished the Evan column, I went to meet Sara at BarF. I told her about my orgasmic distortion and how I couldn't come from sex alone, and she nodded understandingly.

"You mean, you're the same way?" I asked.

"No," she said. "I come from sex every time. I was sympathizing, not empathizing." Once again I'd been sent to the back of the line.

"So, who's on top when you come?" I asked.

"Me. I can only come when I'm on top. I ride the guy and I get off, and then he flips me over and he gets off."

"When did you have your first orgasm?"

"When I was eight."

"What?"

"My girlfriends and I used to get together for these slumber parties and act out little sex scenarios with our Barbies. Then we'd get in our sleeping bags and hump our stuffed animals until we came."

"As if."

"I'm serious. How old were *you*?"

"Eighteen."

"Whoa."

"Thanks a lot."

"I'm sorry. It's just, that's pretty ancient. But don't be bummed. I'm very easily orgasmic. Most women aren't. I read somewhere that seven out of ten women need their clits touched in order to come during sex."

I knew I should have been relieved by that statistic, but I wasn't. I just wanted to be one of the three.

Suddenly this skinny guy in a kente-cloth hat sidled up next to me. "Ariel?" he asked. It was Dan Trier, my resident counselor during freshman year at Brown. I'd never found him that attractive before, but suddenly he looked like a Jewish Ken doll. We hugged and I introduced him to Sara. He didn't seem into her, which was a relief. After they shook hands he turned to me and said, "This is so weird I've been reading you, and wondering when I might run into you."

This dude had been struck by the Steiner Vibe. There was no escaping its wicked hold. I'd found my first victim. My first grist. I couldn't wait to put him through the mill.

"I have some friends waiting for me in the back," he said, "but I play violin for this band, Candidiasis, and we have a gig at BarBara Walters on Wednesday if you two want to come."

"Maybe we will," I said.

But as soon as he left, Sara said, "I think you should go alone. He obviously wants you." So I decided I would. I figured I could make it a joint hookup/music review: write about his playing first, and then his play.

The next morning at work, the Corposhit had me unpack and assemble a paper shredder. The instructions were pretty easy to follow, so it only took about ten minutes for me to put it together. At the bottom of the instruction sheet, it said, "When assembly is completed, shred this page." It didn't sound like the wisest idea but I figured the manufacturers knew what they were doing. I stuck the paper in and watched it fringe up. This was fun. I stuck in a blank sheet of paper and watched it shred too. I stuck in another. It crumpled into a mangled piece, and the message screen flashed, ERROR 49! I lifted the machine off my desk and looked to see if there were emergency instructions taped to the bottom. No dice. I looked in the box, but it was empty.

The Corposhit came out of her office, glanced at the flashing message, and said, "What happened?"

"It jammed."

"Where are the instructions?"

"I shredded them."

"You shredded the instructions?"

"That was the last instruction."

"No it wasn't."

"Yes it was!"

"I don't believe this. Get on the phone and call the manufacturer, and find out what to do when it jams. You're supposed to *solve* problems here, not *create* them." She went back into her office and slammed her door.

"Do you know who I am?" I wanted to shout. "Do you know who it is you're patronizing? The hottest sex columnist in the city! There are guys out there who would *pay* to spend as much time with me as you get to! The least you could do is treat me with a modicum of respect!" But I knew if I said that, she'd can me—and I couldn't risk it. I might have been the hottest columnist in the city, but it would be a while before I was the most highly remunerated.

I called the company and ordered a new set of instructions, and then I hung up and checked my machine. There was only one message, and it was rather strange: "My name's Dana Spack. I'm a fact checker at the *Week* and I want to ask you a question about 'Rockman.' Please call me at the office." I freaked. Had she somehow found out about my distortions? Had some *City Week* spy overheard my conversation with Sara at BarF, figured out who I was, and ratted?

I called Dana back right away. "It's Ariel Steiner?" I uptalked, in spite of myself. "I got your message?"

"Thanks for returning my call," she said. "I was just going through 'Rockman' and I came across something that concerned me."

Oh God. Now I'd have to tell her the sad ballad of my hand dependency. She wouldn't understand. This chick was named Dana. Danas were all easy comers. She'd laugh at me for my deficiency, completely unable to relate, as I wept into the phone and begged her to let my lie run.

"What exactly was it that concerned you?" I asked.

"You mention that the bar where Kevin played was BarBie, and then later you say, 'As we headed up the street to BarNey Rubble.' BarBie is on Eleventh and B, and BarNey Rubble is on Ninth and B. Shouldn't it be, 'As we headed *down* the street to BarNey Rubble'?"

"Why, yes it should!" I shouted. "That's *exactly* what it should be! I'm terribly sorry! I don't know why I made that mistake! I guess I don't have the keenest sense of geographic accuracy! Ha ha ha ha ha!"

"Thanks," she said curtly. "That was all I needed to know."

●

At noon on Wednesday Sara and I went to the distribution box on the corner, took out two copies of the paper, and walked to the Met Life building. That week's illo was me getting fucked from behind by another sideburned guy, with a bubble above my head that said, "What a hunky junkie!"

"I wonder what Evan's going to say at my lesson tonight," said Sara when she finished the column. "I hope he won't want to stop teaching me."

"Why?"

"He's not going to want to associate with anyone associated with you."

"It wasn't *that* mean."

"You call him a junkie and a limp dick and you change only two letters of his name."

"So?"

"How would you feel if someone wrote that stuff about you for the whole city to read?"

"I don't have a dick."

"You know what I mean."

"You think he's gonna be pissed?"

"If he doesn't go ballistic at the junkie and limp-dick stuff, he's definitely going to when he gets to the part where you spit on his feet after dumping him."

"You think it was over the top?"

She held up her thumb and index fingers like she was pinching something very small. I wondered if she was right. What if Evan did do something rash? Would he write in to the paper to call me a lousy lay? Would he out me for my coming lie? I hoped she'd be able to calm him down at her lesson.

We flipped backward from my column to "The Mail." I was hoping to be cheered by some positive response, but I wasn't so lucky.

What's Ariel Steiner's favorite beverage? A *cock*-tail.
What's Ariel Steiner's favorite animal? *Pussy*-cat.
Why did Ariel Steiner cross the road? To get laid.

PETE TERELL, *Bronx*

Ariel Steiner's vagina must smell like the Fresh Kills Landfill. Maybe she could learn a thing or two from those girls in Africa and consider the option of having her vulva sealed for good.

ANDY ZANE, *Park Slope*

"Jesus!" I shouted.

"What?" said Sara.

"How can I go hear Dan's band tonight? He'll never want to hook up with me! What guy in his right mind would want to get busy with a girl who's purported to be a filthy ho?"

"What are you talking about?" said Sara. "Most guys would *jump* at the chance to get busy with a girl who's purported to be a filthy ho." She had a point. So I went.

●

Candidiasis was good, and Dan looked hot playing his violin. I drank three Jamesons over the course of the gig, and by the end I was severely tipsy. When it was over Dan sat next to me at the bar and ordered a beer. I took a handful of peanuts from a bowl on the table, munched them, then leaned in close and said huskily, "Have you ever wondered what honey-roasted peanut tastes like on a woman's breath?"

He reddened and turned his face away.

"What is it?"

"Are you coming on to me?"

It was a little embarrassing to have to be asked that question so directly, but I wasn't going to lie. "Um . . . I guess so, yeah."

"Then I better be honest with you. I've always been really attracted to you, and I think you're sweet, and bright and funny. That's why I invited you here tonight. But there's not a chance in hell I would date you."

"You read 'The Mail' today?"

"Yeah. The letters were pretty nasty. But that's not why I'm afraid to date you."

"It's not?"

"No. I don't care what those people say about you. They're idiots. I'm afraid because I don't want to go out with you, then open the paper the next morning and read all about what we did, with me given some really obvious pseudonym and all my defining characteristics left completely intact."

"How did you know I use really obvious pseudonyms?"

"I didn't, but I guess I do now. Don't get me wrong. If you had a different job I'd be highly interested in pursuing some sort of dalliance. But as it stands, for my own protection, I think it's best that we keep things platonic."

I couldn't believe it. My very first victim had dissed me first. That wasn't the way it was supposed to work. Guys were supposed to be at my beck and call. They weren't supposed to pick up and go. I felt like Madonna after Dennis Rodman refused to go down on her. It was a sick, sick world. My column had gotten between me and my cock.

When I got home from the bar, I called Sara. "How'd it go?" she said.

"You don't want to know," I said. "How was your lesson?"

"Fine."

"What did Evan say?"

"He said, 'I knew what I was getting into when I hit on her. If she needs to make it out like she dumped me in order to impress her readers, that's her prerogative.' I said, 'What about her description of your anatomy? Aren't you worried your friends will read it?' and he said, 'My friends don't really read.' "

I breathed a sigh of relief. There was an upside to the low literacy level of my dating pool. I was safe—for now, at least. But I still didn't have my next column idea—and no new dicks were rearing their heads. I was on the verge of drafting a piece about my first blow job the next morning when I checked my machine and got a message from Faye.

RUN CATCH KISS

True Confessions of a Single Girl

ARIEL STEINER

Don't Call Us

The other day my agent, May, called. She'd gotten me an audition for an independent film about junkie brothers who can't get out of the cycle of destruction. "It takes place in Estonia," she said.

That sounded exciting. An Eastern European drug movie. "Are they paying to fly the actors out there?" I asked.

"What do you mean, fly them out there?"

"Didn't you say it shoots in Estonia?"

"Yeah. Queens."

"I think you mean Astoria," I said, my face falling. But I tried not to get discouraged. Location wasn't that important. It was who you got to work with that mattered.

"Who's directing?" I asked brightly.

"A guy named Ed Pucci. He's the guy who parachuted into Shea Stadium during the 1986 World Series." Any remaining faith I had in the project flew out the window.

My role was Aileen, the widow of one of the brothers, and in the scene I was supposed to mourn to my friend about how awful I feel that I wasn't able to prevent my husband from ODing. The first few lines weren't too bad, but when I got to the part where it said, *"Aileen breaks down and begins hysterically crying,"* I was thrown for one mother of a loop. I've always had trouble manufacturing tears. I can do it in life; I just can't do it on cue.

The night before the audition I sat on my bed and relived bad breakups, sixth-grade ostracizing, public humiliation, lost opportunities, and family crises. But as I remembered these minitragedies, I began to think that in retrospect, none had really been worth crying about. Instead of getting weepy, I just got pissed at myself for being such a wus.

Then I remembered something I read in an acting book once: Laurence Olivier used to make himself cry by thinking about these small, furry ermines in Alaska. The trappers would catch the ermines by putting salt on the snow, and when the poor babies leaned down to lick the salt, their tongues would stick and the trappers would move in for the kill. I tried to envision those adorable little tongues latched to the cold, harsh snow, and the evil trappers harpooning the ermines dead, but it still didn't work. The story got me, but not in the gut. I knew I couldn't rely on that image alone. So I decided to just play it by ear. Feel the feelings and hope the tears came spontaneously.

When I got to the casting office, I sat down in a chair in the waiting room and closed my eyes. Just as I was beginning to relax, I heard quiet sobbing. I opened my eyes. The girl two chairs down from me was mouthing the lines of the scene— and dozens of perfect, glistening tears were rolling down her cheeks. She smiled bashfully at me, as though she was ashamed that her emotions were so easily accessible. I glared back, and then the casting director came out and said, "Ariel? We're ready for you."

She led me down a snaking hallway to the audition room. Sitting behind a table was a six-and-a-half-foot-tall giant with a large-boned, menacing face. "I'm Ed Pucci," he said. We shook hands and he crushed my fingers.

I sat down in the chair across from him. He raised his voice high like a woman's and started the scene: "It's all right, Aileen. It's not your fault."

"It *is* my fault!" I shouted. "Gary wouldn't be dead if it weren't for me!"

"That's not true and you know it. There was nothing you could have done."

I looked down at the script and read the words *"Aileen breaks down and begins hysterically crying."* I tried to picture baby ermines getting stuck to an iceberg, but instead I just pictured Ed Pucci's huge, bearlike frame collapsing onto the field of Shea Stadium. Instead of crying, I cracked a smile. I wiped it away quickly, hoping he'd think it was a wince, lowered my head, and heaved my shoulders up and down so I'd look like I was weeping.

Evidently my trick didn't work, because when I finished, he said, "Good. But I really need to see you cry. This is very hard for Aileen. She feels responsible for Gary's death."

"OK."

"It's all right, Aileen," he said. "It's not your fault." This time when I got to the crying part, I tried to envision my father, my mother, and brother being hacked to death by a psycho killer. But every time I started to get choked up, I would think about how annoying it was that I couldn't cry on cue, and the choked-up feeling would disappear.

I finished sans tears and Ed thanked me in the way they do when you know there's not a chance in hell you'll get it. I walked out through the waiting room past the town crier, and when I got outside I crossed the street and headed toward Port Authority to get on the subway back to work. Two crackheads were fighting in front of the Burger King on Eighth Avenue, and a guy was yelling loudly at someone over the phone. For one split second I wanted to give it all up. But then the yelling guy got off the phone and I stepped up to check my machine.

The Monday night after I submitted the column, I got this E-mail from Turner: "*I liked it, but Steve thinks it's your worst yet. He says you can poke your head out of the boudoir once in a while, as long as you don't make a habit of it. Let's just say you've shot your acting wad for the time being. Don't shoot another for at least a few months.*"

As if that wasn't discouraging enough, the day the column came out my dad left this message on my machine: "I loved it! I mean, really loved it! I called up Mom and read it to her over the phone! Then I made ten copies and sent them to all the relatives. I'm so glad you've finally written something we can show them!"

I shuddered, erased the message and hung up the phone. If my dad was happy with what I was writing, it meant I had to find myself some action, soon. My readers were interested in one thing only—and it wasn't my acting career. It was time to start hunting again. It was time to start humping again.

•

God must have heard my mantra, because when I got home from work that night, I found a letter in my mailbox from Faye. I took it upstairs and ripped it open:

Dear Ariel,
    After thirty years in "the biz," I have decided to retire. It's been a pleasure working with you. Best wishes for the future.
                                                    Fondly,
                                                    FAYE GLASS
P.S. You have been released from your contract with the agency and are free to seek other representation.

At first I felt a wave of disappointment, but after a few seconds it was replaced by an odd sense of relief. In five and a half months of auditioning, I had booked one acting job—for a porn show masquerading as a rock musical. Statistically it wasn't the worst track record, but it sure wasn't the best. Maybe Faye's letter was a blessing in disguise. I would never have to go on a cattle call again. I'd never have to memorize lines, cry on cue, or audition for a stuntman. So I'd never be the Queen of All Media either, but maybe being the Queen of One Medium wasn't the most awful thing in the world. I changed into a short skirt and platform heels, walked to the train, and went to meet Sara at Bar-Nacle.

5

SHE WAS WAITING FOR ME with this new guy she was seeing, Kit. He was the counter boy at her local coffee store, Porto Rico Importing. Every morning on her way to work she would stop in to buy a cup, and then one day he handed her his number with her Ethiopian Blend. I had a good feeling about the two of them. He kept stroking her back while the three of us were talking, and he'd periodically gaze at her with lapdog eyes. He told me he'd gone to graduate school for acting at NYU, and when I said I studied theater at Brown, he said, "I did my MFA with a guy from Brown. Charlton Wakes. Did you know him?"

Did I ever. Charlton and I met working on a black box production of *Long Day's Journey into Night* when I was a freshman and he was a senior. He was notorious for two things: his crass sense of humor and extralong dimensions. He was the kind of guy who never censored his pornographic observations and who looked at women—all women—with a freely hanging cock you could swing on like a vine. But he'd had a girlfriend—a beautiful, siliconed daughter of a California venture capitalist—and I'd been going out with Will, so I never made a move.

Maybe I could now, though. This could be my chance to snag a babe and get some good material, both at the same time. "I do know him," I said. "I used to be really hot for him. What's he up to?"

"He's in a show at SoHo Playhouse."

"Is he still going out with Victoria?"

"No, they broke up after he graduated. He's a free man. In fact, he's been complaining about how lonely he is lately. Why don't you call him?"

When I got home I took out the number. His machine picked up. I breathed in deeply, sat down on the couch, and pushed my voice down into the back of my throat, secretary style. "Hhhhhi, Charlton. It's such a cold, cold night, but I feel toasty warm. I'm under the covers in my warm house in my warm bed. It gets even warmer down here when I think of you. You're so sexy, Charlton. The way you strut like a rebel. Oooh, when I start thinking about you I can't help but stick just one finger up inside me and pretend like it's yours. I get so sweaty under these covers. It's so hot down here. I'm so wet, I just—"

The machine cut me off right when I was going to come. Just like a guy. So I called back. "Ahh! Ooh! Oh! I'm coming! You feel so good inside me, Charlton. I want to wrap my soft lips around your pulsing little man Tate, to taste you, to lick y—" I got cut off again.

I hung up the phone and went to bed. Around two in the morning, the phone rang.

"This is Charlton Wakes," he said. "Did you call me?"

"How did you know?"

"Star 69. Who are you?"

"I was in *Long Day's Journey* with you, spring of your senior year. I played the maid."

"I forgot your name."

"Ariel," I sighed.

"Right. Ariel. How'd you get my number?"

"I met your friend Kit at a bar and we found out we both knew you. He said you were on the prowl. Is that true?"

"Yeah."

"So did you like my message?"

"*Yeah.*"

"Did you jerk off to it?"

"*Yeahhh.*"

"Really? Did you come?"

"I almost did, but you didn't talk long enough."

"Your machine cut me off! What was I supposed to do?"

"You could do it live the next time." That gave me pause. "So what've you been up to since you graduated?"

He didn't know about the column. I could hold back and not tell him, but then it struck me that with a guy like Charlton there might actually be an advantage to telling. "I moved here to be an actress," I said. "But then I got this weird job—a sex column in the *City Week*. They hired me to go out with different guys and write about them."

"You're shitting me."

"I'm not, Charlton. I'm totally serious. They're paying me to go out and sleep with handsome eligible bachelors."

"You know, the cast party for our show is this Friday night. Do you want to come? I could get you a comp to the play and then you could come to the party with me afterward."

"OK."

He gave me the address of the theater and we hung up. A few minutes later, the phone rang again.

"Why don't you talk to me now?" he whispered.

"Really?"

"Yeah. It won't take long, I promise."

I considered my options. It was one thing to give a guy phone sex just because he asked for it, but it was another thing entirely to do it as *research*. Whoring myself for the sake of a good character study wasn't nearly as depraved as whoring myself for its own sake.

"What do you want me to talk about?" I said. "I mean, where should I start?"

"Soon."

"All right. I'll tell you about this . . . this guy I'm seeing. His name's . . . Royalton. And he looks a little like you, Charlton. But he's not you. He's Royalton. The other night he invited me over for dinner at his house, and he fixed me this huge meal, with oysters and pasta and wine and cigarettes. Eating those oysters and drinking that red wine made me . . . kind of *hot* for him."

"Uh huh."

"After we finished eating, we were sitting at the table sighing and loosening our belts, and he stood up and reached over me to get this napkin, which was sitting on a shelf behind me. As he was reaching, his arm kind of brushed against my breast, you know, by accident, *swiped* my *nipple* the tiniest bit . . ."

"Mmm hmmm."

"And it just made me *crazy*, I mean it really made me hot, because my ex-boyfriend used to play with my tits for hours on end and he made them really sensitive. Now, even if somebody just brushes against one of them by accident, it makes me insane!"

"Talk about fucking him."

Damn, I thought. *I always get carried away at the tit part.*

"So I went over to the bed and lay down to rest my head, and Royalton lay down next to me and started playing with my tits. No, that's not what happened at all! I mean, *I* started playing with his big, hard cock—"

"Yeahhhhhh."

"You wouldn't believe how big his cock was, Charlton. It was really big."

"I know."

"I mean, it was just bulging against his pants. His pants were getting so tight on him that I wanted to free it. To let it loose. I started stroking it and it got so hard in my hands that suddenly, I couldn't take it anymore! I just pulled up my skirt—I wasn't wearing any underwear, by the way—and plopped smack down on that glorious cock! I began to bounce up and down, like a little girl romping with her dad, and pretty soon I could feel him get ready to pummel me—"

"Make it that he came from you blowing him."

"Um, but I was tired of sex. What I *really* wanted to do was take him in my mouth. I got off him and took it in both of my hands, then leaned down, opened up, and pressed my lips real tight around the tip. I used my lips to cover my teeth 'cause I didn't want to bite him, no, 'cause that would hurt! I took him in my mouth so very, very deep and played with the little spot at the base of it, right above the balls, pressed that spot with my tongue—"

"Mmmmm."

"I had a feeling he was gonna come soon. *Was he?*"

"I think so."

"So I worked it good, licking it and kissing it and tickling his balls the whole time! I could feel him start to tremble and shake. His cock was stiff as my back, and suddenly, he started to shoot the warmest come—"

"Uhh!"

"Come as warm as soup—"

"Uhhhh!"

"All the way down into my throat, and it tasted so sweet and good."

"Unnnnnnhhhhhhhhhhhhhhh."

He was quiet.

"How was it?" I asked.

"You should charge."

"You think so?"

"Definitely. Were you playing with yourself too?"

"No, Charlton. It was more of an . . . artistic orgasm for me. I'll see you Friday."

●

The next morning at work I wrote a transcript of the phone sex, as best I could remember it, on a notepad on my lap. I knew not to type it on the computer because with automatic saving, you never know what could wind up on the company hard drive. Right as I was in the midst of the "little girl romping with her dad" part, the Corposhit came out of her office without any warning and I had to jerk my swivel chair forward under the desk so she couldn't see what I was doing.

Since I'd started the column, I'd been a little nervous about the possibility of her finding out and firing me. But the great thing about New York City is that it's really a thousand separate cities. People live in their own individualized universes, and the different universes almost never intersect. Midtown middle-rung corporate administrators don't read downtown weeklies unless they're highly atypical, and I could always count on the Corposhit for being one hundred percent typical.

Friday night after work, I changed into a white sparkly crop top from the French Connection and slim red cigarette pants. I had to admit I was pleased with how I looked. Because the shirt was cropped it made me look skinnier than I was, and the pants hugged my ass 1950s-bad-girl style.

Charlton's show was about a trailer park family that worships Elvis. Charlton played the dad. As soon as he came onstage in his white-trash strut, with his overgrown facial hair, blackened teeth, and wad of chewing tobacco in his mouth, I juiced up like never before. When a guy's a matinee idol to you, he stays one.

After the play I went to the dressing room. Charlton was standing in front of a mirror without a shirt, wiping his fake stubble off his face with a Kleenex. His pecs were toned and he didn't have any chest hair.

"Hi, Royalton," I said.

He turned and appraised me, top to bottom. "You look good," he said. The outfit had worked. My matinee idol was about to become my boy toy.

We took a cab together to the West Village, where the party was, grabbed two beers, made our way through the crowd, and sat down on the couch side by side.

"It's really good to see you again, Charlton," I said. "I've thought about you many times over the years."

"Yeah?" His eyes narrowed and he leaned in close.

"Yeah. I had a huge crush on you when we were doing *Long Day's Journey*. But I was afraid to even flirt with you because I'd heard Victoria was incredibly jealous."

"She was. It's one of the reasons we broke up."

"When did that happen?"

"A few months after I graduated."

"Have you seen anyone seriously since then?"

"A couple girls, but nothing long-lasting. How about you? You seeing anyone?"

"Of course not. I'm a sex columnist, remember?"

He leaned back on the couch, cocked his head to the side, and said, "I'm not surprised that's your job. There's something about you that really makes men want to jerk off when they're around you."

"What?"

"There's something about you that makes men want to jerk off."

He was right—I mean, my experiences had proven him true—but no guy had ever spelled it out like that before so boldly and brashly. "Jesus Christ!" I shouted.

"What?"

"You're not supposed to say that—even if it's what you really think! You're supposed to tell me, 'There's something about you that really makes men fall in love with you.' "

"I'm not in love with you," he said. "But I really wanna jerk off. I have such a boner right now. There's a yard out back. Do you want to come down with me?"

He was crude, lewd, and socially unacceptable—lousy boyfriend material but ideal column material. What was that Voltaire quote—"Once a philosopher, twice a pervert"? What was wrong with a little good-natured romping, as long as I understood my own motives? Besides, I *wanted* him. It wasn't like I wouldn't get anything out of this deal.

I followed him down the steps and around to the back of the house. We sat on a wooden picnic bench, straddled it, and faced each other. He took my neck between his hands and leaned toward me with his mouth open. I expected him to be a messy kisser, but he wasn't. He was warm and sleek and not too wet. I wrapped my arms around his back and felt his muscles. He reached behind me and unhooked my bra in about one second. I felt like Susan Sarandon with Kevin Costner. It was very impressive. It's such an erotic downer when you're going at it and the guy can't unhook your bra. He lifted the bra up, massaged my breasts, and sighed.

"I hope you like them," I said. "They're real."

"I can tell," he said.

I fumbled with his fly and slid it out. It was solid and smooth, just like his chest. He unzipped my pants and slid his hand down my underwear. It felt OK, but it was hard to get the angle right when my pants were on and I was sitting on a bench.

"What are you thinking about me doing to you?" I whispered, placing his other hand on his dick.

"You're blowing me." That was a shocker.

"What else?"

"You're taking me between your tits." He tried to stick it there but then some drunk guy from the party stumbled over to us and I had to push it away. The guy wandered off, I leaned toward Charlton, and whispered, "My tiny little open kisser could suck you so right. I bet girls want to blow you all the time. I bet they beg you to let them. Don't they, Charlton? Don't they?"

"Uhh! Uhhhh! Unnnnnnhhhhhhhhhhhhhhh!" he cried, and shot it out onto the bench. Three piddling puddles of pud juice. "Jesus Christ," he said. "I can't believe you got me that horny."

"Me neither," I said.

He buttoned his fly and we went back up to the party. When we got to the living room I sat down on the couch and he started dancing with one of the girls in the cast. Suddenly she pulled away from him and yelled, "Charlton! Charlton! You have some bubble gum on your pants!"

"Oh my God. I do?" he said, looking down. "I'm so embarrassed!"

I blushed and hung my head, sure it was a come stain. The girl would ask Charlton what he'd been up to, he'd point to me, everyone would turn and stare, and then I'd have to tell them all about our secret bench jerk.

He futzed with his fly, and for a moment it looked like a huge stretchy film of bubble gum was coming out of his pants. But then I looked closer and I could see it was his ball skin. *He was pulling his ball skin out of his fly to make it look like bubble gum.* And he had this glint in his eye that made it clear this was a stunt he had pulled before, a stunt he was *known for.*

"Do it again, Charlton!" his friends chanted. "Do it again!"

As I watched him pull it out a second time, a sick smile spread across my face. With this coup de grâce, Charlton had revealed himself to be not just foul-minded but severely demented. The more perverse the fodder, the better the story. After "Don't Call Us," this ditty would be a hell of a comeback. As the crowd roared again at Charlton's testicular exhibition, I slipped out the door and went home to write.

●

I finished the column quickly, but after I sent it to Turner I got a heavy feeling in my stomach. In the heat of the moment, when I'd been whispering and Charlton had been stroking, I had felt excited, high, revved. But now I just felt weary. It had been a long time since I'd jerked a dick that belonged to someone I loved. A long time since I'd held someone, been held. I was a hopeless romantic trapped in the body of a seething hussy. I missed intimacy. I wanted passion and companionship and deep discussion and lots of compliments delivered to me regularly without any misgivings or posturing. I wanted sidewalk embraces and hand holding and hair caressing and eight-hour lovemaking and dozens of phone calls and every cheesy line uttered in a John Hughes or Cameron Crowe movie. But I didn't know how I was supposed to get it. If I couldn't beat the boys, wasn't it wisest to join them? And get paid for it in the process? I turned off the computer and looked out the window at the lights on the expressway.

●

The Wednesday "The Bubble Gum Ball" came out was the day before Thanksgiving. Every year my parents, Zach, and I go to my grandparents' house in Philadelphia, and this year wasn't any different. The Corposhit had given me a half day and I was supposed to go straight to my parents' to drive to Philly.

On my way out of work to the subway I stopped at the *Week* box and took out the paper. First I flipped to the column. The cartoon was me sitting on a bench grabbing Charlton's dick, with three droplets of come landing right on my face. I flipped back a few pages to "The Mail" and scanned the columns for my name, but there wasn't a single letter about "Don't Call Us." I wasn't surprised. I shut the paper and started to read the cover article—an interview with a Republican party bigwig—when something caught my eye. Across the bottom of the front page, in huge white letters, against a bright red banner, was

ARIEL STEINER YANKS CHAIN, p. 28

I put my hands to my head and tore out a few clumps of hair. Once my parents saw that banner they'd be certain to read the column—and it would be too disgusting for them to handle. At least my other ones had involved *intercourse*. Sex was conventional, but phone sex and an outdoor hand job were far more tawdry.

When I got to the building, my mom and dad were packing the rental car (they don't own one because my dad can't drive) and Zach was sitting in the backseat. As I put my suitcase in the trunk, I eyed them suspiciously. But they were total poker from brow to chin. I didn't know if it meant they'd read it and didn't care, or were so upset they couldn't speak.

They didn't give any more clues over the hour-and-a-half drive to Philly. The whole ride there, neither they nor Zach mentioned a word about it. I had requested their silence, but now that I was getting it, it bugged me. I wanted to know what they really thought. Were they telling themselves it was all fiction? Did they think I was losing my mind, or exaggerating? Several times over the course of the ride, I heard the words "How 'bout that jerk-off?" forming on my tongue, but somehow, I couldn't spit them out.

When we pulled up to my grandparents' house, my mom and dad got out of the car to unload our bags. Zach started to get out too, but I tugged on his arm and whispered, "Do you know if they read it this week?"

"Dad and I did, but mom didn't. He doesn't bring home the ones he thinks will upset her."

"She doesn't go into Manhattan to look them up herself?"

"No. She says if he doesn't show them to her, there must be a good reason."

"What did you think of it?"

"That phone sex stuff was hot. I was reading it on the train home from school and I got a boner, and then I was like, Whoa. My *sister* wrote this, and I have a *boner,* and it wigged me out."

We followed my parents into the house and as soon as I made it inside the door, my uncle Paul shouted, "Hey, Ariel, how's your sex life?"

I raced past him into the bathroom to escape, but on the way there I ran into a group of my mom's cousins, and they hit me with an onslaught of jibes so idiotic it was scarcely to be believed: "Why don't you ever send us any of your columns?" "I hear you're shocking the city!" "Little Ariel's not so little anymore," and on and on. I grinned like I had a sense of humor, but I wanted to tell them all to leave me the fuck alone, at least I liked my job, at least I wasn't a *teacher* like all of them.

My mom was raised a secular humanistic Jew, so most of her relatives are hippyish and easygoing. The men all wear Clark Wallabees and have beards, and the women wear loose dresses from crafts fairs and lots of pewter jewelry. Everyone is quick with the one-liners, and in general I think they're pretty funny. But not this time. I almost wished I was a topless dancer or something. Then no one would have said a word—because it would have been too upsetting to talk about. But since my career was on the cusp of respectability, they felt they had a right to make fun of me as much as they wanted.

On Thanksgiving afternoon we played the family football game, the Toilet Bowl, in a field across from my grandparents' house. The family has been playing it since 1945. We're the Jewish Kennedys. Until the late sixties, it was the Fathers versus the Sons, but then, in the seventies, the daughters wanted to play, so now it's the Parents versus the Kids. I hate the Toilet Bowl for two reasons: (1) I suck at football and (2) I can't stand doing anything I suck at. But I play every year anyway because I'm a girl and I don't want to lend credence to the stereotype of girls hating sports.

Unfortunately, my decision to play turned out to be a lousy idea. My team wound up losing—and it was mostly due to me. I accidentally ran the wrong way with the ball and on the next down, the Parents scored what became the winning touchdown. On the way back to the house after the game, my cousin Eddie said, "Maybe you should stick to the writing."

After Thanksgiving dinner (turkey, matzoh kugel, yams), we gathered in the living room for the entertainment segment. My little cousin Reva did gymnastics, Zach played "Layla" on the guitar, and my thirteen-year-old cousin Sam played violin. When he was done, everyone applauded enthusiastically. After the applause faded there was one of those awkward-crowd moments where no one can think of anything to say. The room suddenly got silent and then my grandmother said, "Why don't all the kids go around the room and tell us what they're up to? It's so hard to keep track nowadays."

"I don't think that's a very good idea," I said.

But all the old folks shouted, "Come on! Come on!" and before I knew it, my cousin Nessa was explaining how much she was enjoying her job at the Department of Energy and her sister, Rachel, was going on about her job teaching inner-city kids in Chicago. I stared down at the carpet, awaiting my turn in dread. After Rachel came Eddie, who was a sportscaster in Bergen

County, and then it was my turn. The room got hushed and everyone smirked excitedly, like they couldn't wait to see what kind of spin I was going to come up with.

"Um . . . I'm a temp," I said. "And I write this newspaper column."

"We hear it's very racy!" shouted my aunt Vivian, and everyone immediately erupted in raucous laughter. The gales went on uninterrupted for a full minute. It was like a collective orgasm—they'd been waiting all day for a chance to ridicule me in unison, and now they'd finally gotten it. The only ones who weren't laughing were my parents. They just held hands tightly and looked around the room with twin winces.

In twenty years my relatives had gone from applauding my naked dance to guffawing at my unconventional career choice. They were mocking the same exhibitionistic spirit they had once adored. I wished I was two again.

●

All Friday morning I kept checking my machine, in the hopes that I'd get a message that would bring me back to the city. Around noon, I did. It was from an AM talk-radio producer named Jack Dunleavy. "I got your number from Bill Turner," he said. "I produce *The Norman Klein Show* on WTLK and we're wondering if you're free to come on tonight from eleven to midnight, to talk about your column. The other guest will be the performance artist Fran McLaine."

I'd never heard of Klein, but McLaine was notorious. She was the one who smeared Carnation instant breakfast all over her asshole at one of her shows, then got on the blacklist of the conservative Southern senator Tyrone Welts. I was honored to be asked to appear with such a controversial figure, and plus, there was no way my parents could hear the show in Philly. So I called Dunleavy back, told him I'd do it, and took the Amtrak train home.

●

The show had already started when I got to the radio station. Fran and Norman, this gray-haired guy in his fifties, were sitting in the studio with headphones on. Next to the studio was an engineering room, where a heavy, bald guy in his sixties was sitting in front of a control board and a skinny guy in his thirties was answering a phone.

Through the sound monitor, I could hear a caller giving Fran flak about the instant breakfast incident. "You're filthy and depraved," he was saying.

"Thanks," she said.

I looked at her through the window and tried to picture her naked in front of lots of people. It wasn't easy. She looked more like a soccer mom than a performance artist.

They broke for a commercial and Norman beckoned me in. He shook my hand and said he was a very big fan. "What do you do?" asked Fran.

"I'm a columnist for the *City Week*."

"I've never heard of it," she said.

"It's distributed in green boxes on every corner in downtown Manhattan," I said.

"I don't live in the city. My husband and I moved to Scarsdale once we had our second child."

Norman passed me a set of headphones and I put them on. When we came back on live, he said, "Ariel Steiner has just joined us in the studio. Ariel is the author of the *City Week* column 'Run Catch Kiss.' She seeks out the most disgusting and unsuitable mates she can find and then writes about them. You could say Ariel and Fran have something in common: Fran's a performance artist, and Ariel's entire life is performance art."

I wasn't totally sure I agreed, but this was talk radio and you can't go objecting to the premise of your visit. There was a screen by the ceiling with a display of all the callers' names who were waiting to go on the air. As soon as Norman introduced me, the monitor began blinking like crazy. I'd had no idea I was so well known. But all the callers wanted to talk to Fran. For half an hour I sat there silently as she fielded obnoxious calls from conservative idiots. Thanksgiving with my family was starting to look pretty appealing.

Finally Fran left because she had to get home to her kids. "Fran has gone home," Norman said into the mike. The monitor went blank. "But Ariel Steiner, author of the *City Week* column 'Run Catch Kiss,' is still here." I glanced up at the monitor. Still blank. I looked at Norman. His forehead was shining.

I had always assumed I had thousands of readers, but judging by caller response, maybe I'd been wrong. Maybe the only people who read me were the ones who wrote in to the paper. My delusions of grandeur were finally getting the better of me. Not a single person would call, Norman would have to make up his own questions to compensate for the empty phone lines, and everyone out there in radio land would know I was a last-minute guest, a nobody, a pale imitator of the famous Fran McLaine.

"In your column, Ariel," said Norman, "you've written about going out with junkies, cross-dressers, and socialists, and this week you wrote about jerking a guy off at a party. What I'd like to know is, is everything you write really true?"

There was no way I was going to tell him I'd made up the part about coming from sex. Or that Evan had dumped me, not the other way around. I had to be the raunch queen people expected me to be.

"Yes," I said emphatically. "Every single thing. Especially"— I thought for a second—"especially the parts that make you hard."

"Wow," said Norman, blushing. "I feel like we're on Howard here."

"Look at you, Norman," I said. "Your face is so red, it's adorable. You're pretty sexy." I didn't think so at all, but I had to get people calling in. "Would you go on a date with me sometime?"

"I'm not sure. It's kind of a scary thought, actually. What if you wrote about me?"

"You shouldn't be afraid of that prospect. You should delight in it. Wouldn't it be an ego trip to have our date put up for public consumption? Isn't there a part of you that would enjoy being fodder for my fictive world?" I didn't know what the hell I was saying, but it sounded good, so I kept talking. "It's a voyeuristic culture we live in. We live through tale telling and I'm asking you to be in my tale."

"You make it sound sort of appealing. It's an interesting predicament. I'd be upset if you wrote about me in a way I didn't find flattering, but at the same time I'd be upset if you didn't write about me at all."

"Aha! So you do want to go out with me! Oh, Norman, I can't wait! You know, I've always had a fetish for older men." He reddened again. "I'd like to bring out the dirty side of you. I bet there's a naughty boy aching to get out of your old-fogy exterior."

"Old fogy? Am I supposed to be flattered by that?"

"I'm just being honest. I can't wait to be alone with a hot-blooded man like you."

"Boy, we oughta open a window in here. Should I go out with Ariel? Call in and voice your opinion. The lines are open. We'll be right back after these station messages." I looked up at the monitor. It was starting to fill up.

"You've got quite a mouth," he said, taking off his headphones.

"I just want to make good radio. I hope you don't mind my kidding around."

"Not at all. This stuff is terrific. Usually we just talk about politics." He put his headphones back on. We listened to the commercials and stared at the walls.

"OK—we're back on WTLK with Ariel Steiner, author of the *City Week* column 'Run Catch Kiss.' Let's go to Teddy in Rego Park. Teddy, you're on the air."

A high-pitched man's voice came on. "Yeah, I've been listening to this show for a while now and I just want to say that I think Ariel is a well-spoken, intelligent young woman."

"Thank you, Teddy," I said.

"And she's so *nasty*. I love it." Now I was the one blushing. But it was a good blush. They were eating me up.

"Thanks for calling, Teddy," said Norman. "Bert in Queens, you're on the air."

"Yeah, hi," said Bert. "It seems like what these girls—Fran and Ariel—are talking about, the topic of the evening, what it all comes down to, is empowerment of women." It was quiet.

"And?" Norman asked. "Is that all you wanted to say?"

"Well, yeah. Some men are afraid to see women get empowered. They're scared of chicks like Fran and Ariel."

"You're not, though, are you, Bert?" I asked.

"No, I'm not."

"That's good. I'm glad you're not. I like you, Bert. I like you very much. You're not afraid of empowered women. That is so appealing. You know what they say. A man of quality is not threatened by a woman for equality."

He chuckled. "How'd you like to come over my house after the show, Ariel?"

I looked at Norman nervously. "I . . ."

"I wouldn't hurt you. I wouldn't even touch you. I would just sit on the couch with a bowl of Cheetos in my lap, and you could take off your clothes, put a lamp shade on your head, and stand there, completely still. I'd eat the Cheetos and look at your body. Where's the studio? I'll pick you up."

Norman cut in. "I'm sorry, Bert," he said, giving me a worried glance, "I can't tell you that. John in Washington Heights, you're on WTLK."

"Ariel, have you ever gotten it on with a woman?"

Now this was an interesting question. The truth was, no. The furthest I'd gone with chicks was kissing, and you could hardly count that. It was three times, with three different women at Brown, and each time I'd been drunk and stoned and they had too. But there was no way I could admit to my limited experience. After all, I had a bad reputation to protect.

"Of course I have, John," I said.

"Yeah?"

"Yeah." But I didn't know what to say next. There was a full second of dead air. If I didn't come up with something soon, he'd know I was lying. I had to think of a steamy chick story. And since I didn't have any of my own, I figured the next best thing was to borrow someone else's. "Oh yeah," I said. "Some of my earliest sexual experiences were with other girls. When I was eight my friends and I used to make out together at slumber parties."

"For real?" asked Norman.

"*Very* for real. We'd make our Barbies play out little sex scenarios with each other. Then we'd take off our shirts and touch tongues. And sometimes we'd lay in our sleeping bags and hump our stuffed animals until we came."

"Wow," said John. "That's . . . something else."

"But that was just the tip of my lesbian iceberg! When I was fourteen I hooked up with my best friend. Dana. She was sleeping over my house one night and we were talking about how we liked boys to kiss us, when she leaned right in and Frenched me. At first I was weirded out, but then we started fooling around and I was amazed at how much more she knew about my body than the boys did. From then on, every time she slept over we'd hook up. The greatest thing about it was that my parents never suspected a thing." I didn't know if this stuff sounded even vaguely believable, but it was late-night AM radio and I didn't expect the callers to be astute enough to know I was lying.

"Would you be interested in getting it on with me and my girlfriend sometime?" asked John.

"Sure. Leave your name with the engineer and maybe I'll give you two a call."

"Frank in Ozone Park, you're on WTLK."

"Ariel, would you say you're looking for a long-term relationship?"

What could I say? "Of course I want one, but since my boyfriend dumped me three years ago, I haven't been able to get a guy to stick around longer than his third ejaculation"? I'd come off like a total loser. I wanted to sound in control, like a happy-go-lucky single chick who preferred promiscuity to monogamy, who was alone by choice, not by default.

"Looking for a relationship?" I said. "No way in hell! I'm categorically opposed to monogamy. It reins in people's freedom."

"You really think so?" said Frank.

"Oh yeah! There's nothing worse than seeing two people who are together only out of fear! I'd rather be on my own than be with the wrong guy. And the best part about being single is, I

can do whatever I want with whoever I want, whenever I want."
Hoo-ah! My improv skills were coming in handy.

"Would you call yourself a slut?" asked Frank.

"Absolutely!" I shouted.

"And you're not ashamed to say that?" asked Norman.

"Why should I be ashamed? I'm proud of my sluttishness. Why let only one guy have my body when I can share it with the whole wide world?"

"Can I leave my number with the engineer too?"

I'd done it. He'd fallen for my act. Like Bukowski had said, "Beautiful lies. That's what they needed. People were fools." No one listening to talk radio at eleven-thirty at night wanted to hear about someone else's loneliness. I had given them what they were looking for. I had made them think there was a woman out there who wouldn't ask anything of them, who wasn't looking for commitment. I'd invented a dream girl.

"Edna in the Bronx," said Norman, "you're on the air."

She was a middle-aged woman with a whiny voice. "Norman, I like your show very much. But I don't like your guest one bit. She's a cheap girl, Norman, a very cheap girl. What do you look like, Ariel?"

"Why?" I asked. I had a feeling I knew what was coming.

"I'll tell you why. Some women, like John-John's wife, for example—"

"Carolyn Bessette Kennedy?"

"Yeah. Carolyn Bessette Kennedy. She doesn't go around talking about sex, because she's so beautiful, she doesn't have to stoop low to get attention from men."

"Are you asking if I'm ugly?" I asked.

"Yes, I am."

"Ariel is a very attractive young woman," said Norman.

"Well, that's surprising," said Edna, "because in my experience, those who talk about it never do it. If you were beautiful as John-John's wife, you wouldn't feel the need to talk trash. It's disgusting to hear a young woman with such a filthy mouth."

"Oh, Edna," I said, "if you're saying women should just shut up and look good, you're living in the Stone Age. Carolyn Bessette Kennedy is not exactly a shining role model. I think the public fascination with her is just another sign of our increasing tendency to worship mediocrity and laud peroxided women who build entire careers out of looking bored."

(I didn't really say that. What I actually said was, "I hate Carolyn Bessette Kennedy! I'm sick of hearing about her! I hate her!" But my thoughts were eloquent, I swear.)

"Well, I think you're a tramp," said Edna. "And I think someone should wash your mouth out with soap!"

"Thanks for calling, Edna," said Norman. "Let's go to Ariel in New Brunswick. Now, Ariel, you say your boyfriend is abusive to you?"

"Yeah." It was a guy's voice. Not just a guy's voice, but a guy who was making no attempt whatsoever to disguise his gender. I'd met guys named Ariel before—it's a pretty common Hebrew name—but I didn't know if this was a gay guy Ariel or a trickster.

"Are you a woman, Ariel?" asked Norman.

"Yes," he said.

"Are you aware that you sound just like a man?"

"I hear that all the time," he said. "Anyway, I have this boyfriend, he's really mean to me, verbally and mentally; he abuses me. He drives me crazy sometimes, he just—" Another guy's voice came on in the background. "Get off the phone, you no-good whore! I'll kick your ass!! Bitch!"

Norman disconnected them quickly, gesturing to the engineer to make sure the swear words got dumped in time. I couldn't help but feel a tad unsettled. Here was a man pretending to be a girl named Ariel who went out with jerky men. I felt replaced somehow. I wanted to say something that would give us the last laugh on them, something cunning, witty, and in sum.

"See, Norman?" I said. "You're beginning to look like a more and more attractive date—now that I'm reminded of what the alternatives are. Those two represent what my generation has to offer, Norman. Those invective-spewing fools."

"That's a backhanded compliment if I ever heard one."

"I don't mean it in a backhanded way. I really like you. So, what do you say? Should we go out?"

"I don't know. What if I fell in love with you? Then I'd wind up getting hurt. You said yourself you don't believe in monogamy."

"At least you'd get a good *shtup* out of it."

"Good point."

"You could show me the town and I could show you my tits."

He gestured to the engineer, who was fiddling frantically with some buttons, and said, "Uh oh, Ariel, we're going to have to dump that."

"Oops, can I not say 'tit' on the air?" He waved to the engineer again. "Oh my God, I'm so sorry. I'm like Madonna on *David Letterman.*"

"That's OK. Just don't do it again. Tom from East Orange, you're on the air."

"I got one question. If there was a small town, right? Say there was a small town, and the fate of the town depended on the outcome of a football game. If the entire fate of everybody's future depended on the town winning this game, who would play—men, or women?"

There was a pause. Norman and I looked at each other.

"What are you getting at, Tom?" asked Norman.

"I'm saying women are weaklings. Men are stronger than women. I am sick of hearing women like this Ariel say women and men are the same."

I wanted to set this guy straight, tell him what a raging idiot he must have been to call a radio station just to say women are weak. Tell him that, judging by the desperation in his voice, it sounded like he probably hadn't gotten laid in a long, long time.

I opened my mouth to start in on him but the closing music was coming on and he had already hung up. "That's all the time we have left," said Norman. "Thank you, Ariel Steiner. Tune in tomorrow night when our guest will be East Village witch Darcy Kaplowitz."

●

On the cab ride home from the radio station, I started to feel totally schizoid. I didn't know who I was anymore—me, or Ariel Steiner. Ariel Steiner was the girl on the show. She was the cool and outrageous sexpot of lower Manhattan, even though I lived in Brooklyn. She wasn't looking for any relationship deeper than her own vagina. She sought quick dick and nothing more, didn't speak to her lays in the morning, and fucked to come, even though I couldn't. Half of me despised her and the other half wanted to be her.

When I got into the apartment, the light on my answering machine was steady, unblinking. No Sara, no boys. I didn't feel like a cool and outrageous sexpot without any messages on my machine. I took off my coat and sat on the couch in the dark. Then I went to the phone and called Charlton.

"Hey, Ariel," he said. "I loved that column you wrote about me. It made me, like, relive the whole experience."

"I'm glad you liked it. Do you want to get together again?"

"Yeah. What are you doing tomorrow night?"

"Nothing."

"Can you meet me on the steps of Port Authority at five o'clock?"

I had a feeling he wasn't going to take me to *The Lion King*. "Why do you want to meet there?"

"It's a surprise."

"Why?"

"If I told you it wouldn't be a surprise. But I'll give you a hint: you might get some good material."

"Can't I just come to your place?"

"No. If you don't want to meet me on Forty-second Street, that's OK. But I'm not gonna meet you at my house."

And even though I knew exactly what he had in mind, I didn't refuse him, because I wanted him to want me, even in the most degrading way. Besides, he was right about the material. I had to come up with a column by tomorrow—and it would be way too boring to write about the radio show. This was all in the interest of research. I was Ariel Steiner, sex journalist. Ariel Steiner sought out adventure at all costs. She rubbed her face in the grimiest, most low-down centers of debauchery and quick pleasure in the city, then came up smiling. She wasn't scared of sin; sin was her whole MO.

●

He was eating a hot dog when I got there, and he had a slightly sinister smile on his face. "Where we going?" I asked.

He pointed across the street to a black-and-yellow sign: SHOW WORLD CINEMAS, MOVIES 25 CENTS.

We crossed the street and went in. Through the door was a combination newsstand/sex shop, with dirty magazines laid out on a counter and sex toys hanging on the walls. There were two Pakistani men behind the magazine counter. I glanced at them nervously, expecting them to raise their eyebrows at me, but they didn't even look up.

Charlton thumbed through some magazines while I stared up at the vibrators and dildos. I owned a vibrator, but it was this tiny sweet pink thing called Mini Pearl that I'd ordered from a mail-order company in San Francisco. These cocks were terrifying. I walked over to Charlton. He was looking at a magazine open to a photo of a woman handcuffed to a bed, lying on her stomach, getting fucked by a huge bulbous, veiny cock.

"What do you think of that?" he said.

"I think we should go in," I said.

He led me to a tall counter with a fat, dark-skinned black man sitting behind it. Charlton gave him some money and bought some tokens. We went through a turnstile and came to a staircase with a sign next to it that read, *LIVE GIRLS UPSTAIRS. MOVIES DOWNSTAIRS.*

Charlton gestured to the sign and pointed up with a hopeful

look. I shook my head no. There was a limit as to how far I would go in the pursuit of good fodder. I didn't want to see real women, wonder if they had kids, what their lives were like, how they'd gotten into this. Movies were safer, more pretend.

To the right of the staircase was a hallway with rows of booths on either side. We walked down the aisle in search of an empty room. In between the doors there were signs reading, *One Person Per Booth.*

"How are we going to get around that?" I said.

"Just sneak in behind me," he said. An attendant walked by, wheeling a bucket and mop. When he was safely out of sight, Charlton went in one of the doors and I slipped in after him.

The room was tiny, maybe four feet by four feet. It smelled of disinfectant. The walls were Formica red, and to the right of the door there was a small ledge to sit on. The only noises I could hear were the distant moans coming from the movies in the other booths. Charlton locked the door and sat on the jerk-off ledge, I leaned against the door, and we looked at the screen. A message flashed, PUT IN A TOKEN on a green background, while upbeat electronic music played. To the right of the screen were a token slot and buttons numbered one through four.

He put a token in the slot and four boxes appeared on the screen, showing the different movies you could choose from: Asian chick getting fucked by chubby white guy doggie style; tennis court with two pairs of doubles going at it; man walking in on his wife masturbating in the bathroom; and black woman on a couch getting eaten by a black guy with a gold marijuana-leaf ring on one of his fingers.

"Which one do you want to watch?" whispered Charlton.

"I don't care," I whispered back.

He pressed the button for the one with the Asian chick. The small box turned full-screen. It looked kind of scary large. The guy's ass was facing the camera, and in the background was the girl's head, angled sideways so we could see it. She kept saying "Yes" and "More," but her face was contorted with something that looked closer to pain than pleasure, and the guy's butt was so pale and ugly that I didn't exactly envy her.

Charlton pressed a new number and the image switched to a white woman with a white band in her hair sucking the cock of a bearded Latin guy. Her mascara was runny from having the dick near her face. Charlton pressed another one and the movie changed to an Asian girl on a bed, eating a white girl who had shaved pubic hair.

"You wanna sit on my lap?" asked Charlton. I went over and

straddled him, so my back was to the screen. "What are you doing?"

"I don't want to watch."

He shrugged, leaned toward me, and kissed me, and then he lifted up my shirt and bra and squeezed my breast. I rubbed myself against him, closed my eyes, and tried to pretend we were anywhere else in the world but Show World. Every few minutes the token would expire, the Ms. Pac-Man music would come on, and he'd have to lean over to put another token in the machine. The periodic interruptions did not exactly make for a sexy mood.

After a while I opened my eyes. I noticed that his were closed. "Why'd you take me here if you're not watching the movie?" I asked.

"It's the sounds that turn me on."

"The sounds? But they're so fake."

"I know," he said, grinning. "That's exactly why they turn me on."

He kissed me some more and I started to get hot. I could feel him get harder. He pulled me tightly to him. Then he reached into his pocket, took out a condom, and gave me a look. I stared down at the square of plastic and I thought, *Other girls would be scared to do this, but not Ariel Steiner. Ariel Steiner can fuck in a porno booth and come out feeling liberated, not gross.* I wanted to be able to do it. I wanted not to be afraid.

We both stood up and I pulled down my jeans and underwear, but only to below my butt. We switched places and I sat on the ledge. I was scared there might be some leftover come on it from the last guy that would get inside me and kill me, so I slid forward and angled my body up as high as I could.

Charlton pulled down his jeans and boxers, rolled on the condom, leaned over me, shoved it in, and began to pump away, one hand bracing himself against the wall, the other playing with my breast. Soon the token expired and the music came on again. I listened to the blips and bells and stared up at Charlton's sweaty face, and I felt like I was fourteen again, lying there on the beach, waiting for the moan, because that was how I'd know it was finally over.

I didn't want to be this miserable. I wanted to love it. I was fucking without caring, just like a guy. Wasn't this the sex columnist's dream?

Suddenly there was a knock on the door. A West Indian–accented man's voice said, "You gotta put in another token."

"Just a second!" yelled Charlton, staying inside me and searching his pockets for another token. I got this vision of the attendant walking in on us, finding me there on the ledge, my shirt half up, my bra shoved above my breasts, my pants halfway down my legs, Charlton poised above me. The attendant would yell out for the other pervs to come look, and they would all open their red doors and gather in the doorway to stare. Charlton would keep on thrusting, delighted to put on a show, as the men crowded into the booth, their tongues lolling out of their mouths, their eyes bloodshot from their own spunk. I'd jump up, plow through them, and run off toward Port Authority, pulling on my clothes, humiliated and totally alone.

I couldn't let that nightmare come alive. I yanked Charlton out, stood up, buttoned my jeans, pulled down my shirt, and ran down the hallway. But when I came to what I thought would be the street, I just saw the turnstile where we entered. I tried to go through it but it wouldn't turn. The magazine men and token taker looked at me. I did an about-face and ran back down the way I came. A mustachioed guy in a business suit was about to go into a booth and he gave me this half-quizzical, half-bemused look. I rushed past him and finally came to a door that exited onto Eighth Avenue. I walked a few paces down the street, breathing in deeply, and for once in my life that New York City smell of exhaust, hot dog, and cigarette made me relieved and not disgusted.

I noticed there was a Ben & Jerry's ice cream store across the street. I thought about the strangeness of that, of the new Times Square and the old Times Square peering at each other from across a divide, like a showdown, to see who would perish first.

Charlton emerged from the door. "You wanna go to another theater?"

"No," I said. "I think I've had enough." I walked down the street and into the train.

●

At the Broadway–Nassau Street stop, my father got on. I wanted to bolt into another car but there wasn't any time. He saw me through the window before the doors even opened.

"Look who it is," he said. I scooted over and he sat down next to me. Could he tell where I'd been by the look on my face? What did I smell like? Spermicide? Lysol? Sex?

"Where are you coming from?" he asked.

"Uh . . . a friend's house. In Hell's Kitchen. What about you?"

"The office. We drove back from Philly this morning so I could get some work done today. How was the radio show?"

"It was fun. A lot of freaks called in." He raised his eyebrows and nodded like he wanted to hear more, but I couldn't tell him much else without saying I'd pretended to be an early comer and a bisexual just to impress the callers, so I didn't elaborate. He stared at me for a moment, waiting for me to continue, and then he took out a *New Yorker* from his briefcase and started to read it.

He was my own father and we couldn't sustain a conversation for more than a few minutes. It didn't used to be like that. When I was a kid, he was my best friend. Every spring weekend we would ride our bikes across the Brooklyn Bridge to the Lower East Side and run errands for my mom. We'd buy pistachios and clothes and fish, and then we would stop at the Chinatown branch of the New York Public Library and he would check out mystery books for himself and Judy Blume books for me. When I got older, he would take me to art house cinemas, like Theatre 80 and the Quad, to see Hercule Poirot movies and *Magical Mystery Tour* and *Sgt. Pepper,* and on the bike ride home we would talk about the movies, and I would feel brilliant and funny and loved.

When I busted my chin open, I was with him. It was the summer between fifth and sixth grades, and he, my mom, Zach, and I were renting a house in Vermont for a few weeks. One afternoon he and I decided to go for a bike ride while my mom and Zach went to a beach. My mom drove us to the rental place and then we waved good-bye to her and rode off together on a perfectly paved black path. After a few miles, we came to a steep downhill. I coasted way ahead of him, enjoying the speed and the breeze. I heard the wind singing through my helmet and felt my T-shirt rippling against my chest, and I felt strong and free and totally invincible. Halfway down, the bike started going too fast, and I began to spin out of control. "I'm going too fast!" I shouted, and in the distance I heard him calling, "Touch your brakes!"

But my brakes had been testy all morning—whenever I used them, the bike would wobble—and I was convinced that at this speed, braking would make me spin out of control. I held on and hoped for the best, but I catapulted forward over the handlebars, slammed down onto the blacktop next to the bike, and rolled down the hill, feeling my elbows and knees break open, positive that when I stopped moving I'd be dead.

When I finally came to a halt, I heard him pedaling up behind me and his bike clattering to the pavement. He rushed up beside me. I stood up slowly and we inspected my scrapes. I had huge strawberries on my elbows and knees, but that seemed to be the worst of it until he said, "Your chin's bleeding pretty badly."

"Do you think I'll need an operation?"

"I hope not," he said, then lifted the bottom of his polo shirt to his mouth, bit into it, tore off a strip, and tied it under my chin and around my head.

I hated seeing him with that torn shirt. It made me feel like we were victims of a tragedy, and I didn't want to feel that way. He helped me pick up my bike and we began walking down the road to find some help. He said he'd noticed a car pass us with a family in it, about ten minutes ago, and he thought maybe their house was nearby. We wheeled our bikes in silence for a while and then I started to weep. I hated myself for ruining the afternoon, for making him worry, for being stupid enough to fall. "I'm sorry for not touching the brakes," I said. "I'm sorry I didn't listen to you."

"Shut your mouth," he said. And it stung, but in such a familiar way it felt like a salve. I was a fuckup and he was my hero, and when he was cruel, it only made me love him more.

I looked over at him reading his magazine and I wanted to tell him the truth about where I had been. And instead of telling me, "You don't have to tell your parents everything," he would forgive me and say it would all be OK, and then I would explain that he wouldn't have to worry anymore, because I was going to change, and stop humiliating him, make him proud—the way he used to be before the column, before the mess.

As the train pulled into High Street, he put the magazine into his bag and said, "Feel like coming over for dinner? I'm sure Mom and Zach would love to see you."

I saw myself going over for dinner and I saw it being the same as it was in the car to Philadelphia. We'd talk about everything except my column and I wouldn't get up the courage to ask what he really thought. It would just be more of the feeble jokes and one-liners, and the prospect of another evening of that was more painful than the prospect of no contact at all.

"Actually, I'm kind of tired," I said. "I hope that's—"

"It's fine," he said. "I understand." The doors opened. He gave a little wave good-bye and walked out.

●

When I got to my building I found two more fan letters, forwarded from Turner, in the mailbox:

Dear Ariel,
    Reading your column is the highlight of my week. I think it's brave of you to admit to having a sex drive, to admit that girls want to get laid just as

much as guys do. Don't pay any attention to those Victorian-minded assholes out there. They're just lonely and bitter. Stay as strong as you are.

> Your Loyal Fan,
> CAROLINE SEEGER

Dear Ariel,
 Sometimes I hate you, sometimes I love you, but mostly I just want to be you.

> DENISE VENETTI

I took the letters up to the apartment, put them in the folder under the bed, and sat down at the computer. For my father I wanted to be good, but for my readers I had to stay bad. I was the girl women wanted to be. I was the sex no one else was having. The city was counting on me to live out its lowbrow urges. I had to write about Show World, but I had to tell it like it wasn't.

RUN CATCH KISS
True Confessions of a Single Girl
ARIEL STEINER
Smutlife

[*Note to my parents:* D.N.R. (Do Not Read)]

I've always wanted to have sex in a porno movie booth, so last week I finally did. I called up the testicular exhibitionist Royalton Shakes and told him to meet me at Show World Cinemas on 42nd and Eighth. When I arrived he was munching on a hot dog and wearing a huge bright smile. We went inside the entrance and looked at the dildos together and laughed about how big they were. Then I led him to the turnstile and we bought our tokens. I winked at the token man on my way in.

We went into a booth, locked the door behind us, and sat down side by side on the jerk-off ledge. I put in a token and chose a movie with two chicks. I love watching chicks get it on. Then I pushed Royalton to his knees facing me, pulled down my jeans, and hiked my legs up against the opposite wall.

The two girls were roommates and one had always been secretly attracted to the other, so one day she finally admitted it to her roommate, and that's how they got together. I imagined Royalton was my roommate and I was the girl in the movie. He was such a terrific muff muncher that it only took three tokens to make the kitty purr. "That was fabulous," I said. "Now you pick a movie."

He chose one with two guys. I didn't pass judgment. They were going at it in an alleyway. There wasn't much dialogue other than "Oh, yeah." Royalton pulled his pants to his knees and I knelt down and took his huge and beautiful member between my eager lips. Boy, did it taste good. I love giving head. It's my favorite thing in the world. I could do nothing all day except give head and my life would not feel incomplete.

But soon his cock grew too huge for even *me* to stand, so I pulled my mouth off, turned my back, placed one hand on either side of the screen, and leaned right over. He growled like a wild pig, placed his hands on my hips, and drove right into my Lincoln Tunnel. I love sex doggie style. It's my favorite thing in the world next to giving head. I could do nothing all day except give head and do doggie style and my life would not feel incomplete.

My face was just a few inches from the screen so I could see the men up close and personal. This experience was turning out to be a million times more exciting than I ever could have imagined. One cock in my face, one inside me, the smell of other men's spooge in my nostrils, the noises of all the lust films playing in the different booths.

As Royalton continued to rip me in two, I periodically reached into my jeans to insert new tokens. These regular interruptions only heightened Royalton's fervor. Just as the man in the movie let out a low moan, Royalton let out one of his own, and I felt his tremendous trunk begin to pulse. His rigor mortis so thrilled my gleaming manhole that I was surprised to find a tremor rushing through me as well.

He sighed and I sighed, and then he slid the pup out, smooth and slow. I turned to face him and gave him a doting look, glad that I had finally lived out my fantasy, glad that he had been there to help me do it.

We dressed quickly and walked out onto the street. There was a Ben & Jerry's opposite the theater, so we went inside and he bought me a Vermonster. It was messy and white, and as it dripped down my chin I regretted that I hadn't let him jizz in my mouth, because nothing makes me grin like the sweet fresh taste of seed.

I shared this thought with Royalton and he suggested we return to the theater. We wiped our mouths and went back to Show World. Luckily, our honeymoon booth was still empty, so we went in and picked another movie, and I sucked him till he came in my throat.

———————

6

WHEN I FINISHED THE COLUMN I turned off my computer and went to get something to eat. A new bar had opened around the corner, on Court and Nelson, and I had seen a sign in the window that said they sold hot knishes, so I walked over. Most of the men there were middle-aged Italian locals, but at the end of the bar a young guy in a button-down plaid shirt was smoking a cigarette and sipping a beer. I panned down his body like the camera in *Thelma and Louise* for the shot of Brad Pitt when I suddenly realized I *knew* that chest.

It was Jake Datner, my boyfriend for a very brief period during tenth grade. We met at a Saturday-night youth-group sleepover at his temple, Rodeph Shalom, and I was immediately bowled over by his self-deprecation and biting wit. We flirted all throughout Havdalah services, and when it was time to get ready for bed, he put his sleeping bag next to mine. At two in the morning he woke me up and kissed me, and we snuck off into one of the Hebrew school classrooms to dry-hump on the floor behind one of the desks.

From then on we met every day after school at his apartment on West End Avenue to fool around in his room before his parents came home, and we talked on the phone for an hour each night. But after a month we somehow ran out of things to say, so we amicably and mutually decided to end it. Later that year he dropped out of youth group and I never saw him again.

I'd heard he went to Harvard but I hadn't spoken to him since we were fifteen.

Maybe it was fate that I had decided to come to this bar on this night. Maybe it was God's way of helping me pull my head out of the sand. I sat down next to him. He looked up, startled, then smiled when he recognized me. "Hey, Ariel," he said. "Long time no see. I've been reading your stuff. You're a good writer." I slit my eyes to see if he was insinuating anything sexual, but he didn't seem to be. "I was reading this article in the *New Republic* about Maureen Dowd and female journalists and it made me think of you." He reached for his bicycle messenger bag, pulled out the magazine, and handed it to me.

"Can I keep it?" I said.

"Sure."

Maureen Dowd can suck my left one, but I was nonetheless impressed by the gift. The act of him giving me his *New Republic* proved that he either had a brain or was clever enough to know I'd be impressed by the gesture. The dick of his IQ grew hard as a rock in the pussy of my heart.

"What are you doing in this neighborhood?" I asked.

"I live on Third Street."

He lived in Carroll Gardens! It *had* to be an omen that I'd come to this bar. Our relationship would be so convenient! And my dad would love that I was dating a guy I met in youth group. It would mitigate all the *tsuris* I'd given him since I started writing "Run Catch Kiss." Surely he wouldn't be embarrassed if my column described hot sex with a Jew, a Harvard grad, a *good guy*.

As Jake and I continued to talk, I realized that he still possessed all the traits I'd liked about him when he was fifteen. He was charming and funny, and he'd held on to his Yiddish-film-star good looks—pale skin, pink lips, long lashes.

I asked him what he did for a living and he said he wanted to be a playwright but was supporting himself with a job in desktop publishing. I told him how I got my column and he said, "You have a lot of guts." I liked that. It had been a long time since a guy had been more taken by my ambition than any of my other qualities.

But after we'd been talking about half an hour, he said, "I'm pretty tired. I guess I should be getting home soon."

"I'll walk you there," I said.

As we headed down the street, I slowly inched closer to him until I was rubbing my side against his. He stopped walking and looked at me. I pushed him against a building and dove for his mouth. His lips were full and extrasoft and he was not a biter. I remembered what a skilled kisser he'd been back in youth group. He held my neck while he did it, and after a while he pulled away and stared at my face. I knew that was a good sign, because when guys just want to use you, they don't pull away to stare at your face.

"I'm so glad I ran into you," he said.

"Me too," I said.

We grinned like ninnies and kissed again, and then I pushed my voice into secretary register and said, "Jake? Would you like to *be in my column?*"

He blushed and said, "Maybe." It wasn't the most encouraging answer, but it wasn't the least, either. I wrote down my number on an ATM receipt and he said, "I'll call you tomorrow."

●

The next night he invited me over and I sat on his couch and told him the stories of every guy I'd been with since I moved to the city, except the Show World one. He listened calmly, like he wasn't freaked in the slightest. That was probably because he'd read them all already, but I was flattered anyway.

He told me about this mutually self-destructive relationship he'd had at Harvard and it made me like him even more. We got into a discussion about the grossest lies people used in dumping us, and agreed that "It's not you, it's me" topped the list. I asked him to give me a tour of his apartment, and minutes after we got to the bedroom we were horizontal on his futon. He played with me for forty minutes until I came, and then I sucked him a little and finished him off with my hand. Right as I was falling asleep, he whispered, "Ariel, you bewitch me." I almost died.

●

The next night I slept over again. When I woke up in the morning he was looking at me with a worried expression. "What is it?" I asked.

"I don't mean to jump the gun or anything," he said, "but there's something I'm concerned about."

"What?"

"That you're going to write about me. Relationships consist of the said and the unsaid, and every relationship needs to have some unsaid. If you write about me I'll know your unsaid, and it could be bad for us."

This was not what I wanted to hear. I had already been plotting out the beginning of my next column: I was going to write about me asking him to be in it and him saying maybe. It would be totally meta-, and meta- was very cutting edge these days.

"But I'm feeling good about you," I said. "I *like* you. It's only in bad relationships that there's a huge gap between the said and the unsaid. Wouldn't it be OK for me to write about you if I wrote *good things*?"

"No," he said. "It still makes me nervous. I want you to promise never to write about me."

"OK," I said dubiously. "If that's what you want."

"It is. I don't want to be just another story to you."

I understood what he meant. He wanted me to affirm that he was different from the boys who could be reduced to a thousand words. He was asking me to put him in a different category than my litany of rock-tool flings by not making our relationship public. He'd made himself patently clear: if I wrote about him in my column, I'd never get to see his again. I had to honor his request. Yet honoring his request left me with a huge predicament.

I was on the brink of Serious Change, and I wanted my readers—and parents—to know. I was tired of carrying the metropolitan smut torch. I didn't want to mine my past again and pretend I was still single when I wasn't. But if I couldn't write about Jake, and I didn't want to distort the truth anymore, I wasn't sure what else I could do.

That afternoon Corinne Riley, the *Week* senior editor, left a message on my machine inviting me to a book party at a SoHo gallery for a famous lecherous writer. She said there would be food and booze and interesting people. Maybe the party could be the answer to my Jake problem. Maybe something exciting would happen—like a brawl between two hot young novelists—and I'd be there to document it. That column could be the beginning of a whole new bent for me. If I played my cards right I could slowly transform myself from pomo ho to shrewd, keen observer of the urban literati.

I called Corinne back immediately and told her I'd go. "Wear something cute," she said. I opted for a tight black minidress with plastic gold beading around the neck, black stockings, and the red go-go boots.

The entire place was swarming with fops and anorexics. I felt completely out of place and Corinne was nowhere in sight. I headed straight for the bar, pounded wine, and wolfed down cheese sticks, trying to act like an independent, important sex columnist who didn't need to talk to anybody in order to feel cool. All these skinny women with bad posture and British accents kept traipsing past me, and each time one went by I'd get an incredible urge to stick my finger out and try to topple her.

Forty-five minutes later I spotted Corinne coming through

the door. She was wearing a print blouse and a knee-length tweed skirt with black motorcycle boots. I stumbled over and said, "I'm so glad you're here. I'm drunk." In my eagerness to hug her, my wineglass tipped and some of it spilled on the floor. She grabbed my napkin and leaned down to wipe it up. That was when I noticed she was wearing garters.

"Wow," I said. "Garters."

"I always wear garters," she said. "They're much less restrictive than panty hose."

"I'm wearing control-top tights," I said, lifting my skirt to show her.

She laughed. "You shouldn't wear control-top with a dress that's so short. The control part shows under the hem. It's tacky." This chick meant serious business.

A few minutes later the crowd started moving toward a podium, and the lecherous writer began to read. I wanted to be a shrewd, keen observer of the urban literati, but his voice was so droning it made me want to go to sleep.

"Let's get out of here," Corinne whispered.

"OK," I whispered back. So my next column wouldn't be about the party. Instead it would be a vivid portrait of a strong female beat writer trying to make it in a prejudiced and ugly world.

We headed outside and I linked my arm through hers. When we hit Prince she said, "Let's stop in the J. Crew store. I want to check out some clothes." She took jackets and sweaters off the rack and held them up to me, telling me which ones I'd look best in. As she lifted up a black cashmere sweater I noticed that she had beautiful nails. Long, painted, and filed.

"Have you ever been a hand model?" I asked.

"Yeah," she said, "for a couple years in high school, but then I ran into some cuticle problems and had to give it up."

"Do you think *I* could be one?" I asked, proffering my hand.

"No," she said, inspecting it and pursing her lips. "You have dyke hands."

"What?"

"Dirty, stubby nails. Dyke hands." She turned her back and headed for another clothing rack.

Was she trying to find out which league I batted for? Was she indirectly propositioning me? Or was she just one of those ultra-hip straight girls who felt comfortable throwing the word *dyke* around?

We left the store and walked to a café on Greene Street. She bought us cappuccinos and we sat down at a table in the back. We dished about Turner and Jensen, the conservative politics of the paper, and undergarments.

"So, when you buy garters," I said, "do you buy them with matching underwear? Or do you not care about that?"

"I rarely wear underwear."

Ooh boy. "Are you wearing any tonight?"

"No." She smiled lasciviously. It seemed like she was flirting with me. I was a solipsist but these signs were loud and clear. And I knew Jake wouldn't mind if I told him I hooked up with a chick, because guys never mind when their girlfriends cheat on them with chicks. More often, they want *details.*

Before I could decide what to do, though, she stood up, said, "I should go home. I have to finish this piece on squatters," kissed me on the cheek good-bye, and walked out the door. I couldn't believe it. The broad had been rattling my chain all along!

But on the cab ride home I realized there was a way I could make a play for Corinne without having to ask her consent. If I wrote a column about the two of us getting it on, I could accomplish three simultaneous goals: keeping my column spicy, staying in the relationship with Jake, and fictitiously living out my long-held lezzie urges. It was a totally different thing to fictionalize an affair with a man than to fictionalize one with a woman. The former was lame; the latter was subversive. If I pretended I was bi, "Run Catch Kiss" would grow in popularity among lesbians, bi-curious girls, straight men, and maybe even gay men. Turner and Jensen would eat it up. It would be the twist of all twists: the straight slut bends.

I called the Corinne column "Dyke Hands," named her Beat Writer, and said that after the book party I took her back to my house and fisted her until she female-ejaculated on her face. I hoped it sounded convincing.

But there was a rub. I'd have to trust that she wouldn't squeal about the fiction to Starsky and Hutch. She seemed cool enough not to—but maybe it was best to call her, just in case. I picked up the phone.

"There's something I have to talk to you about," I said.

"What?"

"I wrote this column about the two of us hooking up, and I want to know if you'd mind me printing it."

"You fabricated a liaison?"

"Yeah."

I heard her exhale on a cigarette. "Is it hot?"

"I hope so."

"Does it sound authentic?"

"I don't know. I used my imagination."

"What do you call me?"

"Beat Writer."

She laughed. "Go for it."

"You won't tell Turner I made it up?"

"No."

"Promise? Because they told me I wasn't allowed to lie."

"My lips are sealed."

After I hung up I called Jake to tell him what I was planning. He said, "I can't wait to read it." Everything was under control, and I was five days ahead of schedule.

But the next day "Smutlife" came out, and I had a new set of worries. The first was my dad. I had to find out if he'd heeded my "Do Not Read" warning. I checked my machine twelve times that afternoon to see if he left a message, but by four-thirty he still hadn't. So I called him.

"Don't worry," he said. "I didn't. Larry Stanley tried to read it aloud to me, but I put on my Walkman and cranked up NPR so I couldn't hear him."

"Thanks."

"But my eye couldn't help but catch the first sentence. Mom and I don't want to tell you how to run your life, but we're at our wits' end. We don't know if you should be in therapy or if we should." I could see him running his hand through his hair.

I had to let him know I was OK. He had to know I was growing up in life, if not on paper.

"I'm actually seeing someone new," I said. "And I'm really happy."

"Who is he?"

"He was a guy I dated in youth group. Jake Datner."

"This is the best news I have heard in months! I can't believe it! I am just so thrilled for y—" His voice cracked. He had to stop talking and take a few deep breaths. He cries at everything. Every hokey human-interest tale they air on NPR, Hallmark commercials, sappy movies. He even cried at *Splash*. "What I mean to say is," he said, clearing his throat, "I'm just . . . delighted."

When I walked into BarBarella after work, though, and saw Jake sitting at the bar, I wasn't sure how long he and I would last anyway. His mouth was turned down at the corners and he had two empty shot glasses in front of him. Before my butt cheeks were fully planted on the bar stool he said, "Your column really upset me."

"I thought you were OK with my mistakes," I said.

"I am," he said. "I just didn't know you'd made so many."

You would think a guy who was seeing a sex columnist would figure she'd been around the block once or twice. But Jake was a Guy in a Relationship, so he desperately needed to cling to the two big Guy in Relationship myths: (1) that his girlfriend is an innocent flower whose sexuality he is bringing out and (2) that he is the bigger player in the pair. If a guy feels for one instant that his girlfriend's sexuality has already been brought out by other guys, or that he's the lesser player, he freaks. That's why, when a girl asks a guy how many girls he's slept with, he'll give her the real number, then smile proudly, but when a guy asks a girl, she'll gauge his tolerance level, then reduce accordingly.

"Jake," I said, "are you afraid of me?"

"I think I am," he said.

"What can I do to make you less afraid?"

"Have you been tested?" He sure didn't mince words.

"Yes."

"Since that guy in the porno booth came in your mouth?"

"He didn't come in my mouth. I made that part up."

"Why?"

"To make a better story."

"Did you go to Show World?"

"Yes."

"Did you have sex with him?"

"Yeah, but protected, and he didn't come anyway, because an attendant interrupted us in the middle and we had to leave."

"Oh." He didn't say anything for a second and then he sighed and said, "It's not just the testing I'm worried about."

"What else is it?"

"I feel like I could never be enough man for you."

"You could. You are!"

"Why?"

"Why?" I repeated dumbly.

"What is it you see in me?"

"You're . . . decent."

He winced. "That's the kiss of death."

"What do you mean?"

"I've had more girls tell me I'm decent than any other guy I know. When a girl says that, she might as well be saying she could never fall for you."

"I'm not telling you you're decent in a blow-off way. I'm telling you you're decent *and* that I want to keep seeing you. But I don't want you to be afraid of me."

"I know," he said. "I'm sorry." He squeezed my hand and leaned in to kiss me, and everything was semi-OK again.

The next three nights in a row, we went out together, to dinner, drinks, and a movie. I loved all the relationship perks—dressing up for him, getting calls from him at work, making out in backseats of cabs, falling asleep next to him, eating breakfast at The Fall together. My entire Perfect Guy dream was finally coming true.

Until we hit a bump. We were fooling around on his futon Sunday night when suddenly his interest disappeared. I never know what to do when that happens. It's generally a lose-lose situation. If you don't say anything the guy gets upset and embarrassed, and if you say something the guy gets upset and embarrassed.

"Is everything all right?" I asked.

"Fine," he said, jumped out of bed, put on some boxers, and went into the living room.

I put on my clothes and followed him in. He was sitting on the couch, lighting a cigarette and twitching his leg. "What's going on?" I asked.

He sighed, knotted his brow, and looked at me mournfully. "There's something I've wanted to tell you but I couldn't seem to find the right time."

"What is it?"

"I'm bipolar."

"You have an apartment in L.A.?"

"No, I'm manic-depressive. I just started taking Paxil a couple days ago. One of the side effects is . . . so that's why that happened."

"How long have you known about this?"

"All my life, really, but technically, about a few weeks. That's when my company put me on staff. I got health coverage and I started seeing a shrink on the plan, and he said I was bipolar and prescribed the Paxil."

"Do you feel like it's helping?"

"I'm not sure. And I don't like this side effect. I'm thinking of going off it."

"Are there other drugs you can take that might not—"

"This is the first one I've tried. I'm gonna talk to the shrink about it." He got up, went to the kitchen, and came back with a bottle of beer.

"Are you sure you should be drinking if you're on an antidepressant?" I asked.

"Don't tell me what to do," he spat.

"I'm just trying to—"

"Well, stop trying." He turned on the TV.

This was awful. Jake was supposed to be the answer to my problems—not a new problem. I went into the bedroom and got under the covers. He came in a few minutes later and crawled under next to me.

"I'm sorry I snapped at you," he said quietly.

"You should be," I said.

"Ariel . . ." He got that pleading look in his eyes again. "Please don't give up on me."

"I'm not," I said. But the mood had dampened, and we fell asleep with our backs to each other.

●

On Monday morning I got a strange call from Corinne. "There's something we need to discuss," she said sotto voce.

"What is it?"

"Turner's been acting funny today."

"What do you mean?"

"He came up to my desk a little while ago and asked if 'Dyke Hands' was true. I told him yes but I don't think he believed me. He said, 'She seems like such a breeder. It's hard for me to believe she's bisexual.' "

"He said that?"

"Yeah. I don't know what you want to do about it, but I thought I should warn you."

"Thanks," I said. I hung up and chewed my pencil. It didn't take me long to come up with a plan.

●

After work I went to the *Week*. Corinne was at her desk. I looked to my left toward Turner's office and spotted the top of his head protruding from behind his computer. Perfect timing. I crossed behind Corinne's desk and stood over her chair, my back to Turner. "Are we in his line of vision?" I whispered.

"Not yet," she said. "Take a step to your left." I did. "OK. Now we are."

I sat on her lap, stared at her, and laced my fingers through hers. She had dark pretty lids and long lashes. She smirked at me, getting off on how nervous I was. But I screwed my courage to the sticking place, shut my eyes, and lunged for her. Unbelievable. She had incredible technique—not too much tongue, all the action in the lips. Our chests touched as we held each other, and I felt two hard spots between us. I wasn't sure if they were her nipples or mine, and not knowing kind of turned me on. She put her hand on the back of my neck. I pulled her in closer. This was a dirty job, but someone had to do it.

We smooched for another two minutes and then I swiveled her around and stole a glance into Turner's office. He was looking right at us, his face redder than a nursing mother's teat. Bingo. I yanked my face away, leapt off Corinne's lap, and straightened my clothes. Turner came out.

"Hello, Bill," I said, turning to him. "I didn't know you were, um, in there."

"Me neither," said Corinne, pulling out her compact and putting on a fresh coat of lipstick.

"Well, I was," he said. "You two should try to show a little more discretion. People have to get work done around this place. You don't want to throw them off balance. It could affect the quality of the paper."

Operation: success.

"I'm really sorry, Bill," I said contritely. "I guess I just got carried away."

"Me too," said Corinne. "It won't happen again."

"Good," he said, went back into the office, and shut the door. I winked at Corinne and gave a thumbs-up and we went out to get a drink.

●

On Wednesday at noon, Sara and I picked up two copies of the paper and went to the Met Life building. There was only one letter about me in "The Mail":

Why don't you print a photo of Ariel Steiner so if I ever see her on the street, I can run away?
                                    NAME WITHHELD UPON REQUEST

This time I didn't get upset. I actually smiled. I had enemies all over the city, but none of them ever seemed to stop reading me. And how intimidated could I be by a guy who didn't have enough balls to let the paper print his name?

When I got back to work there were four messages on my machine about "Dyke Hands." Corinne: "The whole office is asking me how you were, and I'm telling them 'the best of my life.'" Jake: "I hate to admit it, but it turned me on." Zach: "My friends want to know if you're a bulldagger. Dad told me you had a boyfriend, though. Are you bi? It's cool if you are. I just want to know." And my dad: "Please call me as soon as possible."

"I only read it this week because I thought it was going to be about Jake," he said when I got him on the phone. "But it sure wasn't. What's going on?"

I had to set him straight. "It was fiction," I said. "The character is based on someone real, but she's just a friend. We didn't— I mean—it's not—"

"Oh, thank God," he said and breathed a huge sigh of relief.

●

That night I went over to Jake's. As soon as I walked in he pulled me right into bed and dove for my muff. I guess he hadn't been kidding when he'd said the column turned him on. He'd been going at it for about five minutes when I reached down and shifted his head a little. Suddenly he jerked his face up and scowled at me. "What are you doing?" he shouted.

"Moving your head."

"Did it ever occur to you that it might be just a tad unromantic?"

"How are you supposed to learn what I like if I don't show you?"

"There's a difference between saying what you like and traffic-copping me."

He put on his boxers. "Where you going? To the living room? Like you always do? To watch TV?"

"I'm not watching TV," he said and went into the living room. I put on my underwear and T-shirt and followed him in. We sat on the couch.

"Did you go off the Paxil?" I asked.

"Yes," he said. "Yesterday."

"Are you sure that was a good idea?"

"Leave me alone," he said. That pretty much answered my question.

He opened a bag of pot that was sitting on the coffee table and started to roll a joint. As he lit it, a piece of ash fell off the end and scalded my thigh.

"Ow!" I screamed. "Did you do that on purpose?"

"No," he said. "It was an accident. I'm sorry."

"You treat me like shit and we've only been going out like a week. Most guys take months."

"I don't treat you like shit."

"Yes, you do. I wish you'd go back on the drugs."

"How can you be so insensitive to my illness?"

"Because it's driving me crazy!"

"Jesus! We're fighting like an old couple."

"Are you aware that when you say things like 'We're an old couple' it doesn't make me feel very—"

"Are you aware that when you direct me in bed it doesn't make *me* feel very good either?"

In the John Hughes movie of my life, that would have been the moment where Molly Ringwald Me told off Andrew McCarthy Jake and stormed out of the apartment, finally realizing we had no future. In my moment of sudden enlightenment and empowerment, Andrew Jake would become so transfixed by Molly Me's feistiness that he'd chase me down the street, grab my arm passionately, and say Andrew's last line in *Pretty in Pink*: "I believed in you. I always believed in you. I just didn't believe in me." Then he would bend to kiss me and his eyes would be all crinkly and warm like Andrew's, and we would kiss an incredible, nonhalitotic kiss under a hot blue rain as "If You Leave" swelled up in the background.

But I knew my life wasn't a movie. I saw myself leaving the apartment and I saw myself sleeping alone again. I saw the victory being a hollow one that in the end didn't make me feel independent and powerful but instead made me lonelier than before.

We sat there silently for a few minutes and then he put his hand on my knee. I wanted us to stop fighting. I wanted him to like me again.

I put my hand on his crotch and he kissed me. It got superhot superfast, the way it always does when you're hating each other, and before long I was lying on top of him. "Should I get a condom?" he asked.

We hadn't gone all the way yet, and I had a feeling it would be a mistake to do it now, but I nodded anyway. He went into his room and came back with one, got on top of me, heaved up and down silently for a few minutes, then came. He knotted the condom, put it on the table next to the pot bag, sat up, and lit a cigarette.

I went into the bathroom, ran the tap water, sat down on the edge of the toilet, and started to cry. I didn't want to be crying. That was what you did when you were going out with a dick, and Jake wasn't a dick. He was just troubled. I had to be understanding. Relationships were about compromise. I had to think longhaul. I tore off a piece of toilet paper, wiped my face with it, and went back into the living room.

Over the next few days we fought every time we got together. He would snap at me about something small, I'd snap back, and then a second later he'd hug me and say, "I don't want to lose you," or, "Please don't be mad at me," and I'd find myself forgiving him.

I knew I wasn't happy, but I was afraid my dad would be disappointed if we broke up. I wanted him to see I could be good at monogamy. I wanted him to see that despite my mistakes I could learn how to be a Relationship Girl.

But my dad wasn't the only reason I was afraid to cut Jake loose. I had this huge, lurking fear that if I broke up with Jake, no one else would want to be my boyfriend. I'd just go back to jerking off jerks and writing about it, till eventually I died—wide, notorious, and alone. Jake was mean, hard to be around, and mercurial, but at least he was sticking. Having a boyfriend was much more important to me than having a good one.

The only possible upside to the tormented coupling was that it would have made terrific copy. But I was too afraid to ask Jake to reconsider his vetting, because I thought it might make him dump me. So that week, instead of writing about my awful, real, heterosexual relationship, I wrote about my fantastic, fictitious, lesbian one. And the next week I wrote the first-blow-job story after all.

The dyke ditties elicited a few incendiary letters:

So Ariel Steiner fucks both women and men ("Dyke Hands," 12/4). Does she do children too? Celery? Furniture? I eagerly await the column where she gets boned by her Chihuahua.
                                        HOWARD KESSEL, *Upper East Side*

What's up with this muff diving, Ariel ("Pap's Blue Ribbon," 12/11)? I thought you were straight. Maybe you should change the name of your column to "Run Snatch Kiss."
                                        ALVIN SIMMONS, *Canarsie*

I might have been able to take a little more pleasure in the abuse if it had been in response to real events. But my column was getting so far removed from my life that I began to wonder if it was worth it to be going to all those lengths to please a guy who wasn't exactly pleasing *me*.

The Sunday I wrote the blow-job column ("Making Head-way") I went to meet Sara for dinner at Café Orlin on St. Mark's. I didn't want to talk about Jake, so as soon as we sat down I said, "How are things with Jon?" (She'd broken up with Kit a few weeks before and immediately gotten back together with Jon.)

"Weird," she said. "Our relationship has always had a pretty high quotient of warped power games, but now it's getting out of control even for us."

"What do you mean?"

"We went out to the movies two nights ago, and then after-ward we went back to his place and had really violent sex, where he strangled me as I kicked him, and then we both came. I left his house feeling pretty good about things, but he hasn't returned any of my calls since then."

Usually, when Sara told me about her guy problems, I would try not to be too judgmental, because I hate it when I tell a girl-friend about some guy and she says, "He's an asshole. Get rid of him." Like that will help. Like my problem is that I don't *know* he's an asshole, when my real problem is *knowing* he's an asshole but not understanding how that fact should make me not want to see him. It sucks when your girlfriend tells you you're completely self-destructive, even when you know she's right.

But hearing that things had gotten this ugly with Jon made me start to seriously worry about her. "Why are you staying with him if he treats you so horribly?" I asked.

"Because he's the Prick I Think I Love."

"Why don't you find another prick who doesn't also strangle you?"

"Because I love him. Why are you asking stupid questions?" The waiter came to take our order. I got salad, salmon, and a gin-ger ale. Sara got coffee. I hoped she wasn't having eating prob-lems again. "Anyway," she said, "things are looking up. This is the first time he's given me the silent treatment in days."

"If you think things are looking up because he hasn't given you the silent treatment in days, don't you think that might be a sign of a problem?"

She leaned forward in her chair and hissed, "You don't think you have problems yourself?"

"Of course I do. I'm just saying maybe yours are bigger."

"At least I thrive on drama, mind games, and misery. I'm a *genuine* masochist. You're just fronting as one. That's far worse." We sat there staring at each other. She lit a cigarette.

"Maybe we should look on the bright side," I said. "We could be in relationships that are even more unhealthy than the ones we're in now. Have you ever heard of Maimonides's ladder of charity?"

" 'Course. We studied it in Hebrew school."

"Well, remember how he ranked different levels of charity? Two-way anonymous giving is more noble than one-way anonymous, and one-way anonymous tops nonanonymous?"

"Yeah."

"Maybe we could design a ladder of self-destructive behavior. The bottom rung would be obsessing over a guy who's verbally and physically abusive, goyish, has multiple substance issues, and doesn't want to see you. One rung up would be a guy who's only verbally abusive, goyish, substance-abusive, and doesn't want to see you."

"And above that would be an occasionally verbally abusive Jew who has only one substance problem and calls once in a while."

"Exactly."

"That reminds me," she said, getting up from the table.

"Where you going?"

"To check my machine."

"Does he know how often you check your machine waiting for a call from him?"

"I don't tell him. Maybe we could make another ladder of self-destructive behavior. The first rung would be calling *his* machine obsessively, and above that would be calling *your own* machine obsessively. Calling your own machine isn't as bad as calling his, because it's a private obsessive practice. He can't know about it."

She walked over to the phone, punched in her personal security code, then checked her reflection in the metal, picked something out of her teeth, and came back to the table.

"He wants me to come over," she said.

"Are you going to?"

"Hello?"

"Listen, if for some reason, on your way to his house, you have a crisis of conscience and realize this is something you want to get out of, I'll sit here for another hour and you can come back."

"I'm not coming back," she said.

"I didn't think so. But I thought I'd make the offer anyway."

She put on her coat, put some money on the table, and started heading for the door. "If he chokes you too hard," I called after her, "kick him in the balls."

"I *ask* him to choke me," she said, turning around. "It makes my orgasms hotter."

"You could die like that. That's what happened to this guy in the British parliament."

"You could break your neck eating your own pussy," she shouted, *"but that's never stopped me before!"* People started to look up from their tables. "I'm an independent woman!" she yelled. "Master of my destiny! Hear me roar!"

Something about the way she said, "Hear me roar," made me get choked up as I watched her go out the door. I waited for an hour, but she never came back. I told myself there was no need to worry, because in the end, her survivalist instincts would save her. They always had in the past. But I wondered how many times someone could put herself through the ringer and still come out unscathed. And I wasn't just thinking about Sara.

It might have been a little easier for me to pull myself out of the ringer if New Year's hadn't been coming up. That ill-fated eve has been loaded for me since I first saw *When Harry Met Sally...* in ninth grade. As I watched Billy Crystal run through the city in search of Meg Ryan so he could kiss her under mistletoe, my romantic expectations of the holiday soared to the sky. Every December since then, I have prayed to meet a young Billy by the thirty-first, who will race through the streets in search of my mouth. But somehow I always wind up alone and in a party hat, watching the ball fall on TV and blowing my nose. I knew I should break up with Jake, but I wanted to have a romantic holiday—and he and I had already arranged to go out for dinner, rent *When Harry Met Sally...*, and go to bed early.

But although I am occasionally superficial, I am not a very good procrastinator. So when I got home I called Jake and asked if he'd meet me at the bar where we'd first run into each other. We made small talk for a few minutes, and then I blurted, "I've been thinking a little lately."

"About what?" he asked.

"I just . . . I'm not sure about things. I think it might be a good idea for us to take a little time away from each other."

"What are you trying to say?" he asked, looking me dead in the eye. He wasn't making this easy.

"That maybe we shouldn't see each other so often."

"Are you breaking up with me?"

"I don't know."

"It's a simple question."

"I guess I am," I said, sighing. "But it's not you. It's me."

He started to laugh bitterly.

"It's not a lie!" I shouted. "I really mean it! You deserve a woman who could love you. And I just don't know if I'm her. But

I don't want you to hate me!" I started to cry. Which was pretty
ridiculous, since I was the dumper and not the dumpee, and when
the dumper cries, it always looks disingenuous. "I'm sorry," I
said, put some money on the bar for my beer, kissed him on the
cheek, and left.

7

ON THE WALK from the bar I bought a pack of Camel Filters. When I got home I put on "It Ain't Me, Babe" and smoked out the window. I tried to let Bob's masculine toughness and isolationist inclinations seep into me through osmosis as I listened—"Go 'way from my window,/Leave at your own chosen speed./I'm not the one you want, babe,/I'm not the one you need"—but in the middle of the second verse I dragged in too hard on the cigarette, broke into a fit of coughing, and stubbed it out.

I turned off the music, shut the window, and stared at the phone. I had to tell my parents about Jake sooner or later, and I didn't see the point in delaying. Better to devastate them now than let them harbor hopes of the two of us getting serious.

My mom answered. "What's new?" she said.

"I broke up with Jake."

"Why?" said my dad. They always do that, both come on the line when I think I'm talking to only one of them.

"Because it wasn't working. We got along at the beginning, but then we started fighting all the time and I realized I'd be happier without him than with him. Also, he was manic-depressive."

I waited for my dad to start in on me, but it was my mom who spoke first: "It sounds like you made a mature decision."

"What?"

"She's right," said my dad. "It doesn't make much sense to stay with someone who's not making you happy."

171

"You mean you're not upset?"

"No."

"You're a very independent person," said my mom. "You can't stay with someone if the situation isn't right. A lot of people can, but not you."

I wanted to tell her that nine times out of ten, when the situation wasn't right, it only made me want to stay more, but I didn't want to pop her balloon, so instead I just said, "Thanks."

●

The next day at lunch Sara asked if I wanted to come busking with her. She and Jon had had a huge argument the night before and she'd decided playing music in public would be good therapy. My musical ability was mediocre at best, but I thought it was important to support her, so after work I went home, got my clarinet, and went to meet her at the West Fourth Street stop.

As I headed down the platform to the passageway at the southern end, I heard this slow, mournful accordion. Sara had never played for me before and I'd always assumed she wasn't that good. But her music was discordant and aching, and she was singing in a clear, high voice—a ballad about losing the man she loved. I reached the entrance to the passageway and saw her sitting on a stool, the accordion in her lap, her open case in front of her, filled with change. Two teenaged boys, a businesswoman, a homeless man, and an MTA worker were watching with expressions ranging from delight to disgust. She finished the song and the woman applauded, but no one else did.

"How's it going?" I said, standing next to her and opening my clarinet case.

"Not bad," she said. "I've made like two bucks so far."

"How long have you been here?"

"An hour."

I wet my reed and attached it to the clarinet. Sara struck up a Klezmer song—"The Wedding Dance," she said. It was incredibly fast and complicated. I had only studied clarinet up to sixth grade and I'd never taken any music theory, but I did my best to follow along, and three out of every four notes I chose sounded OK with hers.

In the middle of the song a rushed yuppie man walked briskly past and threw a quarter toward the case, but it landed on the floor, about a foot away from the homeless guy. The guy's eyes lit up when he saw it, and then he slowly extended his calf like a ballet dancer, until his toe was on top of the quarter, and pulled it back toward his body at the rate of about an inch a minute. Although he was pretending to be engrossed in the music, his motions were so deliberate that it seemed like he wanted to call attention to his thievery. When his foot was positioned back below his knee, he bent down in the same showy style, picked up the quarter, put it in his pocket, then continued to watch us for a few minutes before ambling slowly down the platform.

Sara and I laughed and kept playing. We played for two hours—some more of her songs, plus "Amazing Grace," "Hatikvah," Tom Waits's "The Piano Has Been Drinking." We decided to end our set with "Train's Gonna Carry Me Home," an old gospel tune she'd learned from Evan. I played the verses but sang along on the chorus. It was "I'm going home" repeated eight times, and although I knew it was about Jesus, I didn't feel guilty for blaspheming. The melody was simple and sweet, and the more I sang, the more it comforted me. Our voices filled the passageway and Sara looked beautiful playing, and for the first time in a long time I didn't feel lonely.

When we finished the song, we counted our loot. Thirty-four dollars for three hours—seventeen dollars each. That was better than minimum wage. We were rich! We packed up our instruments and walked outside. There was a Häagen-Dazs across the street, and even though it was forty degrees outside, we decided to buy cones with our new money. We ate them in the window as we watched holiday shoppers go by, and then it started to snow.

•

The next night, Tuesday, was the *City Week* Christmas party. All the other columnists were going to be there and I wasn't sure whether to dress like my cartoon. I opened the closet and began riffling through the clothes. The first outfit I tried was my blue-and-white striped polyester tee, with the butterfly collar, and the brown, ribbed mini, but that was too slutty. Then I tried the white, flowery Nick Fenster dress with red boots—but I decided it made me look fat. I even considered the nurse outfit for a second, but it seemed a little obvious. And then I spotted something lavender all the way to the right. It was a thin velvet gown I had gotten at a boutique in Providence. I slid it on. It was a little loose—I'd been in the high 130s when I bought it—but not so loose that my assets weren't visible.

The party was scheduled from seven to eleven, in the *Week* offices. I got there at eight so I would look fashionably late, but only about a dozen people were there, so I went into the bathroom and sat on the edge of the toilet to kill some time. When I came out of the stall I found Corinne putting on lipstick in front of the mirror.

"Hey, lover girl," she said, kissing me on the cheek. "How are you?"

I looked at the floor beneath the stalls to make sure we were alone. "I'm dumping you the week after next."

"Thank God. I was going to break up with you soon anyway. You were getting way too needy."

"Thanks."

"No problem."

"But will you do me a favor? Come around with me tonight, like we're still seeing each other. For Jensen and Turner's sake. Be my reverse beard."

"Your *shave,* you mean?" she said, grinning.

"Exactly." She took my arm and we ventured out into the office. She led me over to a pale-faced slender guy in his early thirties in a fedora.

"Ariel, this is Dave Nadick," she said. The suicidal! I'd expected him to look tough and haggard, but instead he seemed almost vulnerable. He had tight, smooth, pale skin and wide eyes. I shook his hand and he leaned forward, took my hand in two of his, and said, "Pleasure." I couldn't believe what a gent he was.

Corinne pulled my arm and led me across to the bar, where a bespectacled man in a jacket and tie was chatting with a short guy with bleach-blond hair. "Len Hyman and Stu Pfeffer," said Corinne. The suburban dad and the punk rocker. I shook their hands and introduced myself.

"You don't look anything like your cartoon," said Hyman.

"Neither do you," I said. Hyman's illustrator drew him like a nerd, but in life he wasn't bad-looking. He was much younger than I expected and he had a thick shock of hair and soft eyes.

Stu Pfeffer gestured toward a tall, elegant woman standing next to him. "Ariel, this is my wife, Linda."

"You're . . . *married*?"

"I try to keep it low-key," he said quietly. "It's bad for my image." I nodded understandingly.

A girl my age with a Betty Page haircut and large pointy boobs came over and embraced Corinne. "This is Dana Spack," said Corinne.

"It's nice to finally meet you in person," said Dana. The fact checker. The easy comer. I wouldn't mind it if this chick gave me a few orgasm tricks. But before I could ask, she waved at someone across the room and pulled Corinne over with her.

I tried to beeline for the food table, but halfway there Jensen grabbed my arm and introduced me to a slim brunette by his side. "Ariel," he said, "I'd like you to meet your illustrator, Tessa Tallner." It was incredible. She was the real live version of the cartoon version of me—the cropped hair, the upper-lip mole, the slender bod, the small, perky tits. Suddenly I understood just who this chick had been drawing all along: herself.

"I hope you like my drawings," she said.

How could I tell her they had almost sent my parents to early deaths? "I sure do," I said. "You do a *terrific* job!" Then I scurried toward the food.

Just as I was chowing down on a samosa, this tall brown-haired guy in his thirties sidled up next to me. "How is it?" he said.

"Not bad," I said.

He reached for one. "What's your name?"

"Ariel Steiner." He seemed to color slightly. "What's yours?"

"Fred Sadowsky."

It rang a distinct bell in my mind, but for the life of me I couldn't place it. "That sounds really familiar," I said. "Have you written something for the paper before?"

"In a way," he mumbled.

"What do you mean?"

"I've written several letters to 'The Mail.'"

Now I knew who this guy was—the asshole who said I was a victim of bad parenting! *"You wrote one about me!"* I shouted. "It completely humiliated my father!"

"It was meant to be humorous."

"Well, it wasn't. It was horrible! I can't believe they invited you to this party. What—did they send out a form letter to every psychotic jerk who's ever sent in an obnoxious letter?"

"No. They invited me because they're running something of mine next week."

"What?"

"I've written two dozen letters over the past few months, and last week I got a call from Turner asking me to write a story for them. So I sent in a piece about my first colonoscopy and they're putting it on the cover."

Suddenly Turner came over with this thin guy in his early thirties. He was tall and fair with a black wool cap on his head, blond eyelashes and eyebrows, and a crooked nose. "Ariel," said Turner, "this is Adam Lynn. He's a friend of Nadick's, and he wanted to meet you." Fred Sadowsky sidled away.

"I just wanted to tell you how much I enjoy your work," said

Adam, shaking my hand. "I was looking around the room trying to guess which woman at the party was Ariel Steiner, and when Bill told me it was you, I was really surprised."

"Why?"

"I don't know. I guess because I didn't expect you to be so attractive." Turner grinned and disappeared. "I always pictured Ariel Steiner as mean-looking and cruel, sort of a snide party girl, and you look . . . innocent."

"That's a backhanded compliment if I ever heard one."

"I don't mean it in a backhanded way. I mean I think you're . . . pretty."

I thought he was pretty too. Especially with that huge crooked schnoz. "Did you break your nose?"

"Yes."

"How?"

"In a fight."

"Was it over a woman?"

He nodded. My interest was piqued. I did not want to jump the gun, but here was a dish of a guy who was violent enough to have damaged his face because of a woman. I couldn't help but get wet.

"What happened?"

"I was in a bar in Rome and I was flirting with this woman and this guy came up to me and tried to talk to her. I swung at him and he punched me in the nose."

"Wow," I said. "What were you doing in Rome?"

"I was on tour with my first novel."

"What was it about?"

"A young guy coming of age in the city."

"Have you written any others?"

"I'm working on one now, about a man and woman who break up, then each go insane. Have you always been a writer?"

"No, I started out as an actress, but when I got the column it made sense, because I've always had this movie of my life running in my head anyway, and the column was just a chance to *show* it."

"I know just what you mean. I have one of those movies, too. Even when something really tragic is happening to me, I'm seeing it happen from outside myself, instead of feeling tragic."

"That's exactly it!" I screamed, and it was that incredible feeling of someone understanding you instantly and wanting to skip the getting-to-know-each-other part and do the vows right then and there.

But then he put on his coat and said, "I should be going soon. I have to meet some friends. It was nice talking to you."

"You too," I said. So that was it. He'd just walk out and we'd never see each other again.

But he didn't leave. He kept standing there, looking at his feet, and then he said, "I was wondering if . . . you could give me your number. And we could go out. For coffee." I covered my face with my hands in delight, but he misread it as annoyance and said, "I know what you're thinking. The whole city wants a piece of you."

"Yeah," I said, "and everyone who wants one says, 'The whole city wants a piece of you,' before he asks for his slice."

"I know that too. I feel like an idiot."

"You shouldn't. I want you to call me."

"You do?"

"Yeah." He smiled, took my number, and left. The room spun and I wasn't even drunk.

●

On December 30, he picked me up in his car and we drove to a café in his neighborhood, Williamsburg. I'd never dated a guy with a car before. It wasn't a nice car, though. It was a beat-up sedan from the seventies, and it looked more appropriate for an old husband than a young novelist, but it made the date feel datey and I liked that.

When we got to the café he ordered a coffee and I ordered apple pie and tea. We sat down at a table by the window and suddenly I got nervous. And whenever I get nervous, I get mean.

"Are you bald under that cap?" I asked.

He grinned sheepishly and took it off. He was bald. Shaved bald, though. I didn't mind. Shaved bald is hotter than half bald. But instead of telling him that, I said, "You look like Nosferatu."

"What do you mean?" he said.

"Your nose and head are both so pointy. How old are you, anyway?"

"How old do you think I am?"

"You look like you could be anywhere from thirty to fifty."

"I'm thirty-two," he said. "Thanks a lot."

"You're welcome," I said.

"How old are you?"

"Twenty-two."

"What kind of name is Ariel?"

"Hebrew. It means *lion of God*. It's also one of the names for Jerusalem."

"That's right," he said. "I forgot. We learned that in cheder."

"Did you say cheder?" I asked tremulously.

"Yeah. My father made me go to an Orthodox Hebrew school till my bar mitzvah."

My underpants slid down to my ankles. "Where's your family from?" I asked.

"My mom's side is Russian, my dad's is Polish. *Lynn* used to be *Linowicz*. People always assume because of my blond hair and blue eyes that I'm not Jewish. I always tell them that—"

"Someone in your family got a little too friendly with the Cossacks."

He took on a grave expression and said, "That's *exactly* what I say. How did you know?"

"I guessed." I smiled proudly. It was only our first date and already I'd stolen his line. "So, where did you grow up?"

"Connecticut."

"Where'd you go to school?"

"Yale."

My vulva throbbed with glee. He was not only a Yid, but an Ivy Leaguer. I could already see the *New York Times* wedding announcement in my head.

●

When we got back to my house he stopped the car and said, "I had a great time with you tonight."

"Me too." We stared at each other for a second and I knew that if we were going to kiss, this would have been the moment to do it. But for some reason I didn't feel ready. For the first time in my life, the feeling of knowing I could kiss a guy was more exciting than the prospect of kissing itself. "Good night," I said, then got out of the car and walked up the stoop.

As I was opening the door, I heard him call, "Have a good New Year's!"

"Thanks," I said, stopping dead in my tracks.

"What are you doing for New Year's, anyway?"

I considered the possibility of lying to him, making him think I had plans, but something about Adam made me want to tell the truth. "Nothing," I said. "I have *no plans*. Not a single one. I'm a sex columnist and I don't have anything to do on the sexiest night of the year."

"I was invited to a party in Fort Greene. Why don't you come with me?"

"Really? I wouldn't want to pressure you . . ."

"I'll pick you up at eight."

●

I opted for the black minidress, a little bit of makeup, and a dab of Body Shop White Musk behind each ear. The doorbell rang at five to eight. He was dressed up, in pressed pants and a collared shirt. Some light brown chest hair was protruding from his collar. Usually chest hair grosses me out, but on him it didn't. I wanted to bury my face in it and smell his neck.

When we got to the party he introduced me to the host and hostess, and then we sat down in a corner of the living room and I asked if he knew how they met.

"No," he said.

"Isn't it funny how couples always seem to meet under the most innocuous circumstances?"

"I know what you mean. Maybe we should take a poll to find out exactly how all the couples here got together."

We spent the rest of the night going up to every duo at the party and asking for their first-encounter stories. We heard about people meeting on Greyhound buses, through mutual friends, self-defense classes, and infidelity. The guy and girl would overlap and argue about the details of their meeting, just like in the opening sequence of *When Harry Met Sally...*, and when they finished they would look at Adam and me and ask how we met. We'd color and exchange glances and then one of us would say, "Actually, we're not going out," and they would smile knowingly, like they knew it was only a matter of time.

At five to midnight everyone went down to the basement and stood around the TV for Dick Clark's countdown. As I watched the apple slowly slide down the pole, I tried as hard as I could to think of New Year's as a Hallmark plot and nothing more. On the stroke of midnight all the couples embraced and started to dance, but I kept staring at the TV. Then I heard Adam say, "Happy New Year, Ariel," and he leaned over and kissed me lightly on the cheek.

As soon as his lips touched my dimple, I could feel a blush rise from my neck to my chin to my forehead. I lowered my head quickly so he wouldn't see. I was ashamed that one little cheek kiss could make me turn so red. But then it hit me that if a guy could make me blush from putting his lips on my cheek, it was probably a very good thing.

At one-thirty, he drove me back to Carroll Gardens. When we were a few blocks from my place, I said, "Why don't you come in for some tea?"

He parked the car on Clinton and Third, and as we walked to my house, he put his arm around me. The streets were covered with snow, and every single yard on the block was lit up with plastic reindeer, Santa figures, and lights. One even had a sleigh with a microchip in it that played Christmas melodies twenty-four seven. I despise Yuletide about as much as I love New Year's, but tonight the neighborhood looked like a wonderland, glowing and magical and alive.

When we got into the apartment I put the water on the stove and Adam sat on the couch. "Do you like Bob Dylan?" I asked.

"He's OK, but I've never been a big fan. Most of the Dylan I've heard has been from his later years, when you can hardly understand what he's saying."

"Well, then, you are in for a treat." I put on *Another Side of Bob Dylan* and sat down next to him. "All I Really Want to Do" came on. When Bob said, "All I really want to do is baby be friends with you," I looked at Adam expectantly, but then the water boiled and I had to get up. I poured two cups of almond tea and brought them over. We sat side by side and sipped it as Bob whined on and reveling noises floated up from the street.

But as Bob made his way through "Black Crow Blues" and "Spanish Harlem Incident" and Adam and I small-talked without smooching, I started to fear he wasn't into me. Despite the fact that he'd asked me out, invited me to spend New Year's with him, and come back to my apartment. Maybe the reason we hadn't kissed in the car that night was because he didn't want to. Maybe he only liked me as a friend.

But then he put his hand on my hand—silently, without any particular flair or finesse. He just rested his right palm on the top of my left, threaded his fingers through mine, and looked at me. I kept staring ahead, as though I was utterly fascinated by the counter on the disk player. He stroked my fingers for a long time and then he moved his hand to my wrist, and then up to my neck and the side of my face. He ran his thumb against my cheek and over my ear. I turned to face him and he kissed me with such tenderness that I swear I could feel his soul entering my body.

I moved my mouth to the neck I had been thinking about since he first picked me up, and it smelled so sweet and clean I felt like staying there for a month. He put his hand on my breast and then he got on top of me and moved around, but just as we were getting frisky, the mattress slid off the frame onto the floor. I led him to the bed, and on the way I turned out the lights and put on the lanterns. We got under the covers and rubbed and murmured and moaned until the sky began to get light. By the time we kissed good night, it was four-thirty in the morning. I turned my back to him, he spooned me, and I fell asleep fast and smooth.

When I woke up, he was staring at me. "I can't wait to see you again," he said.

"You want to see me again?"

"Of course I do. Don't you?"

"Yes! I just wasn't sure if you—"

"Well, be sure."

Suddenly, all the months of fighting with Jake, closing my front door to guys I knew would never come back, and having quick, awful sex came back to me, and before I knew it I was crying. "I'm sorry," I said, wiping my face.

"Why?" he said.

"I don't want you to think I'm . . . unstable."

"I don't. It's been an emotional night for me too."

"It has?"

"Yeah." He held me close for a while and I cried into his chest. "Why don't you go back to sleep?" he said. "I'll go out and get us some coffee."

I put on my robe, walked him downstairs, then locked the door behind him. Half an hour later, he still hadn't come back. I started to worry that he would never return. Just like the rest. He'd fled my house without even having the decency to say good-bye.

The doorbell finally rang and I raced downstairs to get it. "What took so long?" I asked as we headed up the stairs.

"I'm sort of embarrassed to tell you."

"What is it?"

"To tell you the truth, it was so I could . . . um. This is hard to say."

"What?"

We sat down at the kitchen table. "So I could . . . use the bathroom. I know that might sound strange, but I just didn't quite feel comfortable, you know, here, with the bathroom right next to your bed. The door's so thin. You can hear everything. I wasn't going to tell you this, but I wanted to be upfront with you because I thought it was better to be honest about my hang-up than to lie about it. Do you think I'm weird?"

"Not at all," I answered, smiling my best encouraging smile. But I *did* think he was weird. Way weird. As relieved as I was that he'd come back, I hadn't been prepared to deal with such a mother of a neurosis so early on, especially not one with such heavy Freudian implications. But it had only been the second date, after all. It was understandable that he didn't feel completely comfortable around me. I tried to relate. "I know why you were embarrassed," I said. "Things are new. It takes time to feel totally at ease around someone. I hope one day you and I can cultivate an intimacy so deep and honest that we're not ashamed to fart in each other's presence."

He laughed and said, "Me too."

I took the coffee and bagels out of the bag and we started to eat. Halfway through my bagel I got so hot for him that I had to move from my seat to his lap. We kissed in a much more openmouthed and raunchy style than we had the night before. He stood up, guided me to the wall, and pressed himself against me. I closed my eyes and tilted my head back, and suddenly I realized I was hovering above the floor. My passion had caused me to levitate. It was surely a vision from God. But then I looked down and saw that he had lifted me up by my crotch, with his hand. So it wasn't a vision from God—but it was significant nonetheless. He had made me rise, literally and figuratively, and when a man makes you do something in both of those ways, you know that man's no joke.

I closed my eyes again and he kept thrusting against me and kissing me until his whole body shuddered and he let out a sigh. He lowered me down.

"Do you want a towel or something?" I asked.

"It's all right. I'll just let it dry."

"I can't believe you lifted me up like that. I didn't know novelists had such strong arms."

"Before I was a novelist, I was a fencer." My clit ballooned out and punched me in the face.

After breakfast he drove me to the F stop because I was supposed to go meet Sara for coffee. When we got to the station I said good-bye, leaned over to kiss him, and tried to get out of the car. But every time I put my hand on the door handle, he would pull me back and kiss me more. Finally I wrenched my lips away and got out. As I headed down the subway stairs, I heard him say, "Shane! Come back!"

"Who?" I said, turning around.

"You've never seen *Shane*?"

"No."

"It's the greatest Western of all time. There's this little boy in the movie who idolizes Shane, and at the end, when Shane rides off into the distance, the boy says, 'Shane! Come back!' in this sweet, vulnerable voice. I feel like I'm him."

I smiled and went into the station. He kept calling "Shane! Come back!" behind me until I got down to the platform and couldn't hear him anymore.

8

ON SUNDAY I wrote a column about the New Year's date. I dubbed Adam Novel Lover. It came to me as soon as I sat down at the computer, and once I saw it on the screen, I knew it was perfect. When I finished writing it, I took a deep breath and called him.

"Is it positive?" he asked.

"Of course it is."

"Is there anything in it that might upset me?"

"No. It's all good."

"OK."

"So you really don't mind?"

"No. I find it flattering."

After I E-mailed it in, I went to meet Adam at a Mexican restaurant in Williamsburg. Over dessert, he gave me a copy of his first novel, *Bedskirts*. "Don't be scared," he said. I wasn't sure what that meant, but when I got home that night and opened it, it became pretty clear.

I read it in the bathtub in one quick sitting. The book was weird. On many levels. It chronicled a litany of sexual interactions more grotesque and freakish than my own—unprotected, frequent sex with whores, men, and transsexuals. His stories made mine look like very silly putty. And I had no idea how much to believe.

183

In the morning he called me at work. "What'd you think?" he said.

"It was . . . beautifully written."

"And?"

"And what?"

"It frightened you, right?"

"Right."

"No one wants to date me after they read it."

"How much is true?"

"I don't want to say."

"Have you really had sex with whores, men, and transsexuals?"

"Most of the book is rooted in real-life events."

Suddenly I understood how Jake felt when he read "Smutlife." "Have you been—"

"Yeah. But the last one was a few years ago, and although there are only one or two incidents that might . . . I've been thinking I should go again. Just to be sure. What about you?"

"Same."

"Maybe it's something we should do, then. Before we . . . I mean, *if* we. You know."

I had a heavy feeling in my stomach for the rest of the afternoon. I didn't want to go through the agony of having to wait to hear if I would die. I felt like it would be God's cruel joke to make me sick right when I'd met someone I really liked, his punishment for my stupidity and wicked ways. But as scared as I was, I knew I had to do it. So I called up my gynecologist and made an appointment for that day after work.

As she stuck the needle in my arm to draw the blood, I turned my head to the side and prayed to God to make me OK. *I promise I will never mess up again*, I thought, *if you let me be all right this one time*. I tried to picture all the guys I'd had semiunsafe sex with, glowing and healthy and totally disease free, holding one another's hands and skipping joyously through plush green fields. But then the boys got so turned on by the hand holding that they started to make out. The make-out got more and more intense until finally they jumped in a pile and engaged in a huge, unprotected anal extravaganza, followed by a collective heroin party with shared dirty needles.

The doctor put some gauze on my puncture and bent my forearm back to stop the bleeding. "I should know within two days," she said. "Call me Thursday." She put the vial in a little Ziploc bag and then she said, "The lab's right around the corner.

Would you mind walking your blood over yourself? It'll speed things along."

I took it, walked to the lab, and handed my fate to the technician. She filled out some information on a form, then said I could go. On my way out the door she shouted, "Good luck!"

●

The day "Novel Lover" came out, the doctor left a message on my machine saying, "I just wanted you to know everything's fine." I felt like I'd just squeezed out a five-thousand-pound shit.

I called Adam at home right away. "I found out I'm negative!"

"I knew you would be," he said. "I got tested too. Yesterday. I'm OK."

"Why didn't you tell me?"

"I wanted to wait to tell you until you heard. You were brave to do it."

"So were you."

"What do you want to do tonight?"

"Celebrate."

●

At ten o'clock, after he finished teaching (he taught writing twice a week at a community college), he came to my place. We got in bed and rolled around and I got so excited I slithered down. I had stuck it in my mouth before, for a few seconds—but this time I wanted to go whole hog. Right as I was eye to eye with the hole of his head, I remembered the scene in his book where his protagonist got his dick sucked by a Lower East Side whore and I had to back away and take a deep breath. He was negative, and that was all that mattered. I slowly inched closer, traced my finger over the line where his foreskin had once been, and said to myself, *I am going to love this penis. Become its buddy. Build some serious cockraderie.*

Then I opened my mouth and said, "Ah." He stroked my hair while I did it. Usually when guys stroke my hair while I'm giving head it makes me want to stop, because it feels so disingenuous. I know they're not feeling tender and it makes me angry that they're pretending to. Yet there was something about the way he did it that made me feel like he was truly appreciative, and that made me like it even more. The whole act didn't take very long, maybe twelve minutes or so. His semen tasted better than any I'd swallowed before. Maybe there were advantages to dating a vegetarian.

I lay beside him and rested my head on his shoulder. "Did you enjoy that?" he said.

"Yes," I said, and it wasn't a lie. We fell asleep in each other's arms, but the next morning we hit a hurdle that made our HIV tests look like a piece of cake.

RUN CATCH KISS
True Confessions of a Single Girl
ARIEL STEINER
Stench of a Woman

The morning after our first date, Novel Lover left my house to take a shit in a diner because he was too ashamed to do it in front of me. I told him not to be embarrassed about his bodily functions and he said he'd try. Over the last few weeks, he's gotten less bashful. He's able to do it in my bathroom, as long as I play music while he's in there and leave a pack of matches on the toilet so he can eradicate the gas with the flame as soon as he finishes.

But recently I started having some trouble of my own. Whenever Novel Lover sleeps over, we go to a café by my apartment for breakfast in the morning. I order oatmeal with milk and he orders a bagel with butter, and then he drives me to the subway station where I leave for work. On the ride the other day, I felt the milk from my oatmeal start to churn in my stomach. I winced and grimaced and crossed my legs, but it was to no avail. I let a silent one rip, I mean, really rip right out with vigor and abandon.

I was terrified that Novel Lover would smell it, so I pushed my window button calmly and quietly, opening it all the way, then assumed a casual expression and looked out onto the street. After a few seconds, Novel Lover reached over to *his* window button and opened every single window in the car. Then he pushed the lighter into the dashboard, waited for it to warm up, and waved it around my pelvis like a magic wand.

"What are you doing?" I asked.

"I don't have any matches, so I'm using the lighter."

"But a lighter doesn't produce flame. The principle doesn't hold!"

"This is a dire situation. It calls for desperate measures." He waved it between my legs and all around the front of the car. There was some ash embedded in it that burned and choked me as he waved, but I felt the punishment was worth it.

When we got to the subway station, I got out of the car

and waved good-bye. As I walked down the stairs, though, my smile faded away. Truth be told, the entire episode made me kind of tense. I felt nasty and gross and foul for my boyfriend, and it really bummed me out.

That night we had plans to go see *Donnie Brasco*. I put on a hot-pink miniskirt, a ribbed tee, and black boots, hoping the outfit would make him forget about the gas crisis. It seemed to work. He wolf-whistled when I opened the door. We kissed in the foyer and I felt his interest against my leg.

It was hard to focus on the plot of the movie. Something about that foyer kiss and watching Johnny Depp on-screen for two hours made me kind of itchy. We drove back to my house after the flick, and pretty soon we were tearing each other's clothes off. I scooted down and bathed him with affection.

When it was over, I lay next to him and gave him a look as hard and sweet as his cock. His eyes were drooping, but that didn't bother me. I buried my head in his neck and he put his arm around me. All was quiet and right until suddenly and without any warning, I let out another silent one.

I tried to make like nothing had happened. I just buried my head deeper in his neck. But when you do it under the covers, there's no cloaking the odor. It just sits there, brewing, expanding, getting fatter and meaner till the stench is so potent it starts to make you quake. Novel Lover's eyes opened slowly, and then he turned over onto his side, subtly easing his nose in the opposite direction.

"I think our sex life is really good," I said. "I feel like we have something really special. I mean, I could live out some of my most secret fantasies with you." I put my hand on his Member Only. It grew firm and proud. "Oh, Novel Lover, you have such a beautiful, healthy cock."

Right when I said "cock," I let another one rip. This one wasn't silent. He ran to the bathroom and came back with the matchbook. He lifted the covers, lit a match, and waved it around underneath. It sparked. This was mortifying. He blew out the match and lay back down next to me.

"Anyway," I said, "your cock is large and very nice. I think about it a lot during the day and"—I leaned in and whispered in his ear—"I get very sweaty."

I took it in my hand and it firmed up once again. Novel Lover put his arm around my neck and I slid my tongue in his mouth. He kissed back passionately. I trumpeted. He put his pillow over his face, reached for the matchbook, and lit another one. As he swirled it around under the covers, I saw that he was trying very hard not to laugh. After a while he couldn't help it anymore. He just started chortling, right in my face, waving his hand back and forth in front of his nose, groaning and wincing. My boyfriend was laughing in my face because I smelt like ass. It was so humiliating.

I knew I should have been able to laugh right along with him, but somehow I just couldn't. It had been easy telling Novel Lover he should feel comfortable cutting the cheese in front of me, but it was another thing entirely for me to feel comfortable doing it in front of him. I realized that my wish for a shame-free relationship was really a one-way street. I wanted Novel Lover to think of me as a chick with mystique, as his own personal Parker Posey—cute, clever, and hot. But I'd suddenly turned from a pert Posey into a putrid Posey. A stench of a woman.

I looked over at him dolefully. "Don't be so glum," he said. "It's not a big deal. It's funny. Really." He hugged me. But I didn't feel much better.

Suddenly he got out of bed, raced into the bathroom, and shut the door. I heard him run the tap water. "Could you please put on some music!" he yelled.

I didn't. I just lay there, hands crossed behind my head, waiting, listening. When I heard a flush, I opened the door a crack and threw in the matches.

———————————

Once Ariel Steiner gave us free porn. Now she details for her readers the ins and outs of her gastrointestinal problems ("Stench of a Woman," 1/15). What has become of my favorite downtown slut? I'm happy you've found a guy you like, Ariel, but please, give us the skinny puppy on what you and Novel Lover do horizontally. Sorry to say it, but the farting stuff just doesn't do it for me the way your old columns used to.

TONY VALENTI, *Astoria*

●

That was the last letter I got for a month. I tried as hard as I could to make my life of stability interesting, but as my column began to metamorphose from a kiss-and-tell-a-thon into a diary of monogamy, my readers stopped responding. After "Stench of a Woman," there was "Oil Me" (about a trip Adam and I took to a Long Island spa), "Holy Matrimony!" (about a wedding we went to in the Berkshires), and "Foul Play" (about a little spat we had after watching a basketball game on TV). I told myself I was doing the city a service by chronicling a real, adult relationship. Surely some of my fans were interested in the trials and tribulations of modern couplehood, but each time I turned to "The Mail," there were never any letters about me. Turner stopped sending complimentary E-mails, Sara nicknamed me June Cleaver, and my parents started calling every Wednesday night to *kvell*.

I tried to make myself believe the downcurve in reader response wasn't that important in light of the fact that I'd finally met my Perfect Guy. But right around Valentine's Day, Adam and I ran into an issue that made me wonder whether we were meant to be together after all. We had decided not to make love until we were both completely ready, because we both thought waiting, which he called "circling the airport," would make it more meaningful. When we first discussed it, it had sounded like a good idea, but after five weeks of doing everything else, I had started to get antsy.

So one night I woke him up, handed him a condom, and asked if he wanted to. He put it on and got on top of me. It started out OK, but then he got faster really quickly and I could feel my body just go into nothing mode. The I'm-not-feeling-anything-and-you-better-notice-or-else-I'll-hate-you mode. He just kept going, though, calmly and placidly, and it only made me shut off more. Finally I said, "I think we should stop."

"Are you OK?" he said, lying beside me.

"Yeah," I said. "It's just that I thought it would be perfect—

because we waited so long. And when it wasn't, and I didn't like it, and you couldn't tell, I started to resent you."

"How could I notice if you didn't say anything?"

"I don't know. But I didn't want to have to speak. I wanted you to be so attuned to me that you could tell it wasn't doing anything for me." I buried my face in the pillow. I'd completely ruined our high romantic expectations. We'd never be able to have sex again. We'd try to work on getting our passion back, but to no avail. He'd finally break up with me and start going out with a girl who loved sex any time of day, any position, with any guy.

"It's OK," he said, rubbing my back. "Not everything's perfect the first go-around. We can think of this as . . . our first hump." I giggled.

When I woke up the next morning, I looked at him sleeping and thought about his first-hump joke, and suddenly I knew that I loved him. It just hit me all at once, and so I immediately decided to tell him. I was certain that if I was feeling it, he had to be too.

As he was parking the car in front of The Fall, I inhaled and said, "There's something I want to say."

"What is it?" he said, turning off the engine.

"I . . . love you."

He smiled, squeezed my hand, and said, "Thank you."

I wanted to smash my head through the windshield. Everything was completely ruined. I'd beaten him to that Line of Seriousness—which meant I'd be certain to drive him away. Everyone knows that whoever reaches the Line of Seriousness first always winds up getting dumped in the end. Because when you start out with a gap in affection, the gap just grows and grows, until finally it's unbearable for the less-feeling one to stand his lack of feeling any longer. Eventually he's forced to end it, and the more-feeling one is forced to flee the state.

So I said, "Jesus! You didn't say it back! I thought you were going to say it back! Now I wish I hadn't said it!"

"I'm glad you did," he said. "It's good that you said it. It makes me happy."

"I'm glad you're happy," I said. "But I was hoping you loved me. I'm never going to say it again."

"Why not?"

"Because when a woman is clever and withholding, it makes her man love her even more."

"I don't want you to be clever and withholding. I don't want you to play tricks."

"But playing tricks is the only way to hold on to someone you . . . like."

"That's not true. All the people I know who act according to rules instead of gut just wind up deceiving themselves and getting more miserable than they were at the start. I care about you deeply. You know that. It's just that those words are very loaded for me."

"Why?"

"My mother was incredibly smothering, so I always experience a woman's love for me as pressure. It took me a long time to be able to say 'I love you' to Laura." Laura was his girlfriend for two years at Yale.

I told him I understood. I told him there *wasn't* any pressure. And then I told myself I was taking the word issue too seriously anyway. Because *I love you* never means *I love you* anyway. Usually, it means, *I want to hear that you love me*. It's a cue and nothing more. Sometimes it means, *The sex we're having right now is feeling incredibly animalistic and nonemotional and I'd like for it to feel warm and romantic instead*. And sometimes it just means, *I really want to get off the phone*.

But as hard as I tried to convince myself that I didn't care if he said it back, it killed me. If he couldn't say it now, when would he? How long would I have to wait? A year? Five years? Forever? I had never imagined my Perfect Guy as someone with intimacy issues. I had just taken it for granted that once I fell in love with him, he'd fall in love right back and lavish me with affection, no holds barred.

As soon as I got to work, I dialed Sara at her desk. "I was just going to call you," she said. "I have to tell you something about Rick." Rick was this former navy officer she'd been seeing. They'd met at a party a week and a half before.

"What is it?" I said.

"Last night I was sleeping and I woke up because I thought I heard Rick say, 'I love you.' I pretended to be asleep, but in the morning I confronted him. 'Did you say something to me last night,' I said, 'or was I dreaming?' 'I told you I loved you,' he said, 'but I didn't want to say it out loud because I was afraid it might frighten you.' *Can you believe it?* We've only been going out eleven days and he's already saying he loves me. Isn't he amazing?"

"He sure is," I said. But smoke was coming out of my cartoon ears. It wasn't fair that she could get a guy to say it so quickly and I couldn't. It just wasn't just.

"How long did it take Adam to start saying it to you?" she asked.

"Um, actually, he doesn't."

"What?"

"I said it this morning and he said he wasn't ready to say it back."

"Really?" she said. "I felt *sure* you two were saying it to each other. I was convinced it was a phrase you exchanged. Wow. I see you guys in a totally new light now."

"It's not what you think!" I shouted. "It doesn't really bother me *that* much! It's a delicate sentence! It's hard for some people! A truly good relationship is good because of what you feel inside, not what you call that feeling. Anyone who attaches too much importance to those words has incredibly warped priorities. Don't you get it? I mean, don't you see that?"

"Um, sure," she said. "Of course."

When I got off the phone, I took out a notepad, put it on my lap, and wrote a column about the love issue. I called it "The Line of Seriousness." But when I read it over and envisioned him seeing it in the paper, I got queasy. I wasn't sure I wanted him to know just how upset I was about his slowtoexpressloveia. I was afraid it might make the situation even worse. But my sentiments were real, and I didn't want to tone them down for his benefit, so I E-mailed the column to Turner and hoped everything would work out.

It didn't. The day the column came out, Adam called me at work. "Is that what you really feel?" he said.

"What do you mean?"

"Does it really upset you that much that I can't say it?"

"No!" I shouted. "It doesn't upset me that much! I mean, sure, it bothered me *a smidgen,* but what I was going for in that piece . . . I mean, what I was aiming at was to *exaggerate* my fear. You know, for *comic effect.* To make it out that I was like totally bummed about you not saying it. I'm not *really* that bummed. Not at all."

"Good," he said.

Over the next couple weeks I tried to think of other things to write about besides my insecurity, but that was the only aspect of my life that interested me. My next column, "Green Girl," was about the rampant jealousy I felt whenever Adam and I went to a party and he talked to another woman. Then there was "Breathing Room," about the time I asked him to move in with me and he said he was nowhere near ready, and "The Phantom Woman," about my fear that he would leave me for a woman who had all the confidence I lacked.

The only bonus to my incessant insecurity-chronicling was that it finally created some reader response. Turner forwarded me personal letters like "Why are you sticking with Novel Lover, Ariel? He doesn't seem to appreciate you at all" and "If you want a guy who treats you right, you can always call me." And in "The Mail" even my diehard detractors began to take pity on me:

> Ariel Steiner could get any guy in the city. Why she's sticking with such a commitmentphobic, neurotic weirdo like Novel Lover is a mystery to me.
>
> FRED SADOWSKY, *West Village*

> At first, I thought Ariel Steiner had finally met her match. But now I've changed my mind. Novel Lover is a screwup, Ariel! He's never going to give you the love you're looking for until he works out his issues with his mother. This is a common problem with Jewish men. Trust me, I know. Tell Novel Lover to get a good therapist and then come back to you.
>
> HOWARD KESSEL, *Upper East Side*

As exciting as it was to be getting letters again, they only made the Adam situation even worse. Each Wednesday when a new reader weighed in on our relationship, Adam would call me at work and ask anxiously, "Do you think that guy's right? Do you feel like I'm not giving you enough love?"

"Well, maybe you could give me just one percent more," I'd say, and then he'd let out a long sigh and hang up quickly.

We were eating dinner at a Lebanese place on Atlantic Avenue the night "The Phantom Woman" came out when he said, "There's something I want to talk to you about."

"What?"

"Lately I've been feeling like you're playing me too close. Men need to be able to chase in order to feel good about themselves, and I haven't been able to chase you lately. I want you to try to wait for me to come to you. Like in *Field of Dreams*. 'If you build it, they will come.' I *will* come. I just need to feel like coming to you is a choice that I'm making. Like I'm the one soliciting you, instead of you always soliciting me. I don't think I should sleep over tonight."

"Why not?"

"Because I have to wake up in my own bed to do good work on my novel."

This was a strange tune. He'd never had a problem sleeping at my place before. "OK," I said. "Then I'll sleep at yours."

"I don't think that's such a good idea either. I want my apartment to be my own space, my cave."

"Cave? *Have you been reading John Gray?*"

"I was leafing through the book the other day at the supermarket, and it's not all crap. There are some very wise things in there. Men need a place they can call their own."

"All right," I sighed. "But what about tomorrow? Will you sleep over tomorrow night?"

And then he uttered the six words that every woman loathes to hear: "Let's just play it by ear."

"Why are you feeling like this?" I said.

"I don't know."

But *I* did. Although he never said it flat out, I knew the cause of his claustrophobia: my column. It was slowly driving him away. He wouldn't have wanted to drift if I hadn't been hitting him over the head with the fact that I was getting afraid. There was no gap between what I felt and what he knew I felt. I had been letting him know on a weekly basis, and in no uncertain terms, that he had all the power, and when a guy knows he has all the power, he flees. I couldn't let Adam flee. He was the love of my life. He just didn't know I was the love of *his*. I had to find a way to even the scales.

I got the idea how to do it after we saw the Sam Shepard one-acts at the Public. Sam Shepard was my second-biggest matinee idol after Nick Fenster. My lust for him first sprouted when I saw *Baby Boom* at age thirteen. As soon as Diane Keaton awoke in Shepard's veterinary office and his creased brow and tender eyes appeared on that screen, I knew it wouldn't be long before I got my first period.

Sophomore year at Brown, I was assigned *Fool for Love and Other Plays* for a playwriting class. I was sitting on my bed reading *Curse of the Starving Class* one night when I found myself flipping back at the cover to stare at his photo. His chin was resting in his hand, and it looked like he was thinking, *You're a very naughty girl.* I *was* a naughty girl. I stuck one hand down my pants and held the book with the other, and imagined the two of us going at it on his veterinary examining table, with various farm animals—and a nude and eager Diane Keaton—periodically wandering in to join in our country romp.

So when I read that three of Shepard's plays were running on a bill at the Public, I got a pair of tickets for Adam and me. The first two were decent but didn't blow either of us away. At intermission, we went out into the lobby, and I was leaning against a pillar, absentmindedly stroking his dome, when I suddenly saw him point straight ahead and exclaim, "There's Shepard!" I followed his finger. Lo and behold, it was no lie. Sam Shepard himself was heading for the door.

"I wonder if he's leaving," Adam said.

"He's probably just going for a smoke. Shepard smokes," I sighed.

I was right. Through the glass, we watched him light up. He stood just to the left of the revolving door, leaning against the wall of the Public, tall and intense, smoke curling out of his mouth.

"Should we follow him?" Adam asked.

"I don't know," I said.

"I can't talk to him. What would I say?"

"I don't know, but *I'm* going to go outside."

"Do you want me to come with you?"

The truth was no. Adam might have been the love of my life, but I was on my way to flirt with a living icon. I didn't want my boyfriend coming along for the ride.

"It's up to you," I said, and went through the revolving door. It was a cold night and I was wearing a thin G.I. Joe T-shirt, so my nipples perked up immediately. I turned to Shepard so he could see how hard they were, then crossed over to his left so I would be out of Adam's view. I wanted Adam to watch Shepard smiling at me and not be able to see what I was doing that was making him smile.

"Hi," I said.

"Hi," said Shepard.

"So, what do you think?"

"About what?" He dragged in on a Marlboro while keeping his noncigarette hand tucked in his armpit. Somehow I always knew he'd be a Marlboro man. His fingers held the cigarette so hard the filter was flattened between them. I noticed that he had a beautiful healthy head of hair, soft and brown. His cheeks were sunken and his front teeth were crooked. I was juicing hard.

"What do you think about the plays?" I asked.

"What do *you* think?"

"Um, I liked the second one better than the first."

"Why?"

Christ, this wasn't any fun. I didn't want to critique the evening. I wanted to tell him about my veterinary fantasy. I wanted to ask him what it was like touring with the Rolling Thunder Revue and tell him that "Brownsville Girl" was one of my all-time favorite songs. I wanted to tell him that a few years before I'd seen this movie on TV starring him and that French twat Julie Delpy, where they have a torrid affair without knowing they're father and daughter, and that I'd masturbated to his love scenes, imagining *I* was his long-lost daughter lover.

"Why?" I repeated. "Because the first one was a little more static, more one-level, I guess." There was another pause. He ashed. "Do you live in the city?" I asked.

"No."

"Where do you live?"

"In the Midwest." I could tell he was protecting his anonymity. He knew it was important not to reveal his state of residency because I could be a psycho with a secret plan to stalk him, Jessica Lange, and their kids in a bizarre *Cape Fear* replay.

The revolving door turned. Adam came through, holding a cup of coffee in his hand. "This is my boyfriend," I said. I was acutely aware of the way the word "boyfriend" sounded in my mouth.

"Thank you for your plays," said Adam.

Uch. I knew I wasn't exactly spitting out the witty ones myself, but that kind of banal compliment struck me as the last thing a tough ex-cowboy like Shepard would want to hear. Adam made some boring comments about the one-acts and then there was a lull. I had to fill that lull! If Shepard got tired of us, he'd go back inside and my only interaction with a major seventies rebel and number four on my list of sexiest men alive, right after Johnny Depp, Fred Ward, and Ed Harris, would end on a disappointing note. I had to think on my feet.

"Do you have a tattoo?" I asked.

"Yes."

"Where?"

He didn't answer. He just looked at me quizzically, a little embarrassed. I knew I'd overstepped my boundaries. Gotten too personal. I was drowning standing up.

Adam jumped in to save me. "She wants to know because I told her this story about how once I was in Elaine's and I saw you, and I called this friend of mine who loves your work and said, 'Sam Shepard's here!' and while I was on the phone with him I noticed that you had this tattoo on your left hand that my friend has too—a crescent moon. So I said, 'And you won't believe it! He has the same tattoo on your hand that you do!' And my friend said, 'Why do you think I have it, man?' "

We both looked eagerly at Shepard for his reaction shot. He smiled halfheartedly and flicked what remained of the cigarette out into the snow. He flicked that butt like he'd been flicking butts since before he could walk.

"Well, nice talking to you," he said, keeping his left hand tucked in his armpit, and revolved through the door.

Adam and I looked at each other. "I think we did all right," he said. "I think he liked the tattoo story."

"I think he thought it was stupid. Why'd you come outside?"

"Well, I was in there imagining you talking to him and I just thought, *I can't pass up an opportunity like this,* so I came out. I know you probably wanted to be alone with him. I'm sorry."

"I'm sure."

The third one-act, *Action,* was kick-ass great. Shepard like it ought to be. Violent, alive, and intense. Adam was into it too because both the actors in it had shaved bald heads. On our way out we saw Shepard in the lobby. He smiled and said, "What did you think?"

"That was great!" I yelled.

"That was something else," said Adam.

"Well, thanks for coming," Shepard drawled lowly.

That night in bed, Adam and I had the best sex we'd had since we'd gotten together. We did it missionary, with my hand on my clit, and then he flipped me over and tweaked me till I came. I thought about Shepard the whole time through so my orgasm was long and intense.

The next morning, after Adam left, I sat down to write my column. The part about meeting Shepard was easy, but when I got to the part where Adam and I were in bed, I didn't know what to do. Maybe he'd get upset if he knew I'd been thinking about Shepard. Maybe it was best not to include that part. But then it struck me that including it might be a wiser move than I knew. Adam would get totally jealous when he read it! He'd despise Shepard and at the same time, realize how much he loved me!

As Novel Lover ran the back of his hand across my nipples, I imagined that they were the butts of two Marlboros being pinched between Shepard's rough, callused fingers. As we rolled around under the covers, I fantasized that after I came through the revolving door, Shepard took one look at me, lifted me up, carried me to the wall, pulled down his pants, then drove his Midwestern member into me hard and fast, right there on Lafayette Street. Novel Lover flipped me onto my stomach and ground my beef, and Shepard in my mind flipped me down onto the snow. Novel Lover's train came a-running, and Shepard's tooth of crime came prancing into the blue bitch of my cowboy mouth. I let out a yelp, Novel Lover moaned, and I squeezed him out, soft and easy.

●

On Monday night, Turner sent me an E-mail saying, "Good column, kid," and Corinne left me a message saying she thought it was my best in weeks. Maybe what was good for my relationship was just as good for my career.

The afternoon it came out, Adam called me at work. "Hey," I said coolly.

"I just wanted to say, *great* column this week."

He was trying to be clever, I could tell. He didn't want to let on that I'd made him jealous. Two could play this game as well as one.

"Thanks," I said.

"You captured Shepard really well."

"I tried."

"And that part at the end where you fantasize about him when you're in bed with me . . ."

"What about it?"

"Hilarious. Absolutely hilarious."

"Hilarious?"

"Oh my God, it cracked me up. I read it over lunch and nearly spit out my food, it was so funny."

"You thought it was *funny*?"

"Wasn't that what you were going for?"

"I guess so, but—"

"I'm telling you, Ariel, you're a brilliant comic writer. You're like the nineties Elaine May."

"I'm glad you thought it was funny," I said slowly, "but it was also *true*."

"I know! That's what made it so funny."

"So it doesn't bother you that I—"

"Not at all! As a matter of fact, *I* was thinking about someone else that night too."

"You were?"

"Yeah," he murmured.

"Who were you thinking of?"

"Jessica Lange."

I banged the receiver hard against my skull, hoping I'd get a blood clot and die. Not only had my plan completely backfired, but now I would have to wonder whether Adam was thinking about Jessica every time we did it. I couldn't believe he was so forgiving. I couldn't believe it was so hard to get a rise out of him. I had to up the ante.

The next day I got a message from Jason Levin, the monogamy-opposed ISO man. "I've been union organizing in Chicago for the past few years," he said, "but I just got a teaching job in the South Bronx and I moved to Park Slope a few weeks ago. I've been reading your column and enjoying it immensely. I was hoping we could get together for a drink, tonight maybe, if you're free." I called him back immediately and we made plans to meet at a Korean bar on First Avenue.

"You look good," he said when he walked in.

"Thanks," I said. "So do you." That was a lie. He seemed shorter than I remembered, and haggard, and he had a slightly desperate, frenzied gaze in his eyes.

"You seem more mature. More grown-up."

"Monogamy will do that to a girl."

"Who is this Novel Lover, anyway?"

"His name's Adam. He's a writer. What about you? Have you been seeing anyone lately?"

"My girlfriend broke up with me two months ago. We were together for a year and a half." So that explained the desperate gaze. Men who aren't used to being single always look shell-shocked when they first get back on the saddle.

"I'm sorry," I said.

"Yeah. How long have you and Adam been together?"

"A few months."

"And you're happy?"

"Oh my God, yes! I'm totally in love with him. He really knows how to treat a woman right. He respects me. He's such a refreshing change of pace from all the jerks I dated in the past."

"What's that supposed to mean?"

"You said you were against monogamy when the truth was you couldn't fall in love with *me*. If you knew that, you should have dumped me after a week, instead of duping me into thinking we had something."

"I'm sorry," he said. "I didn't mean to hurt you. I was just really confused. I didn't know what I was doing." He leaned in close. "You have such pretty eyes, Ariel. I never noticed them before."

"There were a lot of things you didn't notice about me," I said.

"I know," he said. "So you're really in love with this guy, huh?"

"Yeah. Totally. Why do you ask?"

"Just wondering."

For the next hour and a half we just made small talk, and although it was pleasant enough, it made me realize Jason wasn't nearly the genius I'd made him out to be. He was bright and articulate and he still had this shy, charismatic charm, but he didn't seem as brave or brilliant as he used to. He just seemed like a moderately intelligent, moderately attractive single guy.

When we finished our drinks he walked me to Second Avenue so I could hail a downtown cab. "I had a good time with you," he said. "We should hang out again."

"Let's do that," I said. We kissed good-bye on the cheek and I went home.

As soon as I got to the apartment, I typed a column about our meeting. Except this was the ending:

> We stood at the corner of Second and Seventh, facing each other. Cab after cab sped by, but I made no effort to hail one. The drink had made me see Mason differently. I didn't worship him the way I used to. I just liked him. He was much more appealing off his pedestal than on. I wondered how it would feel to be with him again—except, on equal footing this time, even turf.
>
> "It was good to see you, Ariel," he said, leaning toward me and pecking me on the cheek.
>
> "You too," I said. I started to turn to get a taxi, but then he put his hand on my shoulder, turned me around, and kissed me on the lips. For the first few seconds I kept my mouth shut, but then he pulled me closer and I opened wide and smooched him tongue and full and loud. It was so good it made my head spin. So good it made me want to do more. But I couldn't. Novel was my Lover, and I knew better than to blow it all on a lay I would regret as soon as it was over. The kiss was just big enough for me to get to sleep without 'sturbing and just small enough for it not to count as an infidelity. "I think I should go home," I finally said. Mason nodded. As I got in the cab, I debated whether to tell Novel Lover. My first instinct was not to, but as you can see, I changed my mind.

As soon as I finished, I stuck the column in an E-mail to Turner, and as I clicked on *send* I got a huge adrenaline rush that made me dizzy and giddy at once. The rest of the week I was sweaty and constipated. The Corposhit would come out of her office and ask me to do copying and have to repeat it a few times before I could hear what she was saying. At lunch, Sara would go on about Rick and I would nod faintly, pretending to listen.

On Wednesday, Sara and I went to the Met Life building with the papers. The illo was me smooching a guy with a huge boner and a bubble above my head of Novel Lover with question marks floating all around him.

"Is it true?" said Sara when she finished reading.

"What do you think?" I said.

"I think it's not."

"You're right."

"Why'd you do this?" I told her about my balance-of-affection plan. She shook her head from side to side gravely and said, "What if he dumps you?"

"He's not going to dump me over a kiss."

"But even if he does stay with you, and gets more affectionate, you'll know the only reason was because of a lie. Where's the victory in that?"

I spent the rest of the afternoon trying not to think about what she had said and checking my machine to see if Adam had left a message. But the only one I got was from Jason: "Liked your column, Ariel. It came as a bit of a shock to find out what had transpired, but I have to admit, I was flattered by your distortion. Call me sometime."

That night Adam and I had plans to meet at Souen, this vegetarian restaurant on Thirteenth Street, after his class. When I walked in he looked a little pale, but then again, he always looked a little pale. I kissed him on the cheek and sat opposite him. "I've been doing a lot of thinking," he said.

"About what?" I asked, with some serious vibrato.

"I think you know."

"Yeah. I guess I do know."

"There's something I've been meaning to tell you for a while now, and reading your column made me decide to tell you."

This was a strange tune. "What is it?"

"I kissed someone else too."

"*What?*"

"It was about two weeks after you and I started seeing each other. Remember that night I said I wanted to stay home and watch that Knicks game?"

"Yeah."

"Well, I didn't. I got together with Laura for dinner, and she invited me to her place. We wound up talking about old times and then we started kissing. It got pretty hot and she asked me to spend the night, but I realized it wasn't right, and then I left. Are you mad?"

Mad most certainly was not the word for what I was feeling. *Suicidal* was far more accurate. I wanted to pick up a butter knife and lob it into my flailing heart until my aortic valve dangled on the table. He'd totally nailed me. I couldn't tell him how hurt I really was, because on paper, we were even-Steven. And I couldn't tell him my kiss had been a lie, because then I'd have to explain my secret plan.

"I . . . I guess I'm a *little* mad," I said carefully.

"You're allowed to be," he said, patting my hand.

"Are *you* mad at *me*?" I asked hopefully.

"No. Mostly, I'm just incredibly relieved. It's comforting to know we've both made mistakes. God, I'm hungry." He opened his menu. "Getting this stuff out has really worked up my appetite. I'm gonna start with some miso, then maybe go for the curry rice noodles. What do you want?"

I wanted to crawl on the floor and curl up into a fetal position. This was a travesty beyond belief—and there was only one remedy. I had to outcheat him. Concoct an infidelity so insidious that there was no chance he'd have done the same thing himself. I could write that I did two men at once. But then he'd *definitely* dump me. There was this successful young novelist Adam was always telling me he despised—I could write that I fucked him. Except Adam knew the guy well enough that he might confront him and find out it wasn't true. My infidelity needed to be as believable as it was chilling. I had to drive Adam to the brink of insanity. It was the only way I could make him love me back.

9

ON FRIDAY, Sara invited me to a party at Rick's apartment. Before Rick was a naval officer, he was a Seattle rocker, so he was subletting a huge loft on Leonard Street from a famous indie singer friend. I went over around ten. The lighting was dim, Beck was blasting from the stereo, and everywhere I looked there were boys. Languid boys with soft, golden hair, in T-shirts emblazoned with vacuum-cleaning and auto-body-repair logos, in gas-station-attendant outfits with names like *Leroy* sewn on the lapels, boys fellating Rolling Rocks in less-than-innocent ways, slender boys, music boys, tempting boys.

I scanned the room for Sara and Rick but didn't spot either of them, so I went into the kitchen to get something to drink. As I was removing a beer from the refrigerator, this short cutie in an Epcot Center T-shirt came up to me with an opener. "Let me help you with that," he said. I angled the bottle toward him and he popped it open. "Thanks," I said, leaning against the refrigerator door.

"Are you a friend of Rick's?" he asked.

"I'm friends with his girlfriend, Sara. What about you?"

"I don't know anyone here. A buddy of mine invited me but he hasn't shown up yet. I like your T-shirt." It was tight and white and it said *Diva* in red letters across the chest.

"Thanks."

"I like your eyes, too. I noticed them as soon as you came in the door. You're very beautiful."

Whoa. "You're beautiful" was a phrase Adam rarely used with me. When I got dressed up he would say I looked pretty, and sometimes he would say, "I like that outfit," but he never looked at me at random moments and told me he liked what he saw. I always tried to tell myself it didn't bother me, but now that I was hearing the words come out of someone else's mouth, it did. When a random schmo makes you feel better about yourself than your own boyfriend, it kind of means there's a problem.

"If you don't mind my asking," said Epcot, narrowing his eyes, "do you have a boyfriend?"

His gaze was steady, unflinching. I wasn't sure what to say. One part of me wanted to lie, but the other part knew I'd never be able to pull it off. Besides, maybe he'd be more interested in me if he knew I was taken.

"Yes," I said. "As a matter of fact, I do."

"Have you been with him a long time?"

"Three months. But it's been a very intense three months."

"I know what you mean. I've had two-month relationships that were more intense than yearlong ones."

"I didn't mean intense in a good way," I said slowly. "We're actually having some problems."

"Like what?"

"I don't feel like he loves me, I get insane with jealousy each time he talks to another woman, and I'm constantly terrified that he's going to dump me."

"That sounds like something I read in the *City Week*. Have you ever read that paper?"

"Um. Once or twice."

"Well, this girl in the *Week* writes this column about her boyfriend, and it's obvious from reading it that they're going to break up any day now. The guy sounds like he's completely afraid of commitment and probably shouldn't be involved with anyone, and she's just way too insecure for it to work."

"Gee."

"But last week she kissed this other guy, this ex of hers, and I'm kind of curious to see what her boyfriend does about it. I can totally relate to what she's going through."

"You can?"

A huge bearded guy in a Massive Attack T-shirt came in the kitchen and headed for the refrigerator. I moved across to the sink and stood next to Epcot. My arm hairs touched his.

"Yeah," he said. "I was in this relationship a couple years ago with this girl who was kind of cold to me. She had just gotten out of something else and she was protective over her space, but

I wanted to spend all my time with her and I felt like if she really loved me, she wouldn't be so distant. Did you see *Paris, Texas*?"

I started to say, "Shepard wrote it," but bit my tongue after the "Sh" to keep my cover, and nodded instead.

"Well, you know that monologue where Harry Dean Stanton talks about tying a cowbell to his wife's ankle so if she ever tried to get away from him, he would hear her leaving?"

"I love that monologue!"

"That's how I felt about my ex-girlfriend."

"I know just what you mean, man," said Massive Attack, raising his bottle and taking a swig, and then skulked out.

"Anyway," said Epcot, "it was insane. I couldn't stand the thought of her leaving me. I became consumed by my own fear. I lay awake some nights convinced she was cheating on me, and sometimes I'd call her just to make sure she was in her own bed. It was pretty ugly."

"I'm sorry."

"Yeah. Well. It's been four years since she dumped me, and I think I can safely say I'm over her. I'm Ben, by the way. What's your name?"

I inhaled. "Ariel Steiner."

The Rolling Rock in his hand started to shake. "Jesus! Are you kidding?" I took my wallet out of my jeans and handed him my driver's license. "You're not." He blushed and shook his head. "I'm so embarrassed about what I said. I mean, I don't necessarily think you and Novel Lover are doomed. Maybe it'll work out. I think I was just imposing my own feelings about my relationship onto yours."

"I think you might be right, though. I think we might be doomed after all."

"Relationships take a lot of work."

"I know, but maybe there's such a thing as too much work."

Three cute girls in tank tops came in, their arms linked. They began playing with the magnetic poetry on the refrigerator and giggling loudly at each other's creations.

"Do you want to get out of here?" said Ben.

"What do you mean?"

"Do you want to get a drink, maybe?"

I wasn't sure. He was so off-balance, unstable, and romantic hearted that it made me think we were kindred spirits. And all we were doing was getting a drink. That was no sin.

"Where do you want to go?" I said.

"BarCode," he said. "It's on First and Fifth."

The bar was downstairs from a restaurant. It was tiny, with just a few tables and small red love seats around the perimeter of the room. The only people in the place were couples, and most of them were sucking face. It was a little intimidating.

He ordered a Jameson for me and a martini for himself, and we sat down on a couch in the corner. "Tangled Up in Blue" came on the stereo and he started singing along.

"Are you a Dylan fan?" I asked.

"God, yes. The biggest. I'm kind of obsessed. I have four biographies, a picture book of photos of him, *Tarantula,* all his albums, and about two dozen bootlegs I ordered over the Internet."

My thighs began to quiver and I took a sip of my drink to calm myself. As I lifted my head, he said, "Wow. What a great chin scar. How'd you get it?"

"Bicycle accident."

He reached his hand toward my face and ran his thumb over the scar. I lowered my head and looked at him. He didn't take his hand off. He just moved his thumb from my chin to my lip. I opened my mouth and licked the tip. Then I closed my eyes and sucked the whole first joint. He started to lean in. When he was about two inches away from my mouth, I backed away. A thumb suck was one thing but a kiss was another. It was much easier cheating on paper than in life. Despite what Adam had done to me. Despite the fact that he'd given me a free dick pass.

"This isn't right," I said. "I'm in love with someone who's going to put me under the bridge, but it doesn't make me love him any less."

"I understand," he said. "But can I at least give you my number?"

"Sure."

He wrote it down on a matchbook and gave it to me. I stood up and put on my coat.

"It was amazing to meet you, Ariel. I hope things work out. Give me a call if you feel like it."

I stood up, rushed out of the bar, and got in a cab. When I got home, I turned on the computer. I had chanced upon my pièce de résistance. With Ben the sentiments had all been there—the attraction, both physical and emotional, the feeling of intense temptation—just not the cheating itself. I had all the elements I needed. Writing the actual sex part would be a breeze. I'd found my perfect faux fuck.

The beginning of the column was the way it really happened:

meeting Ben at the party, telling him about the problems Adam and I were having, and leaving with him to go to BarCode. Except this time, when he leaned in to kiss me, I didn't back away:

> Before I knew it, we were kissing, and Len's hand was slowly creeping up my skirted thigh. His mouth on mine did not feel weird; it felt right somehow, and familiar. We held each other for a long time, and then he asked if I wanted to come back to his place.
>
> "Yes," I said. "Very much."
>
> He had a *Don't Look Back* poster above his bed, just like me, and as soon as I saw it I started to think maybe my Perfect Guy would have to be a much bigger Dylan fan than Novel Lover. Novel's favorite singer is Sarah McLachlan.
>
> Len went over to the stereo and put on *Blood on the Tracks*, and as the opening strains of "Tangled Up in Blue" came on, he led me to his bed and began to unbutton my jeans. I pulled off his shirt and got on top of him, and that right feeling stayed so strong that before I knew it, we were knocking boots. But as soon as he pulled out, a wave of guilt washed over me. How could I have betrayed Novel Lover so thoughtlessly and cruelly? Didn't he mean anything at all to me? Wasn't our relationship even the tiniest bit sacred? I quickly put on my clothes and ran out the door.

●

For the three days after I sent in the column, I tried to act tense and preoccupied around Adam. Except it wasn't really acting. I *was* tense and preoccupied. He kept asking what was wrong, but I just told him I was premenstrual and tried to look like I was lying.

On Wednesday Sara and I read the column together, and I watched her jaw hang open from the beginning till the end. "So, what do you think?" I asked.

"From knowing you, I can see it's completely inconsistent with your character to do something like this, but it reads like it's true."

"Thank God."

"You mean you made it up?"

"We went to the bar but I didn't fuck him. I didn't even kiss him."

She closed her eyes, pinched the bridge of her nose, and said, "I've seen you shoot yourself in the foot a thousand times before, but this time you've severed your entire lower leg."

"What are you talking about?"

"I guarantee Adam's going to break up with you."

"Then I'll just tell him I made it up."

"He won't believe you. He'll think you're just saying that to get him to stay."

"I'll call Ben and have him tell Adam nothing happened."

"He still won't believe it. He'll think Ben's just lying to protect you. It's over. I never thought I'd say this but you've lied too well."

●

That afternoon I got messages on my machine from both my dad and Zach. "What's going on?" said my dad. "I didn't want to say anything about last week's column, but after reading this week's, I felt I had to call. I wouldn't put it past you to do what you did, but to inform Adam in such a recklessly self-destructive way—*that* does not sound like you."

"What up, sis?" said Zach. "Didn't anyone ever teach you not to cheat and tell? Or at least not to cheat and tell the city?"

But by the end of the day Adam still hadn't called. That could only mean bad news. When I got home from work, though, the phone was ringing. "I'm on my way," he said.

When I opened the door, he looked somber. Very somber. We walked up to the apartment and he sat on the couch. I sat on the other end of it, two feet down. He crossed his legs, then crossed them the other way. The refrigerator hummed loudly. Finally, he cleared his throat.

"I have something to say," he said, "and I don't think you're going to like it."

I knew what that meant. Sara was right. I'd botched everything up. My faux fuck would fuck me over. My not cheating and telling. Welcome to Dumpsville. Population: me.

"What is it?" I asked.

He turned his head toward me slowly. "Laura and I did more than just kiss. We made love."

●

I choose the Whiskey Bar of the Paramount Hotel as the setting for my breakup with Adam. It's two weeks after his admission. I have not told him my own infidelity was a lie, and I have made him believe I've forgiven him for his. Tonight, however, he will learn the truth. I'm dressed up, dressed to kill: knee-length black silk skirt, formfitting V-neck cashmere pullover, garters, and platform heels. Everyone else in the bar is well dressed, warm breathed, and laughing. They throw their heads back in joy because they are happy with their mates. He looks at the people happy with their mates and realizes how lucky he is to have me. He has no idea what I have in store for him.

He buys a whiskey sour for me and a vodka tonic for himself, and as I sip my drink I look around the room and see all the men that are better looking than Adam. I am counting the minutes till I am free of him. When our glasses are empty, I suggest that we check out the lobby.

We link arms, waltz in, and sit on a long lavender couch. I look ahead, with a slightly cross-eyed, half-dead, Kate Mossian gaze. Adam looks at me. He thinks I am beautiful, even though my lipstick is smudged and my eyes are getting red from the drink, and I'm beginning to smell from the sweat that comes from knowing I'm such a cruel, cruel bitch.

He's looking at me adoringly now, but I'm looking up toward the windows of the restaurant on the next floor. All the people at the tables are clear skinned and mean. They look down at me and know I'm about to break some serious *corazón*. They support me in this endeavor, even though they realize I will never be able to get a table where they are eating because I am not tall enough.

He leans in to kiss me. I turn away. He looks at me, startled. *Why,* he thinks, *whatever is going on?* He tries again to kiss me, more viciously, but his breath is so rank from the alcohol, his eyes so desperate, that I can't continue with the ruse.

"Adam," I murmur. "There's something I've been meaning to talk to you about."

"What?" he asks, his voice quivering and whiny.

"See, I, we, it's just—nothing." Excellent. Now I've planted doubt in his mind. Now he's terrified of what I'm going to do to him, and I've put the onus on him to drag it out of me.

"You can tell me," he says.

"I really didn't want to ruin this evening, but . . ." My voice trails off.

"What is it?"

"Our relationship has been going downhill for a while now, and you've been completely oblivious."

"Oblivious to what?"

"See what I mean?"

"What are you talking about?"

"I never cheated on you." His jaw drops. "That's right. That column was all a sorry ruse. A sad attempt to make you reveal your deep-rooted, undying love for me. But all it did was make you reveal your total lack of respect. I lied when I said I forgave you. I never did and I never will. How could you have taken me so lightly? How could you stoop so low?"

"I—" His lower lip is shaking.

"It's over, Adam. Over like clover. You're a sad remnant of a once-pathetic past, and being near you makes me realize I can achieve much more. See the guy with the mustache up there, having dinner with that redhead? He's been eyeing me all night. When I put you in a taxi home, he will tell his date he has to use the toilet, come down here, escort me to the ladies' room, and very quickly and quietly kneel down, open his mouth, and bring me to a thrilling climax with much more skill and accuracy than you ever could. He knows how to treat a woman. And you don't. Your company is a constant painful reminder of my former naiveté. You are a walking regret, and the thought of letting your thing anywhere near my glistening jewel makes me achingly ill. Do you have a light?"

He doesn't want to be kind to me but he's more attracted to me now than he's ever been before. He lights my More. I don't smoke Mores but I brought them along just for this occasion.

"I wish I could say I'm sorry," I tell him, "but I'm not. In fact, I blame you. If you had recognized what an incredible catch I was, you never would have cheated on me in the first place. I feel no shame in letting you go. You are my biggest mistake. Let me hail you a cab."

He is stunned. He wants nothing more than to fuck me or hit me or both. He is slowly recognizing that it will take him years to get over me and that there is nothing he can do to change my mind. I rise slowly from the couch, take his arm, and escort him to the door. A cab is waiting, light and welcoming. There is a Virginia Slims ad on top of it. The woman in the ad looks at me. She is on my side, even though she can't let her husband know she smokes. I open the door and slide Adam in, then slam the door and stick my head in the front window. I give the cabby the address and slip him a twenty. He smiles appreciatively at my figure and I slink back into the lobby.

My guy and the redhead are no longer at their table upstairs. I worry that they have left. But then I spot them at a couch across the room. He is still watching me. I sit, tap out another More, light it, and inhale meanly and slickly. The redhead goes to the ladies' room. I pray she's taking a long, slow shit.

He crosses the room, sits next to me just as I've taken a drag, grabs me firmly and confidently, draws me in close, and presses his lips against mine like in an old movie. I pry his mouth open with my tongue and exhale into his throat. He inhales, then blows the smoke out through his nose, kisses me again, and whispers, "I'm sending her home soon. Don't move."

The door to the bathroom opens. He dashes back over to his couch. She emerges. I know she does not wash her hands after she makes. I see that her dye job is cheap. She sits with him for a few more minutes, and then he takes her outside and puts her into a cab. He comes back into the lobby, sits down next to me, and tells me his name.

●

"Laura and I did more than just kiss," said Adam. "We made love."

My body shot out the window and slammed down onto the sidewalk with such force that my guts splattered on every car from Cobble Hill to Red Hook.

"I know this must be hard for you to hear," he said, "but I've been turning everything over in my head, and I really think we can work through this."

"Work through this?"

"Yeah. As angry as you must be at me, and as angry as I am at you, at least we can take comfort in the fact that we've both erred. To err is human. We're human, Ar."

I could hear the words "I didn't err!" forming on my tongue, but I stifled my gag reflex and tried to deep-throat them.

"What I'm trying to say is," he said, bowing his head, "I forgive you. Do you forgive me?"

I wasn't sure. What did his fuck mean? Had he done it because he was secretly unsatisfied with our sex life? Were all his problems saying "I love you" due to the fact that, deep down, he was still in love with her and always would be? Could a person be too much of a patsy—even me?

But maybe his hookup had been just that—a hookup. Didn't fifty percent of all Americans cheat on their spouses at some point? Maybe this wasn't any different. Maybe I had to think Christian on this one and turn my cheek, when what I really wanted was an eye for an eye.

"What was it like?" I said. "I mean—are you wondering if you two should be together again? Do you miss her? Do you still have feelings for her?"

"Not at all. Not at all! Afterward, I felt really miserable. What about you? Are you really into this guy?"

"No! It was totally sexual and nothing else! It . . . it didn't even feel like it was happening."

"Good. So do you forgive me?"

I hated myself for being so weak willed, but at the end of the day, I didn't love him any less. I still wanted him in my life.

"I . . . guess so," I said glumly.

He took a piece of my hair in his hand and caressed it, then rubbed my cheek and said, "You know, a lot of couples would break up after an ordeal like this. I mean, it would be so easy to just call it quits after this kind of crisis. To say, 'To hell with this. Obviously something here is just not right.'"

"I know just what you're saying."

"But we're more sophisticated than that. I think this experience could be good for us. It can make our bond a lot stronger. If we can get through this, we can get through anything."

"That's . . . one way of looking at it."

"We're so brave. We're pioneers, really. Do you realize how mature we're being about this? It takes a lot of courage to think long-haul, and that's just what we're doing. Your honesty is much more important to me than your fidelity. I'm just glad we can be upfront with each other, instead of having to carry our secrets around."

"Terrific."

"It *is* terrific. I feel so much lighter now, knowing you know. Knowing you forgive me. Don't you feel lighter too?"

"Featherish."

"It feels great to be straight with you. This is so healthy. You know what I feel like doing right now?"

"What?"

"Guess," he said, then began kissing my neck.

The whole while through, I pictured him with Laura. I had never seen a photo of her before, but I'd developed a very vivid image of her in my mind: blond and waifish, with Uma tits, buns of steel, and abs of lead. Unshaved pits, uncombed hair, and a natural, Aryan, Vermont-farmish beauty (even though he'd told me she was from Detroit).

As he ground away on top of me, I pictured him grinding away on top of this amalgam of all the *Little House on the Prairie* sisters, and I pictured her whimpering and yelping and clawing at the air, coming fifty times in a row, and him feeling like the stud of the universe because of it.

He came quickly and fell right asleep. I wanted to smother him with a pillow. My cat had cornered me. There was no way I could one-up him now. You can't outcheat a fucker. There's just nowhere else to go. Except maybe anal. And I didn't have the energy to pen that one. All this fake philandering had wiped me out—and for nothing. He'd been unfaithful but I loved him too much to break up with him, and I could never tell him the truth. I looked at his sleeping face and wondered how Laura had tasted.

●

Sara called me at my desk as soon as I got to work in the morning. "I have something to tell you," she said.

"Me too."

"You go first."

"No, you. I *guarantee* mine's worse than yours."

"OK." She sighed. "Rick and I broke up last night."

"Why?"

"He decided he wants to move back to Seattle to pursue his music career again, and I told him there was no way I was leaving this city. So we're ending it. He's moving next week."

"I'm so sorry."

"It's OK. I've been thinking about everything, and as good as the sex was, I'm not so sure we had the longest shelf life. I mean, I'm going to be severely catatonic for the next few weeks, but in a way, I think it makes a weird sort of sense. What's your news?"

I told her.

"He *what?*"

"Yep."

"You have to dump him!"

"I don't want to dump him!"

"But he *cheated* on you! Don't you feel any anger?"

"Of course I do, but I've decided to forgive him."

"You are really pathetic."

"I know."

She was quiet a moment and then she said, "Well, if you're going to stay with him, there's only one way you can do it and still maintain a shred of dignity."

"How?"

"You go fuck Ben for real."

"Sara!"

"That'll level the scales. There's your balance of affection. You have nothing to lose. Adam already thinks you did anyway, so why not?"

"Because it's cheating!"

"Hello! Don't you think the sanctity of your pairing has been the tiniest bit marred already? You'll feel so much better afterward. If you ever had a motivation to stray, you've got one now."

I wondered if she was right. Was I pathetic for forgiving him so easily? Would it help to go sleep with Ben? Or would it just make me feel worse than before?

That night, Adam and I were supposed to meet at P.S. 122 to see a performance art show. I got there a few minutes late, expecting him to be waiting for me. But he wasn't. After five minutes, I was irritated; after ten, antsy; and after fifteen, worried. I started to imagine all the horrible accidents that could have befallen him, and then it occurred to me that maybe he was with Laura. Maybe she was sucking his dick right this very second, under a hemp comforter on a frameless futon in some rent-stabilized East Village studio with lots of wall hangings and cats. I'd never be able to compete with that tight Aryan mouth, those pert nips. I was allergic to cats.

Suddenly Adam came rushing up the street. "I'm sorry I'm late," he said. "I couldn't find a parking space."

He kissed me. I smelled his neck. Nothing foreign, nothing sweet. I was ashamed to have jumped to negative conclusions so quickly. Just because he'd wandered once didn't mean he would again. His fling was over. It was me he wanted now. I just wasn't sure I still wanted him.

●

After the show he suggested we go back to his place. When we got up to the apartment I went into the kitchen to get some water, and as I was opening the refrigerator he came up behind me and wrapped his arms around me. "I'm so hot for you," he said. "I was thinking all day today about being with you."

I closed my eyes and tried to pretend everything was the same between us, but then I got this image of him with Laura again and I couldn't get it out of my mind. I took out the water, moved down the counter away from him, and poured myself a glass.

"What is it?" he said. "Don't you want me?"

"I don't know," I said, turning to face him.

"What do you mean, you don't know?" He got this wounded look in his eyes.

"I've been feeling really angry at you," I said. "Can't you relate to that *even a little*?"

"No. I've totally forgiven you. I feel like I'm seeing you in a new light. I just . . ." He embraced me and kissed my shoulder. "I can't keep my hands off you."

I closed my eyes. For months I had been wanting him to touch me like this, to need me like this, but how could I enjoy it when all I could think about was *her*?

"Maybe we should just go to sleep," I said.

He gave me the hound-dog gaze again and said, "Fine."

"Adam—"

"No. If that's what you want, then fine." He went into the bedroom.

I walked into the bathroom and brushed my teeth. I looked at my face in the mirror and saw a frightened, miserable person behind two sad eyes. I felt ashamed for not being able to tell him the truth, but I didn't know how I could. He was warming to me. He wanted me. My lie was bringing him closer. In a completely demented way, my plan had worked. If I could just get Laura out of my mind, maybe he and I could work everything out.

I went into the bedroom. He was lying in bed reading John Fante's *Ask the Dust*. When I came in he didn't look at me. He just put down the book wordlessly and went to the bathroom. I took off my bra and jeans but left my T-shirt on, got into bed, and faced the wall. A few minutes later he came in, turned out the lights, and got in next to me, his back to mine. I tried to breathe slowly and relax, but my heart was pounding and my palms were wet. I tossed and turned for the next hour, but I couldn't tell if he was awake or asleep.

"Adam?" I finally whispered, my back still to him.

"Yes?"

"Are you having trouble sleeping too?"

"Yeah."

"What should we do?"

"I think I should drive you home."

We shifted onto our backs and lay there silently for a while, and then I got up and put on my clothes. He dressed next to me and we went down to the car.

●

He came over the next night, and as soon as we got upstairs I pulled him to the bed. All day at work I had been feeling violently jealous, and I had decided to show him I was better than Laura. I wanted to make him come so hard he'd forget all about her. We got under the covers and he lifted my shirt and buried his face in my breasts. But after just a few minutes he took his mouth off my teat and said, "There's something I want you to do."

"What?"

"I'm a little embarrassed to tell you."

"What is it?"

"Well, I was thinking today, about what . . . happened between you and Len."

"Ben," I said. "His real name's Ben."

"Whatever! So it was making me really upset. I guess this

isn't as easy for me as I thought. Anyway, I got to thinking, *How can I make myself less jealous?* and I got an idea."

"What?"

"I was wondering if you could . . . tell me about what happened. Talk about it, while I lie next to you and . . ." He looked away.

"Play with yourself?"

He nodded. "I know it sounds bizarre, but I really think it might help me come to terms with this."

Jumpin' Jehosophat. This was some sick-ass shit. But how could I protest? He was looking to me for help. Maybe this little exercise would bring him closer.

"Um . . . where do you want me to start?" I asked.

"Start in the bar when you kissed," he said, adjusting himself under the blanket.

"Are you sure you want to do this?"

"Yes."

I cleared my throat. "So . . . um . . . after the party, we went to BarCode, and we had a couple shots, and we were looking at each other, and he put his hand on my thigh and kind of leaned in toward me."

He closed his eyes. The blanket started rippling slowly. "Did it feel good?"

"*Really* good," I said, cringing. "And as he leaned in, he pulled his chair closer to mine and leaned his body against mine, and I could feel him, you know . . ."

"Get hard?"

"Exactly. That. Against me."

"I bet he was really hot for you."

"Mmm hmm."

"And you were hot for him, too."

"Mmm hmm. I really was. Boy, was I. So he asked if I wanted to leave and I said yes and we went back to his apartment."

"Where was it?"

"A few blocks away."

"Was it a nice place?"

I turned to him abruptly. "What does that matter?"

"I'm just trying to imagine it."

"It looked like any other East Village studio! It had a dimmer! The bathroom had no sink!"

"OK!"

"So as soon as we walked in, we started kissing, really violently and passionately. All I wanted was to rip his clothes off and jump his bones. We raced over to his futon and—"

He opened his eyes. "I thought you listened to *Blood on the Tracks* first."

"We did. I mean, his stereo was right next to his bed. He put on *Blood on the Tracks* and *then* we got into the bed. Then he went down on me—"

"You didn't write about that."

Uh oh. I was forgetting my own details. "No. I didn't. But he did go down on me."

"Oh."

"Does that bother you?"

"A little. I mean, that's so much more intimate than just sex."

"Should I stop?"

"No. I need to do this. Tell me about him going down on you."

He closed his eyes again. I sighed. "It was really good. He licked away at me so diligently and terrifically that I came within like three minutes . . ."

Again the blanket stilled. He turned to me. "Three minutes? You never come that quickly when *I* do it."

"Did I say three? I meant thirty."

"Oh."

"So, after I came, he put on a condom and slid it into me, and it wound up being this incredibly easy and simple procedure? Because of how ready I was? How wet I was from just having come?" The blanket was vibrating more quickly now. "He pushed my thighs all the way up over my head and I almost coughed on his cock he put it in so deep."

"Oh God, Ar . . ."

I looked over at him, his eyes shut, his face contorted, the blanket trembling violently, and I decided the situation had gotten just a little too weird. My own boyfriend was about to jizz over an infidelity that didn't even take place. What was next? Would this cheating stuff become a regular part of our dirty talk? Would I have to keep inventing lurid new details just to keep exciting him? Would it get to the point where he suggested the four of us get it on together, for therapeutic reasons? I knew it probably wasn't the best timing to spring the truth on him when he was three seconds away from spooging his brains out, but somehow I just couldn't let the game go on.

"I'm sorry," I said. "I can't do this anymore."

The blanket stopped moving. He glared at me. "What do you mean?"

"I never had sex with Ben. I didn't even kiss him. And I didn't kiss Jason either. It was all part of this stupid plan."

His eyes grew wide as his dick. "What are you talking about?"

"The moment I said, 'I love you,' and you didn't say it back, I knew you'd never catch up with my devotion. I'd always love you more. And I hated it. Because I wanted you to be as passionate about me as I was about you. So I made up the kiss to make you jealous, and then when you said you kissed Laura, I had to come up with something better, so I wrote that I fucked Ben. Sara thinks I should dump you. She says I'm a sucker for staying with you."

"You're not a sucker."

"Yes, I am. I should hate you for what you did."

"Didn't do."

"What?"

"Laura's a lesbian. She's been living with her girlfriend for two and a half years."

Holy Moses. "You mean you didn't kiss her, either?"

"No! I only said I kissed her to get back at you because I was so hurt that you kissed Jason! And then when I read 'Den of Len,' I decided to tell you I fucked her. Because unless I made you think I cheated on you too, you would always have more power over me."

"I thought you didn't believe in those kinds of games!"

"In principle I don't, but in practice it's a totally different matter."

I looked at him for a second, trying to take it all in, and then I had a terrifying thought. What if even this wasn't the truth? What if he was such a skilled manipulator that he'd changed his story when I changed mine, because he was too afraid I'd dump him for fucking Laura? What if they really *had* done it and this was nothing more than another web of lies?

"Wait a minute," I said. "How do I know you're telling the truth now?"

"Do you really think I could have made up a story this twisted?"

"People do it all the time! I should know!"

"I swear nothing happened!"

"Why should I believe you?"

"You could call Laura up and ask her if she's gay. It'll be a little embarrassing to have to explain why you need to know, but you could do it."

I looked at him hard. I didn't see any deception in his eyes. "That's OK," I said. "I don't want to."

He smiled and pulled me toward him, and down onto the bed, and smooched me like it was our last night together on the eve of world war. It was a different kind of kiss than any we'd had before, more intense than that first night together, even. He didn't feel closed off. He felt like he was with me, completely. Suddenly I tasted something salty in my mouth. At first I thought it was coming from me, but then I realized I wasn't crying.

"Are you OK?" I said.

"Yeah," he said. "Just incredibly relieved. I'm glad you didn't cheat on me. That column made me so jealous."

"It did?"

"It made me want to punch him in the face."

"*It did?*" I asked gleefully.

"Yeah. I couldn't stand the thought of losing you. Of you being with anyone but me. I adore you. I . . ."

"What? What? You what?"

"I . . ." He took a deep breath. "I . . . yuv you."

"Do you have something caught in your mouth?"

"No. It's just easier for me to say it in baby talk, for some reason."

It wasn't exactly the romance movie of the decade, but it was a start. He'd said it with a severe speech impediment, but he'd said it. We kissed again and he hugged me so hard I could feel a few vertebrae crack. I stared at him and for the first time I didn't see any fear in his eyes. I just saw love. I mean *yuv*. And it wasn't a wild, reckless love that was there only because I'd tricked him. It was an open, real love that was there because he'd sensed what it would be like not to have me, and it had made him afraid. He loved me for me, not for my lies.

I'd been waiting years for the moment when I'd see that look in a pair of male peepers, but now that it was finally happening, I was afraid a genie would tap me on the shoulder and tell me this was another girl's life; we'd gotten switched at the wish center and I'd gotten hers instead of mine. It didn't happen, though. No matter how hard I looked, the love didn't disappear. I started to cry, and as soon as I stopped, he started again. "It's like crying Ping-Pong," he said.

In the romance movie of the decade, that probably would have been the moment where we made perfect, soft-lit, missionary love as a really nauseating Phil Collins song swelled in the background. But even though Adam probably had a wicked case of blue balls from his interrupted stroke session, he didn't suggest it, and neither did I. We just lay there holding each other for a long time, until finally we fell asleep.

10

IN THE MORNING, we went to The Fall. We kept putting down our newspapers to smooch and nuzzle, like every couple in the café I had envied from afar. But once, midkiss, I farted, and Adam walked to a table across the room, and I realized we'd never be completely like those other couples.

When I got home from the café there was a message on my machine from Turner. "Call me as soon as possible," he said. "I'm in the office."

I dialed. "Can you come over right away?" he said.

"Sure. What's this about?"

"I'd rather discuss it with you in person." No good news has ever come after those eight words.

When I got to Turner's office, he led me down the hall into Jensen's. We sat down on the couch across from Jensen. *Both* of his eyes seemed crossed now.

"I received a rather disturbing call at home this morning," he said. "From a Mr. Richard Sand. Ben Weinstein's lawyer. Weinstein claims your last column was partially fabricated. He says that although you did meet at a party, nothing sexual actually transpired. In fact, he has a live-in girlfriend, who was away the weekend you met him. The girlfriend came back yesterday, read your column, figured out it was him because of the Epcot Center T-shirt and the *Paris, Texas* reference, and hit the roof. Ben tried to tell her it was made up, but she wouldn't believe him. So he called his dad. Emerson Weinstein, the bond trader. His dad hired Sand and they're threatening to sue us for libel unless we print a retraction. What's going on?"

I should have known it was a mistake to mess with that conniving little shit. I couldn't believe I'd been duped so hard. You couldn't even trust your own *boy toy* to be upfront with you. But there was nothing I could do about it now, except 'fess up. I looked from Jensen to Turner slowly, then sighed and told them the boring true story: the party, the bar, the thumb sucking, Ben's invitation, my refusal, and the cab ride home. Their heads drooped lower and lower as I went on.

"Why did you do this?" asked Turner when I finished.

"I have a perfectly reasonable explanation!" I shouted.

"We'd love to hear it."

"I was feeling incredibly unsure of Adam's devotion, and I decided I had to do something that would make him jealous! But I couldn't bring myself to actually cheat on him, so I wrote that I did!"

"*That's* your explanation?" sputtered Jensen.

"Yes."

"Do you have any idea what's at stake because of your sophomoric power games? You could shut down the paper!"

"I—"

"What about your other columns? Have you lied in any of them?" asked Turner.

"I didn't lie, per se. I . . . heightened, maybe."

"Didn't we make it clear when you started the column that you had to tell the truth?"

"Don't tell me you guys really thought everything I wrote was true! *Nobody's* that depraved!"

"We thought you were!" shouted Jensen. "Why do you think we hired you?"

"I—"

"How much 'heightening' have you done since you started?"

Suddenly I started to panic. Maybe it was best to remain silent. That's what the perps always did on cop shows, and this was beginning to feel like an interrogation scene. Jensen was the bad cop and Turner was the good one.

"I don't know if I should say," I said.

"You'll only make things more difficult if you don't cooperate," said Jensen. I waited for him to grab me by the hair and slam my head down on the desk.

"I'm sorry," I said, "but that's all I'd care to share."

"Fine," said Jensen, rising and twitching. "You're fired."

For the first time in twenty-two years, I couldn't speak. I nodded blankly, trying to keep my face from exploding, and walked out toward the elevators.

As soon as I got down to the lobby, I started bawling. The only good thing that had ever come out of my twisted existence had been yanked away from me—all because of Ben Weinstein's jealous whore of a girlfriend. It didn't make sense. His affection had seemed so genuine. He'd even given me his phone number. I pulled out the matchbook, raced down the street to a pay phone, and dialed. A voice mail came on. "You've reached Ben Weinstein," he said. "I'm either away from my desk or on another call, but leave a message and I'll get back to you." He'd given me his *work* number, for chrissake! What a sneaky, manipulative asshole! Thank God I hadn't *shtupped* him!

I headed slowly down Broadway toward the F stop, and when I got on the train, I saw this girl my age, wearing a bike messenger bag slung over her shoulder, reading the *Week*. I moved next to her to get a better look. She was reading "Den of Len." Her mouth was slightly parted, and she had this look of half terror, half amusement on her face.

I wanted to sling her over my shoulder and cart her into Jensen's office so he could see what a huge mistake he was making. Didn't he realize how many readers he was about to lose? I had made people laugh! I had made them spurt! Without me, all the city's young hipsters would have to reach into the dusty shoe boxes underneath their beds and take out their long-abandoned smut sources. Girls would brush off their tattered copies of Anaïs Nin's *Little Birds,* Judy Blume's *Forever . . .* , and *My Secret Garden,* and the boys would return to their *Hustler*s and *Penthouse*s. The guys who wiped their asses with my columns would have to go around crusty, and the ones who used the *Week* as a spooge target would have to go back to staining their walls.

The city would collectively grow more tense and miserable, couples would return to the lousy sex they were having pre–"Run Catch Kiss" because the men could no longer fantasize about me while they were fucking their girlfriends, and pervs would go back to harassing women instead of going home to read my column. Muggers would grow restless and violent, the crime rate would soar, and the entire town would become the inferno it was before I came along. It was going to get Hobbesian.

When I got home, I called Adam. "That's crazy!" he said. "Don't they realize that all their columnists embellish?"

"I guess not."

"But you're—"

"The greatest stroke writer since Miller. I know."

"I was going to say, 'one of the top reasons people read the paper.' "

"Oh."

"Maybe this isn't the worst thing in the world. This shift could be good for you. Madonna reinvents herself every few years. Now you have a chance to."

"What am I supposed to reinvent myself as? A freelance perjurer?"

"You can do anything you want. Just wait. I have a feeling everything's going to work out for the better."

I didn't.

After we hung up, I called my parents in the country. My dad answered and I told him the news. "I have to tell you," he said, "as angry as I am at those muckrakers, I'd be lying if I didn't admit to a faint sense of relief."

"What do you mean?"

"For one thing, I'm thrilled you haven't cheated on Adam. Mom and I were afraid you'd wrecked the entire relationship. For another, this is great for us. Larry Stanley won't bother me anymore, Mom can start going to Women's League for Israel meetings again, and Zach's friends will stop calling him slutbrother."

"It's nice to know you support me when I'm down."

"I don't think you'll have to struggle to get other employment. You've got a remarkable ability to fuse trash and lies. Have you considered a career in advertising?"

I dialed Sara next. "I already know," she said.

"How?"

"Roy Cohn Junior just called. He asked me to give him the real names of all the guys you've written about so he can contact them."

"Did you?"

"No. I said, 'Suck my dick. If you're going to burn her at the stake, it'll have to be without my help.' "

"You told him to suck your—"

"No. I said the other part, though."

"What do you think he's gonna do?"

"He's probably going to go to each bar you've mentioned and interrogate the regulars until he deciphers your pseudonyms. Which won't be too difficult."

"You really think he'd stoop that low?"

She didn't answer.

●

Over the next few days I got some strange messages on my answering machine. Charlton left one saying, "I just told it like it was. I had to. I hope it doesn't mean we can't still be... friends." Corinne said, "I'm really sorry, but what could I do?" Jason said, "I wish it really had been true," and Evan said, "I was glad to set the record straight. I lied when I told Sara your column didn't bother me. It did."

On Wednesday at noon, Sara and I trooped to the *Week* box on the corner, removed two copies of the paper, and walked to Grand Central Terminal. I had decided an occasion like this merited royal surroundings. We bought sandwiches and sodas at a deli in the station, sat down against a wall under the towering ceiling, and opened up.

From the Editors

In her "Run Catch Kiss" column "Den of Len" (March 12, 1997), Ariel Steiner claimed she met a young man at a party, went with him to the East Village pub BarCode, then went to his apartment and engaged in sexual intercourse. This was a fabrication. Although she did attend a party on the night of Friday, March 7, 1997, met a man named Ben Weinstein, and left the party to converse with him at BarCode, Steiner and Weinstein did not have sex. Although Weinstein briefly inserted his thumb into Steiner's mouth while they sat on a couch in the bar, that was the only penetration that took place over the course of the evening. And although Weinstein does in fact have a poster from the D. A. Pennebaker documentary *Don't Look Back* above his futon, Steiner could have had no way of knowing that, as she did not once set foot in the apartment he shares with his girlfriend of a year and a half, Jennifer James, who was away that weekend visiting her sister Sheila in Akron.

As of Saturday, March 15, Steiner has been dismissed from her position as *City Week* columnist. We retract "Den of Len" and apologize wholeheartedly for any shame or embarrassment its publication may have caused Mr. Weinstein and Ms. James. We have launched an investigation to determine the veracity of Steiner's past columns, and at this point can share with you the following information: At least three of them over the past six and a half months—"Rockman" (November 13, 1996), "Smutlife" (December 4, 1996), and "The Kiss" (March 5, 1997)—were partially fabricated; and at least three others—"Dyke Hands" (December 11, 1996), "Pap's Blue Ribbon" (December 18, 1996), and "The Last Muzzle Guzzle" (January 1, 1997)—were wholly fabricated.

To all those who were misrepresented in Steiner's columns, we offer our humblest apologies. We are currently reorganizing our fact-checking department to insure that such a situation never arises again. Once again, we are sorry.

—STEVEN JENSEN IV, *Editor in Chief,*
and WILLIAM H. TURNER, *Associate Editor*

I swooned sideways onto the marble floor. "What are you so upset about?" said Sara. "It wasn't that bad!"

"That's exactly what I'm upset about!" I said.

"What?"

"I thought they were really gonna rake me over the coals. But that retraction was completely devoid of a single good zinger!"

"You're saying you wished they'd been meaner?" she asked incredulously.

"*Yes!*" I wailed. "I gave those guys six and a half months of my vaginal secretions. The least they could have done was ended my career with a bang."

"I can't believe you," said Sara. "You used to *complain* about the nasty letters, and now you're complaining because the retraction wasn't cruel *enough*." She was right. It was totally inconsistent, but I couldn't help it. I just wished Jensen and Turner had had the balls to fry me with some flair:

From the Editors

At some point or another, every newspaper editor makes a major hiring mistake. Whether it's because the editor was pulling a little too hard on the bottle before the interview or simply because the prospective employee had really nice gams, it happens. And once it does, all that editor can do is pray that the hire never screws up badly enough to get the paper in trouble. So far, we've been lucky. But then we met Ariel Steiner. And the bitch set us up. Like Jesus, we were nailed to the cross. And now we bleed, we bleed, we bleed.

In her March 12 "Run Catch Kiss" column, "Den of Len," Steiner claimed she got booty when in fact she did not. One lie would have been bad enough—but then we found out that she'd fibbed in half a dozen others, too! A downtown penis probe elicited the following information.

Evan Draine (aka "Kevin," of "Rockman") acknowledges having had a sexual relationship with Steiner but contends that he chose to end it, not Steiner. "Ariel's a sweet girl," he said, "but she got way too into me too fast. I had to break it off. My music is my life. I broke up with her in a diner in Carroll Gardens. She definitely didn't spit on my feet. As I recall, she looked pretty depressed. And she made something else up too. If she came while we were kicking it, she sure didn't show it. I never felt contractions, she didn't make any loud noises, and afterward, I didn't notice any nipple flush."

Charlton Wakes ("Royalton," of "Smutlife") claims: "First of all, I didn't go down on her. She didn't ask, so I didn't offer. We did get it on in a booth at Show World, but then an attendant came to the door and said we had to put in more tokens, and Ariel freaked out and bolted. We didn't go to Ben & Jerry's either. And she never blew me. Although I sure wish she had."

According to "Beat Writer," of "Dyke Hands," "Pap's Blue Ribbon," and "The Last Muzzle Guzzle" (*City Week* senior editor Corinne Riley), "I did have an affair with Ariel Steiner. But she didn't proposition me. *I* propositioned *her.* I'm not ashamed. I'd do it again if I had the chance. I'm proud to count myself among the minions of Ariel Steiner's lovers. For a chick who claimed to have no prior experience with women, she sure knew her way around my cooze. I consider the cunnilingus I received from Steiner to be among the best of my short thirty years. And I once dated Chastity Bono."

The fabricated segment of "The Kiss" was the kiss itself. Jason Levin ("Mason Bevin") contends, "Actually, I had a cold sore at the time. I was definitely attracted to Ariel that night, but I wouldn't wish herpes simplex one on anyone, much less someone I consider a friend."

Finally, playwright Sam Shepard offered this response to "Sam My Man": "I never told her I lived in the Midwest. I live in rural America, and I'd rather not be more specific. But I did meet that girl outside the Public. I remember her quite well, actually. She was a bit pushy, but sweet and self-possessed. I found myself thinkin' quite a bit about her . . . poise . . . on my trip home from New York, lyin' on a motel bed in Dubuque one starry, starry night."

How did this little schemer get away with her tricks? We've been asking ourselves that same question. Although we do have a fact-checking department, it is set up to monitor the work of journalists who have a modicum of respect for basic ethical principles such as fairness and honesty—not career scammers like Steiner. However, we take full responsibility for our mechanism's failure to deliver and are currently launching a deep, probing investigation so as to guarantee that we are never Steinerated again.

As for what could possibly have motivated this senseless young hussy to act with such a brash lack of integrity, we, like you, can only speculate. Like the weimaraners on the television commercial who are told the food they are offered is 100 percent beef, all we can do is bark in unison, "Lies! Lies! We can't believe a word you sa-ay!"

—STEVEN JENSEN IV, *Editor in Chief,*
and WILLIAM H. TURNER, *Associate Editor*

When I got back to my desk, the Corposhit was waiting with a computer printout in her hand and a grim look on her face. She handed the papers to me and leaned against the edge of my desk. The printout was from the famous Internet gossip site "The Dirt Disher." Under the headline CITY WEEK COLUMNIST DISMISSED FOR FABRICATING was the following:

The *City Week,* a Manhattan alternative weekly, printed a retraction of one of its articles today, "Den of Len" (March 12, 1997), by the *Week*'s 22-year-old sex columnist, Ariel Steiner. In the column, Steiner recounted a tale of sexual intercourse with Ben Weinstein, 28, son of Wall Street bond trader Emerson Weinstein.

"I'm not saying I didn't meet her," said the younger Weinstein. "I did. But I totally wasn't attracted to her. In fact, I found her much more disappointing than her cartoon. I have a girlfriend. I love her. I'd never stray. Never." According to sources close to the Weinstein family, the family threatened suit unless the *Week* agreed to print a retraction.

The retraction states that Steiner was dismissed on March 15, following a partial confession. The *Week* is currently pursuing an investigation into Steiner's past columns and has already concluded that at least six of them were all or partially fabricated. *Week* editor in chief, Steve Jensen, supplied this comment: "We love printing vitriol, but it better be true vitriol."

I looked up at the Corposhit and handed her the papers.
"So it's you?" she said.
I nodded.
"I didn't know you wrote a newspaper column."
"I didn't think it was relevant," I mumbled.
"I wish you'd told me. Evidently, I was missing out." She smiled faintly, then wiped the smile away, pointed to the paper, and said, "This is not good news. I just got a call from my supervisor about this item. He said I had to let you go. It makes the company look bad to keep you on, even in a menial position. We're a publishing house, after all, and to keep you among our ranks would give out the wrong impression. Pack up your things. I'll call your temp agency and let them know what happened. I hope you understand."

She went into her office and shut the door. I lowered my head toward the blotter, breathing in the ink and hoping the chemicals would kill me. Then I opened my top drawer, swiped a few pens and notebooks, and put them in my bag. I might need those pens someday. It could get to the point where I couldn't afford stationery supplies. I had enough money saved to support myself for a month, max, but then I'd have to find myself another job. What if my temp agency fired me? What if they decided I was unemployable? I put on my coat, glanced at the Corposhit's closed door, and went home.

●

When I got to my apartment, the machine was flashing like crazy. The *Times,* the *News,* and the *Post* all wanted my comments. *Ego,* the celebrity glossy, was doing a story on me and wanted my version of the events. My dad wanted to know if I'd seen the "Dirt Disher" piece. A *Voice* reporter was doing an article called "Why the *City Week* Is the Worst Paper in the Country" and wanted me to attest to Jensen and Turner's shoddy fact-checking policies. Ned Slivovitz, the tabloid talk show phenom, wanted me to come on and duke it out with Weinstein. The head of a production company called Wet and Slippery had some ideas for script collaborations. And a gossip columnist for the *Daily News* wanted confirmation of a rumor that I had actually gotten it on with *both* Ben and his girlfriend. At the same time.

I had always dreamed of arriving home to a wildly blinking machine, but these weren't the messages I had hoped to get. This wasn't the kind of fame I had envisioned. This was the cheapest and most insidious form. I didn't want to go on schlock TV to be ridiculed by an audience of inbreds. I wanted to be remembered as a writer, not a liar.

I erased the messages, went into the bathroom, and threw some cold water over my face. When I lifted my head and caught a glimpse of myself in the mirror, I did not like what I saw. My upper-lip hair had grown so long I looked like Lonnie Barbach. My shoulder-length mop was mushrooming out and the ends were split-ended and dead. Perhaps it was time for a salon trip. It wasn't like I had anything better to do.

Corinne had written about a place in Trump Tower a couple issues ago that she swore was the best in the city. Cuts were ninety bucks each, but she said it was worth it because there was a French dude named Pierre there, who made you feel like royalty. I called up, made an appointment, unplugged the phone, and walked to the train.

●

Pierre was about thirty-five, good looking, and effeminate in that generic French effeminate way that made it hard to tell if he was gay or straight. "What are you looking for today?" he said.

"Something short, and new."

" 'Ave you considered putting in some color?" he asked.

"No. Why?"

"Because some blond would look very pretty on you. A few streaks. For the spring. A little drama."

I had never lightened my hair before, because I had always seen it as a form of Jewish self-hatred, but now that I was jobless, on the verge of financial ruin, and a target of a media witch-hunt, my moral integrity kind of flew out the window.

"What the hell," I said. "Let's do it."

Two hours later I walked out with a chic bob, six blond highlights, and waxed lips and brows. I loved the new me. I knew it probably hadn't been the wisest move to blow a portion of my scant savings on beauty, but I figured it was worth it. If I was going to be homeless soon, at least I'd look good begging for quarters.

That night Adam slept over, but when I woke up the next morning the bed was empty and the doorbell was ringing. I decided he was probably having shitting anxiety again and had gone to the diner. When I went down to get the door, though, he didn't have the cleansed and refreshed look he usually did after he'd taken a dump. His head was stooped, his shoulders hunched. He looked like a war messenger telling some mom her son had been killed. Then I realized why. In his left hand were the *Times,* the *News,* and the *Post.*

We marched upstairs and sat down at the kitchen table. He passed me the papers one by one. All three had articles on my dismissal—and op-ed pieces that speculated on my possible motives for fabricating:

Ariel Steiner's predicament sheds light on our increasingly fame-obsessed culture, in which young journalists will do anything at all—even concoct a fictitious love affair—just to get their Warholian fifteen minutes.

●

Raised in the elite neighborhood of Brooklyn Heights in an upper-middle-class Jewish family, educated at Brown University, Ariel Steiner was taught from an early age that she had to succeed in order to win her family's love. Baby boomer parents need to examine the pressure they put on their children if they do not want to rear an Ariel Steiner of their own.

●

Ariel Steiner was merely a pawn in Steven Jensen's randy game. The issue is not "Why did she lie?" but "Why does sex sell?" In an increasingly voyeuristic culture, it's no wonder that nearly every alternative newsweekly in the nation now employs a female sex columnist to chronicle her weekly exploits. The current governing mantra in American journalism is "sleaze over substance." Steiner simply took that mantra a little too much to heart.

All in all, the editorials weren't nearly as bad as I had expected. But it was the accompanying photo in the articles that kicked me in the gut. Each paper used my graduation portrait from Brown. The portrait company had slotted me at 9 A.M., but I slept through my alarm that morning and rolled out of bed at ten to nine. I hadn't had time to shower, much less put on makeup. So I arrived at the shoot with a huge frizzy head of hair and dark circles beneath my eyes. The stylist winced when she saw me and handed me a comb. But a comb is about as effective on a Jewish girl's hair as Binaca on a Bowery bum's breath, so I cast it aside and took my seat under the lights. I did my best to make up for my lack of attractiveness with an enthusiastic smile, but it came off looking forced. The cumulative effect was a half-comatose, heavy, and constipated serial killer. I was a veritable visual atrocity.

And now every guy out there who had ever wondered what I looked like was going to see that Medusa and think she was me. I could hear the wilting noise of thousands of New York City boners going limp. "Oh God," I moaned to Adam, leaning my head against his shoulder and staring at the three identical witches.

"Ar?" he said. "There's one more."

"What do you mean? I read all three papers." He gingerly reached for the *Post,* flipped backward to the gossip page, Page Six, and passed it to me.

LADY DYE

We hear that print isn't the only arena in which former *City Week* sex columnist **Ariel Steiner** messes with the truth. She was spotted at the midtown salon Enrico Faberge yesterday, getting her hair highlighted by popular coiffeur **Pierre**

Thibaut. What color did the former smutwriter go with? "I suggested a blond tint to bring out her natural highlights," said Thibaut. "It's a very natural look. You can hardly tell it's not real." How very fitting.

I put my hands to my cheeks like that guy in the Edvard Munch painting. How had they gotten that shot? Had someone hidden a spy cam in the blow-dryer—or had the sixty-year-old dame in the chair next to mine really been a paparazzo in disguise? And how could Thibaut have ratted? Who could a girl trust if not her stylist?

"*I can't fucking believe this!*" I shouted, looking at Adam.

He was smiling.

"You're *laughing* at me?"

"I'm not laughing at you. I'm laughing at the situation. You have to admit it's a little amusing."

"*No, it isn't!*" I said, whacking him on the arm.

"I'm only laughing because I know this will blow over soon. And even if it doesn't, you can take comfort in one thing: it can't get any worse." But of course, he was wrong.

●

After he left I took a shower and tried to get a grip. There was nothing I could do about the articles or the photo, but there was one area of my life in which I could still take some control: finding a new shit job.

I got dressed and plugged the phone back in. I started to dial my temp agency and then I got a call-waiting beep.

"Did you see the papers?" said my dad.

"Yeah."

"Couldn't you have sent them one of your acting head shots?" asked my mom.

"Mom! It doesn't work that way! You can't choose the photo they run of you!"

"I tried to explain that to her," said my dad, "but she wouldn't listen."

"How are you holding up?" asked my mom.

"OK. The only one that really got to me was the Page Six item."

"What Page Six item?" said my dad.

"In the *Post*."

"Hold on. I have it right here. I'll bring it to Mom." I heard the static as he walked the cordless into my parents' bedroom.

Then I heard some rustling papers. My dad said, *"Gevalt,"* and my mom said, "Why didn't you tell me you colored your hair? I want to see it!"

"I have slightly more important things to worry about. The Corposhit fired me yesterday once she found out about the retraction."

"I'm sure you'll be able to find something else," said my dad. "You can do anything you want. You have an Ivy League degree."

"So does Ted Kaczynski."

"Chin up," said my mom.

"We love you," said my dad.

"I know," I said.

I hung up and dialed Frances, the woman at my agency. "We tried to reach you all afternoon yesterday," she said, "but there was no answer."

"I must have forgotten to turn the machine on. Did Ashley tell you what happened?"

"Yes. While we're disappointed that the assignment ended, we discussed your . . . case . . . and decided we'd like to keep representing you. A few women in our office were big fans of your column, and they want to help you however they can. But we've decided not to try to place you in the publishing world, so you don't wind up in the same situation again. I was able to get you an assignment at a bank starting Monday."

"What is it?"

"It's the same kind of position you had before. Similar responsibilities—memo and letter typing, light word processing, phone answering."

"Does my boss know who I am?"

"We told her your name and she didn't seem to react."

"What's the rate?"

She cleared her throat. "I'm afraid it's a tad lower than the one at McGinley Ladd."

"How much lower?"

"Eleven an hour."

"Eleven an hour?"

"It's in the back office of BankAmerica. They don't pay as much in back offices."

"Where is it?"

"Long Island City."

"Queens?"

"That's correct."

Two weeks ago I'd been the most controversial columnist in the city, and now I'd be getting eleven bucks an hour to answer phones in an office in Queens. After taxes, it would probably be closer to seven. This was baby-sitting money. But how could I refuse? They might not be able to place me anywhere else. I had to be grateful for whatever I could get. I told her I'd take it, and went to get some breakfast at The Fall.

I bought a coffee and a bagel and sat down on a couch. There was a middle-aged guy sitting next to me, reading the Metro section of the *Times*. He flipped through the pages, then pulled down the paper, glanced over at me, and looked back down at the paper. I slunk in my seat and turned my head the other way, but the bastard wouldn't give up. "Excuse me," he said, "but are you—"

"Yes!" I shouted. "I am! Are you satisfied?" The counter boy turned toward us but I didn't care. "What is it you want to know? Why I did it? Come on! I'm ready. Hit me with your best shot!"

"Actually," he said, "I never heard of you before today. I just wanted to say I think you look much better with short hair than long."

"Oh," I said, my face burning. I could have handled him mocking me, but it was much more difficult to handle him not knowing who I was. I stood up with as much dignity as I could muster and walked home.

When I got back to my building, Al was sitting on the front stoop. He didn't look happy.

"Hi, Al," I said.

"You didn't tell me you were a sex columnist when you rented the apartment," he said.

"That's because I wasn't."

"I was looking for a nice girl when I put that ad out. But you're not a nice girl at all. This is a family neighborhood. I knew something was wrong when that guy rang my bell in the middle of the night. I can't have a loose woman as a tenant."

"But I don't even have the job anymore! And besides, I have a boyfriend now!"

"It doesn't matter. Your face is in that article. People will see you coming out of my building and they'll recognize you. I don't want to be known as the guy who rents his apartment to a tramp. I want you out by Sunday."

I had never signed a lease on the apartment. Al had said, "Paper isn't necessary. I trust you," and I'd been stupid enough to buy it. So I had no legal recourse. I went upstairs, called my parents, and said, "Get my bedroom ready."

●

For the next three days I packed my things and let my machine take calls from tabloid papers and TV shows. It got easier to ignore them over the course of the weekend. It would have been one thing if Diane Sawyer wanted to go head to head with me, but the callers sounded so seedy I knew all they really wanted to do was mock me. I could just see myself as the featured guest on *Ned Slivovitz* for a show called "Cheaters, Liars, and Scumbags."

On Sunday afternoon Adam came over with a U-Haul and we loaded it and drove to Brooklyn Heights. My mom and dad were in the country with Zach, so Adam and I had to lug everything up in the elevator ourselves. When we finally got everything into my room, he sat on the edge of the bed to rest and I leaned over and started to unpack. He grabbed my ass, turned me around, and bit my left tit. I pulled his pants down and got on top of him. "Where are the condoms?" he whispered.

I climbed off him and reached for the box I thought I'd packed them in, but it turned out to be filled with kitchen utensils instead. I ripped open the one next to it but that was just linens. I had a momentary image of myself dashing into my parents' bedroom and taking my mom's diaphragm out of her bedside table, but that was too disgusting even for me.

"Let me just check one more," I said. As soon as I opened it, I struck gold. The Lifestyles were sitting right on top. I ripped one off and tossed it to him. He rolled it on, I straddled him and started to bounce. He grabbed my shoulders and then moved his hand down to my breasts. I angled myself forward for the extra clitoral stimulation and closed my eyes. His nip squeezing felt so good that it made my whole pelvic region get warm. *"Don't take your hands off my tits!"* I hissed, my skin beginning to flush. I started to breathe superfast and tilted my head back, and just as I was about to cross that glorious hurdle in the sky, I heard the front door to the apartment open.

"We're home!" called my mom.

Adam jumped up and put on his boxers, and I collapsed on the bed with a groan. I'd been two seconds away from my first orgasm from sex alone, and my own parents had coitus-interrupted it. There really was no place like home.

●

When I got off the subway at the BankAmerica building the next morning, I looked down at the directions Frances had given me: "Go through turnstile to steel door next to ATM." That was odd. The office was on the same level as the subway. Meaning in the basement.

As all the suits around me went up the escalators into the building, I went down a dingy, humid hallway toward a steel door marked *Building Services*. I heaved it open. Sitting behind a high gray desk, under a flickering fluorescent light, was an incredibly overweight woman about my age with long black hair and the foulest body odor I had ever inhaled.

"Can I help you?" she said.

"I'm here for Ruth Jennings," I said. "I'm her new secretary."

"She's not here yet. Why don't you take a seat and wait? She should be in any minute."

I sat down on a couch and listened to bizarro Elvira take phone calls. Her responses didn't sound much like those of a typical secretary. "What floor's the leak on?" she'd say, or, "So the toilet's been overflowing for half an hour?" or, "*Which* elevator is stuck?" Then she would scribble down some notes, get on a walkie-talkie, and tell someone named Tom or Alario to go handle the problem.

It didn't take me long to realize just what *building services* was a euphemism for: *maintenance office*. That was why it was in the basement. That was why this girl reeked to high heaven— because the only people she ever came in contact with were poop moppers. This job lent a whole new meaning to the term *Corposhit*.

The door opened and a short, fiftyish woman with cropped brown hair came in. "Ruth, this is your new secretary," said the girl.

"Oh, yeah," said Ruth in a husky, nicotined voice. "I forgot you were starting today. What's your name again?"

"Ariel."

"That's right. Ariel. Follow me." She led me to the back of the office and sat me down in front of a desk with a computer and a typewriter. I spent the rest of the morning calming frenzied and wet staffers, typing bid rejection letters, and bantering with the BankAmerica janitorial staff. At lunch I went up to the cafeteria, ate a frozen yogurt, stared out the window at the S trains clattering by, then headed glumly back to Asbestos Central. I came home that night dizzy from the air and light deprivation, and when I sat down at the table Zach said, "Something smells funny."

After dinner I went into my bedroom and lay down on the bed. I looked over at my computer. I hadn't used it since I had written "Den of Len." I got up slowly, went toward it, and turned it on. But I was dead inside. I had nothing to say. It was Henry Roth city. I turned off the machine, lay down on my bed, and faced the wall. After a few minutes something made me roll back over. I looked at the typer again. It seemed to be beckoning me back. Perhaps I had left it too hastily. It was begging me to do something I had not done—and I knew just what it was. I walked back over, knelt down by the wall socket, and yanked out the plug.

●

On Wednesday morning I took overflow overflow calls from Elvira and talked socialist politics with the BankAmerica janitors. When the clock struck noon I got a funny pang in my stomach. It felt strange to know that soon Wednesday would be like any other day, and the *City Week* like any other paper. After work I made a detour in midtown to pick up a copy, and I read "The Mail" on the train ride home:

I don't care if she made them all up. I live alone. Bring her back!

SY RIZZUTI, *Park Slope*

Ding dong, the witch is dead!

TIM FELLOWS, *Upper East Side*

Now that I know what Ariel Steiner looks like, it doesn't upset me so much that you canned her. How could I ever have enjoyed her column again, with the image of that hulking she-cow in my head?

PATRICK FERBER, *Chelsea*

I put the paper in my lap and sighed. The abuse was a hollow pleasure when I knew it was bound to end. There might be a few more weeks of castigation, but eventually my readers would forget all about me. I'd never be defamed again. No longer would my dating life be a subject of public debate. No longer would men compare my genitalia to rotting garbage. The days of ridicule, vilification, and humiliation were over. It was horrible. What was the point of being alive if no one was around to hate me for it?

●

On Friday at ten to five, I brought my time sheet into Ruth's office for her to sign. She was halfway through her John Hancock when she leaned down and squinted at the paper. "What's your last name?" she said. "Steiner?"

"Yeah."

"That rings a bell."

"Maybe that's because my temp agency told it to you when they called." I was sweating like a whore in church.

"They didn't," she said. "They only told me your first. I'm sure I've heard the name Steiner before. Something I saw in the paper, I think."

"I have no idea what you're talking about."

"It was the end of last week. Thursday or Friday. I should have it here somewhere." She leaned down and reached into her recycling bin. I did a quick prayer to make the incriminating issue magically disappear. But no such luck. She pulled out Thursday's *Daily News* with a self-satisfied smile and began riffling through the pages. "Here it is!" she shouted. *"Downtown Rag Cans Fibbing Squibber."* She turned it toward me so I was face-to-face with my photo. "You're saying this isn't you?"

"OK!" I shouted. "It *is* me!"

She shook her head from side to side. "I don't know if I can keep you on now."

"What?"

"How can I trust you?"

"Easily! I'm not a liar in life! Only on the page!"

"But you just lied to me ten seconds ago."

"You don't understand—"

"How can I be certain you'll take accurate messages? Or fill out your time sheet honestly?"

"I would never withhold anything from you!"

"I don't like how this smells, Ariel. I don't like that your agency didn't mention anything about your past, and I don't like the fact that before you came here, you were a porno writer. I'm a Catholic woman. It makes me uncomfortable."

"They weren't pornos! It was first-person journalism with an emphasis on my romantic trials and tribulations!"

"Like I said, pornos." She stood up. "Why don't you go?"

"Now?"

"Yes, now. I'll call your—"

"Agency and let them know what happened. Thanks."

●

When I got home, the apartment was empty. Zach and my parents had gone to the country for the weekend. I kicked off my flats, went into my bedroom, and looked at myself in the mirror.

Was it my imagination, or had I gained a few pounds since I'd started at BankAmerica? I was morphing back into the self I'd worked so hard to destroy. I wanted to feel successful again, and talented. I wanted to do something that would give me a sense of control.

I sat down at the computer and pressed the *on* button. Nothing happened. At first I thought it was God sending me a sign, but then I remembered I'd left it unplugged. I stuck the cord in the wall and tried to write, but again nothing came. I was drier than my grandmama's cunt.

Maybe the key to unblocking myself was to try a new tack. Like nonfiction. If I could get an article into a glossy magazine, I could kill two birds with one stone: open my creative floodgates and salvage my marred reputation. My name was a million times better known than other freelance writers'. There were bound to be some editors out there who'd want me on their roster.

I started to brainstorm about possible ideas to pitch, and within a few short minutes I had come up with a very impressive list: female versus male masturbation habits; infidelity; anal sex as the new yuppie trend; aphrodisiacs and voodoo; and feminist porn. I typed pitch letters for each topic, and addressed them to *GQ, Elle, Esquire, Cosmopolitan*, and *Vogue*.

●

Adam came over for dinner that night. When I told him Ruth had fired me, he said, "That's the dumbest thing I've ever heard. What does your writing have to do with your ability to radio janitors?"

"I think it was the content of the columns. She said it offended her Catholic sensibilities."

"But you're not even writing it anymore."

"I guess she didn't believe in absolution."

"Are you going to try to get another temp job?"

"I don't think so. Temping is too demoralizing. I'm thinking I should try something less soul draining, something a little more challenging."

I didn't exactly have Hebrew-school teaching in mind.

●

In the morning, after Adam left, I called my parents in the country and told them I'd gotten the sack. "This is perfect timing," said my mom. "I was working on the synagogue bulletin yesterday, and Elliott Nash, the principal, asked if I knew anyone who might be interested in a religious-school teaching position.

One of their teachers quit suddenly, for no apparent reason, and they need someone to take her place for the last two months of school. It's twelve hours a week, and it pays thirty an hour. Why don't you go over to the synagogue and talk to him? Morning services should be getting out now."

Compared to taking leakage calls, teaching rugrats didn't seem like such a lousy option. And thirty bucks an hour was damn good money. If I saved enough of it, I could move into my own place by the end of the spring.

As I entered the synagogue, I heard the closing lines of "Adon Olam." A few minutes later everyone streamed out of the sanctuary into the reception room and raced for the challah. I joined in the *motzi*, ripped off a piece of bread, and approached a middle-aged woman with a kid. "Excuse me," I said. "Do you know who Elliott Nash is?"

"He's right over there," she said, and pointed to a goateed guy in his early thirties. He wasn't bad looking. He had clean, tight skin, a decent build, and twinkling eyes. Maybe there were some perks to this job. I threw back my shoulders and sauntered over.

"Mr. Nash," I said, "I'm Ariel Steiner, Carol Steiner's daughter. She mentioned that you have an opening in the religious school, and I wanted to speak to you about it."

"I'm delighted you're interested in the position."

"Really?"

"Yes. Why don't you come in tomorrow morning for an interview, at eleven, say? I'd rather not discuss business on Shabbat."

When I got to the synagogue the next morning, we went up to his office and I told him how I'd gone to Hebrew school as a kid, been president of the youth group, and worked as a counselor at a Reform sleep-away camp the summer after ninth grade. When I finished talking, he nodded and said, "You're hired."

"You mean that's it? I don't need a license or anything?"

"No. There's no license required for teaching religious school. It's a bonus, but we don't demand it." He took out the textbooks and showed me where the last teacher had left off. I stood up and headed for the door, but just as I was about to leave he said, "Ariel?"

"Yes?" I turned around.

"I just wanted to tell you, *I was a huge fan!*"

"You mean—"

"Of course I knew. I just didn't want to say anything before the interview because I was afraid it might make you uncomfortable. I was so upset when they fired you. I thought it was a ridiculously misguided decision."

"So you really don't care about my past?"

"As far as I'm concerned, it's completely irrelevant. You're no longer working for the paper, your parents are members of the synagogue, and all I really care about is whether you'll be devoted to the kids."

This guy seemed too good to be true. Maybe he *was* too good to be true. Maybe the only reason he liked my column was because he was some kind of perv, or pedophile. What if he was secretly fondling the kids on the *bimah* right in front of the ark, under the eternal light, when he was supposed to be disciplining them for bad behavior? What if he was hiring me in the hopes I'd join in his game? I could bust him for the criminal he really was, save the synagogue, and become a neighborhood hero. Who knew where this job might lead?

●

I arrived for my first Hebrew class fifteen minutes early and waited for the kids to file in. They came in clusters, chewing neon gum, wearing Yankees T-shirts, hitting one another, and generally looking like the last place they wanted to be was Hebrew school. As they took their seats at their desks, I heard one of the boys whisper, "I hope she's not a bitch."

The bell rang. "Hi, everyone," I said haltingly. "My name's Ariel. I'll be teaching you for the rest of the semester." Then I took their attendance, passed out the dittoes I'd prepared, and told them to work silently. After two minutes they started balling them up and throwing them at one another.

"Stop that!" I shouted. I picked up one of the crumpled papers, brought it over to the kid who'd thrown it, opened it up, and smoothed it out in front of him. "Now get back to work," I said, walking back to my chair.

"Fuck you," he whispered.

I turned around slowly. "What did you say?"

"Nothing," he said. The kids next to him tittered.

"I think you said something."

"He said, 'Fuck you,' " chirped the boy next to him.

The entire classroom erupted in squeals. "That's it!" I shouted. "You two are going to Elliott's office!"

I escorted them down the stairs to Nash's, but when I opened the door, it was empty. I had one of the boys check the men's room, but after a few minutes, he still hadn't come out. I hoped Nash wasn't in there doing something horrible to him. I knocked on the door gingerly and pushed it open. The kid was kneeling on the floor facing one of the urinals and using it as a chin-up bar. I whisked him out, brought both the boys back up to the classroom, sat them outside the door, and said, "Sit here and be quiet until class is over."

"Thank you," said Urinal Boy.

"What do you mean, 'Thank you'?"

"Now we don't have to learn Hebrew. Thanks!"

"I changed my mind," I said. "You're coming back in with me." We opened the door and went in. It was like a scene out of *Shock Corridor*. Someone had written PENIS BREATH on the chalkboard, one kid was hiding under the table, one was banging his head against the wall, one was doing a split on the floor, and the rest were throwing not only dittoes but sharp pencils, text-books, pieces of chalk, erasers, and articles of clothing.

No wonder their last teacher had quit. When I went to He-brew school, the most obnoxious we ever got was flicking small pieces of mucus at each other and eating Chinese spare ribs on the front steps. What was becoming of my old neighborhood, my old shul? I walked slowly through the maelstrom toward my chair and clapped my hands to get their attention. I shouted, *"Be quiet!"* but they ignored me. Finally I gave up, rested my head in my arms and let them keep messing around until the period ended.

●

When I got home my family was gathered around the dining room table. "How did it go?" asked my dad.

"I don't want to talk about it," I said.

I went into the bedroom and threw my bag on the bed. There were three business-sized envelopes on the pillow, from *GQ, Es-quire*, and *Vogue*. I ripped them open one by one. The wording was slightly different for each, but they all amounted to the same central thought: Are you out of your mind? We can't run nonfic-tion by a confessed fabricator!

"Did you see the mail I put in there?" called my mom from the dining room.

"Yes, I fucking saw the mail!"

"Someone's testy," I heard Zach murmur.

I sat down on the edge of the bed and stared at the rejection letters. I wanted to keep a positive attitude, but how could I? I knew the score. If those three magazines all had the same thing to say, the others wouldn't say anything different. My journalistic career was over—pure and simple.

But I had to look on the bright side. The disgrace couldn't last. It might take a few months—but eventually my name would lose its taint. It had to. This was an attention-deficit world. And besides, there were tons of once-shamed has-beens who'd been able to jump-start their careers later in life. Vanessa Williams. John Travolta. Even Judd Nelson. I was living in the era of the comeback. It was far too soon to lose hope.

The next day, Hebrew school went a little better. I got through half of the ditto before the kids started throwing things at one another, and no one said, "Fuck you." But then I took them down to the sanctuary for *tefillah*, the prayer service, and when we got to the Kaddish, Urinal Boy (whose name turned out to be Ezra) and his friend started shouting each Hebrew word that sounded vaguely like an English swearword—like *"TUSH b'chata"* and *"b'rei SHIT"*—and poking each other in the ribs. I finally had to pull them outside, and again they thanked me.

●

On Wednesday after class, I went to meet Adam for dinner at Souen. He hadn't gotten there when I arrived, so I picked up a copy of the *City Week* from the stack in the foyer and sat down at a table in the back to wait. I started to flip forward to "The Mail" when something on the bottom of the front page caught my eye:

"WHEN NAVAL LOVER TOLD ME HE WAS MOVING BACK TO Seattle, I went to the bathroom, stuck my finger down my throat, and vomited into the toilet. It wasn't the first time I'd made myself puke, though. I've been doing it on and off since I was thirteen years old . . ." Sara Green, "I-Level," p. 27.

"Jesus H. Christ!" I shouted, quickly flipping forward to the story. It was called "Purge-atory" and it was a very depressing account of Sara's breakup from Rick, her bulimia, and all her problems with men and self-hatred. It was god-awful. Hackneyed and sensationalistic—the worst confessional journalism had to offer.

The door to the restaurant opened and Adam walked in. He kissed me on the cheek and I passed him the paper. "What is it?" he said. I pointed to the teaser on the front. He squeezed my hand and opened to the story.

"So?" I said when he finished. "What do you think?"

"Honestly?"

"Yeah."

"I think it's pretty good."

"Are you out of your mind?"

"I found it very heartfelt. She's working a lot of things out here. I think it's an intriguing portrait of a self-destructive young woman."

"It's horrible!"

"If you weren't so competitive you'd be able to see how good it is."

"I can't believe you're siding with her!"

"See what I mean? You turn everything into a contest."

"No, I don't. It's just hard for me to respect someone who's blatantly riding the coattails of my fame."

"All Sara's doing is capitalizing off her natural assets. What's wrong with that?"

"That part about how much she loves anal sex—she's shilling for the patriarchy in the most obvious way!"

"If that's not the pot calling the kettle black . . ."

"I'm not saying I didn't shill! Of course I did! But at least I was a *skilled* shiller!"

"I can see why this might be hard for you. But Sara's going to want your support. You're her closest friend."

Not for long, I thought.

But when I got home and my mom told me Sara had called three times, I felt guilty for being so hard on her. Just because Sara was totally talentless didn't mean I had to ditch her as a friend. I took the cordless into my bedroom and dialed.

"I had a reason for not telling you in advance," she said.

"What's that?"

"The day I found out they were running it was the day you got fired from BankAmerica. I didn't want to upset you any further. So what did you think?"

"I thought it had some . . . strong moments. But Sara. *Naval Lover?*"

"That was their edit! I named him Dick, but they changed it!" I gritted my teeth. So Turner and Jensen were out for my blood. "There's something else," she said quietly.

"What?"

"I had a meeting at the *Week* today and they've offered me a regular column." The box was kicked out from beneath my feet, the noose tightened around my neck. I died a quick, painless death, spasming for a few minutes before my body stilled and swung slowly in the breeze, in front of fifty thousand delighted onlookers.

"Did you take it?" I whispered hoarsely.

"Of course I did. They're paying me three fifty a week. I could use the money."

"They're paying you *three fifty*?"

"Yeah. They offered me two fifty but I said I wouldn't do it for less than three five."

The rigor mortis kicked in and I began to spasm violently in the wind. "I thought you wanted to be a musician!" I shouted.

"I can be both!"

"How can you do this to me?"

"This has nothing to do with you! This is about me! You don't own the paper! Jesus. I was hoping you'd be happy for me."

"How can I be happy when you're *stealing my life*?"

"How can you be so recklessly self-centered?"

She was right. I was being self-centered. And the truth was, it wasn't fair to blame her. The real culprits were Jensen and Turner. What kind of skanky, low-budget pornographers were these guys anyway? Didn't they have any integrity? Any standards? They'd spread open the legs of any girl who stuck her feet in the stirrups. They could find "talent" in the work of the dippiest chippies in town.

"I'm sorry," I sighed. "This is a little hard for me. But I *am* happy for you. Really."

"I'm sure you mean it."

"I do! What are they going to call your column?"

" 'Sex und Drang.' "

" '*Sex und Drang*'?" I cried.

"Yeah. I kind of like it. It's a little cute, I know, but I think it'll grow on me."

"It's . . . not bad," I said, crossing my fingers. "What's your first column going to be about?"

"My fucked-up relationship with Jon."

"Sounds terrific," I choked, hung up, and went to work on my Hebrew lesson.

●

Over the next month, as Sara chronicled lousy dates and drew hate mail from my once-faithful detractors, I watched Jewish twelve-year-olds flick chalk and curse. The week after "Purge-atory" came out, one guy wrote a letter calling Sara "a bigger bubblehead than Ariel Steiner—which I didn't think was possible," and Name Withheld said she "should make an appointment for a hysterectomy as soon as possible, to insure that her spawn will not wreak havoc on the earth." She went unlisted the next day.

Turner and Jensen hired a new illustrator for her—a semifamous cartoonist with a monthly 'zine, Mike Cella, who was known for drawing dead women better than anyone else in town. He gave Sara huge bulging breasts, long shapely legs, and a full pouty mouth. I couldn't stand it. Even her *cartoon* was hotter than mine.

But after the first few columns came out, my jealousy began to fade. I was monogamous now. Adam and I weren't having any problems—aside from the fact that we always had to go to his place when we wanted to have sex. As far as readers were concerned, my life was over. If I had kept writing the column, it would have lost steam, and Turner and Jensen probably would have fired me eventually anyway.

Besides, I tried to tell myself, I was doing noble work. I was nurturing young minds instead of young cocks. My daily moron-sitting was a mitzvah. I was making up for the shame I'd brought upon my family by doing something positive for my community. I was reaching the kids even if I didn't seem to be, and years from now they'd remember me as a great mentor.

I tried to be inventive with my little demons. For one of my Judaica classes, I let the kids act out a *bris* with a doll. I wrapped the doll in felt and said it would represent the foreskin, so at the moment of circumcision, the *mohel* would cut off a piece with a pair of scissors. Naturally, when we got to the role assigning, they all wanted to be the *mohel*. I picked the calmest and most mature kid in the class, a boy named Jesse. But as soon as the mother and father approached him with the doll, he put on this ghoulish face, said "Give me da baby!" in a Transylvanian accent, and began violently stabbing at it with the scissors. I had to wrench it away and stop the skit right there.

One April day I was on my way out of the synagogue when Elliott pulled me aside and said, "I'd like to talk to you upstairs." We went up to his office and he gave me a rueful look. "The religious school committee had an emergency meeting last night," he said. "One of your students, Ezra Rothman, was reading the *Post* for the sports stats and accidentally came across that item about you yesterday. He told his mother and she called the emergency meeting."

"What item in the *Post*?"

"You didn't see it?"

I shook my head no. He reached into one of his drawers and handed the paper to me. I knew which page to turn to. On the bottom right corner of Page Six was a grainy shot of me exiting the synagogue, next to an item that read:

SPOTTED: Former *City Week* sex columnist **Ariel Steiner**, on her way out of **Temple Ahavat Shalom** in Brooklyn Heights, where she's currently working as a religious school instructor. Personally, we wouldn't let her near *our* kids, but maybe **God** has taken a more generous attitude. We can only wonder what career move is next for the reformed sex writer—rabbinical school?

I stood up abruptly, crossed to the window, moved the curtain aside, and looked across the street. There was a man leaning against a lamppost, but he didn't have a camera around his neck. Halfway down the block was an unmarked van. Maybe my paparazzo was hiding in there. Suddenly the lamppost man looked up—right at me. Maybe it was him. Maybe he was using a tiny spy camera. I quickly dropped the curtain, panting. I felt like Malcolm X in that famous photo. Except Jewish and without the gun.

"What was that all about?" said Elliott.

"Nothing," I said, sitting back down.

"Anyway," he said, "Mrs. Rothman convened the meeting and said she didn't feel comfortable with her son being taught by a former pornographer. She brought up the mock circumcision as an example of your negative influence."

"But the kids loved that class!"

"I tried to defend you, but there wasn't much I could say. They took a vote on whether to dismiss you and I'm sorry to report that the outcome was not in your favor. This is still a rather conservative neighborhood. But I know a lesbian rabbi in Park Slope who says her religious school would be happy to hire you in September."

I nodded, picked up my bag, and walked out. I wasn't just a failed writer; I was a failed shul marm. It didn't get much more humiliating than that. And from a financial standpoint, this was the worst possible timing. April 15 was coming up, and I barely had enough in my bank account to pay my taxes. Steven Jensen the neo-Nazi didn't have enough integrity to put his columnists on staff, so none of my taxes had been withheld. I needed a job that provided a quick cash flow. I also needed a job that didn't include cleaning up spitballs as one of its main responsibilities.

On the walk home from the synagogue I started thinking about my marketable skills and realized there was still an area of shit work I hadn't explored: waitressing. I had shied away from it in the past because I always suspected I'd be far too neurotic to pull it off, but these were desperate days. Besides, it was one occupation in which my reputation couldn't matter. No one could rightfully argue that my past made me unfit to serve salads. All that was required was a polite manner, a sense of balance, and an ability to take accurate orders.

I picked up a copy of the *Voice* at a newsstand on my way to the apartment and scanned the BAR/REST ads. One read, "NoHo Café, busy downtown restaurant, sks exp'd & enthusiastic waitstaff for day shift. Personality & flexibility a must. Apply in person with Tasos, weekdays from two to four." The address was on Lafayette Street.

The next day I took the train over. It was a small place—a dozen tables—and the prices on the menu outside were pretty moderate. I walked in. It was dark and a little smoky. Only a few of the tables were taken, and at the bar was a broad-shouldered man in his thirties going through a stack of applications several inches high. "I'm here about your *Village Voice* ad," I said.

"Take one of these," he said, sliding me a blank application. I filled out my name, address, and phone number, and then I got to the first question. "Define the following: haricots verts, demiglace, steak au poivre." I racked my brain for any remnants of high school French. I knew *vert* meant *green* but I didn't know what the hell *haricots* were. *Demiglace* meant *half ice cream,* but that didn't seem to make any sense. And I had no clue about *poivre.* This baby was harder than the temping test. I left all three lines blank and moved on to the next question. "Name three types of gin, three types of vodka, and three types of rum." Too bad I'd been drinking nothing but Jameson for the past year. "Name three wine regions in California and three in France." I figured I'd start with California. Napa. That was one, but the only other regions of California I could think of were the Haight and Venice Beach. Maybe France would be easier. Bordeaux. Cannes? Did they make wine there? Nice? Cognac? Was Cognac a place—or a thing? I went to the "Employment History" section, left that blank too, and slid the application back to Tasos, facedown.

"Thank you," he said. "Let me get a picture of you." He picked up a Polaroid camera sitting on the bar and said, "Stand against the wall."

I backed up and tried to smile confidently. Just as he was about to take the shot, he lowered the camera and wrinkled his brow. "I know you," he said. "I've seen your face."

"People say I'm the spitting image of Carol Kane in *Hester Street.*"

"No. I mean you look familiar."

"Some even say I look like Meg Ryan. I don't think so at all, but maybe it's the dimples."

"No." He walked over to the bar and glanced at my application again. "Ariel Steiner!" he said, his jaw dropping. "You used to write that smut for the *City Week*! What are you doing applying for a waitressing job?"

"I've been having some trouble getting steady work since I left the paper," I mumbled.

"What do you mean?"

"I'd rather not go into it."

"I used to read you all the time. I was really disappointed when I found out you'd made them up. I thought they were true." He grinned and gave me a once-over. I pretended not to notice. "So, you have no waitressing experience whatsoever."

"That's correct."

"Tell me why I should hire you, then."

"Because I'm an incredibly fast learner, I'm quick on my feet, you used to be a fan, and I really need the money."

He crossed his arms and leaned back. "Do you have any idea how many people have applied for the job?"

"No."

"A hundred and twenty-five."

"I'm sure there's a lot of competition, but I promise I'll do good work." He shook his head. "Think of this as payback! You're giving me something in return for what I gave you. You're throwing me a bone in exchange for me having thrown you a . . ." I batted my eyes.

He snickered. "When could you start?"

"As soon as you want me to."

"How 'bout tomorrow?"

"That's fine."

"The base is five-fifty an hour and the shift is ten-thirty to four-thirty. With tips you'll probably average about a hundred a shift. I'll have you trail Christina tomorrow and Thursday, and on Friday you can start on your own. There's no pay for the trailing unless she tips you out. Wear black pants. I'll give you a shirt when you get here."

"Thank you so much. You won't regret this."

"I hope you're right." I pumped his hand and skipped out the café down the street.

I showed up the next morning ready and raring to go. Christina was a struggling actress from Chicago and she was very sweet and patient. She taught me the computer system, table numbers, seat positions, and showed me how to fill out a dupe.

While she took orders, I stood off to the side, listened to customers' questions, and took notes on all her answers. I went to Adam's that night and I had him drill me on the menu and wine list until I knew it by heart. I was going to be the best damn waitress in the city.

I trailed Christina again the next day, and then on Friday I got my own shift. My first customers were a yuppie couple. The woman was coiffed and bitchy, but when she asked how the Chardonnay was, I was prepared and I told her woody and full, and I brought everything at the right time, and they gave me a decent tip.

Around twelve-thirty, as I was setting down salads for a three-top by the window, I noticed that a new deuce had been seated at table seven. Two middle-aged men. I fetched their menus, and as I approached the table, I almost shat in my pants. It was Jensen and Turner. But before I could turn around and tell Christina to take them, Jensen had recognized me. A sinister smile crept across his face. Turner just blanched.

"Well, if it isn't Little Miss Pants on Fire," said Jensen. "What are you doing here?"

"What does it look like?"

"I thought you were teaching religious school."

"Not anymore," I mumbled, setting down the menus. I looked both ways and waited for a flash to go off. Page Six would eat this scene up. "Would you two care for any . . . drinks to start?"

"I'd like a Dewar's on the rocks," said Jensen.

"Bill?" I said.

"Water's fine," he mumbled. "Just fine."

I went to the computer and entered the drink order. Then I poured their waters, walked over to the bar, and picked up Jensen's drink, momentarily considering the possibility of spitting into it. I brought it over and said, "Are you ready to order?"

"I think we are," said Jensen. "Bill? Why don't you start?"

"I'll have the garden salad," said Turner, closing his menu and handing it to me, "and a grilled chicken sandwich."

"You have a choice of dressing with the salad. Blue cheese, Russian, vinaigrette, creamy vinaigrette, Caesar, honey mustard, or fat-free honey mustard."

"I'll have the creamy vinaigrette."

I turned to Jensen. "The arugula salad, please," he said, "and a cheeseburger."

"What would you like on your salad?"

"What are the choices again?" He smirked.

I sighed. "Blue cheese, Russian, vinaigrette, creamy vinaigrette, Caesar, honey mustard, or fat-free honey mustard."

"You say the honey mustard's fat-free?" he said.

"That's right."

"Why should I believe you?" he shouted, breaking up into a fit of hysterics.

"The fat-free honey mustard, then," I said, digging my nails into my pencil, "and how would you like your burger?"

"As rare as your honesty!" he hooted.

"I'm sorry," I said tightly. "Does that mean medium rare? Medium?"

"Extra rare!" said Jensen. "Oozing rare! Fucking *kobe* rare!"

I took Jensen's menu, entered the order into the computer, brought the dupe into the kitchen, and attended to two of my other tables, trying to breathe slowly. I picked up Turner and Jensen's salads and grabbed a pepper grinder on my way over. "Some fresh pepper for your salad?" I said to Bill.

He shook his head no and began eating very vigorously. I turned to Jensen. "Some fresh pepper?"

"Absolutely."

"Say when," I said, and began grinding it out onto his plate. As it sprinkled down onto his greens, he stared up at me with a cherubic grin. I wanted to aim the shaker into his eyes till I blinded him.

"When!" he finally shouted. "You said to say when so I'm saying when! Ha ha ha ha ha!"

"Enjoy your lunch," I whispered, and headed into the kitchen.

Five different times throughout the rest of the meal, Jensen beckoned me back with little requests—more water, another drink, another tray of bread, some barbecue sauce, and a clean fork. Each time he saw me heading into the kitchen, he'd signal me, as though he was deliberately trying to throw me off track. By the time they were on their coffee, I was nearly conniptive.

Finally Jensen asked for the check. I totaled up the bill on the computer and brought it over. He already had a corporate card ready. I took it to the machine and swiped it through, brought him the receipt, then went into the kitchen to pick up another order. When I turned toward their table again, they were gone. I hurried over and opened the bill holder. The total had come to $45.78. On the blank line to the right of the word TIP, Jensen had written, OF THE DAY: GET A LIFE. And next to GRAND TOTAL, he'd put, "$45.78."

I sank down into Jensen's chair. It was still warm from his ass heat but I was so bent out of shape I didn't care. An old woman was calling for me from across the room, but I couldn't get my legs to move. I just sat there immobile, staring at the bill till it got blurry.

Suddenly Turner appeared opposite me and leaned over the table. I wiped my face with the back of my hand. "Steve's still in the men's room," he said. "He'll be out any second. I feel terrible about this. I'm so sorry this had to happen. Here." He held out a twenty.

"I don't want your money," I said.

"Please take it," he said.

"I said I don't want your goddamn money!" I shouted, standing up. My head was spinning. Patrons started to look up at me. Christina came out of the kitchen and stopped in her tracks. Tasos stepped around the bar. Jensen emerged from the bathroom. I looked around the room at everyone, untied my apron, threw it on the floor, and bolted out onto the sidewalk.

Halfway down the block, I realized my tip money was in my apron pocket. I couldn't afford to leave it there. I had always dreamed of quitting a job in such an abrupt, dramatic way, but now I'd have to ruin the glory by going back. I did an about-face, trudged in past everyone, crouched down sheepishly, removed my bills from the apron pocket, and walked out.

I headed briskly down Lafayette Street. When I got to Prince, I spotted a diner. I went in and sat in a booth. The place was pretty empty—a lone man in his fifties was eating a sandwich, a hipster couple were drinking sodas, and an elderly Italian woman was sipping soup. I looked at my reflection in the window by the booth. My eyes were bloodshot from crying, my cheeks flushed, and there were two large sweat stains under my armpits. Who would have guessed that this haggard lump of B.O. and Gilda hair was once the hippest young hussy in town?

The waitress handed me a menu. I ordered a coffee and she went behind the counter. I took out my tip money and laid it on the table. It came to $24.40. For three days of work. Christina had chosen not to tip me out. Maybe I should have taken Turner's twenty after all.

I shoved the money back in my pocket and the waitress came over with the coffee. I poured in some milk and took a sip. It wasn't bad, for diner coffee—strong and not too bitter. But you know you're in a sorry state when the only thing you have to be grateful for is a decent cup of Joe. I had no money, no job, no permanent home, no professional future, and a name that brought nothing but shame. My best friend was profiting off my failure, even a maintenance office wouldn't employ me, and although I'd finally found someone to share my life with, it wasn't much of a life to share. It was an outrageous and obscene story, twisted and degrading, and one hundred percent true. I couldn't have made it up any better myself.

Suddenly I got an idea. I took a napkin from the dispenser and a pen from my shirt pocket.

I was only twenty-two and already I was infamous.

I reached for my coffee. Right as I lifted the mug to my lips, the waitress rushed by with two burger deluxes and jostled my elbow. The mug jerked toward me and hot coffee spilled all over my crotch and thighs. I yelped in pain, grabbed the napkin, and dabbed my legs with it furiously. Then I realized what I had done. I looked down at the napkin. It was brown, soaked, and steaming, and the words were blurring into oblivion. It was just my luck. I'd written my first sentence in months—and turned it into a sponge. I set a new napkin next to the old, copied the sentence over, and kept going.

About The Author

AMY SOHN writes the "Female Trouble" column for *New York Press* and has also written for *Details* and *Feed*. She lives in Brooklyn, New York.